PRIVATEERS

PRIVATEERS

CHARLIE NEWTON

BLACKTYPE PRESS

Published by BlackType Press, Austin, Texas
www.charlienewton.com

Edited and Designed by Girl Friday Productions
www.girlfridayproductions.com

Editorial: Ed Stackler, Erin Cusick, Amy Snyder
Interior Design: Paul Barrett
Cover Design: David Drummond
Illustrations: Robert Bucciarelli - RobertBDesign
Cover Image Credits: © Shutterstock / NataLT;
Shutterstock / Vixit; Shutterstock / STILLFX

ISBN (Paperback): 978-1-7344368-0-8
e-ISBN: 978-1-7344368-1-5

LCCN: 2020900870

First Edition

Printed in the United States of America

"It is a Rotten Bargain that threatens the very underpinnings of our democracy, the unholy union of government, business, and organized crime."

US Senator Estes Kefauver, 1951

Odricks Corner, Virginia

February 1986

Thirty degrees and ice.

Two unmarked sedans are parked on an isolated road. Two men stand at the front fender of the rear sedan, a file open between them. The American taps a gloved finger near an eight-by-ten photograph that would make most men vomit. He says:

"*Gibbets*. One-man conical death chambers. Used them to execute pirates back in the 1700s."

The Brit at his shoulder shakes his head, says: "Taken *three* weeks ago." The Brit's accent is a mush of Britain's colonial-era geography.

The American looks up, then quickly away.

"Clothes are current. Still have human meat in 'em. There's a map drawn on the back; shows the airstrip where we think our plane landed. We need to know where; need to get our guy out."

The Brit is a "green card," a private contractor. The American is a direct employee of the US government and bound by all the laws of his agency. At a minimum, his government career will be over if he's connected to the photograph and its implications.

The American continues explaining gibbets, buying time for a way out. "Gibbets fit tight, head to toe. If the executioner hangs your cage high enough, birds peck at your eyes while you're still alive, and whatever else they can reach. Hang it lower, like these unfortunate fellows, it's the rats and bigger scavengers that do the chewing."

The Brit nudges the photograph, refocusing the American on why they're talking. "That's the last contact we had with our agent and cargo. Came to us in a plain brown wrapper. We think it's Cuba. Maybe near Cienfuegos. But we can't figure gibbets lining the runway as Castro."

"Plain brown wrapper" could mean anything from an anonymous envelope to a dead man's pockets.

The American uses a penknife to flip the photograph to the map drawing. He inspects the drawing, flips back to the photograph, eyes the horror shot from a different angle. "Definitely not Cuba. I'd say Haiti. Mangrove jungle. Got that vibe."

"Haiti?"

The American frowns, glances at the tree line ten feet away for threat. The Brit would absolutely know what a gibbet is—the British Crown was infamous for using them when the English ruled much of the planet. And he'd know what Haiti looks like.

Some still refer to men like the Brit as "privateers," a legal status coined in the 1600s that four hundred years later means the same thing: a private contractor with letters of marque and reprisal—clandestine "permissions" to operate outside the law in specific situations.

Another substantial difference between the two men is murder. The American, James W. Barlow Jr., is a lawyer, a University of Chicago debate-team valedictorian who killed one man by accident last week in a downtown Buenos Aires crosswalk.

The Brit has attained no academic honors; his degree is a hodgepodge from the London Day College in Bombay and later Hong Kong, and Appalachian State in North Carolina. His name is Sile Howat. He has killed a number of people, all of them on purpose.

Barlow checks the tree line again. "Yes. Haiti."

Howat shrugs, staying with his story that he doesn't know from gibbets or Haiti.

Barlow folds his penknife, then thumbs his gloved fingertips clean of any residue. "In Haiti—if that's where your photo was taken—there's a fellow who'd be responsible for that brand of madness. The drum-beaters call him 'the Gryphon.' Gibbets have been the Gryphon's signature since . . . for a while."

"You're sure? Your people would agree?"

"*My* people? No one I know would set foot in Haiti right now. The entire island is on fire. Fifteen minutes ago, I heard all three sides of their presidential 'election' were *eating* each other."

Howat leans closer, as if confused. "But your section's active in Haiti, isn't it? Like the Contras are in Nicaragua?"

"If you mean cocaine, this conversation's over."

Howat swallows a laugh. "I mean one of those 'presidential candidates' is your guy, right? Luckner Cambronne?" Howat reaches under the photograph for a sheet of paper. "You'd better look at this."

Barlow draws a Browning .22 semiautomatic from his coat pocket and shoots Howat four times in the head.

CAMAGÜEY BREAKS, CUBA

(TWENTY YEARS LATER)

Chapter 1

SUSIE DEVEREUX

August 2006

Boyfriends lie but good binoculars don't. Our 45-foot Hatteras falls down a wave and bucks hard to the lee. We bottom in the trough and the twin diesels dig in. The combination bangs my appendix scar into the galley table and a Benelli shotgun halfway out of its wall clamps.

I plant two size nines that have sailed oceans of bad water to get here, then retrain my binocs on Cuba's Cayo Confites. At the cay's south end, a pile of bleached rubble peeks above the shore break. *Right where said rubble's supposed to be.*

Spindrift splatters the galley windows. I tight-dial the 7x50s to be sure. *Bet your ass—screw that, bet your last life jacket. After five years, the good guys have just found an unfindable eighteenth-century light-house, forever forward known as "**X marks the spot**."*

I shout up through the galley door: "Gentlemen! Believe we've done her!"

A chill stands the hair on my neck.

I refocus the 7x50s; spread my feet wider. Something's wrong with this picture. *Trap* replaces *treasure*.

Thunder pounds to the west, then rumbles louder until it booms over us. Shakes the boat like a one-jolt earthquake. Behind the thunder, the horizon line now includes a low three-hundred-mile ribbon of midmorning black.

Huh? Don't you fucking dare.

Major storm was not the NOAA forecast. I recheck the NOAA data, then the black ribbon at the horizon. *Higher? Already?* On a good day, Cuba's Camagüey Breaks are treacherous but navigable. On a bad day, the Breaks are suicide. Trap versus treasure officially drops to distant second. I pull a Vectormaster Storm-Runner and recalculate today's weather implications using what I see, not what was forecast.

The math on our available fuel and time required to reach known hurricane holes produces one option. It has two parts: Hail Mary and Hold On.

Both eyes squeeze shut. Why does bad news always add up? In my defense, the NOAA forecast was for a "minor tropical depression." But based on what I'm looking at, my forecast is we've got two hours. Then this storm will swallow the bottom half of central Cuba, and us.

The binoculars lower themselves to the galley table; I scan the cabin for ruby slippers I can click three times. When those two hours are up, it'll be noon; what remains of the sun will be gone. Our world will be full-gale winds, seas as high as a two-story building, and absolute black dark. And being the smartest girl on the block, I sailed us to this very spot on purpose.

A wind gust rocks us to starboard. I hate being stupid—and I have some experience. And I'll really hate being dead at forty-two, the new thirty-two.

My name is Susie Devereux—we probably won't know one another long, so don't worry about pronouncing Devereux. For posterity, I'm the American girl who lost the 1994 Rugby World Cup in Edinburgh, and who will now almost certainly perish at sea. Although it's fashionable to blame one's parents or one's neighborhood for life's disasters, I can't. I was raised to do what I do.

I was born in Chicago and lived there forty-eight hours. From hour forty-nine onward, my childhood was the cold water from Glasgow to Rotterdam, the warmer ports from Marseille to Morocco, and the warmer-still from Charleston to the green heat of Jamaica. My parents were captains, contrabanders, and adventurers, and so full of all things fabulous that I never wanted to leave them. They schooled me on *the life* from the day I could reach a gunwale and name three of the Beach Boys.

I glance the photo of my parents on the foredeck of their last sloop, *The John B*. The conditions that are about to kill me require that I ignore every warning Mom and Dad taught me. I wince at their photo and whisper, "Sorry."

Pocket lightning flashes in the storm wall like fortress cannon. Thunder pounds us a foot deeper in the blue water. I should make the SOS call; us wrecking isn't a 100 percent; small craft have survived worse; God does protect the ignorant. At the very least, I should warn my partners, two of the three "Witches of Eastwick," who both think I'm lots smarter than I am.

I radio-call Anne Bonny in Kingston. No answer. Then Florent Dusson-Siri on mainland Cuba. No answer. I radio-click our coordinates, send the SOS, then squint at the poems, maps, and charts strewn across the galley deck.

Goddammit, if I'm gonna drown, I need to know why; I need the answer so Anne and Siri can survive this adventure, then toast me from their mega yacht that this treasure will buy.

I squint harder at the papers, try to see the clues the way the author did when he wrote them eighty years ago, thinking he could survive double-crossing a Sicilian crime king who could spot a lie at a thousand yards.

The poems don't answer. Why answer a brunette too stupid to be a blonde?

Their murdered author doesn't answer either. When he was alive, Eddie O'Hare was a shitheel Chicago lawyer who ran a racetrack with Al Capone. And fancied himself a poet-raconteur.

My teeth clamp, teeth that an Iraqi detainee broke and I paid plenty to make pretty again. Unfortunately, I was an idiot then and I'm an idiot now. Shoulda been doing nails in a mall, in Kansas, but only with supervision.

Thunder pounds high and hard. The clues on the deck that are about to kill my friends up top and me down here are clear on only four things:

1. Know less than 100 percent of the puzzle—you die.
2. The gold "liberated" from Haiti's Banque Nationale in 1914 was no longer aboard the USS *Machias* when it ran aground, crewless, outside Charleston harbor.
3. Seventeen years later, Al Capone bought the gold at 20 cents on the dollar from two capital-murder defendants. They were represented by Eddie O'Hare and his law partner, James W. Barlow Sr.
4. Al Capone never saw the gold. O'Hare snitched him into Alcatraz, then buried it, waiting for Capone's mafia partners to die off or move on. O'Hare's poems tell you where.

"Susie! Boat's coming!"

I vault stairs to the main deck. Two sandy-haired, shirtless renaissance men stand the flying bridge above me, both lean, wearing faded military boat shorts, both accustomed to risk in foreign waters. (My head's still on my neck because they led the team that rescued me from Abu Musab al-Zarqawi.) Of the pair, Tommy-the-American is the lesser boatman, but the better diver and fighter. And the man I share my hopes, dreams, and bathwater with.

Cyril, the Afrikaner, leans into the throttles. Over his broad naked shoulder, he shouts: "Astern."

Tommy braces backward into Cyril's instrument panel, binoculars already focused into the eastern horizon. "Coming high and dead-on. Could be Cubans, circling back from mid-channel—Nope. Hull's red, deep V."

My stomach sinks. "You sure?"

Tommy shouts above the roar: "Roger that."

Red is very, very bad. Think pirate flag, but in the fiberglass era— the devil's front man. I yell up at Cyril: "Run us for the flats on the backside of Cayo Romano. We'll get 'em in the shallows. Get the sun or the storm in their eyes."

Cyril rams the throttles and veers due west into the wind. Tommy throws me the binoculars, jumps to the deck, then snakes to the stern between the fifty-five-gallon high-octane fuel drums, metal-detection equipment, and diving gear.

The binoculars confirm the bow of the deep V is a vivid scarlet red and closing.

Tommy pops the lid on the transom bait box, grabs two rebuilt MAC-10s, four thirty-round magazines, and two metal ammo cans of .45 ball. Each can holds a thousand rounds. He hauls one can up to the bridge, drops it and a MAC-10 with two extra magazines next to Cyril, then jumps back to the deck and bumps my shoulder.

"The Gryphon?" he asks.

"Don't want it to be. She's fast, though, whoever she is." I duck from the deck to the galley, stuff the maps and poems into a waterproof chart bag, then a .45 Auto into the waistband of my jean shorts. I sling a bandoleer of shotgun shells over my shoulder, then unclamp the pistol-grip Benelli 12-gauge.

On deck I brace into Tommy, rescan with the binoculars, then yell up to the bridge: "It's him. The Gryphon."

Cyril points starboard and shouts: "Two more."

Tommy frowns hard at the three boats. "Eleven goddamn days and a world full of ocean . . . he's not here by accident."

I agree. "Part of the last clue must've been fake, a plant. Fucking monster put us here to rob and kill us. Storm's his enemy too, though. Get the weather between him and us and we have a chance."

Tommy slides his two extra magazines into his shorts, drops to both knees, and opens his can of .45 ammo. Cyril yells down, "Give the bastard the file."

Chop buckles my knees. "Won't be enough."

Tommy drops the bolt on his MAC. He spent five years in the Teams and three in Delta, and offers no argument.

I flip off the Benelli's safety. "Our partners in Chicago made a deal for our heads—Barlow Jr. or Grossfeld. Promise me you'll kill 'em both if I can't."

"Never did like those guys."

I kiss Tommy's cheek, then the Benelli's barrel, then pull a big-bore derringer the Afrikaners call a "suicide special" that I go nowhere without, check the chamber, slide the derringer back into my front pocket, and tell the three boats charging at us: "The Gryphon's hands never touch me again."

Tommy yells over me to Cyril. "Make the fucking boat go faster and we don't have to give him anything."

Our Hatteras crashes west across the channel. The Gryphon's three chase boats close to shooting distance, running hot on the same high-octane avgas we are. One chase boat splits to port, one stays dead astern, one splits to starboard.

Fifteen rounds rake our water to port. Another fifteen rake to starboard. Tommy opens fire on the starboard boat. His first five-round burst walks up the waves; his second burst rips the boat's hull and bridge.

Cyril opens fire to port. That boat fires back, hits Cyril three times, then explodes in a fireball. Cyril tumbles eight feet to the deck.

Tommy rams a second magazine and empties it dead astern at the middle boat.

The starboard boat rakes bullets across our bow. I climb to the bridge, jam the throttles, ram a full magazine into Cyril's MAC, and fire to starboard. We're almost to the reef. Tommy pivots to the starboard boat and empties his third magazine. The starboard boat has three black men firing full-auto from so close their faces are clear. Their boat hits a reef, flips, rolls airborne, lands, and disintegrates on impact.

I spin the wheel left, then right, crush the throttles, and kick my last magazine down to Tommy on the deck. We slug deep into a wave that knocks me into the windscreen and slices my temple. I re-right the wheel. Bullets rip through the instruments and windscreen. I yell, "Shoot back, Tommy! They can't risk hitting the avgas drums."

Tommy's down, leaning against the transom. Blood streams his face and splatters his chest. Our engines cough. The last chase boat is fifty yards back and closing. Tommy wipes at the blood, mouths, "Love you," kisses at me in the air, uses both hands to push the MAC under his chin, and pulls the trigger. Empty.

He blinks; his eyes try to focus, rise to me . . .

I point the Hatteras straight at the rocks of Cayo Romano, jump down, pull the derringer, and kneel inside Tommy's knees. My lips kiss his until he smiles. I put the barrel under his chin, say, "Know I loved you, all I could," close my eyes, and bend backward. "Godspeed, baby. We'll dance together on the other side." I pull the trigger.

The bow of the chase boat rams our stern.

My Hatteras hits the reef, goes airborne as it splits down the centerline, explodes below deck, and blows me over the side. The avgas drums ignite and the fireball kills everyone above water.

JOHNNY'S ICEHOUSE, CHICAGO

(THREE YEARS LATER)

NOW

Chapter 2

BILL OWENS

August 2009
6:00 a.m.

If you grade on a curve, stay clear of the neighborhoods that have five-pointed crowns spray-painted on the walls, and don't say "Outfit" unless you mean clothes, the West Side of Chicago is no more difficult to navigate than Beirut during a cease-fire.

When I was a kid in the '70s, West Madison Street was skid row. Now it's home to the United Center and Johnny's IceHouse. The reason hockey players with a past, or a future, come to Johnny's IceHouse is the bright-white ice oval at its center—a training rink that is to pro hockey what Gleason's and Stillman's Gyms were to boxing.

I'm not here to play hockey—pre-sunrise at age forty-four—before I go to work in the concrete and rebar. I'm here because I've got some karma I bought a long time ago in the West Indies. Karma I'm still trying to buy back. Ten Commandments kind of stuff. The silver neck chain I wear isn't jewelry; it's a talisman for night terrors.

Did I plan a life that required a talisman to sleep at night?

Nope. Actually, the teenage plan was to accomplish the opposite—become a "beloved" songwriter and/or save the planet (Peace Corps, Nobel Prize)—the Boy Scout trip but without the shorts. For better or worse, my plan was designed to dodge the gangster-in-training program that quickly swallowed most of my friends.

So me and the Plan went in search of the world I'd read about in the library. Unfortunately, we hit some bumps along the way. I was young, didn't quite know how to steer yet. Not an excuse; there aren't any good excuses when innocent people die, and you don't.

Which explains why we're here.

At 6:00 a.m.

The rink at Johnny's is cold, silent, and empty other than a pack of small round-faced misfits at the blue line: twelve total, all rolling around in hockey pads and jerseys like a dozen eggs that escaped their carton. They are Grossfeld's Flyers. Although no eggmen (or women) will actually ever *play* hockey, this is the happiest he or she will be today.

"Mr. Owens!"

Shit. Eye roll.

Out of shadows, waddling her Nurse Ratched shoes toward me, is a third-generation civil servant from County Protective Services who doesn't think hockey and Down syndrome are a natural match. Her name is Ms. Balloon-Ass Law & Order. She has a large Cook County sheriff with her, same as last time. I'm six foot; he's taller, heavier, and has a Glock 19 on his hip. Mr. and Ms. Law & Order stop at fistfight distance.

She slaps my work shirt with another subpoena. "Third and final. Court date is twelve days."

"Wow." I fake a smile. "Twelve more days? Still won't grant you the emergency restraining order?"

"Check the judge's name, asshole." Ms. Balloon-Ass Law & Order's posture is not encouraging. "Think jail. 'Child endangerment.' Maybe prison."

"Maybe you'll come visit? I'll introduce you around?"

"Twelve days." She turns, doesn't look at the Flyers she's here to save, and walks out with her gunfighter in tow.

Grossfeld's Flyers are a special-needs hockey team that my erstwhile business partner, Dave Grossfeld, and I organized, sponsor, and for all practical purposes, raise. As wards of the state, all twelve live on the dwindling largess of bankrupt government—state, county, and city—and the corrupt, petty politicians who make up the Illinois and Chicago brain trust for administering funds that neither entity has. If not for my monthly stipend to the Flyers' expert wrangler / bus driver / daytime den mother, Patty "Prom-Night" (don't ask)—an army medic who left a butt cheek and two ribs in Iraq—the Flyers could not train daily to become the Wheaties-box Special Olympians they will surely be.

Ha, you say?

The Flyers may be a one-team league, but they're sufficiently popular to have a coach: Johnny's best, ex-pro Kenny Rzepecki. They also have friends on the Blackhawks starting roster, and a nemesis, Ms. Balloon-Ass Law & Order, whom you just met. She thinks fluorescent-lit dead-end corridors and institutional dayrooms are the way to go.

I slide Ms. BAL&O's subpoena into my jeans pocket behind today's *Daily Racing Form.* This is her big-moment, final court-filing to disband the Flyers, hang my partner and me with a permanent NCO (no-contact order), and reduce Coach Rzepecki's afterlife chances for something better than eternal purgatory to zero—like me, Kenny's got some karma issues. Mine forged twenty years of night terrors. The ether's way of asking for payment for my little brother, Michael, and a Down syndrome kid who went down with him, both innocent, both murdered by Caribbean hitmen who mistook Michael for me.

Coach Rzepecki's Right Guard deodorant announces him as he appears at my shoulder. He frowns at act III of *The Eggmen Fold,* leans a bad hip against his hockey stick, and says: "Flyers need a new lawyer, a pit-bull bitch protecting her pups. I know a woman; comes in here with your pal Todd Smith. Not gonna be cheap, or pretty."

I float hopeful eyebrows at *woman.* Women of a certain type find me interesting for a week or two.

Coach Rzepecki cold-eyes my primp. "She's into money; ain't gonna care that you modeled underwear."

"Really?" I pat a reasonably good set of aging-action-figure abs, daily armor against past-life indiscretions that crisscross my back. "You know someone else who's graced the Sears catalog? On three occasions?"

"Twenty years ago, when the pay was fifteen bucks and you keep the shorts."

"*Fine.* Assuming your NHL customers at the Blackhawks can live with 'not pretty,' how much does a pit bull cost nowadays?"

"Thirty thousand to beat the no-contact order—"

"*Thirty?*" I step back so the number hits someone other than me.

"Fifteen more to keep the Flyers on the ice and you and Dave un-charged; and five more to convince one of Toddy Pete Steffen's insurance companies they should write medical." Coach Kenny nods at the blue line. "Should one of the Twelve Days of Christmas get hurt."

"Jesus Christ. *Fifty grand?*"

Kenny goes blank, not taking responsibility.

I glance for the rich patron saint who looks after God's misfires . . . the glance lands on empty seats like it does most places Mother Teresa doesn't frequent. "Your fifty include full absolution from Francis Cardinal George? We could take that to Taylor Street or Chinatown; Outfit guys pay for that kind of paper."

"No paper. And the insurance itself is extra."

"God *damn*, man; was your fucking lawyer raised by wolves?"

"Hey, don't fuckin' cry to me. Wanna dump your kids back to the projects, up to you."

"*My* kids?" I flip Kenny the bird and walk away.

Then back. "How the fuck am I the guy—"

I walk away again, eyes up in the rink lights, then back. "Their parents didn't want 'em; the city couldn't give a shit; but *I'm* the guy?"

Kenny stares at me, then the night-terrors talisman around my neck that I've unconsciously gripped with a specific hand.

Exhale. Neck-chain release. "You have how much of the fifty?"

"I have the ice-rink job; and like you, some history I wish I didn't; and morning doughnuts. And every so often, Blackhawk players who tear-up easy." Stare. "Same as you do, tough guy."

"Allergies." I wipe one eye; blow air through my lips. Ice glance. "Little shits are kinda cute, you gotta admit."

"*Cute* is a topless auto-shop calendar girl. Yes or no on the pit bull?"

I look at the spot Ms. Balloon-Ass Law & Order just vacated, then the eggmen and women. "Fifty fucking grand? Really?"

"Plus the insurance."

Headshake. Flyers glance. Our goalie, Lisa "The Wall" Saunders is making snow angels on the ice in front of the net she's guarding. My eyes close. *All good things end. The Flyers had a good run with Dave and me; somebody else could step up . . .*

Without my permission, my right hand checks my phone and the third message from a downtown heavyweight attorney, a summons I had no intention of honoring.

No. Absolutely not. Do not fucking think about it.

The name on the screen means trouble—Levee Grill, back-room-city-politics, organized-crime kind of trouble—trouble way beyond what a regular guy can survive if the dominoes fall wrong . . .

Ice glance: Lisa scrums up to her padded knees in time to block the slowest slap shot of all time. She pumps both arms into the rink lights like she just won the Stanley Cup. Her defensemen mob her.

Fucking shame. Crying goddamn shame. But life's hard, and then you die. Coach Rzepecki glance: he's focused on the Stanley Cup celebration, a smile softening his scarred face.

Don't, Bill. Don't you fucking dare. Mother Teresa has blood relatives, and they ain't you. My mouth says: "Your pit bull take half in ten days, the rest as soon as Dave and I can scrape it up?"

"You mean you, right? Dave ain't scraping up shit and we both know it."

I walk away again, faster and farther this time. *Keep fucking moving, don't stop until you can jump out a fourth-floor window.* I watch my Redwing work boots slow down, then stop, then turn, the steel toes now pointed at Kenny. Someone who sounds like an incredibly stupid version of me says, "Will she take half or not?"

Kenny looks at the Flyers, then nods. "She owes me on something else; I'll spend that. If she needs another reason, I'll give her one."

I glance my phone, feel the suicide *moment of clarity* just before you do the swan dive or pull the trigger, then hear myself say:

"Fuck it. I'll find the money. Tell mama to bite."

**

Traffic downtown adds to my headache. Headaches are God's way of reminding you that accepting contracts from people you know will be trouble is asking for same.

The polar opposite of self-induced headaches is the *Daily Racing Form* (my copy waits un-studied on my passenger seat). It has more pages than the *New York Times*, more numbers than a math textbook, and contains every winner of every race that will be run today. The racetrack's voluminous "newspaper of record" represents a handicapper's hopes and dreams as well as his commitment to achieving them. *I'll find the money*, as spoken to Coach Rzepecki earlier this morning, is the equivalent of setting those aspirations and commitments on fire.

Horns blare. A bus swerves. Brake lights. More horns.

My mission this morning—*I'll find the money*—is inscribed on at least one tombstone in every cemetery, everywhere. Trust me, I know. When I'm not managing the Flyers' front office or at a racetrack, I'm in a cemetery, covered in concrete dust, making a modest living building mausoleums.

Back in the '80s, while a bunch of my mausoleums' residents were doing blow at the North Side's 950 and the Fire Alarm, I was at Oxford—yeah, the one in England—on scholarship, no less, for Advanced Game Theory and English Lit. I can read the writing on the wall pretty well. But *paying attention* to what's on the wall? That's a different construct, up there with "Mind your own business" and "Know your limitations."

But I *did* model underwear. And, for the record, it was twenty-five bucks.

Left turn, finally I'm on Michigan Avenue, two blocks south of the Barlow-O'Hare law offices in the Willoughby Tower, Mr. Barlow is on the sixteenth floor, facing Millennium Park and the fourth-largest freshwater lake on planet Earth. Mega storms crash inland here every year. Fitting, because inside Chicago's city limits, attorney James W. Barlow Jr. does not fear God, or mega storms, or anything else. Why? James W. Barlow's DNA is in the base code of the Democratic political machine that has ruled this city, one way or another, since 1931. For those folks born elsewhere, Chicago runs on bare knuckles and no apology. If you don't favor that style, you're far better off in New York, where they at least hide the guns and knives before they use them.

Barlow-O'Hare's receptionist is a sturdy Scandinavian American blonde in her sixties named Ragnild. She's power-dressed in a whale-blue pantsuit, seated behind a transparent crescent desk, shoulders back, chin up. Her part of the office smells like Copenhagen after the rain. Ragnild accepts an envelope from a five-five alpha male who looks through me to the storm clouds over the lake, then gives her curt FedEx instructions.

Ragnild speaks to me instead, says, "Hi, Bill," winces at her watch, adds, "he's waiting."

I wince back—neither of us care for Mr. Barlow.

The five-five alpha male quits Ragnild's window, focuses on me, isn't any more impressed than the last time we met, then disappears in a waft of scented hair gel and shoe lifts.

Ragnild swivels out of her chair, straightens my bow tie, shifts my seersucker coat on my shoulders, stands back, nods at her work, and says, "Go home; change back into your work clothes. However bad you need the money, you don't need it from here."

I kiss her forehead and quote Elwood Blues. "I'm on a mission from God."

***

JAMES W. BARLOW JR.

Barlow is at his desk. Next to his intercom is an advance reader copy of the nonfiction book *Get Capone*. The intercom announces: "Mr. Owens is here."

"Send him in."

Barlow opens a drawer, places an unopened bottle of Barbancourt Rhum inside on top of a file labeled "O'Hare/Piccard/Grossfeld." He stands, adjusts one red suspender across his starched-white shoulder, then walks to one of the four windows overlooking Millennium Park and Lake Michigan.

The coming storm frames him when the door opens . . .

***

BILL OWENS

My meeting with Mr. Barlow is over.

He catches me at the elevator, says, "Bill—"

"Sorry. The answer's still no."

"Really? I can't imagine anyone more perfect for the job. You have your history all over the Caribbean selling for Myers's Rum. You know a close friend of Ms. Devereux's down there. *And* you need the money."

"Hire a detective from Miami, Nassau, or Kingston. My 'history' in the West Indies includes more than selling rum, and it wasn't pretty."

"Ten thousand plus expenses for a few day's work. *Twenty-five thousand* more if you prove Susie Devereux's alive. Another twenty-five thousand if you can find her."

Barlow pushes a Susie Devereux file and the *Get Capone* book into my chest.

My hands remain in my pockets. The elevator bings. Barlow reoffers the check for ten thousand.

I stare at the check, then Barlow. "Wanna tell me what you're not telling me? Whatever it is that *really* makes me perfect for your job?"

Barlow shrugs innocence.

"Bye."

Barlow blocks the elevator. "Your hockey team, Bill. Without you, they're . . ."

Exhale. "Fifteen thousand for openers. Ten now, five when I get back and tell you I found nothing. But first you explain—here and now—why you want me to travel knowing less than you know."

NASSAU, BAHAMAS

(THREE DAYS LATER)

Chapter 3

BILL OWENS

August 2009
Midnight

Palm trees rustle in front of pastel colonial edifices. A distant steel-drum band adds soundtrack to air you smell only in a flower shop. As they say in the guitar-and-parrot-shirt anthems, "Another day in paradise."

As I stand here wearing Sperry Top-Siders (that should never have walked into James W. Barlow's office), the harbor and dock are mostly shadows, save for the red glow of ganja spliffs and the running lights of the almost seaworthy *M/V Lady Frances* mail boat. The eight-year-old next to me is named Harba Gangsta. I can call him Haba G 'cause we down; Haba G has adopted me "for your protection, and $10."

Haba G points at my T-shirt. "Wasa Grossfeld's Flyers?"

"Hockey team."

Round eyes; confusion.

"Ice hockey." I bend, do a slap shot. "Kids like you, but with Down syndrome."

"Huh?"

The kid's eight, but that's the universal reaction, as in: *What kind of asshole would sponsor a Down syndrome hockey team?*

"You play cricket, right? When you're not running the docks? Hockey's like that, but on ice. Something to do other than sit in a room waiting to die."

"Die? They sick, your team?"

"Sorta. Nobody wants 'em, so I . . ."

Round eyes again.

"Yeah, I know. Long story."

***

One second-thought shy of midnight, I pay Haba G his $10, then another $40 to a shirtless Bahamian captain who looks like he could hula with the Hawaiians and probably does. Captain Stooz points me aboard what a professional seaman might call a "rust bucket" for the weekly run to Rum Cay, 185 miles south.

The ship's horn attempts *throaty*. My left hand grips rusted rail as we slip away into the channel. My right hand grips a freshly acquired Kalik beer. Let's call today a fool's errand. Not that I want to be labeled a fool—I *am* getting paid—but as is often said, if you look around the table and can't find the schmuck, he's you. And for the record, the furniture doesn't have to be a table.

For the next six hours of moonlit trade winds, me, Captain Stooz, and the *Lady Frances* sail through the Bahamas' out islands. I ask my captain to play us some Bob Marley, which he does. The islands twinkle in the breezy dark. Two spliffs into the four that the Stooz-man and I share, I have no trouble singing "One Love" to the dolphins that track us, then testing my hula chops once I feel like me and the dolphins are all on the same page.

***

High noon at sea has more sun in it than my Blues Brothers Ray-Bans can filter. Captain Stooz slides the *Lady Frances* up to the concrete dock at Rum Cay's Grand Hotel Boblo. I am the only cargo that disembarks.

From his pilot-house rail, Captain Stooz repeats, "Careful," and taps the shark logo on his hat. "Weather permittin', be back through the week comin'."

I give him the peace sign.

According to the Stooz-man, the Grand Hotel Boblo has nine bungalow rooms, two bars—one with mosquitoes—a landing strip if you're desperate or fortified with recreational medication, and the best hurricane-hole marina between Hispaniola and the Florida Keys. It was built by a bush-pilot contrabander and a deranged artist who loved limestone, chain saws, and ocean trash that could be massed into giant Burning Man sculptures. But it was the bush pilot's Sicilian girlfriend—a five-foot, stunning bit of business named Yolande Citro—who added the colonial white shutters, pale-yellow siding, pink roof, and high-end escorts looking for a working vacation.

The "hotel" sits on, in, and around a limestone quarry sixteen feet above sea level. Hurricanes pass through often, as do sport fishermen who aren't fishing for fish, as well as modern-day rumrunners (cocaine) on forced holiday from their respective countries of origin and the international police who hunt them. The Grand Hotel Boblo also gets the occasional rock star trolling for trouble they can't find in a tour bus. The sign out front reads:

> Another gringo folly, an alcohol-soaked, sunstroke vision of paradise driven by ego and the lack of any geographic knowledge of the region whatsoever.
> —*James William Buffett*
> *misquoted, as are many, at Hotel Boblo*

Captain Stooz also said that if you stop smiling in either bar at Grand Hotel Boblo, it's only because your cheeks are tired. So the bar is where me and my Top-Siders go.

***

Someone is panfrying fish in the back. I finish my second on-island beer and push the photo across the bar for the fifth time, having added a $20 with each push.

Shrieeeek!

Outside at the hurricane-hole dock is a 58-foot luxury yacht that was Eurotrash posh in the '70s. The five topless girls aboard point at the water. The water's calm, nothing odd, pastel blue—a shark explodes through the blue at a poodle on the yacht's ski deck. The five girls jump backward, and the dog does an Olympic high jump. The shark's sharp half thrashes the ski deck, lucks into the dead wahoo about to be the girls' lunch, chomps the fish, and slams back into the water.

Ooo-kay.

Got it. Don't feed the animals.

I re-push the photo across the bar. This time, my lean, sun-weathered, sixty-something bartender scoops the twenties into his "Fly or Dye" T-shirt pocket. Kayak Jim Jordan smiles and turns the photograph toward me—three women rugby players post-match, arm in arm. He says, "Where'd you get this? Photoshop?"

"A lawyer in Chicago. Said it was taken in '94 or '95 in Glasgow, Scotland. They were playing for a Barbarian team owned by the guy behind them in the photo, a Scotsman named Norrie Rowan."

Kayak Jim smiles again, shaking his head. "The Witches of Eastwick. Wow. Never seen a picture of all three together. If this is real, it's almost as good as that '50s photo of Elvis, Johnny Cash, and Jerry Lee at Sun Records." Kayak Jim points at his wall. "Love to have this up there."

I grin at our good fortune.

Kayak Jim says, "Don't know what a 'Barbarian team' is, but the black babe is Cuban military—Che Guevara type—Florent Dusson-Siri, but she doesn't look like that anymore." Kayak Jim palms the side of his face. "Burned. The redhead is Anne Bonny." Kayak Jim's eyes narrow and he nods southwest. "Women don't come more dangerous than Anne Cormac Bonny. They say she does 'salvage.' Anchors in, or near, Port Royal, Jamaica. But you don't want to find her, even if you could." Kayak Jim taps two fingertips on the last woman. "The brunette is your Susie Devereux. Flashy little number, but no walk in the park either. Scottish Moroccan, pirate from birth, dead three years ago aboard her boat in the Camagüey Breaks." Kayak Jim winces, *sorry.* "Devereux's dead, but I'm keeping your money."

I nod. *Polite* being my default demeanor, and the five twenties weren't my money. "Anyone find her body?"

"Nah. But she's dead."

"Last time Susie Devereux was 'dead,' it was actually the witness-protection program."

Kayak Jim prunes, not a believer.

I repeat some of the info provided with my stipend—a full-on Bond-girl profile that I reread more often than was required for this *I'll find the money* adventure. "Before the US Air Force killed Abu Musab al-Zarqawi in 2006, he put a price on Susie Devereux's head, literally. Al-Zarqawi's al-Qaeda crew tried twice to kidnap her—once in Santiago de Cuba and once in Egypt, where they got her, promising both times to behead her on video."

Kayak Jim's eyes go cartoon-wide. *"The Arab with those sword videos* was after Susie Devereux, *down here?"*

"Scary, huh? Miss Devereux worked as a private contractor at Sheberghan, Abu Ghraib, and Guantanamo. She's good at not being dead when she's dead."

"Never heard any of that. Her boat was here, in and out, five, six times three years back, but she and her crew kept to themselves. Nice enough fellas—an American and an Afrikaner, polite, but serious, you know?" Kayak Jim stops. "Sorta looked like you under that aloha shirt, now that I think about it—middle age, white, good size, good shape, eyes that'd been around the block."

"Really?" I check the Grand Hotel Boblo's backbar mirror.

Kayak Jim says, "Yeah, *really.*"

Me in the mirror looks like Tinkerbell not Captain Hook, the violence of my previous life buried where the mirror can't reflect it and only a psychiatrist or mortician could mine it.

I smile my best Tinkerbell.

Kayak Jim continues, "Given Susie Devereux's reputation, it seemed prudent to let her be. It wasn't a party or a hole-up; they were working."

"Looking for the Capone gold?"

Kayak Jim floats bushy eyebrows. "As in *Al* Capone?"

I nod. The book Barlow gave me, *Get Capone*, was written by a Chicago guy named Jonathan Eig. Reading it on the way here, I found no map to the missing gold—Barlow's convinced it's part of Susie Devereux's story. Unfortunately, I can't use Mr. Barlow's name as support for this conversation, or any other. Pretending to be Eig will be lots easier.

My bartender says, "Son, I've been kicking around down here a long time and never heard Al Capone's name south of Miami. Hollywood puts Capone's hand on every criminal act ever committed by an American, but in these parts, the Golden Age of Piracy was two centuries before Capone was born."

I stay with my employer's theory. "Capone's gold was definitely modern-day. Would've been in the 1920s or '30s."

Kayak Jim says, "The only *modern-day* gold I know about is what went missing from the Banque Nationale d'Haiti during World War One, almost a hundred years ago. A treasure hunter's ghost story."

Gag; cough. Barlow did not mention Haiti. My neck-chain talisman is choking me. Kayak Jim glances at my right hand, the palm now flattened over a name carved across the lifeline.

"Could Susie Devereux have been chasing that gold? From"—I cough again—"Haiti?"

Kayak Jim fisheyes me. "Doubt it. And she never said. And I wasn't in the breaks, but the Cubans say Susie Devereux is dead down island of Cayo Romano. No one over here on the non-Communist side of the channel has seen, or heard of, her since." Kayak Jim polishes the bar. "Why's Susie Devereux worth a hundred dollars to a guy like you?" Small smile. "Whatever kinda guy you are?"

Behind Kayak Jim, reflected in the bar mirror, a truly odd white guy walks past the bar's windows. No shirt, powerfully built, a wad of sandy hair no barber college could explain. I know he's not Eurotrash, because they almost never carry chain saws. The white guy comes through the door, sets the chain saw on the bar next to me, and extends his hand. "Bobby Little, my pleasure to meet ya."

I reach to shake and tell him my fake name. The girls on the boat shriek again. Bobby Little says, "Excuse me" and grabs his saw off the bar.

Three steps out the door, Bobby fires the chain saw. Everything that's alive, in or out of the water, runs for cover. Bobby jumps off the dock, lands chest-deep in the water, and fans the saw like he intends to go diving with it.

Kayak Jim shakes his head. "My partner; nothing to worry about," then asks me again: "Why's Susie Devereux worth a hundred dollars to a guy like you?"

I quit looking at the potential showdown in the harbor between chain saw and shark and ease into my cover story. "I stumbled onto a crate of Capone documents that a US federal prosecutor had squirreled away back in the '30s. Used 'em to write a book about Capone that's about to publish." I push Barlow's copy of *Get Capone* across the bar. "Thinking about writing a sequel; wanted to see if the Capone gold is more than an urban legend."

"You're a writer? Woulda guessed smuggler, cocaine maybe, or guns." Both hands go up. "No offense. What's your name again?"

I lie. "Jonathan Eig."

"No . . . the *Weaponized Accounting* Jonathan Eig?"

I swell on my stool. "Yep."

"No shit? Stay put. Next beer's on me." Kayak Jim walks down the bar and disappears through a gray kitchen door. I check Bobby Little still in the water, now chopping at it with his chain saw. His partner returns with a mangled Jon Eig paperback, a Michael Lewis hardcover, and a 2005 *Rolling Stone* magazine in a clear plastic bag. On the cover: "The Man Who Sold the War." Kayak Jim pushes the paperback at me with a pen. "Would you mind? Make it to Kayak Jim Jordan. I tell all the girls and captains who dock here—tell 'em all the time—read these three, not the Bible."

I sign messy over Jonathan Eig's faded back-cover bio (no photo) that says he was an investigative reporter for a list of big-time newspapers.

Kayak Jim adds: "All you need to know. The whole goddamn world-scenario is Wall Street fiction—Iraq's WMD, the War on Drugs, campaign finance reform—all of it bullshit."

At the far end of the serpentine tile bar, a sun-and-life-mottled captain with navy tattoos sits on his stool unfazed by the shark-poodle attack and the continuing chain saw response. The captain's lack of interest isn't completely out of line; he has a tanned, topless young lady on his lap.

"God bless Buddy Holly," says the captain, raising a Carib beer in a toast. "Best place for facts is always a rock 'n' roll tabloid."

Shouting outside.

Kayak Jim says: "Goddammit," jumps the bar, a revolver in hand, and runs for the dock. The blue water around Bobby Little is red for ten feet in every direction. Kayak Jim aims at the water and shouts at two Bahamians watching the carnage. They jump in, grab Bobby and his chain saw, haul him out, and drop him on the dock. Bobby Little jumps to his feet, points at the dogs on the dock, then yells at the water: "Not the goddamn dogs! Dogs are not fish!"

From behind his topless stool mate, the captain says, "Odd, an educated fellow like yourself down here hunting gold."

I cut back to the captain and his Cinderella.

"Not *hunting.*" My fingers make a crucifix. "Just want to vet the Capone gold story. But if it's true, then the money trail's real, and the money trail is what I'm actually interested in."

"Money *trail?*"

"Same general theory as you'll find in our bartender's reading list." I nod to the ghost of Kayak Jim. "US foreign policy in collusion with Wall Street banks, add Capone as the criminal element, and we're looking at another Iran-Contra or United Fruit—the same crime-business-government three-way that Senator Estes Kefauver called the 'Rotten Bargain' back in the 1950s. The story I'm chasing has the gold embezzled from a bank down here in the Caribbean with the help of a bank in New York."

The captain sips his beer, his chin above Cinderella's naked shoulder. "Never heard about Capone being involved, but your story could be Haiti. Lots of Haitians say gold was *looted* from their treasury, not *embezzled.* The Ida rebels in particular never stop selling that story. The gold *itself* is fact, and it's MIA, but that gold never belonged to the Haitian treasury. That gold belonged to the bank's US investors as part of their reserve requirement."

I squint confusion.

The captain says, "During World War One, Haiti's president was assassinated, chopped into *edible* pieces. The US government feared that a slave revolt, the cacos, led by Charlemagne Péralte, would take power, steal the bank's gold, fill Haiti's treasury, then help the Germans attack America. If it's *that* gold you're talking about, *that* gold has killed everyone said to have touched it, including your Susie Devereux if that's what she was after."

"And the Gryphon?"

Cinderella loses her smile. The captain hardens. He stares and doesn't speak.

Oops. Whoever Mr. Gryphon is, I've overplayed knowing about him.

"Sorry. Didn't mean anything. Heard the name from a Chicago lawyer who worked in DC twenty years ago, that's all. He said this Gryphon guy was a player down here back then. That he might know something about Susie Devereux."

The captain eyes the doors and Kayak Jim returning, then the windows, showing more concern than he did for the shark fight. "I suggest you finish your beer, Mr. Eig, and go wherever it is you're going. Keep that name to yourself and good luck to you."

I conjure a Jonathan Eig apology. "Sorry. Really. I used to be a reporter for the *Wall Street Journal*. A guy hears things, so he asks, that's all. Old habit. No offense." I toast the captain with my beer. "Really."

The already diminished *happy* in the room diminishes to zero.

Kayak Jim changes the subject. "I can tell you about the gold; can't say I don't look when I'm flying that water." Grin. "On December 17, 1914, sixty-five US Marines under the command of one Major C. B. Hatch 'looted' the Banque Nationale d'Haiti. They loaded 1,650 *pounds* of gold aboard the US Gunboat *Machias*—$500,000 worth at $20 an ounce—then sailed immediately from the harbor at Port-au-Prince. Later that day, engine trouble forced the Machias into the old port at Kingston, Jamaica. A day later, the *Machias* docked in Santiago de Cuba at Guantanamo Bay, trying to avoid the hurricane that almost sank her in the harbor anyway. She left Cuba on December 21, 1914; was found adrift off Charleston, South Carolina, on January 3, 1915, a ghost ship—no crew, no US Marines, no gold."

The girl on the captain's lap speaks for the first time, eyes on her beer: "Don't go to Haiti; you won't come back." She raises her eyes to me, staring like the naked and fervent do in Madonna videos. "Ayiti's civil war will start soon, fifty thousand Ida rebels . . . but they won't be *what* kills you; *he'll* know you're coming before you know you're going."

All righty, then.

It makes me ill to say Haiti—and there's absolutely no chance I'd go—but these reactions are too over the top not to press. "Think one of your fellow captains would take me? To Haiti?"

The captain shakes his head. "You don't listen well, do you?"

Actually, the real me does. "It's not that far, is it?" I point southeast.

The captain shakes his head again and nods toward our bartender. "Jonathan Eig, meet Kayak Jim Jordan. Bush pilot. Seaplane. Half owner of Hotel Boblo. And crazy." The captain nods outside at Bobby Little. "And that's saying something. Write down your next of kin; I'll make sure they get word."

***

Rather than do that, I set up my office on the Grand Hotel Boblo dock—sufficiently far back to avoid a shark reprisal—unfold my laptop, log on to Boblo's pirated cell signal, and task Google with "Anne Cormac Bonny, gold, Jamaica." The signal is slow. Three multicultural terriers sniff my laptop and me. They smell like scavenged crabmeat and sweat.

The girls aboard the yacht giggle and shriek and throw food in the water. The dogs eye the food. I remind them, "Shark? Big teeth? Chomp?"

My screen lights up with Anne Bonny's namesake ancestor, the pirate from the 1700s. I add "smuggler, treasure hunter, salvage" and get a *Jamaica Gleaner* op-ed article with a photo, written three months ago. It says that Anne Cormac Bonny is "out of favor with the current government, considered a smuggler and a subversive whose continued presence on our island is an insult to the republic."

Gosh, what a shock. My girl Anne is, as always, the epicenter of *happy.*

Barlow was correct that Anne and I have a history. Why Dave Grossfeld felt the need to share that fact is one of several in-your-face conversations he and I will have when I see him.

Although Anne's one of the reasons Barlow selected me for this mission, he's unaware that we have not spoken since 1986. My night terrors are the reason. If Anne knows that Susie D. is somehow alive, I doubt Anne will tell me unless Susie D. wants me to know.

Anne's picture in the *Gleaner* is in front of the Sazerac Bar, a bar the article says Anne owns in Port Royal, the pirate capital of the world back in her namesake's day. In the photo, Anne hasn't changed much since our days at Oxford—still a shoulders-back flaming redhead, but in a national-pattern sarong skirt instead of a kilt, bathing-suit top, muscled arms and shoulders, and the same full-lipped half-grin that promised way more than a smart person could handle.

I try an email address that my employer said was associated with an Anne Bonny in the "professional salvage" business. The email address produces an automated reply asking for my info and the reason for my enquiry. I type my reason but expect no reply. I try a phone number search. Three numbers with 876 prefixes (Jamaica) match Anne's name. I call—at two dollars and twenty cents per minute—and each number answers with a recording prompting me to leave a message.

Hm.

Kingston would be a three-hour flight in Kayak Jim's single-engine seaplane . . . and seeing Anne again is definitely tempting, but so is *not* seeing her (I do have to sleep at night). And the Glasgow rugby photograph of Anne and Susie D. is fourteen years old, so it isn't like Anne and Susie D. are *current* mates. Then there's the history Anne and I and her boyfriend had in that country I'm never going back to. Seriously unpleasant history I do not care to revisit, talisman or no. And . . . what do the Fates say? Jamaica or Cuba?

***

"The key"—Kayak Jim points at a nine-foot nurse shark patrolling the dock pylons—"if one's intention is to arrive in Castro's Cuba illegally, is to land just before sunset in one of the back bays of the Jardines del Rey. Water's too unpredictable on the ocean side."

"The ocean side would be the Camagüey Breaks?"

"Roger that."

Next to my laptop on Hotel Boblo's dock, I unroll the nautical chart I brought from Chicago. The Jardines del Rey are strung along Cuba's eastern coastline—120 miles of islands and reefs, one of which is Cayo

Romano, where Susie Devereux wrecked. Cayo Romano is two hours from Rum Cay, *if* one has a seaplane and a deranged pilot. I offer the coveted Witches of Eastwick photo and $300.

Bobby Little steps in grinning and takes the $300. "Your contribution to store-bought dog food and this year's Burning Man."

Kayak Jim grabs the photo, then two of the hundreds. "Gas costs money."

Time to fly.

Rum Cay's airstrip is littered with DC-3s (shock)—in and out of the water—planes that might've had more cocaine aboard than they could fly, or maintenance logs that might've been a tad outdated. Carlos Lehder's infamous Norman's Cay (cocaine ground zero in the 1980s) is fifty miles northwest.

Kayak Jim's Cessna 172 Skyhawk vibrates in the water. He wraps a WWI aviator's scarf around his neck, says, "Onward," and gooses the throttle. We're airborne well before our blue-water runway ends at the seawall coral.

The trip to Cuba is loud and low altitude in the copilot seat. "Low altitude" in a single-engine Caribbean seaplane translates to hot, cramped, and National Geographic beautiful.

Two hours into the 250-mile flight, Kayak Jim banks to the south, then due west. He says, "Cuba," to a string of islands, then drops toward the southeastern end.

The pale-blue water is so bright it hurts my eyes. He points across a long, ragged archipelago with a huge inland bay and a mouth to the ocean. On the west side of the bay is a small one-story town. The town's docks are bigger than its buildings.

Kayak Jim says, "Ciudad de Nuevitas," and banks north. "See the railroad tracks? Castro's sugar port. We land in that bay, we go to prison."

I say, "Cayo Romano. I need to see it."

"Dead ahead." He points at an atoll shaped like a winged skull.

Cayo Romano is arid and sparse, dotted with odd chunks of dense green, and no buildings. The Camagüey Breaks side is foamy reef.

Kayak Jim says, "We could land on the back side in the bay after I fly over and spook the birds. If you want to talk to anyone, we're better off back near the fishing village." He thumbs over his shoulder. "You speaka da Spanish? Nobody down there'll be speaking English."

I give my pilot a thumbs-up, certain my racetrack Spanish will carry the day.

**

Kayak Jim taxis me into a protected length of knee-deep water but won't take money to stay. "Not losing my plane. Find a landline; call; I'll fly back. Your best chance to avoid Mariel prison is stay on the bay side of the cays, away from any civilization except fishermen. Castro's defense against beach landings by Americans ain't a joke. And don't ask about the Gryphon; these out-island Cubans are serious *la bruja*— witch—people. A Gryphon question may get you burned at the stake or chopped into fish bait."

"Anything else?"

"Yeah. You know about the Santeria, right? The Palo Mayombe Santeria in particular?"

"Some. Maybe."

"The bad version is Haitian vodou, the blood-and-death shit from up by Souvenance. The Santeria's, in Spanish, got the *orishas*—that's their saints. And their priests, the *palero* and *palera*. Do not step on any saints or priests. Also, anything with 'black' in it you interpret as *Vaya con Dios*—get the fuck outta Dodge."

Kayak Jim's Skyhawk does the into-the-sunset goodbye, then banks southeast.

I walk, climb, and wade what I can of the Camagüey Breaks, looking for my Bond girl's ghost in the sunset and foam. Even the low waves crash. Coral heads appear and disappear in the foam. Susie D.'s coastline isn't one you'd approach on purpose, not in a storm, and not with Susie D.'s history in boats and water. She had to be running, chancing her way through the coral, hoping it killed whoever was chasing her.

I wait for Susie to do the scantily clad *Dr. No* Bond-girl entrance and solve the mystery.

She doesn't.

I spend the night without her, nibbled upon by rock crabs near a maze of inland shallows. The sky is a star carpet; godly, if I were to be honest.

At sunrise, I pee on the crabs for biting me, drink the last of my water, and head for the fishing village.

As I approach, a tiny smiling woman and a boy in mismatched gym shoes meet me.

I mention Susie D.'s boat crash three years ago.

"*Si! Si!*" The boy has a big Cuban voice. "*La bruja Palo Mayombe!* She is alive after the four boats explode! *Vela negra palera!*"

The boy's mother jerks him to her.

The kid points. "There. Between the lighthouses at Cayo Confites and Faro Colón!"

The mother slaps him silent.

In racetrack Spanish, *vela negra* would mean "black candle." *Black candle* and *palera* in the same sentence would be Kayak Jim's "really fucking scary woman."

The boy's mother points me south, where her now-crying son pointed, says, "Faro Colón," and drags her boy back toward the village.

I yell, "*Con permiso, señora?*"

She looks over her shoulder, but keeps walking. I put three US tens—a month's wages—on the high coral, add a busted conch shell on top, and say, "*No problema. Gracias.*"

For three hours, I trek coral and scrub and wade tide-pool ocean to reach the lighthouse at Faro Colón. The tower is a biggie, better than 150 feet, and chalk white. The keeper is outside tending a garden patch with occasional palm trees and breezy white sand. He stands, removes a cane-cutter's *guajiro* straw hat, and welcomes me in Spanish, glancing for my vehicle.

I say thanks, then repeat what the boy told me.

The keeper chills. "This boy is mistaken, a spreader of tales, like all children. No persons survived the explosions. Absolutely no one. Except, possibly a honey-bee-colored woman."

"And?" I offer one US twenty.

The keeper requires three more to utter another word. He 360s our middle of nowhere, then he says, "This woman, who some say *might* have survived—some say this but not me—is taken by *mulañé fletera* into the convent near Camagüey."

At the racetrack, *mulañé fletera* translates to "mulatto prostitute," but this far out in the bush it could mean "President Kennedy." Who the hell knows? I ask, but the lighthouse keeper won't explain.

He points me down the steps of his lighthouse into the low hills and sun glare. "Convento Nuestra Señora de Regla."

"*Señora* who?"

"Señora de Regla. The Black Virgin, the Black Madonna." He crosses himself, points north. "She stands high above Havana Bay."

"Was the woman somebody special in Cuba? Why take her to the Black Madonna's convent?"

The keeper looks both directions, touches the inside of his wrists.

"Her wrists? I don't get it. *No entiendo.*"

"When the mulatta wipe away the blood"—his voice breaks—"they say the woman have the marks."

"What kinda marks?"

He steps backward into the lighthouse.

"What? Like suicide cuts? Stigmata?"

The door slams shut between us.

I knock, repeatedly, wave more twenties, take a wild shot and shout: "The Gryphon?"

No reaction. No faces in the small windows.

In the '80s (my rum-salesman history in the region), I went to Havana six or eight times from Kingston for Myers's Rum. The black statue that stands high above Havana Bay was Mecca to a specific group of people.

The sun rises all the way out of the Atlantic to scorch the air, me, and the sand. I lather on Banana Boat sunscreen, then begin the trek inland from the Camagüey Breaks.

The Cuban sun is hot on my neck. Three hours into the trek, the final miles to the convent begin to feel like the ill-advised, ill-equipped sun-set trip to Dracula's castle. What little I do know about Palo Mayombe Santeria is that it is serious crazy shit in this part of the world—witch dread they borrowed from European religions that already thought burning and drowning their congregations was reasonable. Add the slave trade and African alchemy. No telling what kinda reception they provide Americans "on a mission from God" at a convent that *wants* witches.

Bad thought: Maybe Belushi and Aykroyd imported Sister Mary Stigmata from there.

A rumbling sugarcane wagon rolls up on me and stops in the diesel stink and smoke. The driver smiles down from the faded blue cab. Behind him, ten cane cutters and their machetes ride inside the wire mesh that baskets the wagon bed. I catch a ride for ten fabulous miles, drink all the water I can from the jug the cane cutters offer, and don't mention the convent until the wagon stops to turn off the main road.

I hop out the back, dust off the cane shreds and spiders, say, "*Gracias, amigos,*" then in Spanish ask about Convento Nuestra Señora de Regla.

None of the brown faces answer.

The driver grinds the wagon into gear, waves me up to the cab, points farther west, then touches a red-and-black card hanging from his rearview mirror. On the card is a bell-shaped face with beads around the forehead.

I say, "*Gracias. Vaya con Dios,*" and salute with two fingers.

The driver squints at my mention of God, stares at the inside of my wrist, touches the card again, touches that finger to his lips, then rumbles the wagon across the road.

I choke on the diesel, remind myself that the Flyers need me to do this, then look west where the driver pointed.

I arrive outside the convent at sunset; perfect timing if you're making a horror movie. The good news is there's no "inside" to get trapped in and tortured. What's still standing of Dracula's castle are sections of scorched walls, bits of rubble, and a goat eating weeds and grass. I fisheye the goat—cloven hoof, horns; you know. He makes no move that a real goat wouldn't make. I wander as it gets darker, dragging fingertips on the walls, talking to the scorch marks and rubble.

"So, Susie, did the witches bring you here? Breathe life back into you?"

Night falls. No Susie Devereux. No Dracula rises from the ground; no *la bruja vela negra* appears; and better still, no Sister Mary Stigmata. My issues with night terrors are real, even if this Dracula's castle isn't. Me and my talisman sleep outside the walls just to be safe.

At sunrise, I hunt for any trace of Susie Devereux three years ago; a clue or a connection that might matter. After an hour, I say goodbye to seeing Susie D. alive in lingerie and the bonus from Barlow that would buy a bigger chunk of the Flyers' legal defense fund. My feet say hello to the cracked highway, centipedes, and scorpions that will collectively lead me to water and the airport east of ciudad de Camagüey.

***

The police at Camagüey's airport offer me water and a chance not to go to prison. After I down my third bottle, they ask about my condition. In tourist English, I tell them, "I walked to a convent, then back here, something called the Nuestra Señora or something. Didn't realize it was that far. Never found it."

The police nod. In Spanish, one says, "A convent, yes. But this building burned down three years ago."

"Three years, huh? How'd the fire start? Anybody hurt?"

Shrug. Narrower eyes.

I'm too stupid to shut up. "Any idea where the survivors of the fire went?"

One of the policemen steps forward and says, "Passport, *por favor.*"

He takes me to an airport policeman with epaulets and subordinates who transports me in handcuffs to *el jefe* in Camagüey. Seems I have no entry stamp in my USA passport and no visa. I miss the next international plane while they check and recheck my passport, asking me repeatedly: "Why are you in Cuba with no visa or stamp?"

"Again, *señor*, I came in by seaplane, intended to ask the officials not to stamp my passport so I wouldn't get in trouble back home. You know, '*No estampa, por favor*'? But I couldn't find any officials. I went to the lighthouse hoping he could tell me who to see. Sorry."

"Your intention was to visit Cayo Romano, yes?"

"To fly over it, and we did, twice."

"Before you went to Faro Colón, the lighthouse?"

The lighthouse keeper must have a phone. Duh? "Yes, we flew over Cayo Romano before I walked to the lighthouse."

"And there you ask about a woman." He cuts to the name carved across the lifeline of my right palm.

"No, not her."

"This woman you ask about, she is a survivor of—"

"The wife of a friend was on one of the boats that sank at Cayo Romano three years ago. No one in the USA knows what happened to her." I say a silent thank-you that I am not holding the Witches of Eastwick photo that includes a Cuban revolutionary of unspecified politics. "The wife's name is Lisa Reins, from Moore, Oklahoma."

"Why did you go to the convent?" He points a finger. "The truth, *señor*."

"The lighthouse keeper said maybe there had been a survivor, a 'honey-bee-colored woman,' who had been taken to the convent. Lisa Reins is kind of that color."

They run Lisa's name for three hours, ask about drugs and guns, then take me back to the airport and wait with me until I am buckled into a Cubana Airlines 737 bound for Cancun. God bless, Lisa. She turns men's heads even when you can't see her.

***

The air we deplane into at Cancun International is that unmistakable, musty-mildew-Mexico aromatic cocktail. The police are cruise-ship-destination pleasant. Unfortunately, the restaurants inside are USA chains. I pick the least offensive and drink a showy margarita to my safe passage and the Flyers' partially funded impending victory over Ms. Balloon-Ass Law & Order.

Nubile college girls throng past on "the adventure of a lifetime." None rise to Susie D.

Finishing margarita two, I redebate the trip to Jamaica, fantasizing Anne Bonny in a Maureen O'Hara *Against All Flags* outfit and me as Errol Flynn. I add a possible three-way with Susie D.—on-screen the Bond girls *are* a promiscuous bunch—after I rescue her from some horrible volcano-dwelling villain.

Ordering margarita three, I admit the historical "Anne and me" also included Carel Roos, Anne's Afrikaner boyfriend, a three-way that never made it past two—her and Carel.

I walk across the concourse to the pay phones. But, discretion being the better part, I call my employer in Chicago instead of Anne Bonny, regaling Mr. Barlow's voicemail with my trip to Cuba, then close with, "I'll be by your office in a few days; some of this doesn't belong on voicemail." I hang up, think about direct dial to Kingston, and—

—scurry back to the Corona Beach Bar's plastic sand, where I will stay, listening to the mariachi-pop soundtrack until my flight to Chicago is ready to board.

Two gates down, an electronic departures board blinks a flight to Kingston. I pivot away, being a bit impulsive where women are concerned. My palm with the name grips the Flyers talisman at my neck . . .

The last time I saw Anne Bonny was 1986; I'd been gang raped and beaten almost to death in a Haitian prison. Haiti was on fire and Anne walked into it like she was Joan of Arc and saved my life. Yep, that's what happened. Then Anne and I and her boyfriend's crew of Rhodesian mercenaries began three days that would kill a lot of people.

Like I said, Anne was no Hannah Montana.

I suck down the last of my margarita.

And back then, for a brief, horrible time, neither was I.

CHICAGO

(ONE MONTH LATER)

Chapter 4

BILL OWENS

Today is a race day. I'm feeling better than lucky—the Flyers have prevailed in two court appearances, both of which required me to sit in the witness chair and defend accusations that would cringe an errant priest. Not something you want to endure if the accusations involve children, especially handicapped wards of the state.

But we have prevailed, partially because Todd Smith himself showed up to backstop our new lawyer, and Todd Smith be a playa. Unfortunately, Ms. Balloon-Ass Law & Order has decided to take our victories as personal insults. (As a lowly citizen, I'm supposed to live with the shit they inferred I was guilty of *and* bear the legal costs.) Her continued use of public funds to fuel her attack translates into a second round of *I'll find the money.*

For round two (thankfully, this round won't include a Barlow mission), I am again properly attired in my blue-and-white seersucker suit, a new pair of Sperry Top-Siders, and misted with Old Spice after-shave, walking through a sweltering construction site littered with ruined rebar, masonry sand, and wasted concrete, all of which I have to pay for. I begin a silent duet with my inner Daryl Hall and the svelte "Maneater" on my arm.

The young lady on my arm is nicknamed "Better Offer" because when I dated her, Lisa Reins kept her options officially open until you were both naked. And even then, I was never certain she'd still be there for the big finish.

Lisa's career currently fluctuates between hairdresser, process server, rehab, and escort, the latter for those men or women customers who require thirty years of experience packed into a tight twenty-something's body: education, manners, and no Christian morals whatsoever if there's money involved. Lisa's on my arm today as a representative of my Serenity Mausoleum Corporation. I have high hopes for my company even though it requires an almost constant scramble. And I have high hopes for Lisa's sundress and its impact on angry, unreasonable construction contractors.

Lisa hugs one generous breast into my upper arm and smiles at Lithuanian Ron, the contractor in front of us. Lithuanian Ron is quite large, topped by a square head on a twenty-inch neck.

I say: "It'd be good, Ron, really good, if you could build the wall according to the plans." I show him my rolled copy of the architectural plans that match his. "See, that's why the cemeterians pay *me* and that's why I pay you."

Ron smiles at Lisa and her sundress, glances at the three-hundred-crypt mausoleum we're building, then gives me the silent look subcontractors use when they want to be paid for work they didn't do—part threat, part promise to fix it on the next draw (completed items to be paid).

I answer Lithuanian Ron's silence. "How many of these have we done, Ron? Six? Eight? A hundred? I can't write a draw on that wall; the inspecting architect isn't fondling funeral directors in his back seat, and I don't have pictures. If you're paying your guys this week, better rob a Foremost Liquors on the way home."

Lisa smiles sympathy.

Ron straightens his 265 pounds, eyes Lisa's opulent décolletage, then my well-cultivated look of bon vivant-ness, not the jeans and work boots he normally sees me wearing. Ron spits behind his leg into the rebar, and says, "So, my guys made a mistake. I'll fix it, but you still gotta pay me, cause I gotta pay them." Ron nods at his crew of gorillas five hours short of the Labor Day weekend. All five favor me with the South Side, lynch-mob posture of men who relate to alcohol as a primary holiday companion.

"No, Ron, I don't. Today is a racing day. One I've planned for a very long time. You may have noticed my suit. What I have to do is go to the track and ensure that a huge amount of work is not killed by bad luck."

Ron smiles beyond Lisa at headstones as far as his wide-set eyes can see. "Like dying here can't happen?"

I frown at Ron, a man I know well but don't like much more than the last bite of an average meal. "Maybe you're saying you want a loan? A loan shark I can find you; six for five, pay Loef Brummel back next week."

Lithuanian Ron glances at the *Daily Racing Form* folded once into my seersucker pocket the way a gentrified horseman carries the *Form* on a race day. Ron spits again, this time closer to my Top-Siders. "Ain't me who needs a loan shark; you're who the Micks got by the balls." Ron thumbs over his shoulder. "My guys ain't going unpaid 'cause your debts kill you."

"I don't owe any loan sharks, Irish or otherwise, and if I did, it'd be none of your fucking business."

"Loef Brummel's gonna squeeze you for what Dave Grossfeld owes 'cause Loef thinks you can pay, and he *knows* Dave can't."

Silent alarm bell.

My partner Dave is a man who *was, and is,* dumb enough to borrow from Loef Brummel. I consider my options. And go with the most aggressive, scorched-earth "fire for effect" known to man:

"Ron, I'd like you to meet Lisa Reins."

***

Unrumpled by a physical altercation, I'm now northbound in my aging but immaculate Citroën C5, doing seventy toward Arlington Park for a race-day Ritual that must be followed to the letter. This Ritual properly aligns the heavens and removes all bad juju including Lithuanian Ron's suggestion that Dave Grossfeld might be on the arm to Loef Brummel. While this is a troubling addition to Dave's behavior the last few days, a *suggestion* of trouble is not going to ruin a career-betting proposition that's been thirteen months in the making and will fund the Flyers' defense fund well into whatever idiot sphere Ms. Balloon-Ass wants to visit.

My cell phone rings just south of the 294/Kennedy interchange for O'Hare. A Baird's Bread truck swerves into my lane to avoid a forced airport exit. I dodge the truck and answer: "And it's a good morning to ya, whoever ya are."

Loef (pronounced "Laif") Brummel's tone is icy. "Meet me at the Brehon."

"I'm out on the West Side, Loef, headed to Arlington. Can we do it tomorrow?"

"No."

"Later, maybe? After six?"

"Thirty minutes."

"Ahh . . . are we good, Loef? Something wrong?"

"Nothin' but sunshine." Click.

Sunshine and loan sharks are a non sequitur. I envision Loef alone at the Brehon after I don't show.

Nope.

I veer east off 294 onto the Kennedy, hang up, and punch Dave's cell on speed dial. Fucking Dave . . . me and Loef Brummel in the same sentence is *not* what my afternoon plan had in it. Dave's phone goes to voicemail. My childhood friend and errant partner hasn't answered my calls for two days. Calls I've been making since Dave's secretary called, saying, "Dave's in the TCI"—(Turks and Caicos)—"changed his mind at the last minute and entered this year's tournament. Said to tell you he has a big job, like the Sportsman's"—(a racetrack)—"move in '03, but has to have your help to close it. Please call him ASAP."

I try Dave's satellite phone. It rings ten times. Fucking Dave. Since he retired from the NHL, Dave's big into ocean sportfishing. His 48-foot Viking, *Slap Shot Terror*, is docked in the TCI south of the Bahamas, where Dave spends four weeks a year that are more like eight. Dave being MIA isn't unusual; Dave putting me on Loef Brummel's plate for dinner is.

***

In the summer, the Brehon Pub props open all its doors. The 150-year-old building smells clean and airy, front to back, but it's surrounded by two hundred years of Chicago history, much of it neither clean nor airy. The sounds of the city roll past the doors. Canaryville's top loan shark isn't here yet. Canaryville is Chicago DNA for hard-ass, working-class, kill-you-twice-a-day Irish.

Two cars pull up in tandem out front on Wells. The doors of the tail car pop open. Four of Loef Brummel's guys leap out. Two sprint to the passenger door of the first car, rip it open, jerk out a white man, and sprawl him to the sidewalk. Both guys take turns slamming size twelves into the man's head while their associates glare witnesses away. The stomping doesn't stop until the man's face is unrecognizable.

Loan Shark 101—pay them.

All four guys, plus the driver of the first car, get into the tail car and leave. The man on the sidewalk bleeds in three directions and doesn't move.

A young waitress I haven't seen before runs past a bar customer to help. He grabs to stop her but misses.

I feel the threat behind me before I see it and cut to the Brehon's side door on Superior.

An Irish gentleman of about fifty leans into his steps as he approaches. He's a hard 175 pounds, dressed better than I've seen him act, and capable of killing people in volume. The summer Donegal cap cheerfully dipped to the left eye doesn't change that. Loef Brummel stops at conversational distance, looks the remaining waitress away, then chins at me. "Step into my office."

People in the crime business call this Irishman a dead-serious gangster, a throwback to the straight razors and ice picks of the Levee era in Chicago, but one who will listen to reason if it's about money. I know Loef from the track, used to work his horses. He likes me, so I might live five minutes longer than someone he doesn't.

Loef's office for this meeting is a wall-attached table at the front with a good view of Wells Street and no way to get to him from behind. We sit; I glance him outside at the body on the sidewalk. He shrugs.

Customers at the Brehon's long bar stare at the body, but none leave their stools to assist the waitress. Proof that Loef occasionally does business from here.

I raise my index finger, step off the stool to the pay phone, dial 911, tell CPD they have a dying man on the sidewalk, and ask for an ambulance.

When I return to the table, Loef's head is canted five degrees off-center. "Wanna tell me anything, Mr. Bill?"

"Like what?"

"Your partner, Dave."

"Huh? Like Dave and . . . *you*?"

Loef nods.

"Is Dave jammed? Must be, or he wouldn't be talking to you."

"Dave isn't talking to me, you are."

Silent alarm bell no. 2. "Far as I know, Dave's fishing in the TCI, the tournament he does every year." I glance at the sidewalk, hoping for EMTs.

Loef nods again. His eyes don't blink.

Mine do. "What?"

"You tell me."

"Like I said, Dave must be jammed. End of story."

Outside the Brehon, two women hover over the waitress and the body on the sidewalk. One has her phone out but drops it and puts both hands to her mouth. The other woman stoops to assist in the triage. Sirens blare; EMTs arrive.

Loef says, "When's Dave back?"

I lie, "Wednesday," then quote Dave's secretary. "Dave says he has a big job about to pop."

"You sure?"

"I'm not sure of death or taxes."

Loef stares at me, then two squad cars arriving. His thickened bottom lip pushes forward. "Your Dave's in for a hundred; owes the vig three days ago. Comin' back next Wednesday means you're late three days on the first payment and you're gonna miss the second."

Heart spike. "A hundred thousand *dollars*? My Dave?"

Nod. Icy stare.

"Tell me you're lying." I point at Loef. "You're after Dave for something else."

Two-inch headshake.

"No. Goddammit." I glance the bar for a clue on the real story, then the sidewalk. "Dave didn't do that. He didn't."

"Ain't just Dave."

I lean back. But distance won't change the unspoken indictment: Dave and I are partners; I run Serenity Mausoleum and own 50 percent, so in loan-shark world I cosigned Dave's debt and I have to pay it if Dave doesn't.

"Loef, no, man, don't go there. Whatever Dave's doing with you has nothing to do with Serenity." I look right at Dave's loan shark and lie. "I bought Dave out a month ago. Me and him are all done."

"Not what Dave says, or the *Tribune* covering your court cases over the cripples. You two still got the hockey team. You're partners."

Before I can begin to negotiate or beg for Dave's life, and by default, my own, Loef wants a breakdown of the problems at Grossfeld's Moving and Storage that are none of his business, or mine.

I pull my phone and call Dave. Voicemail.

Loef asks, "Dave doing more blow than usual?"

"Not that I've noticed. Didn't see any chop scratches on his desk last time I was at Grossfeld's, but that's been a while."

"Who's the finance company on Dave's trucks?"

"If you sell his trucks, he'll never be able to pay you."

"Finance company?"

"Liberty Loan. Cosmo and his sons, same guys who do my construction loans."

"Get me my vig by Saturday night—that's tomorrow. Twenty thousand for the payment you missed three days ago, plus the twenty thousand that's due on Tuesday—or the trucks get lost before Cosmo can repo 'em; I got a buyer lined up for $40K. Pays you up through Tuesday."

"*Me?* Forty K? The trucks are almost new, have to be worth a hundred, maybe two if the loans are current and sold with titles."

"If you can do better, do better. Either way I want my vig tomorrow."

"Why the fuck would you lend Dave that kind of money?"

"I didn't." Loef nods out the window at the sidewalk. "One of my associates did."

I lean closer. "You know the insurance companies won't pay. All grabbing the trucks does is guarantee a gunfight."

Loef's eyes narrow. "I'm gonna forget I heard that."

"C'mon, man. Nobody wants trucks right now. And Dave's company doesn't have $40,000—for vig or anything else. You gotta wait for his big moving job to work out."

Headshake. "Sell the shit his customers have stored in Dave's warehouse." Loef presses his spatula-tipped finger on my hand. "Or rob one of them nigger-gang dope banks . . . Dave was one violent motherfucker back in the hockey days. But what you don't wanna do, William, is not pay me, and we both know why."

"Quit saying *you*, okay? It isn't me, it's Dave and . . . whoever. And I have to be alive to save Dave's idiot ass. Again. If possible."

"Nope. Dave conned one of my crew. I got partners in street money, nothing I can do. You and Dave are partners, just like I am with my people, so you're on the paper; owe what Dave owes."

"No! Bullshit. Fuck your partners. Absolutely not. I didn't agree to—"

"Get the fuckin' money, Bill." Loef chins at the window. "We just showed you."

I lean in again, this time to argue for *my* life.

Loef shoves me back. "Dave's buying kilos of coke in the Bahamas— Rum Cay—not fish. Outta my hands." Loef gets up to leave before the cops come in to interview for witnesses.

I grab his arm. "Rum Cay? Coke deal? What do you mean?"

Loef looks down at my hand on his arm, then up my seersucker sleeve to my face. I let go and lean back. "*Cocaine* is Dave's sure-thing big job?"

"I told you, Dave conned that fuckin' cheat on the sidewalk. *The cheat* says it's blow. He's supposed to get a private piece of Dave's deal for putting out my money on deals we don't do. Coke makes sense why Dave'd pay the vig; he makes two, three hundred easy if he don't put it up his nose."

My stomach knots. "Dave's into this coke deal alone?"

"Don't know. Could be Dave's trickin' with your lawyer buddies again."

"Who?"

Loef eyes me like I know, like *I'm* part of it, turns for the Brehon's side door, and doesn't answer.

Fuck. Gotta be James W. Barlow Jr. The same lawyer who thirty days ago paid me to find Susie Devereux. *Starting at Rum Cay.* Two days after my return I reported to Barlow. He was oddly complacent about my lack of success, offered no explanation about "marks" or "the Gryphon" or "Haiti," paid me the remaining $5K, patted my shoulder, and sent me out the door.

More police cars screech-stop out front.

Clock check: *Shit*; racetrack.

I bolt for the side door, hit speed dial for Dave's satellite phone, get no answer, then call Kayak Jim at the Grand Hotel Boblo, and get voicemail. At the door to Superior Street, I call James W. Barlow Jr.

Ragnild says, "Sorry, Bill, Mr. Barlow's in court."

"It's urgent, as in life or death."

"I'll text him. Be careful."

"Thanks. Make sure he knows *he* has a problem."

Fast-walking Superior toward my car, I try to make fact out of fiction: Barlow sends me to Rum Cay, a sand-pile atoll in the middle of nowhere, on some bullshit-story recon job three weeks before Barlow's crime partner, Dave Grossfeld, borrows the $100K, then goes to the very same Rum Cay in person.

Supposedly, Dave's at Rum Cay to do a cocaine deal using loanshark money on a fuse so short Barlow and Dave had to believe their deal was a lock. Except no dope deal is a lock, and both Dave and Barlow know that.

How would me *not* finding Susie Devereux or *not* talking to Anne Bonny help seal Dave and Barlow's coke deal?

No fucking way Dave's doing a coke deal; he's doing something else with Susie Devereux.

But what? And why would Barlow pick me to participate?

At my car's fender, I flatten against the paint to avoid a Lycra-clad bicycle messenger flying past, then key the driver's door. Above my hand, my reflection shimmers in the window. Things have changed.

Bill Owens no longer looks like a gentleman horseplayer late to a career-betting opportunity; he's more of seersucker bobblehead holding a suicide note.

***

3:30 p.m.

Traffic's been shit for an hour. I'm four-tasking, foot on the gas, foot on the brake, steering one-handed and speed-dialing with the other. Post time for the feature is five o'clock. I should already be there. I blast onto the shoulder, spit gravel the last half mile to the Arlington Racecourse exit, loop all the cars in the turn lane, split oncoming traffic, and veer into the clubhouse entrance.

At the gate, I throw $10 at a guard I don't recognize, mash the gas, fly up the drive, and skid-stop at valet.

Out of my car, I pat Jimmy-the-Golden-Arm's palm with $10, flash my owners badge at the front gate where the Ritual has to begin, then sprint to the grandstand apron.

At the apron I touch the outside rail, then fast-walk across the parking lot to the barns on the back side, swallow the mandatory lunch at the track kitchen (hot dog with relish, no mustard), run through the barns to the barn that has my three horses, touch it at its corner nearest the finish line, and finally, stop to stand on the four linoleum tiles in the grandstand where I last saw my father.

Done. Exhale. *Thank you, God.*

I speed-dial Dave's sat phone again and get no answer again. Same for Kayak Jim at the Grand Hotel Boblo. The horses are in the gate for the seventh race, the race before ours. The gate bangs open like a cash register drawer. Track announcer John Dooley's baritone booms: "AND THEY'RE AWAY . . . POCKET ROCKET BREAKS ON TOP."

Pocket Rocket is a speed-horse front-runner. He smokes the opening quarter in .22 flat with two horses on his neck, then the half mile in .45 battling the same two horses. I want today's surface conditions to tire the front-runners in this race, then the feature race. Pocket Rocket spills out of the turn, digs in, shoots past me at the rail, and wins by five.

He didn't tire. Frown. Today's surface favors speed. We'll have to beat the conditions, not just the favorite. The tote board blinks the opening odds for the feature. The 8 horse, Free Town Lady, blinks "25 to 1," proper odds for an off-the-pace long shot on a speed-favoring day.

To me and my trainer/partner, Tee-Red Bernis, Free Town Lady isn't a long shot. She's our thirteen-month reclamation project, a bay four-year-old filly who's about to pay telephone numbers instead of the more accurate even money.

Our plan was to bet $3,000, a whole lot for Tee-Red and me. And a major win for the Flyers.

Loef Brummel's existential threat straightens my back. I admit the un-admittable: the only way out of the loan shark's threat is a full-on violation of everything Richard Blaine in *Casablanca* taught me were the rules of the road. I make the first of nine calls to bookies in three states, betting a total of $15,000—$12,000 more than I have.

I hang up on the last call. The acid in my stomach climbs to my throat. A win will reap what Dave owes, plus cover the Flyers' defense fund, and $5K for Tee-Red and me. Dave's trucks will pay the $40K vig. If Free Town Lady signs our exit visas from Dave's disaster, I will consider my family's debts to Dave paid in full, then choke him unconscious.

Convenient? Fated? That's how fucking Dave would describe my horse being who she is and where she is today. But if you work three jobs to make one living—plan, and save, and scrape—then today's bookie-loan-shark adventure is more like risking your life to rob Peter so you can pay Paul, who *you* don't owe in the first fucking place.

Luckily for Dave, I can control my temper and know something about successful horse-race betting. You'll notice I didn't say handicapping. In current economic and purse conditions, a short-money stable stays afloat on gambling profits. First, you buy horses others think are too broken to fix (cure); nurse them back to health with all the attention, kindness, and skill they didn't receive from their previous owners; then enter them in three or four races that don't fit their skill set, running with equipment like shoes or bits that don't maximize performance.

Then, you enter them in a race that fits, wearing equipment that fits, against a well-bred, expensive horse on a good streak that you think you can beat. This is the proper way to race horses if you care about your money and the animals but not the bookies.

Is that against the law? Technically, no. Do the bookies and bettors care? I think we're a number of death threats past worrying about that.

But you still have to win. From behind, on a front-runner day, after completing a hurried prerace Ritual that some gods might see as disrespectful. Then you have to be granted what is called "racing luck," meaning that your come-from-behind trip around two turns is unhampered by surface irregularities, other horses and their jockeys misbehaving, and karma you may have earned elsewhere.

From the rail, I watch the nine horses entered in the feature stream past toward the paddock to be saddled. Eight of them will try to secure me the suicide gamblers' death penalty. I check the dirt that favors front-runners, then the heavy stretch breeze that favors front-runners, then . . . a svelte little guy staring at me—about fifty, shaved head, surfer shirt, linen jacket, Vans checkerboard slip-ons—staring with the confidence of a larger man. He speaks to his cell phone, pockets it, then gestures for me to wait as he approaches.

He arrives smiling. "Aren't you Jonathan Eig? The writer?"

"Huh?" I look past him, then left, right. Then at the rail behind me. "No. Sorry."

"Yeah, you are." The smile fades. "Or you were, last month in the Bahamas."

I make silent odds on which of the four people in the bar at Grand Hotel Boblo made the call to their handler at the DEA.

"Sorry, you have me confused with a world traveler. I bought this suit on eBay."

He squares up, puts the sun behind him—a professional's mix of caution and aggression.

"What do you want?"

"Wanted to know if I got laid when I was in Rum Cay."

"*You're* Jon Eig?"

"I got a call. In my world, calls have repercussions."

I recheck our surroundings. "Yeah? What world is that?"

"One you don't know much about."

"One among several. Sorry if I caused you heartburn. Ran into your *Get Capone* book in the airport. It said you had the ten thousand documents; perfect cover to ask questions that might have Capone's name in the answers."

Jon Eig waits for more.

"Can't, sorry. Was working for a lawyer." I shrug. "What are you gonna do? They sue you if you break their confidentiality agreement."

"James W. Barlow Jr. He's your lawyer?"

"Might've been. But because he'd sue me, I can't say."

"Worse things out there than being sued."

"Really? Gosh, who knew?"

Eig glances into the crowd, then back. "The gold's probably urban legend. Barlow and his friends aren't."

"Okay . . ."

"Neither am I."

I look at him, notice what might be a gun under the jacket. I look where he glanced. "So, Jon, you out here to bet the kids' baby-food money?"

"Babies are dead. People you're working with killed them."

"Jesus." I add karma distance. "Here's hoping that's a figure of speech. Good luck with . . . whatever it is you're doing."

Eig doesn't move.

I do. Bullshit story or not, the Racing Gods do not reward bad karma.

THE EIGHTH RACE AT ARLINGTON

Chapter 5

BILL OWENS

4:50 p.m.

My hands are sweating. I no longer smell like Old Spice. I should've given more to Catholic charities; should've done more Farm Aid stuff—

John Dooley's baritone booms: "THEY'RE AT THE POST FOR THE EIGHTH RACE AT ARLINGTON."

In the hurricane latitudes, the survivors say, "Hide from the wind, run from the water." Most board up and stay home, fade the risk, and hope to ride out the consequences. Betting horses with borrowed money is similar to betting against a hurricane's path. You make the bet early, then wait for results that will kill you if you're wrong. Prior to today, I have never bet with borrowed money.

I string together the parts of prayers I can remember. Honest, I'll do better. Really.

The tote board blinks the favorite as even money. She looks it, like Secretariat in a dress. Free Town Lady blinks "16 to 1," down from "25 to 1" six minutes ago. All the horses are approaching the starting gate to load. Free Town Lady passes me at the rail, doesn't notice, and bites at her outrider's leg, more full of herself than usual. It's hot. We're going nine furlongs, a mile and an eighth; *calm* would be better.

"THE HORSES ARE APPROACHING THE STARTING GATE."

Just so we're clear, I'm going to church every Sunday, forever.

The horses load into the gate. The favorite goes in smooth with local hero Earle Fires on his back. Free Town Lady goes in smooth. We're in the eight hole but don't run on the front, so an outside post position doesn't matter. We'll run the long stretch to the first turn, then tuck in behind whoever's in front, hope for big fractions for the first quarter and the half mile, then sit down and pull the trigger in the far turn just past the 3/8 pole.

The tote board blinks "Free Town Lady: 10 to 1."

The gate bangs open. "AND THEY'RE AWAY . . . FREE TOWN LADY BREAKS ON TOP, FOLLOWED BY—"

Huh? I weld 6x30 binoculars to my eye sockets. The pack is tight, four wide. We run the grandstand straightaway on the lead and bend into the clubhouse turn, the quarter in .23 flat. Fast but not devastating, but we're not a front-runner, never have run on the front. I will never speak to Tee-Red, my trainer, again. I will feed our jockey and his grandparents to Loef Brummel. I will—

We do the half mile in .46 flat, Free Town Lady and the big-money favorite shoulder to shoulder. I repeat my new Walt Disney mantra: "Fast but not devastating." But up ahead, when they turn for home, is where the front-runners pay for the speed they spent getting there. Speed can hold—like it has been today—if you trained for it, *like the favorite did and we didn't*. I will kill our jockey, then myself. I deserve to die; I bet my life on a guy who wears a size-six hat.

John Dooley booms: "THREE-QUARTERS IN 1:10 AND TWO. IT'S FREE TOWN LADY AND PISHKA'S PILOT—"

Too fast. Too goddamn fast, but perfect had we run from behind. Like we planned. I lower my binoculars so I don't see us spill out of the turn, hang, then fold.

Me not watching lasts a full second.

The closers dig in behind Free Town Lady and the favorite, Pishka's Pilot. The favorite changes leads. Earle Fires asks for it all, too early to mean he has a bunch of horse left. They spill out of the turn. The crowd begins to roar. My throat constricts with an idiot's hope. Free Town Lady doesn't fold. She hits a gear she doesn't have—Oh my GOD—runs the last quarter fully extended, lights out, in .24 flat, hits the wire first in a fucking world-champion life-saving finish! She and I will have children together. We'll live next to the statue erected in her honor. Her jockey and trainer will be in the Bill Owens Hall of Fame. Grossfeld's Flyers win the Stanley Cup and cure Down syndrome. Dave doesn't die, and more importantly, neither do I. Oh my God!

Little red neon word on the tote board:

"Inquiry."

***

I can still see it.

Cut to the chase: We should've won—bullshit, we did win, by nine, but the bold, brave, and beautiful Free Town Lady was taken down on a foul that only fifty-fifty happened. Earle Fires, the affected jockey, will get the Academy Award for "bumped." Midget motherfucker should be an NFL punter or one of those cute little candy-ass soccer players whimpering for a red card. Call me insensitive; I just wanted to be alive tomorrow. Candy-ass midget motherfucker.

Jon Eig joins my exit toward the valet mosh. "Karma's a bitch. Have much on her?"

"Last three chapters of the Bible. I now owe ten bookies and a loan shark."

My feet accelerate. Eig extends his stride without effort. We make the pickup curb without further conversation. I trade five dollars for my keys, key the door to my Citroën, hoping it explodes.

Eig says, "Maybe I can help."

I stop. Think about it. "You have forty thousand dollars? Another twenty thousand next week, and the week after?"

"No. But I might have a proposition. Given that you're already dead, you don't have much to lose."

Sensitive little fucker. "And?"

"I have history that intersects with Barlow's. And his friends. We'll call the relationship 'unrequited.' Why I don't spend much time in public."

I stare at an "investigative journalist" while I consider what type of life-changing betrayal we're talking about. "Well, Jon, you'd have to tell me why you're interested in a really unpleasant criminal-lawyer criminal with a CIA pedigree. *And* your interest would have to pay well and soon, as in by tomorrow, or me as a 'helper' won't do you much good."

"The Capone gold might actually be out there."

"I'll tell Loef Brummel. He'll be thrilled."

Eig glances the valet crowd. "Does Brummel have much pull in Haiti?"

"Ever been to Haiti, Jon? Have any fucking idea what twenty-four hours in that lovely country is?"

"I have. And I'm not interested in returning. You, on the other hand, may have information, or could locate information, that would make it worthwhile to return to Haiti . . . given your current, ah, situation."

"Me and Haiti will not meet again in this lifetime. And I sure as fuck hope not in the next."

"What the hero always says before he goes."

I lean in at him. "I'm not your story's hero. Whatever your unrequited relationship is with Barlow, it's *yours*."

"Not just Barlow. He's part of a larger cancer, and so was I. And now, so's your partner, Dave Grossfeld."

Jon Eig is beginning to sound like the DEA cocaine police. "Jon, the very *last* thing I want to do is get between Barlow, Loef Brummel, and the police, be they federal or local." I point Mr. Eig away from my car door, get in, fire the engine, then drop the window when I'm in gear. "And I strongly recommend you don't either."

Eig tosses a business card in my window. "Barlow's more dangerous to you than Brummel, you just don't realize it yet. If you're alive tomorrow morning, take a look at the history you and Grossfeld have with Sportsman's racetrack. Maybe your history there won't kill you like it did Eddie O'Hare."

I start to drive away, but don't. Jon Eig just used Sportsman's racetrack as a death threat against my future. Dave's secretary just told me Sportsman's was the good news. I feel the hook in my mouth but swallow it anyway.

"All right, what's the fucking Sportsman's story I *have* to know?"

"Capone and his lawyer/partner, Eddie O'Hare, originally built Sportsman's as the Hawthorne Kennel Club. While they were converting it from greyhounds to thoroughbreds, O'Hare snitched Capone into Alcatraz so he could steal the track. For seven years, O'Hare ran Sportsman's as Chicago's premier gambling palace. Was murdered leaving there in 1939."

"I read your book. So what?"

"This part wasn't in it: Eddie O'Hare had a law partner, James W. Barlow *Senior*, father to your current employer. Barlow Senior didn't die with O'Hare and he should've. He didn't die because Capone's accountant, Jake 'Greasy Thumb' Guzik, believed O'Hare stole the gold that Capone bought from the USS *Machias*."

"Meaning you believe it? The gold's real?"

"Capone's accountant thought it was. Enough that he allowed Barlow Senior to stay alive to help find it."

"And you want it."

"I want Barlow Junior."

Greed running second isn't SOP. "Because . . ."

Eig checks the crowd again. "I have some bills to pay that money won't cover. My number's on that card. We're on the same team. For now." He turns into the crowd.

I leave. Shifting from first to second, I upgrade the gold to a real, albeit iffy, possibility—hell, I *know* the Dave-Barlow cocaine story is bullshit.

I check the mirror for whatever "bills to pay" are chasing Eig.

Other than the gold/Barlow Sr. stuff, everything he just told me about Sportsman's I already knew. Sportsman's was my second home; and after my parents died, my actual home. For eighty years, every Chicago celeb and gangster who mattered hung out in the clubhouse, as did I—until it closed. Dave and I worked the Sportsman's "funeral" auction.

In 2003 and 2004, before the city of Cicero started the teardown, Grossfeld's moved miles of the racetrack's stadium-type stuff, left-behinds, and lots of memorabilia. At the auction, one anonymous buyer alone bought five truckloads of mementos, and I helped Dave load them. That buyer was represented by James W. Barlow Jr. He paid Grossfeld's a $50,000 profit for the move.

Frown: Lotta history. Barlow's father, Barlow, me, Dave, Eddie O'Hare, and Al Capone—all of us at Sportsman's . . .

Takes up a lot of space on a suicide note.

***

My seersucker suit is rumpled, as am I. The ceiling above my bed at the Crown Motel in Calumet City is popcorn asbestos, the same view soul-singer Wayne Cochran had the night he intended to commit suicide here, but found Jesus instead. The photo on my chest isn't Jesus or Wayne, it's Susie Devereux, a copy I made and kept.

Why keep a copy?

I'm a guy, how should I know?

Maybe it's the Bond-girl history; maybe the three-country trek I undertook looking for her; maybe she's Ian Fleming's golden girl—

My phone rings. The sound *feels* like the echo in a loan shark's basement; I let the call go to voicemail. It rings again. I call Dave instead of answering, then Barlow. Neither answer. I listen to the new voicemail, an Ireland-Irish voice, rough and cold:

"You or Grossfeld don't make yourselves findable, the Flyers—all fucking twelve—are goin' off the Ashland Avenue bridge. See how your little hockey fucks do in the river."

A normal person couldn't do that. Loef probably has five guys who can. Dave and Barlow's bullshit "cocaine" adventure is now our only ticket out of the cemetery. I call Kayak Jim before I call Patty Prom-Night.

He answers: "Hotel Boblo; how can I help you?"

I blurt twenty questions.

"Yeah, your guy Dave was here. No, I don't know anything about cocaine, his or anyone else's. Yes, I heard him say 'Anne Bonny,' 'James W. Barlow Jr.' and 'Al Capone.' Was talking to a man-size woman, probably Haitian, who arrived and departed by single-engine seaplane. Dave and his boat were gone the next morning, stiffed us on their bill."

"Dave mentioned Anne Bonny?"

"Saw the photo you gave me. Acted like he knew all of 'em."

Dave knows my history in Haiti and Jamaica; helped me survive it when all I wanted to do was die. Now he's down there *using* it?

"Sorry about Dave stiffing you. Don't think he's running on all eight. Send the bill to Grossfeld's Moving and Storage; I'll try to get it paid."

Static, then: "If your asshole friend went to Haiti, it won't be him paying it."

DOWNTOWN CHICAGO

Chapter 6

BILL OWENS

Fish, dressed as tourists, school the wide sidewalks of South Michigan Avenue. I'm on a CTA bus for the final mile in from the Crown Motel, tactical defense against being carjacked to a loan shark's Canaryville basement. We crawl past James W. Barlow Jr.'s building; I palm my face, eyes watering from the bus's industrial-strength disinfectant, and don't see Loef Brummel's hard-ass Irishmen. I speed-dial Dave's satellite phone.

A girl answers singsong: "Hel-lo? Hel-lo?"

"Hi! Is Dave there? Dave Grossfeld. It's an emergency."

Crackle, spit, static. "Who's calling?"

I yell: "Bill." Half the faces in the bus turn to look at me.

The voice says, "Hold on."

I get up, push the bus's stop button, and step down into the rear exit.

The girl's voice says, "Can David call you back?"

"No! Absolutely not. It's an emergency." The bus slows, my audience watches. We stop; I jump out into the sidewalk crowd.

Dave Grossfeld says, "Bruddah, what up?"

"What the fuck are you into? And why am I part of it?"

"How long we been friends, Bill?"

"Fuck you. You owe Loef Brummel $40K *today*. He's gonna put me in the hospital to make sure you get the picture. If that doesn't work, he's gonna toss Flyers off the Ashland Avenue bridge until it does."

"Okay . . . call me back when you calm down—"

"Don't hang up, goddammit!"

Silence, static. "How long we been friends, Bill?"

My teeth grind for the litany. "Since we were kids."

"Right. And when your 'dead' mom shows up outta the blue, who gets her the big downtown lawyer James W. Barlow Jr. for the car accident?"

"You, Dave."

"Who paid him?"

"You, Dave."

"Who got her the cancer doctors she couldn't pay for?"

"You, Dave."

"Who *bought* a fifty percent stake in Serenity Mausoleum so you could spend all your money on trying to save your mother?"

"You, Dave."

"And who needs your help now?"

"You fucking do." I pause for control. "The Flyers, Dave. Their only goddamn sin is they know you. Loef said $100K. One hundred thousand fucking dollars."

Static, crackle.

"Twenty grand a fucking week, Dave. Your loan shark's gonna come get the trucks at Grossfeld's. He does that, you have no way to earn a solution. Two plus two, you're dead two or three days after me."

"I got the big job coming in, through Barlow-O'Hare. Needed the hundred to juice it—"

"Does it pay today? Tomorrow? You're paying Brummel three thousand a fucking *day*."

"Don't worry—"

"Fuck you. What job? When? And don't say the word 'Haiti.' Don't fucking go there. No job's worth—"

"It ain't Haiti, Jesus. The job's like the Sportsman's gigs that Barlow got us in 2003 and 2004, but way bigger. A big auction and we move it all, pay me at least $250K net-net, maybe more. The deal ran late a week. We'll start on Thursday."

"This Thursday?"

"Yeah. Calm down, Bill. Jesus. Barlow guaranteed it."

"Is this your medication talking, Dave? Your loan shark won't care that you were loaded on G-strings and Colombian baby powder."

"I know what I'm doing. Stall Loef; don't let him take the trucks and don't let the sheriffs in the warehouse."

"*Sheriffs*? Are you late to Cosmo, too? Meaning he filed to repossess them?"

"Yeah, he did, the fucking Jew."

"Cosmo's Italian. You're Jewish. What the fuck are you and Barlow into?"

"Couple of high-ups needed to make the right decision. Same as the Olympics."

"High-ups where? In the Bahamas? Carlos Lehder's in jail. The FIFA boss down there only takes bribes on soccer. Is this soccer?"

Static. No answer.

I yell into my phone. "Goddammit, where are you?"

Tourists on Michigan Avenue's sidewalk veer away.

"TCI. The fishing tournament."

Dave's not in the Turks and Caicos. But I can't be direct; he's using a sat-phone frequency that's monitored 24-7 by pirates and police alike. "I watched your loan shark put one of his own guys in the pavement. Okay? For lending you money on a business Loef ain't in. *Okay? We clear?* Loef told me what you're doing, except I did the math, and cocaine isn't what you're doing."

"Fuck Loef Brummel. I'll pay him and he can shut the fuck up." Static. Dave's voice ramps, *"All right!* Got my goddamn marlin, *finally.* Call Loef; tell him I'll be back midweek with all his money." Static. "Honey, toss this goddamn phone over there—"

"Dave!"

Nope, Dave's gone fishing.

I ease back into the crowd, school with them toward Barlow's building, and call Lisa Reins. "How we doing with Lithuanian Ron?"

"Ronny likes nylons, sex toys, and baby talk."

Lithuanian Ron knew Dave was on the arm to Loef Brummel before I did. "Do me a favor, ask him how he knew about Dave, then get back to me."

"Not part of my contract, hon."

"Is now. Your friend—me—has some wolves in the orchard."

"What's my friend want to pay?"

"Take one for the team, okay? We'll talk money later. Just find out, and quickly. Thanks." I button off before Lisa can play me, then look down Michigan Avenue at Barlow's office. I backtrack south, staying mid-throng on the Millennium Park side of the street, hoping to pick out—

On my side of the street, two black guys are checking their reflections in the stainless-steel Cloud Gate sculpture across from Barlow's building. Both are wearing jeans and sport jackets in a crowd of sweltering tourist shorts and T-shirts. Locals dress like that in Jamaica, wear jeans all summer. I never could figure how denim-thermal didn't kill them.

Final glance for the Canaryville kidnap crew.

I don't see them, can't figure that either, sprint across ten lanes of horns and front bumpers, duck into the Willoughby Tower's lobby, slide past a stinky Reuben sandwich and a desk guard who isn't there, then punch the button for the penthouse elevator.

Commotion outside on the sidewalk.

The lobby elevator bings.

Barlow plans to play me, staying outside the target zone while he marionettes all of us inside it. A while back I would've handled this situation differently, a brief, terrible time after the events in Haiti.

The elevator door opens. I jump in, punch "16," see the name I carved across my palm . . . then squint back at Michigan Avenue. Chicago's not Haiti and this isn't the 1980s—

Then why's it feel like it?

Chapter 7

SUSIE DEVEREUX

Saturday, 2:00 p.m.

As it happens, the ruby slippers I wished for in the Camagüey Breaks come in a variety of styles. Yes, the rumors are true. I am alive, and currently on the sixteenth floor of Chicago's Willoughby Tower, most of me hidden behind the stairwell door.

From here, the doors to James W. Barlow Jr.'s office appear more edifice than entry. The doors announce a lawyer who reads John Grisham novels and sees the stunning similarities. Men I loved are dead because of this man and his crime partner, Dave Grossfeld. On the private side of Barlow's doors will be a meticulously suited, middle-aged, cold-eyed fixer whose mirror sees "attractive ex-linebacker," not "position power." I screw the silencer onto my Glock 21 and step out into the hall. In the next thirty seconds I intend to demonstrate the difference.

The elevator pings. I pivot back into the stairwell. A fit forty-something in a rumpled seersucker suit exits the elevator, moving like a man with a mission. Based upon Anne's halcyon description, this is Herself's university mate, Bill Owens. The same man Dave Grossfeld used to credential himself when he called Anne and instigated the hunt for the Capone gold. The man Barlow and Grossfeld used as bait, bait that subsequently lured me into a trap in Miami last night.

Mr. Owens is not bad-looking in person, although I'd be pressing my suit more often. Anne says Mr. Owens is not party to our betrayal. Herself will be pissed if I shoot him with Barlow. Anne says Mr. Owens can, and will, help us.

Bill Owens opens Barlow's doors, then disappears inside.

I lower the Glock and demand the same of my heart rate.

Now that there's time for a proper introduction, my surname, *Devereux*, is pronounced "Dev-a-row." I'm a five-foot-seven brunette, sufficiently rebuilt after the breaks to still use T&A as a negotiating tool if the light's not fluorescent and you're not into nineteen-year-olds.

Early last month I surfaced in Cuba—we'll call me "bait"—took all of thirteen days before Anne's long-ago American friend Bill Owens was in Rum Cay impersonating a writer and looking for me. *Gosh, imagine that?* And now he's here. And unless his stars align, or he's smart enough to do what I tell him, he'll probably die here.

Chapter 8

BILL OWENS

James W. Barlow Jr. smiles at me from behind a three-hundred-year-old cherrywood desk that he says belonged to Alexander Hamilton. Mr. Barlow nods to a secretary who I haven't seen before, thanks her for working the weekend, tells her, "We'll be fine. Please close my door and no need to stay."

Mr. Barlow cuts to me, floats his eyebrows at my slept-in suit and Crown Motel odor. "So, Bill, how goes it?"

"Becoming a bit rough out there, Mr. Barlow. Dave and you, and unfortunately me, might have a problem."

Barlow motions me to sit in one of his $4,000 green leather chairs. He adds, "I certainly hope not."

"Somehow Dave and I *both* end up at a flyspeck in the Bahamas twenty days apart? That's not a coincidence. Last night, the bartender down there quoted Dave as using your name, Haiti, Anne Bonny, and

Al Capone, all spoken to a 'man-size' Haitian woman who came and went by private seaplane with no numbers."

Mr. Barlow nods. "Odd."

"Not *odd*, so let's not burn any more of your valuable time. You might survive Dave's and your adventure, but I won't unless Loef Brummel gets paid. I make it ninety-ten Dave dies either way, and seventy-thirty you follow him."

Mr. Barlow's face remains blank.

"You sent me to Rum Cay; you sent Dave to Rum Cay. Twenty days apart. Why?"

"*I* sent Dave? On that you're mistaken. And you know why I sent you—Susie Devereux and Al Capone's gold."

"Sorry. I just talked to Dave. Dave said he borrowed the $100K to juice two high-ups for a deal *you* put together." I point to framed 1920s jockey silks on Mr. Barlow's wall. "A deal Dave claims is like the Sportsman's moving contract in 2003. I think him being on the arm for a $100K bribe that you told him to pay qualifies you as a direct participant."

"Dave said that?"

Nod. "I need you to give Loef Brummel $140,000 *today* or he'll put me in a coma to show Dave the future. Whether or not you want to explain what all this has to do with Sportsman's is up to you. I need the one forty."

Mr. Barlow does not burn calories to decline my demand.

I continue. "Dave's loan shark told me you're part of Dave's Rum Cay adventure—it isn't just Dave saying so—and after Dave and I are dead"—I point at the Afghan rug under my chair—"Loef Brummel will be standing right here, or in your garage, or in your closet. For that kind of money and street insult, he will skin you naked and nail you to a telephone pole in Canaryville."

Mr. Barlow eases into the professional smile he uses for Levee Grill / Counsellors Row transactions and death-penalty juries. "My relationship with Dave Grossfeld in this matter began at Sportsman's Park in 2003 and ended, I thought, in 2004. I cannot imagine why Dave, or anyone else, would borrow $100,000 from a loan shark.

"Regarding Sportsman's, I represent a client who in 2003 bought five truckloads from the Sportsman's pre-auction—one hundred percent of the contents of the offices and back-of-the-house operations. Last month, six years after that purchase, my client informed me that several items included in the sale-inventory list had not been delivered. At my client's request, I rechecked the paperwork, then contacted Grossfeld's Moving and Storage to adjudicate the discrepancies."

"You didn't tell Dave to bribe two high-ups in the Bahamas for $50K each?"

Barlow frowns. "Please."

"Or to meet there with a Haitian woman whose plane doesn't need ID numbers?"

Barlow reaches for an iPad on his credenza, touches it four times, and hands it to me. "Yesterday, I received this video from my Sportsman's auction client." Pause. "Along with some troubling information relative to the fifteen thousand in fees already paid you."

The screen is grainy, a women's rugby match with audio. The camera is focused on a woman playing defense. The collision she causes at the sideline is fast, brutal, and sounds as bad as it looks. Both players finish facedown in the mud; one recovers to her knees, slowly elevates her chin, and stops. The match ends.

Barlow says, "Susie Devereux. The woman I paid you to find, that you couldn't."

Susie Devereux stands, steps over the unconscious player, and walks straight at the camera. The Scottish Moroccan heritage is obvious and matches the "honey-bee" color of the woman who the Cuban boy said survived the wreck in Cuba. Brunette in a big way; her eyes are wide-set and brown. As she passes the camera on the sideline, her eyes fix on the lens and lock.

Whoa—The rush is 100 percent night terrors, straight up my back, direct from the Corazón Santo. I drop the iPad, hear Anne Bonny in my ear in 1984 as she hustled me aboard a Jamaica-bound ship to escape the brothers Kray in London: "Mind yourself in Kingston, Bill. There are women in the Corazón Santo the devil fears."

Barlow says, "Corazón Santo?"

I must've said it out loud. I mumble the answer, "The triangle that connects Havana, Kingston, and Port-au-Prince. Literally translated, it means 'Sacred Heart.'"

The iPad's streaming in my lap. The video freezes on the final frame—it's the Witches of Eastwick photo I was given—Anne Bonny, Florent Dusson-Siri, and Susie Devereux arm in arm. It's Susie D., not Anne Bonny who has my attention, an instinctive choice that I'd have bet every dollar in my wallet against.

Barlow says, "You're *certain* you didn't locate Susie Devereux?"

"Huh? No, the *maybe* in Cuba was as close as I got. Can I keep this?"

"I'll have my secretary email you a copy."

I hand Barlow his iPad. He doesn't look like he believes me.

"Contrary to your findings, Bill, it appears Susie Devereux is alive; in Hialeah, Florida. Yesterday, Little Haiti, to be exact."

"You know that?"

Barlow continues, sans clarification. "According to my client, Devereux and her partners—the two women in that video, one of whom you already know—have been working with Dave Grossfeld for some time now. This was unknown to me until my client informed me a month ago. I told Dave that if he'd kept anything from the Sportsman's move, it would be considered theft. Dave denied—"

"Dave worked with Devereux? And you didn't tell me? I could've asked him about her before I went to Rum Cay."

Mr. Barlow shrugs. "In retrospect, I shouldn't have believed Dave's denial."

All or part of this story is bullshit. "How was Susie Devereux working with Dave?"

"We don't know. Clearly, Dave was not being honest with me. That's why I paid you to have a look. Dave and Ms. Devereux have found, or are searching for, three items missing from my client's inventory— a 1927 win picture / wall plaque of the greyhound Astor Argyle taken after a dog race at the Hawthorne Kennel Club, later known as Sportsman's . . ." Barlow watches my reaction and doesn't continue.

"Why a greyhound photo?"

"My client did not disclose his original interest, although I suspect it was, and is, related to the Capone gold. The other two items missing from the inventory are hundred-year-old bottles of Barbancourt Rhum . . ." Barlow stares right through me.

I stare back.

He says, "Barbancourt Rhum is the premier product of Haiti, but of course you know that." Barlow glances the cell phone on his desk. "You said you just spoke with Dave Grossfeld?"

"Yeah."

"Good. Let's get Dave back on the line."

I try three times. All voicemail.

"Do you have keys to Dave's warehouse?" Barlow asks.

"Maybe."

"Tell you what, Bill. I'll think about your problem with Mr. Brummel. Why don't you drop by the warehouse and have a look for Astor Argyle and Barbancourt Rhum bottles? Apparently, the items collectively form some sort of message."

"Loef Brummel's gonna put me in a coma. Because of Dave and you. And before you tell me again that you're not involved, that isn't what Dave's loan shark thinks. I want you to know that real soon I'll have to choose between who to be afraid of first—you or Loef. So we're clear, you're gonna come in second."

"Be careful at the warehouse, Bill. I'm sure Mr. Brummel will be about. But finding those missing items would certainly be helpful. I have a feeling our friend Dave knew far more about their importance than he let on."

"Like you're doing with me? On every goddamn thing?"

"One hand washes the other, or will. Or shall we say, *could*."

"Speaking of hands, Susie Devereux had marks on her wrists. That's what they told me in Cuba. What kind of marks?"

"Birthmarks?" Barlow shrugs. "Tattoos?"

"But she had them?"

Barlow nods, then reaches to check the screen of his cell phone. "So I've been told. I have never met the woman."

Heat rises on my neck. I throw Barlow a threat that seems to scare the shit out of everyone else. "And your friend Mr. Gryphon? Should I call him too?"

Barlow holds the smile, unaffected. "By all means, Bill, if you believe that will help."

Chapter 9

SUSIE DEVEREUX

The elevator pings its return to the sixteenth floor. It opens for Bill Owens, then closes behind his broad shoulders and will now lower him sixteen floors to safety. His stars aligned; good for him. Anne's university mate and I will chat, but that will be after James W. Barlow Jr. and I have our reunion.

The elevator begins its drop. I rewrap the gray-checked keffiyeh across my face, hair, and neck, count three, then step to Barlow's office doors, slip through, sprint the carpeted hall to his door, and run straight at his desk with my Glock 21 leveled at his head.

"Good to see ya, James."

Barlow reaches for his desk drawer.

"Bang!"

Barlow jolts backward in his executive chair.

"Don't make me kill you." I round his desk, kick his chair and him toward the window behind him. "My partners would. By 'partners,'

I mean Anne and Siri. Tommy and Cyril are dead in the Camagüey Breaks. You remember Tommy and Cyril?"

Barlow freezes his hands in front of him, inhales to begin his lie—

"No thanks." I aim my pistol at his forehead.

"Susan. Allow me to clear your misconceptions—"

"No. Allow me." I step closer with the pistol. "Here's how we got to the Camagüey Breaks: In 2002, Sportsman's racetrack goes broke. A year later the track is sold to the city of Cicero. You act as Cicero's legal advisor. To pad your fee, you sift through cabinets of papers. In one of 'em you stumble upon Eddie O'Hare's files from back in the day—clues that support the Capone gold treasure stories you'd been party to all your life.

"You take the possibility of the Capone gold to Grossfeld. Dave puts up initial money as his part of the partnership. Anne Bonny knows the Caribbean. Dave uses Bill Owens's name to meet with her in Port Royal; Anne comes to Siri and me in Santiago. We have ideas; the ideas need more capital than Grossfeld has.

"Dave goes to you. You say 'no problem' and deliver the financing. Siri, Anne, and I spend five years chasing the gold.

"But you lied. The money you put up to finance the hunt wasn't yours, it was the Gryphon's. Him and Cranston Piccard are big cats who like to play with their food before they eat it. They get tired of waiting for us to find the gold, or they decided they're being cheated. You and Dave try to give them me and my clues to save yourselves and your shares."

I unwrap the keffiyeh. "Stand up. Walk to your door and close it."

Barlow lowers his hands, feigns comfort while he reads me for weakness. Barlow reads juries for a living; he figures my sentiments correctly, walks to the door, and closes it.

"Sit on the floor; back against the door."

"I think not." Barlow gestures to a green side chair at his desk. "Please. Have a seat, Ms. Devereux. We'll settle our dispute. Like adults."

I raise my chin to show the raw garrote welt that circles my neck. "Last night outside Hialeah Racetrack, two miles from Little Haiti, I 'spoke' with representatives of Cranston Piccard and the Gryphon. They wanted me and the clues."

"I'm sorry. None of this . . . unpleasantness was necessary."

"Unpleasantness? Sit on the floor, your back to the door, or I put a bullet in your stomach, search your office, then grab lunch and eat it while you die."

Barlow frowns and nods toward the chairs. "Please. I'm too old to sit on the floor." He walks to a green chair, sits, and points to the other green chair. "I know you to be an angry woman, but not unreasonable."

I stand behind the other chair, tell him: "Odd, huh? I come out of rehab and hiding—three years of hospitals and hideouts—dangle myself as bait, and bingo, *your* people are everywhere I am, or used to be."

Barlow stares at me, not the Glock, and says, "Dave Grossfeld is a client of this law firm, not 'my people' . . . in spite of the fantasy your friend Anne Bonny continues to conjure. Dave Grossfeld double-crossed you three years ago, and he double-crossed me as well. My part in his treasure hunt was as his lawyer. If he were successful, I would receive a contingency fee. All legal, all aboveboard."

"Oh. So, you're just *Dave's* innocent lawyer. Crying shame the facts don't support that."

"But the facts do . . ." Barlow floats his eyebrows for effect. "Whether you and your compatriots like it or not."

"How about Cranston Piccard. It was him who bought the five truckloads of stuff from Sportsman's, wasn't it? He hired you to front for him. You guessed what he was looking for. Then you fucked him. And us."

Barlow doesn't answer.

I aim the Glock. "One knee at a time, then each ankle, then the shoulders. If you don't die, you'll be in replacement surgeries the rest of your life."

Barlow says, "I have known Cranston Piccard a long time, since the 1980s, my days in Virginia."

"Not Virginia. *CIA*. Both of you. When'd you last speak to Piccard?"

Barlow shrugs, disinterested in remembering Cranston Piccard any further. I don't feel that way. Barlow inhales in mock surrender. "Cranston Piccard is—"

"A fucking hate crime in a tropical white suit." I aim at Barlow's left knee. "A slime-ball bureaucrat conduit-confrere shadow diplomat.

A CIA station chief who went bamboo when I was still a teenager. And not unlike your miserable fucking self, a player in the
government-crime-business partnerships that govern our planet. Piccard's
just bigger."

Barlow feigns frustration.

I show Barlow the suicide attempt that scars one of my wrists.
"You and Dave got our treasure-hunt financing from that fucking red-
market monster, but forgot to tell us."

"You were late on your performance and unresponsive. Numerous
meetings were requested to detail your progress that you declined to
take." Barlow shrugs. "Whoever it was who attacked you, it wasn't me."

"It was the Gryphon's boats that attacked us, and you know it. Him
and your pal Piccard."

"I know no such thing."

I shoot Barlow in the left knee.

Barlow screams, careens out of the chair, and balls fetal. His office
now smells like blood and cordite.

"My friends on the boat . . . they died. Did I just tell you that?" I
scan Barlow's opulent office, adding time and self-control before I continue. "I had to shoot Tommy . . ." Breath catches in my throat. I cough
to clear it. "Tommy was the first man I thought I could marry. And I
had to shoot him so the Gryphon and Piccard couldn't take him alive.
Put him in their goddamn gibbets."

Barlow rocks against the pain, squeezing his leg to his torso.

"The last three years I've thought a lot about how I'd kill you."
Pause, room scan, heart-rate reduction. "And Dave Grossfeld. And
Piccard. And the Gryphon." My eyes return to Barlow on the floor.
"And, gosh, here we are."

Through bit teeth, Barlow spits: "I didn't betray you."

"Three things will save you, *if* I get all three: Give me Astor Argyle.
Give me the Barbancourt bottle. And give me a way to lure Cranston
Piccard and the Gryphon out of the groves. All three, or you die here
on your carpet."

Barlow blurts: "Bill Owens. He has Astor Argyle. And the rhum
bottles, or will. His number is on my desk. He's bringing them to me."

I back away to the desk, reach behind me, and grab the number.
Truth check: "Is Bill Owens the fellow who just left here?"

Barlow nods, face contorted against the pain.

"Where's he going?"

"Grossfeld's Moving and Storage. To get the bottles and the picture."

"Bottles *plural*? You're wrong there; I already have one. It's why I'm here." I scan the office again, looking for the other bottle. "For your sake I hope it's here."

I shoot Barlow in the other knee. He screams and rocks onto his back.

"The bottle, or the next bullet's in your stomach."

Barlow pants, whimpers, then growls: "I don't have it."

I step to the desk, rip his landline out of the floor jack, and begin popping cabinets in his long credenza. Door no. 3 has Barlow's Capone gold file but no bottle. I grab the file, then Barlow's cell phone off the desk and walk back to him bleeding on the rug.

Standing, I straddle Barlow's chest. "As of now, we are officially no longer partners." I make a one-inch smile. "Good news. I can't afford to lose your boy Bill before he finds me the rest of the clues. Meaning there's not sufficient time to kill you the way you deserve. But I *absolutely* intend to kill you. You try not to bleed to death. I'll call 911 when I clear the lobby."

Barlow rolls to vomit, doesn't, and focuses on the Glock.

I squat so he can see my eyes at the other end of the barrel. "I know you're worried about Piccard's madness, and you should be. And you're sure as fuck scared of the Gryphon. But I intend to kill both of them, so think of me, not Piccard, whenever you see a shadow. Sooner or later, I'll be the one with teeth."

Chapter 10

BILL OWENS

The cab south from Barlow's office to my Citroën takes nine minutes and $8. The call to Jon Eig is free. At 4:00 p.m. I exit the expressway. I've added a 9 mm Beretta to my pants.

Two blocks from Grossfeld's warehouse, I pull into an alley that smells like the dumpsters that line it. Jon Eig is parked where he's supposed to be. We meet window-to-window, engines running. I say, "Ready?"

"I told you, I don't do burglaries."

"Not a burglary, Jon, I have keys and the alarm code. Dave gave me permission. You want to jam Barlow; I want to hear your offer. This is where we talk."

Eig says, "I'm listening."

"Is the DEA in this? Barlow-Dave-Bahamas? Is that how you knew I was there?"

Shrug.

"The publicity for *Get Capone* said a US attorney's son slipped you a cache of ten thousand documents. Yes or no, was the gold mentioned and do you believe it's real?"

"Barlow Jr. paid you to go to Rum Cay, a part of the world he'd avoid reconnecting with if he could."

"That ain't an answer."

"Yes, it is. Back in the '80s, your employer lawyered for the CIA. He resigned during the murder investigation of a green-card mercenary named Sile Howat, killed five miles from CIA offices in Odricks Corner, Virginia. Barlow's beat was the Caribbean. He worked with a number of malignant characters before and after Haitian president Bébé Doc Duvalier was toppled in the 1986 coup."

"And you worked with him; knew about the gold?"

"Something new put Barlow back on the hunt, a hunt his father would've put him on while Jr. was at the CIA."

"Anything in those US attorney docs about the Hawthorne Kennel Club?"

Eig reads me before answering. "Yeah."

"I heard that a greyhound named Astor Argyle might fit somehow. Maybe his owners, breeders, who knows? This dog won a big race in 1927."

Eig nods. "You obviously don't play the dogs."

"Thank you."

Eig laughs for the first time. "What? Horses are better?"

"Jesus Christ, Jon, horses are the sport of kings. Greyhounds chase a plastic rabbit—"

"That Eddie O'Hare stole the patent on."

A horn blares on North Avenue. I jolt to the mirror. A white van is parked across North Avenue at the mouth of our alley. Down the block from the van is a taxi, a Flash Cab. Like the one that might have been behind me before and after I picked up my car. Probably coincidence. The cabdriver is waving a car past his cab.

"So," I say, "you heard of Astor Argyle?"

"I know a Chicago cop who has a win picture from the race you mentioned. Biggest dog race ever run at Hawthorne, or in Chicago for that matter. The picture would have Astor Argyle's owners and trainer in the photo."

"Where?" I check the van in my mirror.

"On the cop's wall."

"Where's the wall?"

"Are you willing to wear a wire on Barlow?"

"Everywhere but the steam room. Where's the wall that has the photo?"

"In the Hardscrabble. Bridgeport. Better we take one car. Yours."

"You bet."

Wanting to share my car is proof Jon Eig does not deal with loan sharks. Or it's proof that his current situation is worse than mine. I check the van and the Flash Cab again, then tell Eig to hit reverse and follow me out of the alley, away from North Avenue.

***

In my car, Eig and I exit the expressway south of the river, hit Wentworth Avenue below Chinatown, cut west into what's left of Bridgeport, the working-class, ancestral home of the Daley machine. And now home to one Astor Argyle, everyone's suddenly priceless racetrack artifact.

Ten short blocks south looms Loef Brummel's Canaryville.

The car in front of us stops at Halsted. We're trapped at the light. My pulse adds twenty points. Behind us, Bridgeport is tidy bungalows; ahead the neighborhood changes to three and six flats called the Hardscrabble. A giant shadow paints my hood, the Gothic steeple of St. Mary's on Thirty-Second Street. I glance at Jon. "Why'd you say my history at Sportsman's might kill me."

Eig says, "Because your history is tied to Barlow and his dead father. Barlow's into something that has him making phone calls to serious people; panic kind of calls."

"How would you know who Barlow's calling?"

"Could be somebody's listening. Could be they mentioned something to me. Knowing I have those bills to pay."

I fisheye Mr. Eig, "ex-journalist, biographer," shadow man on a mission. "Have to be awful bad to make James W. Barlow Jr. panic."

Under the Gothic steeple of St. Mary's are four gargoyles. Gargoyles are like *gryphons* . . .

Eig is looking at them too. He says, "Yes, awfully bad."

My Citroën creeps through the red light. We make two blocks and a fast left, then park down the block from Nick & Nora's, one of the best hot-dog storefronts in the city, provided you're willing to eat your lunch this close to Canaryville.

Eig points at Nick & Nora's. "Belongs, in part, to Area 2 Homicide Lieutenant Denny Banahan. He's from Canaryville, made news last year for killing an Outfit street captain and Nigerian heroin kingpin in our version of the French Connection."

Swell, yet another Canaryville happy face, this one with a badge. Seems kinda odd that a guy with Banahan's rep would own a hot-dog stand, but the Canaryville Irish are an odd lot, even the good guys—

Air brakes. Horn.

A hundred feet behind us, a CTA bus is stopped at the corner. Construction workers file out the bus's back door; city workers file out the front. I stare for Loef Brummel's crew. Three of the bus riders walk toward us. My hand goes to the Beretta—

Bus riders, dummy. Loef Brummel wouldn't have his kidnappers ride the bus.

We exit my Citroën and walk across to Nick & Nora's glass front door.

Inside, it's hot-dog steamy; Chicago mustard and onions. One wall is covered with framed photos of Chicago writers, wrestlers, cops, racehorses, and posters from the *Thin Man* movies of the 1930s—Nick and Nora Charles (William Powell and Myrna Loy). Only one framed photograph has a greyhound in it, an eight-by-ten that's probably Astor Argyle.

I cut to Eig—he's looking at something out the window. I cut back to the counter and the woman behind it.

She's late-twenties, artist beret, way too pretty to be making hot dogs in the Hardscrabble. Her iPod earbuds make her head bob to music I can't hear. She smiles big. Too loud, she says: Kings of Leon, then offers me one earbud.

I smile back but decline. Her mustard-stained apron fits tight to a sporty figure and covers a Special Olympics volunteer T-shirt. I point at the Special O logo, then inhale to tell her I can get Flyers tickets behind the penalty box, a meet-and-greet with the players. She and I will—

"Over here." Eig steps through all three empty tables to the greyhound picture. "Astor Argyle."

I check the front window, then step to the wall.

Eig says, "You know Chip Ganassi? Car-racing billionaire. Spent $50 million to convert Sportsman's from thoroughbreds to NASCAR."

"Yeah, know of him. Gets credit for turning a Chicago institution into a vacant lot."

Eig doesn't apologize for knowing the Antichrist. "When I was researching *Get Capone*, Ganassi gave me stuff, this Astor Argyle photo was one of the last things, just before he and Bidwell signed the papers to dump Sportsman's. I thought Tracy Moens should have it for that fabulous *Herald* piece she wrote about all the characters out there, the history. She thought the photo belonged in here, so here it is."

"Ganassi give you any bottles of rum?"

"No."

Eig waits for me to explain, then asks: "Was it Barlow who said Astor Argyle mattered?"

I lean my nose to the glass that protects the photo. "Not the dog itself; the photo. It was in the Sportsman's offices, part of an inventory that didn't get delivered." Inside the frame is a yellowed typewritten card. It describes the half-mile race AA just won in 1:01. The card is dated December 16, 1927. Eight men crowd the photograph, four wearing straw boaters and seersucker jackets. Jackets like mine, but not slept in.

Eig says, "Tracy Moens couldn't figure the black guy in the straw boater, a West Indian by the shape of his face, but no one knows his name." He runs his finger across straw boater no. 2, no. 3, and no. 4. "The other three dandies are Ralph Capone—Al's older brother; artful Eddie O'Hare; and Eddie's law partner, James W. Barlow Senior."

I turn to my really cute date for the next Flyers game and motion for her to pull her earbuds.

She does.

"Hi. We're friends of Denny's." I point at Jon. "Jonathan Eig from the *Wall Street Journal*. Would it be okay if we took this off the wall and looked at the back?" I add a lie. "Jon gave it to Denny six years ago, wants to show me something. Okay?"

"Gotta buy a hot dog." She grins. "One each. House rules."

"Make it ten, with everything." I step to the counter and hand her two twenties. "We'll have a picnic." I match her grin and offer my right hand. "Bill Owens."

"Selah Dune, proprietor, pleased to meet ya."

Eig says, "Shit."

I cut to his voice. He nods out the window at a big-body Buick out front, its doors popping open. My stomach sinks.

I yell to Selah Dune behind the counter: "Unlock the back door. Hurry."

Two blacks from the Buick are already in the street. Both wear suit coats and blue jeans. Under their coats are short-barreled submachine guns with long magazines.

I pull the Beretta, fumble the safety, wave Jon toward the counter, and yell: "Selah! Back door. Right now or we're all dead."

She bolts for the short aisle to the back. I turn to Jon; he's mid-room, reaching for Astor Argyle—

Engine roar; a white van slams into one of the two blacks, then careens into a car parked three cars behind mine. The black who's still standing fires full-auto into the van's driver's side window, steps left to the van's windshield, sets his feet, and blows the windshield apart.

A bloody white guy falls out the passenger side and fires a cut-down shotgun. The blast knocks the gun out of the black man's hands and cuts a big chunk out of his midsection.

"Out the back!" I shove Jon. "Grab the girl."

Two more blacks exit the Buick. Women? One charges Nick & Nora's front door. A shooter from the white van flattens her in the street. Her pistol fires a round that shatters Nick & Nora's door. The remaining black female loops their Buick's trunk, shoots the white guy in the van, then charges Nick & Nora's door. She pancakes before I can fire, shot from behind. Her porkpie hat coin-flips above her dreads.

Eig rips Astor Argyle off the wall.

My Beretta is stiff-armed at the street. Jon knocks me off balance and shoves us toward the back door. I stumble over Selah on the tile, reach down to help her up—she's covered in blood, half her head missing. Jon and I bang through the back door.

Into two empty parking spaces and the side alley. A car I last saw out front at the Brehon squeal-stops inches before it hits us and Nick & Nora's back wall.

I level the Beretta on the windshield. Jon jukes for our building's back corner and is knocked sideways by an Irishman charging out of the Brehon car. Jon kicks the guy in the pelvis, pivots off the guy's hip, and sprints the alley west toward Morgan Street.

The Irishman draws to shoot Jon. I shoot the guy twice, then fan back to his car's windshield, fire twice into the glass, then sprint west behind Jon.

Gunfire erupts out front on Morgan Street. Car doors pop behind me in the alley.

Irish accent: "Stop, goddammit. We'll kill ya!"

I fire blind over my shoulder, keep running, skid at the Morgan Street sidewalk, turn left, tumble over Astor Argyle on the pavement, and land on a knee. I swivel to fire just as an Irishman runs out of the alley.

He blows backward, shot from Morgan Street by a gray-and-white shape behind a flash.

I grab the framed picture, sprint farther south past Nick & Nora's shattered front door, then across Morgan Street through the white and black bodies, and flatten against the front bumper of the blown-apart, bloody van, its driver splattered at the steering wheel.

"Jon!"

Sirens wail inbound. The white flash I saw is a woman in a combat stance. She fires down the alley where I just met Loef Brummel's Brehon crew. A gray-checked keffiyeh covers her face and hair. She yells, "Bill! With me!" dumps her Glock's magazine, slams another, and fires again.

I bolt, sprinting though alleys, over fences, through the old Stearns Quarry, under the Stevenson Expressway, through its homeless camps, and finally to the 'L' station at Archer and Halsted. The Orange Line train is on the platform. I throw a fiver at the attendant booth, leap the turnstile, and do the stairs three at a time.

The train's doors are closing. I jump through. The doors shut; we lurch forward and I death-grip a pole for balance. The train adds speed and noise.

Sweat-soaked and panting, I slide into a seat. The Astor Argyle frame trembles on my knees. My hands are shaking. Clasping them doesn't help. My gun hand is blood-spotted; so are my shoes and shirt. I just shot at least one man dead. Under my shirt, the Beretta digs into my stomach. I straighten, suck air, and cover my mouth.

Five riders stare . . . then look away.

I replay the blood splatter, dead people everywhere, a goddamn horror movie. The train screeches metal on metal. Face wipe. I pat places that hurt but aren't bleeding. Eyes shut; eyes open. Gotta be seven, eight dead. Jesus, Mary, and Joseph. And Eig?

I palm my face; my phone bangs my eyebrow. Huh? How'd that get in my hand? I hit redial for Jon Eig.

The call goes direct to voicemail.

He could've lost his phone. Even so, he'd be able to call me . . . *if* he's okay. I check my phone again for voicemail and messages, find none. I call Dave.

The 'L' veers left. Downtown's skyline appears. We're almost into the Loop—the elevated network of tracks and stations that surround the center of downtown. My cell phone rings, "Unknown Caller" on the screen.

"Hello. Dave? Dave?"

The call disconnects. I stare at the phone; *will* it to talk or ring again.

It does neither. I hit redial but the call won't connect. Astor Argyle bounces on my knees. I'm gonna get the Irish-mob death penalty because of you, dog. Why?

I call Barlow's cell phone; his phone picks up and I shout: "Hello? Hello?"

"Hello?"

"Barlow?"

"Mr. Barlow is on another line. Who's calling?"

The voice is a man, and not polished enough to be a partner or associate working weekends. I look at the other passengers on my train, then Astor Argyle. "I'll hold."

"May be a while." He reads me my phone number. "Is that the correct number?"

"Yeah."

"And your name?"

"Have Mr. Barlow call me as soon as he gets off the line. Tell him it's about Dave Grossfeld."

"We heard."

"Heard? Heard what?"

"Dave Grossfeld is in Haiti, Mr. . . ."

"Smith. Horace Smith. I'm a client."

"Mr. Smith, this is Detective Roger Murphy, Chicago Police Department. What's your relationship to Mr. Barlow and Mr. Grossfeld?"

"Me? I'll let Mr. Barlow explain that. You said Dave Grossfeld's in Haiti?"

"Yes, he is. On his boat. Dave Grossfeld committed suicide an hour ago."

Chapter 11

BILL OWENS

Saturday, 10:40 p.m.

It's been six hours since the gunfight at Nick & Nora's. I haven't panicked like a sane person would. I want to, but haven't. So far, survival—for me and others—trumps the fight or flee.

The hot water's just starting to warm when I finish the speed shower in Lisa Reins's bathtub, sans her Bates Motel shower curtain. Her towel smells like a Victoria's Secret store.

In her kitchen/office, I button the wall-mounted TV.

The sound is off. The screen is a crime scene. The graphic below the close-up and yellow tape reads "Morgan Street Massacre. Nine dead." I hit the sound. The voice says: "Four black, five white, all dead, one of them the business partner of a Chicago police lieutenant." None of them are Jon Eig.

Nine dead would be two more than the St. Valentine's Day Massacre. The reporter speculates that the shooting is somehow connected to last year's "French Connection," an event that turned Chicago's nine-digit heroin trade upside down.

The screen cuts to the WGN studio and "team coverage" that's probably been running all day. Anchor Mark Suppelsa reads a garbled intro I can't hear and the screen cuts to a daytime shot—the front door of a downtown office building and a replay of James W. Barlow Jr. being gurneyed out to an ambulance.

WGN runs a grainy security-camera tape of a male (me) exiting the lobby, then a female in a keffiyeh. Her time stamp exit is fourteen minutes after mine. The voice-over reports that CPD has no ID on either of us, saying that the security desk was unmanned, the guard on duty MIA investigating another incident.

WGN cuts back to the anchor speaking to the camera with a better mic: "Sources inside the Chicago Police Department have confirmed to WGN that 'due to attorney James Barlow's extensive involvement with "questionable" city contracts and high-profile murder cases, CPD's Organized Crime Unit is leading the investigation.'"

My elbows drop onto Lisa's retro Formica table. Lisa Reins isn't home because I paid her $300 not to be; wasn't fair to risk her being beaten to death if Loef Brummel finds me. I pull the pint of Beneagles I bought on the way here, unscrew the cap, and swallow a mouthful. The whiskey shivers me all over. Dave. Dave. Dave. Dead. *In Haiti.* Suicide.

Dave and suicide. *Never happen.*

Me, killing someone, again. *Never happen.* Would've bet my life that it couldn't. And I no doubt have. One hand palms my face, the other sets the pint on top of Astor Argyle, next to my cell phone. Wish I still had a gun.

Why? Gonna kill somebody else?

Exhale. No. But I still wish I had a gun.

When I got off the 'L,' the $600 Beretta—sans barrel—went into an Evanston storm drain. I bought underwear, socks, Top-Siders, a madras jacket, and light cotton pants at Wally Reid's on Sherman Avenue, then threw my "lucky" seersucker suit and shoes in a Salvation Army drop box the Northwestern students use for their commitment to social change. The gun barrel went to a commercial welder I use who melted the barrel into a ball. The ball went into a dumpster. My car, I recovered an hour ago, paying a local Hardscrabble kid $100 to drive it three blocks. I told him it was an "angry husband thing." CPD will already have my plate number but at least I have the car.

Jon Eig, I can do nothing about, other than the three calls I attempted from pay phones. If he's alive, staying silent forever is probably his best bet by a million miles. He sounded like a guy who'd know that. My phone rings for the twentieth time. "Unknown Caller" displays on the screen for the twentieth time. This time I answer.

A harsh Irish voice says, "Dave Grossfeld's dead? In Haiti?"

"Who's this?"

"Your fuckin' ma. Is he, or isn't he?"

"I heard Dave's dead in Haiti, but I don't *know* it."

"And you know who has the money he owes, or his 'fish'?"

"No to both."

The unfamiliar voice says, "You made enemies today. Explain the niggers."

"No idea what you're talking about." I look at my phone. *Over the phone?* Nobody must go to prison in Belfast via a phone tap.

The voice says, "Maybe somebody saves you and your hockey gimps if we know what's goin' on, where the 'fish' are, who the niggers are. We might can keep the gimps off the bridge and the price on you low enough in the ghetto that nobody who's worth a shit chases it. But we gotta know everything."

"*On the phone*, you gotta know everything? How dumb are you Micks? Have your boss find me in an hour. I might know something about Dave by then. Whatever else you're talking about has nothing to do with me."

"Hour's a long time for a guy with your problems."

"Threaten somebody who wants to listen; I have stuff to do."

"Them fuckin' kids of yours don't swim so good. A minute be a long time in the water for them."

Heat burns on my neck. "Let me explain something, asshole. One Flyer gets grabbed or hurt, I walk into the Federal Building, take a reporter with me. When that story breaks, every mother in Canaryville hunts your boss like a pack of rabid dogs."

"Where you gonna meet us in an hour?"

"Right. Great talking to you—"

"Guys are coming for Dave's trucks. Where's the keys and titles."

I picture Dave's office the last time I was there. "They leave the keys in the trucks. No idea on the titles." I button off while the Belfast import is still talking, then frown at my phone. Like the Irish mob can reach into the ghetto to "keep the price on me low." If the dead blacks were GDs or P Stones, the price on me is fifty cents, the cost of a bullet.

My phone rings again, vibrating like a bug against the Astor Argyle frame, "Unknown Caller" on the screen. I glare at the phone. Both hands palm my face; I gotta do something about the Flyers. The phone rings again. I stare at Lisa's kitchen walls, then Lisa's windows, then Astor Argyle . . .

The screen reads: "Rugby Gurl."

I grab it. "Hello?"

"Bill?"

Woman's voice.

"Who's this?"

"We met at Nick & Nora's."

I stand too fast and knock over the chair. "Not me. Never been there."

"Nor have I. So, Bill, you went to Rum Cay and Cuba looking for me. How come?" The accent is satin-smooth American, and maybe Scottish. The rest of the voice is glossy foldout with a touch of three-card monte.

I glance at the kitchen's back door. "No idea what you're talking about."

"Anne and I want to chat. She sends her best."

I flash on the white woman in the combat stance. "Susie Devereux's dead in the Camagüey Breaks. Who are you, really?"

"I think you know better. Call your friend Jon. Ask him who got him away. Then call Anne. Here's her number." The voice gives me an 876 number in Jamaica. "I'm in the neighborhood. We best get together, tonight, after—"

The connection quits.

Eig's alive; glad I didn't get him killed. I take a long pull on the Beneagles, then call Coach Ken, then Patty Prom-Night, neither of whom answer. The message I leave Patty is cryptic but clear enough: "Will explain later. Make your Flyers pickup tomorrow an all-day daytrip. Call the cops and tell them where you're going. And if they ask, you haven't heard from me."

I hang up. My phone lands next to the pint of Beneagles and AA's win picture. I dig out my pen knife and pry open the back of the frame. Tucked behind the shot of Argyle are two eight-by-ten photographs.

Photo no. 1 is two emotionless men standing at a desk, one of them infamous—Al Capone. The photo is dated in white ink with: "Sportsman's Park 1931," the same year Jon said Al was convicted of tax evasion and sentenced to federal prison. The other man is . . . no idea.

I use Lisa's kitchen-table computer to Google: "Images Capone Sportsman's Park 1931."

Google fills the screen with old photos.

Wow. The top row has faces that match both men, even their hats. The second figure in my eight-by-ten is none other than Eddie O'Hare. I read what I can make out in a photographed article. It agrees with Jon that Eddie O'Hare snitched Al into Alcatraz. Unknown to Al, his partner-lawyer had become a federal informant for "altruistic reasons."

Uh-huh. Like lawyers could spell altruistic.

Photo no. 2 has no date. It's a close-up of a desktop at its corner. Atop the desk are two bottles of Barbancourt Rhum. Both bottles sit on a handwritten poem too small to read. The desk is the same in both photos.

Also pressed inside the frame is one ragged sheet of heavy linen stationery—six incomplete lines are arranged in the same pattern as the lines from the poem in the photo:

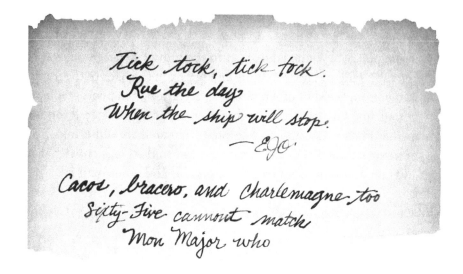

Tick tock, tick tock.
Rue the day
When the ship will stop.
        —EJO.

Cacos, bracero, and Charlemagne too
Sixty-Five cannot match
    Mon Major who

Unlike the poem in the photo, the stationery poem is missing the remainder of its text. I squeeze my eyes shut, then open, then try to decipher the poem.

Back to Google. I type: "Cacos."

Cacos were the peasant revolutionaries who fought against the US occupation of Haiti during WWI, and after.

I type: "Bracero."

A bracero is a sugarcane cutter . . . in several countries, including Haiti.

Cacos and braceros. Two groups of people from Haiti.

Where Dave died ten hours ago. Where "the Gryphon" is.

My stomach votes, demands more Beneagles.

The long pull on the bottle burns my throat. I lay the two photos side by side next to the poem that came with them. Part of the Eddie O'Hare article I just read says he liked handicapping, poetry, and puzzles—not unlike me. That he made his own crosswords and that they appeared weekly in the *Chicago American*.

And like most every regular patron of Sportsman's knows, part of Eddie's Sportsman's history is that "an unknown assailant" shot him dead in 1939 after he left his racetrack office.

I Google for ten minutes, finally find a snapshot of a 1939 article I can read. It says Eddie had a poem in his pocket when he was killed, a poem about time, but there's no poem for me to read.

Back to the poem. "Tick tock" is the first line of this stationery poem. "Tick tock" is a time reference—similar to the theme of the poem that was found in O'Hare's pocket. "EJO" separates the verses. Likely Eddie O'Hare's initials.

Okay, so maybe Eddie wrote a poem about cacos and braceros in Haiti, and time, then hid the poem in a 1927 dog-track win picture with office photos of him and Al Capone and two bottles of Barbancourt Rhum.

Lotta room in that story, including a whole bunch of "Why?" This is not the treasure map I remember from *Treasure Island.*

Maybe work the dates. All three photos were taken between 1927 and 1931.

Okay. And the big news in 1931 was what? The Great Depression, worldwide colonialism, lull between the two world wars . . .

Anne Bonny and I studied a bunch of this at Oxford a lifetime ago. I Google: "Haiti 1927–1931." The first link is "Haiti—Wikipedia."

Of the million sections available in Wikipedia, I jump to "Early Twentieth Century," take another slug of the Beneagles, and read four pages, the gist of which is:

The US invaded Haiti before, or during, WWI, depending on which 'official' version you believe. The German army was funneling support to the rebels, hoping to incite another Haitian revolt. A revolution that would threaten US security and our corporate-banking and sugar investments. The US invaded/intervened, stayed on the island till—

I close the browser. I drank any memory of Haiti out of existence for a reason.

My hand tremor is back. I squeeze my Flyers talisman, stack the photos on the box frame, then my phone, grab the Beneagles, and take another big pull.

The TV keeps talking.

Fuck it. I Google: "Haiti US invasion."

According to the article, the US ran Haiti from 1915 till 1934. The Marines officially landed in 1915, right after the Haitian president was dismembered by revolutionaries friendly to the Germans. The article also mentions the mystery of the missing 1,650 pounds of gold and the ghost ship, the USS *Machias*.

The sheer amount of gold registers for the first time. At today's gold prices, 1,650 *pounds* would be Wall Street kind of money; scorched-earth kind of money. And James W. Barlow Jr. is that kind of lawyer . . . who somebody wearing Susie Deveraux's keffiyeh shot in both knees earlier today. Minutes after I left him.

I glance at the 876 number for Anne Bonny—a guy who makes that call might could get out of the pan with the Irish mob and police, but he'd be officially into the fire.

And your other options are . . . ?

Exhale. I slide my phone to the table's edge and punch ten of the eleven numbers that will connect Anne and me once again, in Jamaica, next door to Haiti. My finger hesitates above the last digit, lucky number 7. I roll my wrist to look at the name carved across the lifeline of my right palm, choose self-immolation, and tap the number 7.

The phone rings three times.

Anne's boyish Irish accent answers, "Grand, Bill, joyous to hear you sane and sober. Liked you better sane and sober, situation being what it was . . ."

Her voice strolls me down the sunny part of memory lane.

"Hi, Anne. I think."

"You *think*? Have you gone timid on us?"

"Always was timid. You and Carel were the pirates."

Anne laughs buoyant and vivacious, an echo of the stunning twenty-year-old redhead she was at Oxford. "Carel was a pretty one, wasn't he? Broke my heart as he always did."

"So you're a treasure hunter? In Jamaica?"

"I am."

"And Carel?"

"Last we spoke he was still roaming the red dirt of the motherland, training their Recce Commandos."

"Kinda surprised you're in Jamaica, still. Are you and I . . . wanted . . . there?"

"If you've forgotten, Bill, the way she works in our esteemed Commonwealth is a person's history can be papered over. Transgressions will stay forgotten until a government minister can require another payment."

"Meaning we . . ."

"Meaning we will always have enemies on the island. And friends. Not the least of which is me."

Nothing's changed; Anne Bonny will walk a tightrope. "Do you, ah, hunt treasure on the come? For a piece if you find it?"

Laugh. "I'm a smuggler, Bill. The treasure huntin's a bitsy sideline, a notion to keep the authorities happy."

"But you know how, I mean, to hunt treasure, if it were around?"

"Oh, she's around to hunt; *finding* her's the problem."

I ask the question that looms between us. "Have you been back to Haiti since . . . we, you know?"

"Since our anniversary? Oh, I've been around her, off her coast. Tortuga, Cap-Haïtien, the wilder parts. Got a Rebelyon gurl in my crew, a nun the last governor hung for accusin' the bishop. But I don't sail Port-au-Prince and the south, other than the hurricane hole at Ferret Bay. Might could now—hell, Haiti's on her fifth government since you and I were there—but sailin' her today would have to be well worth the risk. We'd be facin' six thousand UN peacekeepers, fifty thousand Ida rebels led by an army colonel turned revolutionary, and their boil-pot revolution about to cook off." Anne pauses. "And yourself, William? Susie says you've stepped in it a bit."

I quit memory lane and silently segue to the bloodbath at Nick & Nora's, Dave dead on his boat, Barlow kneecapped in his office. "Things are, ah, fluid. So it is actually your Susie calling me?"

"A fine lass, she is, and can wear pants when it's called for, but you likely already know that."

"No shit."

"Not to worry. Susie's known to be a bit headstrong when the head-masters shake their fingers in her face, but I've only seen her shoot those who won't heed her warning. If you have what we're hunting, it'll be me you'll deal with. No worries there."

"Right. Anne Bonny . . . never an ounce of conflict near her."

Anne laughs again. "But I am a pretty one, still; and we never did see the stars together, although it was on my mind more than one night."

"Spent a few of those myself."

"Make a girl wait twenty-three years, she might think a man's changed his mind."

Anne Cormac Bonny was the most attractive female I'd ever known, on so many levels that no woman since has taken me where I'd imagined she might. "Tempting."

Her voice deepens. "My job."

I laugh small. "Yeah. *Tempting* would be you." I glance the photos and poem. "Is there money at the end of your rainbow?"

"Appears to be. And a fair amount of discord."

Door glance. "How close are you?"

"Depends on you; what you might have and our ability to decipher it. Last time we had this adventure 'figured,' it killed Susie's boat and our mates."

"Sounds high-risk, even for you."

"Don't think we have a choice, William. Our opposition is . . . motivated. If you have the last pieces we're hunting, we'll have the best chance. Greed helps a man make mistakes."

"Like Dave Grossfeld?"

Silence, then: "Aye. Came to me knowing the whole of our story, yours and mine. Said it poured out of you in the night terrors he helped you battle. I forgave you for talkin', your condition bein' what it was."

"Was bad. I'm sorry."

"We are where we are, William. Let's make the best of her."

"Your Susie didn't say what she was looking for up here. Tell me what you guys want and we'll go from there."

"Not possible on the phone. And you'd know that if you were thinkin'. Like it or not, you're already a party. Phone up Susie; have coffee. Tell her I said not to hurt you. We'll all talk after."

I glance out the window at a mixed minefield that I don't know how to walk. "You're guaranteeing my safety?"

Anne laughs again. "Haven't I always?"

***

South of Diversey Avenue, downriver two thousand feet from the Vienna Beef plant, is a WWI railroad bridge built out of red Indiana steel and Northern Illinois aggregate. On the south end, a trunnion-bascule tower rises five stories, including two massive concrete counterweights that haven't been lowered to raise the bridge for as long as I've been alive. The bridge has three tracks and shakes when the trains are inbound. As a kid, I played on every inch.

Mid-bridge in the moonlight and rust, walking toward me on the narrow repairman's walkway, is Anne's partner come to life, Susie Devereux.

Ten feet separate us when I hold up my hand for her to stop on the narrowest length of walkway. Susie Devereux looks female-formidable in the heat and silvery shadows, but far from "safe." Her jeans fit athletic hips, and she's doing a solid impression of wholesome and unthreatening, not that I believe either.

I ask, "Are you armed?"

She shrugs an apology, then shows me that her hands are currently empty.

"Me too. Stay there." I step back, partially shielded by rusted superstructure and the lie that I have a gun. "I'm listening."

She says, "Nice place you picked. They sell coffee here?" Her accent is the same sexy gumbo of American and Scottish that I heard on the phone. "Ours is an amazing story, Bill, *Treasure of the Sierra Madre*, but the tale's on the long side and better with a pint than coffee." She nods west toward the yuppie bars of Bucktown.

I say, "Doubt one pint would be enough. You and Anne are in it from the beginning?"

"And another girl. Five years, give or take."

"Witness-protection before that?"

Miss Devereux frowns. "Your friend Barlow tell you that?"

Nod. "Looks like he and my friend Dave played me, used me as bait."

"You'd be right."

"Barlow said you're off the grid. What's that mean, exactly?"

Miss Devereux doesn't answer, then does. "Wasn't witness-protection. Similar, but . . ." She shows me that her hands are still empty and moves one step closer. "I have family history on the North African coasts; grew up on contraband boats. Went to college, played some rugby with Anne, was eventually recruited as an Arabic translator by an agency whose name you don't need to know. After 9/11, a number of us moved into interrogations as private contractors. Sheberghan, then Abu Ghraib, then Guantanamo."

Same story that Barlow's file detailed for my trip to Rum Cay. "You're gonna waterboard me?"

She smiles crooked. "If sex and drugs don't work."

I can't help the grin. "Barlow said al-Zarqawi tried to kill you. On video."

She nods. "I got sloppy."

"But you're not sloppy now."

She laughs. "You'd be a good judge?"

"I'm working on this Bond-girl fantasy. It'll help me make the bad decision you and Anne want."

"Let me guess, D cup, thong—"

"Close. You were saying . . ."

"I was scuba diving in Zabargad. Saudi jihadists killed three of my friends and grabbed me. The Saudis had me a week. Pre-rape and beheading, they lost a firefight to my rescuers. My contract was shifted to Guantanamo."

"After rugby, Anne and you hooked up at Guantanamo?"

"No. The bad guys tried again in Santiago when I was off-base. Anne was two hours away in Kingston. We talked. She and another girl presented me with a change-of-career opportunity—the Capone gold—and I, again, put to sea under a flag of convenience, convincing two of my rescuers to come along."

"They were with you in Rum Cay and the breaks?"

Susie pats her heart twice. "Two spectacular men I miss every day the sun comes up."

"They knew Anne's Capone gold opportunity could be Haiti?"

Susie Devereux nods again, but smaller, conciliatory, like she knows my history. She says, "Anne told me."

"She did, huh. Love to hear Anne's version."

"Sounded horrible. Sorry it happened to you. And your brother. And the Down syndrome kid."

The deep concern for my feelings probably sounds more believable without the *Live and Let Die* soundtrack behind it. "So, what can I do for you, Miss Devereux?"

"Maybe thank me? For saving your life today? Twice? And your pal Jon's. Those gunmen weren't shooting blanks."

There is no circumstance where I'll admit out loud that I was part of a "French Connection" gunfight where nine people died, including one who didn't deserve it. "I'm thinking the good thoughts."

Susie Devereux loses most of the *wholesome*, hair-flips upmarket brunette an inch, and rests both hands on her hips. Her shoulders rotate back and the T-shirt tightens across her chest. She elevates her chin, exposing a raw neck welt, and waits.

I'm pretty sure no Bond girl could've done that better—somewhere between death threat and NFL cheerleader porn. The bridge trembles, then quits.

She says, "Anne and I are looking for two items. Reliable sources say you have both. If you do, we'd like to buy them."

"How much would you like to pay, say, for one of them?"

"I'd like both." One corner of her smile improves from the flat version. "The items fit together. Like a puzzle. Your forte, according to Anne."

"Let's price them one at a time—"

"Let's not."

The bridge trembles again. The tremble is two trains; one leaving the Clybourn station behind me, the other already past the Ravenswood station behind Miss Devereux. I'll know what to do when both trains arrive; she won't.

"I need $140,000 for Dave's loan shark and $50,000 for my hockey team. That's the price for whatever it is you want."

She nods, but it doesn't look like agreement. "Will one ninety cover everything, Bill? Including . . . today?"

Dry swallow. Nothing will *cover* today for Loef Brummel.

"Didn't think so." Miss Devereux nods again. "I don't have $190,000 on hand, but I do have the same problems as you. The longer I stay in Chicago, the worse my chances are."

The bridge begins to shimmy.

Miss Devereux focuses on the movement, then continues. "I'm sure your Canaryville loan shark is a bad actor, but those black men and women work for a nightmare called the Gryphon who you cannot outrun and neither can I. We either recover the treasure we're hunting and he's hunting, then pick the time and place to bait him into a fight—the highest and best ground—or he'll pick, and we'll lose. That includes you."

"Right. Like Nick & Nora's is the highest—"

"The blacks weren't there to fight. They tried to kidnap me yesterday in Miami. The last one of them alive told me that our friend Dave Grossfeld gave you up, told them you were his guy to read the tea leaves O'Hare left behind. I tailed you from Barlow's; so did they—"

"Dave and Barlow's 'big job next week' was gonna be me reading O'Hare's tea leaves?"

"Yeah, because for the last three years they've tried to figure it without me and couldn't. The blacks' job, then and now, is to deliver you, Astor Argyle, and the Barbancourt bottles to Haiti. Keep you alive until Piccard and the Gryphon can make sense of—"

Deliver me? My knees try to buckle. The bridge shimmies hard. We both flex into our hips. "The blacks are Haitians? Looking for *me*?" Heart-rate explosion. "Explain."

A light appears on the tracks behind her. She leans over the superstructure looking for handholds on the outside above the water, and speaks faster, "Anne and I have a significant portion of the clues to the Capone / Banque Nationale gold. Our adversaries know enough to know the gold trail is real, but not enough to find it.

"Early on we were partners with Barlow and Grossfeld. Unknown to us, the capital they invested wasn't theirs. To get the money, they went to Cranston Piccard, a CIA station chief who'd gone off the rails, and his French Haitian *patron*, the Gryphon. Piccard and the Gryphon had trouble reining in their . . . aberrant behavior."

Miss Devereux looks behind her at the train light.

"Astor Argyle and the Barbancourt bottle hold the last pieces of the puzzle. But the puzzle has endless trapdoors and punji sticks wrapped in O'Hare's poetry, his Chicago references, Haitian-USA history, and American racetrack parlance. If you don't understand it *all*, then the clues and the Gryphon will kill you. My friends and I learned that the hard way."

"Bottle, as in singular?"

"There are two. Anne and I have one. That's why I surfaced as bait; why I'm here. For the second one and the Astor Argyle photo—that we think Dave and Barlow have, or had."

I chin at the wound circling her neck. "The clues did that to your neck?"

"Same people who killed your friend Dave." Her face tightens. "Grossfeld was a hockey player. I'm still here because rugby girls are lots harder to kill." She focuses over my shoulder at a second train coming at her from behind me. "*Two* trains? Could we adjourn to someplace that won't kill us?"

"Are you gonna pay me the one ninety?"

She looks behind her again. "You knew there'd be trains . . . they're your backup."

"Grew up on this bridge playing chicken." The bridge begins to shake. Rumble-and-screech echoes from both directions. I add, "Where you're standing, you can jump or hang. Wouldn't stand where you are, though. The inside train will kill you for sure."

Train lights illuminate us front and back. She jumps over the railing, loses her grip on the top railing, but grabs the rust-pocked I beam at the trestle. Her feet dangle twenty feet above the river.

I flatten on top of the railing, hook it with both legs and one arm, reach down, grab her wrist. It will be almost impossible for her to hold on when the trains cross the bridge.

I yell: "When you lose your grip, grab my arm—"

The trains roar onto the bridge. Her grip on the trestle fails. She grabs my wrist and arm with both hands. The trains screech and rattle past. I say, "Throw your gun in the river."

She loops her legs trying to reattach to the bridge.

"Throw your gun in the river."

"Pull me up! We need the goddamn gun."

"We? My arm's getting tired . . ."

She relaxes. "Okay. Big deal, my new jeans get wet."

She's right, it's not like the fall ever killed my friends or me. I wedge my weight behind the railing, plant both feet on the deck, and use both hands to pull her up far enough that she can regrab the bridge and haul herself over.

Miss Devereux reestablishes on the repairman's walkway. She does not look happy, inhales big—pushes the hair out of her face—exhales big, then:

"Deal. One ninety for Astor Argyle and the remaining Barbancourt bottle. Let's have a look."

"Show me the money. That you said you don't have."

"Anne told me not to hurt you, but she's not here. I may have to make an executive decision."

"Better bring your lunch."

Miss Devereux frowns. "Right. You have a twelve-inch dick. Show me Astor and the bottle of Barbancourt, and I'll show you the money."

"I don't have the bottle . . . yet."

Major frown. Then: "But you do have Astor Argyle?"

I pull the eight-by-ten win picture of Astor Argyle out of my shirt and hand it to her. Her face brightens, not surprising after a five-year chase. Sans threat, her crooked smile is turn-your-head radiant. In the silver moonlight, she holds the picture close to her face, flips it over to see if anything is written on the back, then flips it back and asks, "We know any of these men other than Eddie O'Hare?"

"Al Capone's brother Ralph is the guy on the left. James W. Barlow Sr. is next to him."

"The black man?" She looks above the photograph to me.

I shake my head.

She says, "Has to be a Péralte—the head and face are unmistakable—a family from Haiti whose hands are all over the Capone gold."

I stop myself before saying that for as long as I can remember, and until the day Sportsman's closed, the maître d' at the third-floor clubhouse restaurant was Constantine Péralte, a guy I knew well enough to know his kids' names. His daughter Zelda worked there with him. Miss Devereux is correct, the Mr. Péralte I knew did have an odd-shaped head and face . . . just like the photograph.

I say, "Behind what you're holding were two eight-by-tens and a poem hidden in the frame."

"Show me."

"Show me the money."

"Anne wants you in . . . as a partner. For the same reasons Dave and Barlow did. It's the only way you'll get paid *and* survive all your problems up here."

"I go down there in hurricane season, handicap a guy who died eighty years ago while we dodge a crew of—"

"Yes."

Deep breath. "O-kay." Someone with my voice says: "How would that work, me being partners with you and Anne?"

"And Siri. We take the items to Port Royal, tonight. You help us decipher Mr. O'Hare's poetry, Chicago and horse-racing mumbo jumbo. Best guess? Probably leads us back to Cuba, and maybe Haiti later."

"Anne says Haiti's about to implode."

Miss Devereux shrugs. "When wasn't it?"

Dry swallow. "Not going to Haiti."

"Haiti's already here, Bill. The Gryphon's not going away because we killed a few of his crew. Show me the eight-by-tens."

"Didn't bring them. Sorry."

"And the bottle?"

"I think I know where it is. Maybe. But it's a good, solid maybe."

"Like your twelve-inch dick?"

"That's your fantasy. I do fine with less."

"Okay, I'm on my back; you've been doing 'fine with less' for fifteen minutes; big finish / happy ending for both of us; I say, 'Wow, Bill, that was the best of all time. Could you show me the photos, poem, and bottle?'"

I hold out my hand. "Give me your gun."

"Don't think so."

I vault the railing, toes on the trestle's outer edge, holding on with one hand. "Then give me the magazine and the round in the chamber or you're on your own."

"Bill, we *need* a gun. And bullets." She points at her neck. "We're not playing lawn tennis."

"Magazine or bye."

She pulls a Glock 21, drops the magazine, racks out the .45 ACP round, and puts both on the railing by my hand.

I say, "Step back."

She does. I vault back over to her side of the railing, pocket the magazine and round, then point toward North Avenue. "Grossfeld's. There's two spots there where the bottle could be; I'll call Anne en route. We'll make a deal that doesn't include me and Haiti."

Miss Devereux frowns again. "I'll yell really bad words at whoever tries to kill us between here and Grossfeld's."

"Tell 'em you're a rugby player."

She nods. "Wag your twelve-inch dick. Always works in your 007 movies."

More like my shriveled dick. Only now is the look of the black shooters at Nick & Nora's registering. I'd so completely blocked out my Haitian past that their hats, coats, and sunglasses didn't translate. Same look as the two I saw at Millennium Park across from Barlow's office when I got off the bus.

In my previous life, those hats, coats, and sunglasses were what Papa Doc Duvalier's Militia of National Security Volunteers wore. Tontons Macoutes, they were called. Shadow men, miscreants and sociopaths too deranged for the army, encouraged to roam Haiti's countryside, defending the *république* by whatever means necessary. Papa Doc's son, Bébé Doc, renamed them when he took over from his psychotic father in 1971, but it was the Tontons Macoutes who built me my nightmare fifteen years later in 1986.

Those deranged fucking cannibals up here in Chicago, looking to *kidnap me back to Haiti*, is my equivalent of waking up with the devil straddling my hips.

Chapter 12

BILL OWENS

Four stories above the street, Susie Devereux and I duckwalk one hundred feet of stinky tar roof to the roof's northern parapet. It's midnight; we're directly across from Grossfeld's. We peek.

Four stories below, the weekend-reveler traffic clogs North Avenue in both directions. Idling under the streetlights that define Grossfeld's half block of windows and walls is a dented blue '04 panel van—like the white one at Nick & Nora's. Two white men sit in the van, windows down, smoking.

The front-office section of Grossfeld's is lit, but no shadows move on the window blinds.

I squint. "Gotta be Loef's guys in the van. Here for the trucks."

Susie wipes sweat from her eyes. "They need to hurry up." Her perfume or deodorant is lemon-light but nice, way out of sync with the tar stink and sweat.

Behind Grossfeld's is a wide alley that I can't see.

At what would be the alley's west end, a white guy sips a half pint, looks up and down the north-south side street, then disappears back behind Dave's building.

My madras Wally Reid jacket binds in the armpits. The pants bind at the knees, neither garment made for rooftop recon work. I re-squint

North Avenue for Haitians, then tell Susie, "There's a warehouse trash door that Barlow or Loef won't know about and your Haitian pals shouldn't either—"

"Don't kid yourself, Bill. Before Dave died, he answered every question they asked."

"You know that?"

Susie Devereux hardens to stone. She shows me her wrists. "Yeah, motherfucker, I know that."

The marks on her wrists run up her arm, not across, what a deep, serious suicide attempt looks like. The history in her face looks similar to some of my own. "Sorry."

She says, "Is there *any* reason you can imagine—*any* reason—why Dave would need to talk about that door?"

"A way to get in. But Dave has, *had*, door keys he could give them."

Susie thinks about it. "Your pal Dave thought he was in Rum Cay to buy both rhum bottles for $100,000; a trap the Gryphon set for him and Barlow."

Bingo. That's the missing piece, why Dave went to a loan shark and why he went down there right after I came back without Susie.

Susie scans North Avenue. "The Haitians won't come to Dave's warehouse until Barlow tells them he sent us here. And he will. Barlow will be careful; he knows who he's facing, but the Haitians know where he is. Barlow will be dead by sunrise, or he'll wish he was. And *then* we'll be the only connections left for the Gryphon to hunt."

My stomach binds like my clothes. "You really think there's more Haitians? Four dead today is a bunch—"

"At least two crews. We saw the shooters, his grab team. There's a backup/transport team we didn't see."

"We're facing a goddamn army?"

Susie nods. "He makes them. The Gryphon's a trafficker and Haiti never runs out of poor people. Same as the cartel soldiers on the Mexican border." She turns her back to North Avenue and slides her shoulders down behind the parapet. "It'll be light in six hours. We want to be as far ahead as possible before Barlow spills everything he knows."

I peek back over the parapet. The alley's mouth still has the lookout. The drivers for the trucks are probably back there too. "Okay, I say we climb down, loop the block, call in a fire on this building from the pay phone outside Snyder's."

"A fire?"

"Yeah. Engine Company 35 is just around the block on Damen; take 'em two seconds to get here. The sirens will blow Loef's crew out of the alley. When the fire trucks and cops jam the block, we sneak in the trash door in back."

"I'm not going down there without a loaded gun and you shouldn't either."

I weigh Haitian pirates versus Scottish Moroccan pirates. "If you shoot me in the knees, I'm still not telling you where the rest of Astor Argyle is."

Susie Devereux rolls her eyes in the moonlight, pulls the Glock off her stomach, then holds out her hand for the Glock's magazine. "Scout's honor."

***

12:50 a.m.

Sirens echo outside Grossfeld's warehouse.

Inside, the police and fire-engine lights flash across the warehouse's opaque windows. Heat turbines whir in the barrel-vault ceiling. The floor is a maze of stacked crates and pallets that go on forever, all of it in the deep shadow of low-voltage security lamps. The smell is cardboard and engine oil.

Miss Devereux allows me to lead; clearly she's spooked that the Haitians could be squirreled in here, waiting. Sweat drips off my nose. My eyes bounce left at a noise I can't see, then right, then to Susie Devereux behind my shoulder. If she's queasy, what the fuck should a Boy Scout civilian be?

Fifteen minutes into our B&E, the last siren quits. The red, blue, and white lights continue flashing. By now the firemen know it's a false alarm. The Irish goons probably do too. I refocus on the thirty wall lockers Dave allows the staff to use for free; some unopened for years. I cut the first lock with a bolt cutter liberated from Grossfeld's tool locker. The snap echoes like thunder.

"Jesus."

Susie aims her Glock at the shadows. "Don't think Jesus is down for this one."

I search each locker with a small flashlight.

No Barbancourt Rhum bottle.

"Dave will have a file in his office from the 2003 Sportsman's move." I point for Susie to follow me.

We creep through the warehouse's pallet maze toward the front-office section on North Avenue. I open the connecting door an inch, then squint into fluorescent light.

Susie's hand nudges me on the ass. "On the off chance this isn't a waste of time we don't have, today would be good."

"Feel free to take over whenever you're ready."

"Funny how those twelve inches shrink when it's time to use 'em."

Uh-huh. Some women can kill a hard-on on a sixteen-year-old. I crawl into the fluorescent-lit hallway. Susie stays crouched at the door-jamb, pistol leveled on bad possibilities in both directions. The red, blue, and white lights outside flash across the window blinds.

I crawl past file cabinets and three offices to Dave's. The door is shut. His light wasn't on when we called in the fire. I reach up, turn the doorknob, and squeak the door open.

Dave's blinds are closed. No lights flash against them. I crawl under Dave's window and hunch up behind his desk.

Outside, a shadow darkens Dave's blinds in the middle—a man shape lit by the streetlight above him. Loef's goons are back.

I rifle Dave's top drawer. His Beretta automatic isn't there, but eight hundred-dollar bills are. I pocket them. *Noise?* I stare at the blinds, then the doorway. We do not want to go to a loan shark's basement. I search the other drawers, find Dave's Beretta, drop the magazine—it's full; half-rack the slide to see the round in the chamber. My knees ache on Dave's linoleum. I lean back and sit, straighten one knee, then the other. A Grossfeld's Flyers jersey is framed on the wall, signed by our star goalie, Lisa "The Wall" Saunders.

At the front door, a voice shouts: "POLICE. OPEN UP." The door rattles hard against its frame. "POLICE. WE HAVE A WARRANT."

I jump up, pull Dave's Beretta out of my pants, stuff the gun back in his drawer, and make it to the front door just as it splinters and bangs open.

"DOWN! DOWN! ON THE GROUND! ON THE GROUND!"

Body armor and guns flood the fluorescent-lit lobby. I pancake on the linoleum. Police burst past me in every direction.

"ON THE GROUND!" echoes from the warehouse. "ON THE GROUND!"

Warehouse fluorescents sizzle, then pop on.

The shoes by my face are scuffed and topped by jeans. The voice is familiar. "Working overtime, Bill?" Hands search me up and down, then pull me up by my belt. I land upright with a large man at each shoulder.

Facing me is a heavily armed, square-faced Polish gentleman. He says, "Cannot wait to hear your story. Always good, but this one should be special."

"How you doing, Waz?"

"Wife still thinks I'm Superman. Kids?" Lieutenant Timothy Waznooski frowns. "They like the rap singers better."

"Possibly you should've stayed home more. Played catch and stuff."

Lieutenant Waznooski shrugs agreement. "Softball's dead; even twelve-inch. If my kids go out at all, it's soccer." He points the two cops at my shoulders into the warehouse.

When we're alone, Lieutenant Waznooski says, "Susie Devereux."

I retuck my shirt. "Excuse me?"

"Susie Devereux. The illustrious James W. Barlow Jr. says she shot him twice. Barlow seems to think she's here"—Lieutenant Waznooski points at the worn linoleum between us—"because you are."

I don't glance at the warehouse where Susie's hiding. "Far as I know, I'm the only person here."

"And why is that, Bill? And why does Barlow's alleged assailant care?"

"Maybe you didn't hear, Dave Grossfeld committed suicide. Dave and I were partners. I came down, you know, to sit with his stuff."

"Yeah, we heard about Dave when we were at Barlow's office. As did you when your phone called Barlow's. And we heard about Loef Brummel. Dave really owe $200K?"

"Think it was a hundred. But either way, Dave can't pay. Or couldn't . . . when he was alive."

Lieutenant Waznooski doesn't ask who told me Dave owed Loef because Waz probably knows. "So that leaves you owing the money?" Waz's face prunes. "Can you pay the hundred?"

"I can pay my rent, *most* of the time."

"So why would the woman who shot Barlow be here 'because you are'?"

"That'd be a Barlow question."

"Except I'm asking you. Is she here, Bill? I got eight guys in there looking. Devereux has a serious sheet, lots of black redactions nobody wants to talk about. One of my guys dies, me and the team aren't gonna be happy."

"Shit, Waz, I don't know. Dave's warehouse could hide an army. Dave and I were partners in the mausoleum business and the Flyers. I helped out here *occasionally* when the voice of reason was required. But this place"—I shrug at the rest of the warehouse—"who knows what's in there?"

Waz's tone drops. "Barlow's security tape has you on it. His weekend secretary confirms you were by to see him eleven hours ago. About what?"

"Barlow sent me on an errand a month back and wanted to talk about it." I hold my hand up. "Before you ask, you know I can't discuss his case preparation or he'll sue me into oblivion."

"Barlow's got bigger worries. He's got enough private security on him to protect the president. Way more than he needs if Devereux is all that's after him. Already changed hospitals twice but won't tell us why. How 'bout you tell me?"

Two cops enter from the warehouse. Both are shaking their heads.

Lieutenant Waznooski says "Try harder" and points them back into the warehouse. Waz returns to me. "Neither of your eyes are red from crying. What the fuck are you doing here at one in the morning?"

"Couldn't sleep—"

"Bullshit."

Commotion and loud voices at the splintered front door.

Lieutenant Waznooski turns to a uniformed officer who cocks his head back and says, "Sheriffs and some loan company guys. Say they're serving a repo order for moving trucks."

Lieutenant Waznooski turns to me, floating his eyebrows for an explanation.

I shrug and shake my head.

He tells the uniformed officer, "Keep 'em out till we've searched the building," then points over my shoulder at Dave's office. "That Dave's?"

"Yeah."

"Go."

Waz follows me into the office, flips the light switch, and points at the desk. "Have a seat."

I do and set my hands where he can see them on Dave's desk blotter. My left hand lands on a phone number that begins with 876, the area code for Jamaica.

Lieutenant Waznooski looks at the desktop between us, the fishing trophies on the credenza, the sports memorabilia on the walls, Dave's bar, the Flyers jersey. "We got two of Loef Brummel's crew in a van out front. Know anything about that?"

"Huh? No. Jesus, that's not good."

"No, it isn't, given that Loef lost four guys nine hours ago on Morgan. You saw the TV?"

"I did."

"Banahan's partner, Selah Dune—a girl Lieutenant Denny liked a lot—died inside. Looks like at the hands of the blacks. If forensics prove it wasn't Brummel's people, Denny and Brummel won't have to kill each other." Lieutenant Waznooski stops scanning Dave's office and focuses on me. "Four black, five white, four of them Irish mob. All dead at a place Banahan owns but doesn't run. Media thinks it's a reprisal for his 'French Connection' last year. It ain't."

I do my best totally confused face.

"The mob guys at Nick & Nora's were Irish, not Outfit Italians like last year. None of the dead blacks were Nigerians like last year, and none of 'em were local gangbangers who move the Nigerians' dope." Waz's mouth hardens under his stare. "So, we have the goddamn O.K. Corral in Loef-town, but he's got his guys sitting *here*? On Grossfeld's, waiting for a dead man to come home? Don't think so. And if I was looking for you, this isn't where I'd go. Yet here they are. Tell me what the fuck's going on."

"I don't know. No idea. None."

"Susie Devereux shoots Barlow, then comes *here* looking for you. Why? Loef Brummel's crew dies 4X and the remainder is *here*, looking for her, or you, or both. Why? A fifth grader would say you have something everybody wants—*what is it?*"

I show Waz my palms. "No idea. Honest."

"Wanna walk out front with me? Let the Canaryville boys know you're in here? Won't be good when our cars leave."

"C'mon, Waz. I didn't borrow the money. I don't know Devereux, and maybe it was Barlow who hired the blacks. I build mausoleums and try to race horses, for chrissake. I don't know, okay? And while we're talking, I need a favor."

"From me?"

"Could you step outside and mention to the Canaryville goons that you know one of the Flyers? And that if that kid is the one they throw off the Ashland Avenue bridge, you're gonna start hanging loan sharks from streetlights."

Waz looks at the door to North Avenue. "What the fuck is wrong with you? What kind of asshole puts retarded fucking orphans at risk?"

"*I didn't do it.* Dave did. Can every-fucking-body try to remember that?"

Waz frowns, looks around, and says: "Gimme something with Grossfeld's Flyers on it. That chain you hang around your neck."

"Need to keep that." I unhook the key ring from my car keys.

Waz hooks the key ring into his, says, "This didn't happen. Do not move your feet; I mean it," and walks outside.

Three minutes pass. Waz walks back in, doesn't comment or return the Flyers key ring, and asks: "Ever been in Nick & Nora's?"

My fingerprints will be in there, and my car tag on the street. "Yeah, sure, there and Johnny Ga Ga's are the best dogs in the city."

"After the shooting, a picture was missing from the wall . . . some kinda dog-racing picture. Nine people *died* over a *dog-racing picture*? Ever race dogs, Bill?"

"No."

"Got something against blacks? Women? Foreigners?"

"No more than you do."

Waz doesn't laugh.

One of his guys raps on Dave's open door and says, "Nobody in the warehouse. There's thirty lockers with the locks cut, stuff tumbled out like somebody searched 'em." He hands Waz an old eight-by-ten photograph held by a clothespin. "Found this."

Waz looks at it, then shows me the Astor Argyle win picture. "Imagine that, a dog-racing picture."

My stomach sinks. I shrug. My fingerprints will be on it. Lieutenant Banahan will ID the photo as the one missing from Nick & Nora's, *that also* has my prints and had my car nearby.

I'll be leaving town for somewhere, with or without the Barbancourt bottle, *if* Lieutenant Waznooski doesn't handcuff me now. I grab for the photo. "Can I see that?"

Waz jerks it away before I can contaminate the evidence. The lantern jaw sets and his eyes narrow. "Look, but don't touch."

I refold my hands and lean toward his side of the desk. "No idea. Why would a dog race in 1927 matter?"

"Why would a picture stolen from a mass murder earlier today be here?"

I shrug again. "Don't know? Susie Devereux?"

"How would she get in?"

"Barlow gave her a key? She searched the lockers?"

"Didn't say he gave her a key." Lieutenant Waznooski points at the photo. "Know this black guy? This *foreign*-looking black guy?"

I squint. "Nope. Never bet on a dog race in my life. Hopefully you haven't either."

"Ever hang out with transvestites?"

"Huh?"

"Guys who dress like girls."

Frown. "I know what a transvestite is. Other than Cognac St. Germaine, the piano player at the Baton Lounge, probably not. But who knows anymore?"

Lieutenant Waznooski nods. "The four black shooters? Two of 'em are women?" He frowns. "Not so much."

Waz is wrong; I saw them; they *were* women, just in men's clothes, dressed as Tontons Macoutes.

"All of 'em had marks high under their left arm, welts, like they'd been branded small. Might be an *E* with a cross shoved through it. The coroner says—"

Commotion again at the front door. Two of Cosmo Camastro's sons burst through, yelling: "Fuck you! This ain't no crime scene! You can't keep us out. We got papers for the trucks!"

Lieutenant Waznooski steps out of Dave's office and yells at Cosmo's sons. One is dumb enough to chest-bump Waz and keep yelling. Waz takes him to the floor. Astor Argyle floats toward me like we were separated at birth. I grab Dave's Beretta from his desk, then the photo, step around the three-person scrum and out the splintered front door onto a still-congested North Avenue.

Two steps past the nearest fire truck, I'm spotted by Loef's goons. Luckily, they are out of the van, facedown on the pavement, fully engaged by four unhappy policemen. I hear "Ashland Avenue bridge," like that's where these fellows are headed. I reach the street corner, pull the Beretta, and sprint south for my car.

Black or white, anyone in my car gets two in the chest. I'm *not* going to Haiti . . . or a loan shark's basement.

Chapter 13

BILL OWENS

Sunday, 1:30 a.m.

Eleven miles across the city, I park dark, strip my jacket and shirt, pass out in the Citroën's back seat with Dave's 9 mm on my stomach.

Heat and streetlights wake me.

Watch check—three hours. I'm bleary but un-kidnapped and un-arrested. *Jolt.* Susie should've called. I fumble my phone, almost hit redial on "Rugby Gurl." Wait. I can't put my cell number inbound on Susie's phone; not if she gets ID'd as a shooter at Nick & Nora's. Can't go home, or anywhere else I'd normally be. Need a plan. I try Anne; no answer. Need a pay phone and coffee.

The pay phone outside Top Notch Burgers on Ninety-Fifth accepts my quarter and gives me a dial tone (shock). I dial Susie; she doesn't answer. Would she hide at Grossfeld's? Stay to look for the bottle? Risk the Haitians until daylight? She might; Anne said they believed their *only* chance was if they found what the Gryphon wanted, lured their version of Dracula into the light, and fought him there. I loved the skin in those Hammer Film / Christopher Lee Dracula movies when I was a kid, but hated the scary parts. And now I'm in one.

Face rub. Predawn vampire glance. I squint at the Astor Argyle photo, the black face that Susie made as a Péralte. There is one call I can make. A long shot that might buy me $190K without having to join Anne and Susie's trip into the Corazón Santo.

How fitting. I get to bet my life on a dog race.

***

Standing at the front door of a modest but immaculate red-brick bungalow at 5:00 a.m. on a Sunday is Zelda Calhoun, the widowed daughter of Sportsman's maître d' Constantine Péralte. Zelda's terry-cloth robe is wrapped tight from neck to knee. She's in her bespectacled sixties, can't be thrilled to host a visitor predawn, but does remember me as a customer and friend of her father's.

In spite of the hour and my madras jacket, she says, "Come in. Nice to see you again, Mr. Owens."

"Again, my apologies. It's just, my editor at the magazine . . ."

"The mementos are in here." She directs me through the arched foyer and into an odd but pleasant bouquet of citrus fragrances that highlight her living room. The window AC unit isn't on. "Sportsman's was my father's life. Then, eleven days after the auction, he passed unexpectedly. As I recall, you attended the wake and funeral."

"I did."

Mrs. Calhoun points to the far corner of her father's Sportsman's Park wall of fame that wasn't here when I last came for the crowded, smoky wake. She walks me within three feet of what might be an antique bottle of Barbancourt Reserve du Domaine Rhum. I turn the bottle. It's an old bottle, most of the label gone other than the image of Napoleon's sister, Pauline Bonaparte, and her husband, General Charles Leclerc. Barbancourt is honey dark, not quite as dark as Myers's, but this bottle is ink black.

Mrs. Calhoun asks, "Why such short notice on your story?"

"The internet has changed everything. The magazine agreed to do the feature on Sportsman's because the city just announced they were scrapping the plans for the mall. My article's about why Cicero tore down a landmark—where men like your father were stars—in exchange for a vacant lot."

"Sad." Mrs. Calhoun excuses herself to feed a calico cat that continues to figure-eight her slippers as they walk toward their kitchen.

The seal on the Barbancourt bottle is waxed ruby red and covers the cork. I use a pen knife to circle-cut the wax, then twist the cork till it pops. Smells like rhum, sweeter than most because Barbancourt is made from cane juice, not cane molasses. When I was last involved as a salesman for Myers's, Barbancourt owned the rhum market in Haiti, had been there for 250 years, had a castle where we used to drink before everything went to shit.

I slow-pour thickened liquid into a jumbo 2002 Illinois Derby glass. A long sealed-top glass tube clinks into the Derby glass. *Oh shit* . . . did I just find everyone's magic bullet?

I set down the Barbancourt bottle, cut the seal on the glass tube, and pull out a tightly rolled piece of linen stationery . . . like what was behind Astor Argyle and the two eight-by-ten photos. This stationery is torn at the top. Astor Argyle's was torn at the bottom.

Are we part of the same page as the Astor Argyle poem?

left the ship with skeleton crew.
                    —EJO.

Only the Rhum beards know
The long and the latt.
His partner names
Just bits of the trap.
                    —EJO

The treasure belongs to me.
Be it missing or dead.
I advise the night thieves to be
Of the dark angel, afraid.
                    —EJO.

17°57'51.16"N / 76°47'52.62"W

Fear the feds; fear the sky;
fear the pencilmen; who never die."

I fast-pocket the stationery, pour the rhum back in the bottle, cork it, and snap two photos of the entire wall of fame. In her kitchen, Mrs. Calhoun is brewing coffee on a spotless Formica counter. I make her accept a hundred from the money I found in Dave's drawer.

"No, please. Make an offering at church today. I loved your dad, always great to me. Please."

In my car, under a dome light I shouldn't have on, I try matching the ragged edge of the new poem and the AA poem.

Same sheet of paper.

My God, am I talented, or what? No wonder Anne and Susie D. think I'm the man.

I reread the new poem. Two words: *Treasure* and *coordinates* go super swell together in every swashbuckler I've read or seen. I open my cell phone to Google Earth and type in the poem's coordinates: 17°57'51.16"N / 76°47'52.62"W.

Google's spinning Earth appears. A satellite camera stops in the Western Hemisphere, shrinks toward North America, then south into the West Indies, then deeper still into the Caribbean Sea, closing on Haiti. *Don't you fucking dare*—the camera or connection stutters, then shrinks *past Haiti* to the island of Jamaica, down to Kingston, to—

The connection quits. "Charge Battery" flashes on my screen.

Frown. I plug into the cigarette lighter and restart Google Earth. Eddie O'Hare's eight-decade-old coordinates shrink the world back to Kingston, Jamaica, *not Haiti*, then into Kingston's massive harbor, and stop just offshore, east of what looks like a pier covered by a giant gantry crane. No, it's actually a series of old piers where Ocean Boulevard turns inland just west of downtown. No telling what was, or wasn't, there in 1914 when the gold was stolen, or in 1931 when Eddie snitched Al, or in 1939 when Eddie was murdered.

My heart adds an extra beat. Could we really be looking at $26 million in gold? A partner's share of that could, no shit, buy Dave's debts *and* me Loef Brummel's forgiveness. And the best gunfight, self-defense lawyer in Chicago if Waz and CPD decide I'm their villain for Nick & Nora's. And (insert heroic music here) Grossfeld's Flyers will not only live on, they'll have their own tour bus with bathrooms, a radio show, color commentators—

Google Earth quits again. I restart and zero it back in to Kingston.

Part of the larger harbor *was* there when I worked at Fred L. Myers & Sons in '84 and '85, but this section of Kingston Harbour wasn't like it appears now. Back in the '80s this spot was a dock for ships, historic ships, three-masters, frigates, colonial/pirate stuff, much of it rotting and aground. That's what water does to things—rots them, drowns them. Blink. Makes no sense. A Chicago lawyer / poem writer who was crafty enough to survive seven years after betraying Al Capone into Alcatraz wouldn't *hide* $26 million in gold on a semi-sunken wooden ship.

I dig out the 876 number that was on Dave's desk blotter, scroll up my recent call list—same number Susie Devereux gave me to call Anne Bonny.

Makes sense. If a guy had to hunt treasure in the Caribbean, there'd be no better partner than Anne Cormac Bonny. And Dave betrayed her. *Stupid* on a scale that would insult a box of rocks. Fucking Dave.

And right next to Anne's number on my phone are all the calls from the Canaryville goon, and below those threats, two calls from Loef himself. I glance Zelda Calhoun's neighborhood, where I shouldn't be, where black Haitians wouldn't be out of place.

Shiver. Time to hit the bricks. With all haste and rapidamente.

***

At sunrise, O'Hare Airport's curbside drop-off is already crowded. I recon, then, phone to my face, stroll past two Chicago policemen focused on traffic, and into the international terminal.

Inside, I call Lieutenant Waznooski. "Hiya, Waz, hope you didn't hurt Cosmo's kid."

"Where are you?"

"In the car. If you want to continue our conversation, just tell me where."

"Bring my dog picture back or you're going to Stateville."

"Don't have it, sorry. Like I said, I'm into horses, not the dogs."

"You got one hour. Get your ass to my office by seven thirty and bring the goddamn picture or I'm going citywide as 'armed and dangerous.'"

"Jesus, Waz, don't do that. Your guys tend to shoot those people."

"Your relatives can sue me."

"I don't have relatives."

"You don't have an employer either. Barlow's MIA. Three of his security team are dead."

I spin a fast 360. First for immediate safety, then for my goodbye memories of Chicago.

Waz finishes with: "Seven thirty. And bring me my goddamn picture. Me and my office are the only way you'll ever read another *Racing Form*."

I button off and check the departures board. In spite of weather issues in the Caribbean, there's a one-stop flight to Kingston that boards in forty minutes. Jamaica is 1,800 miles away from a Canaryville basement and the Chicago police. Unfortunately, Jamaica is in the Corazón Santo, across the street from Haiti, closer than I ever imagined I'd get again in this lifetime.

My phone rings. "Rugby Gurl" lights the screen. I answer, "Hey!"

Susie Devereux says, "You safe?"

"Yeah. You?"

"Didn't find the bottle; dodged bad guys all night, but think I'm good now. We have to find the bottle, Bill."

"Barlow's MIA."

Silence, then Susie says, "MIA means dead. And the bad guys now know everything Barlow knew about you, me, the bottles, and the photo."

I 360 again. "CPD's all over this. Wanna tie me to the shooters at Nick & Nora's. Called two of them 'women,' but 'not so much.' That mean something to you?"

"Yeah. Where are you?"

"Running." Pause. "I found the bottle."

"What?"

I scan the airport.

Susie shouts: "Goddammit, Bill, I can't hold my breath forever. Talk to me."

"Poem in a glass tube inside the bottle."

"You found it. Jesus, I may faint. Read me the poem."

I ease backward against the concourse wall. "On a cell phone?"

Silence. "Where are you?"

"Flying to see our friend. Plane leaves in forty minutes. Got you a seat if you can get here."

"Not in forty minutes, but mos def the next thing smoking. God*damn*, I'm happy. Can you make copies of everything? In case something happens?"

"*In case?* Shit, if this Gryphon guy scares you and Anne sideways, I make it more like even money."

"So make copies. Photograph everything with your phone and email me."

"First, we sit with Anne and your friend Siri. All of you tell me we're four equal partners and that I had nothing—as in zero—to do with Barlow and Dave betraying you. Then you tell me who the Gryphon is—"

"I told you."

"No. 'Trafficker' is not gonna be enough. This guy's got the reach of an Old Testament villain."

"Doesn't matter. You're in, whether you like it or not, and so am I. And so are Anne and Siri."

"This airport has planes to lots of places."

Silence, then, "He's a modern-era warlord—cocaine, slavery, currency, human organs—and as bad as I've ever encountered. Anywhere. The only black box in this hemisphere other than Guantanamo—"

"Black box?"

"A secure, deniable site where governments can do black business . . . interrogations, red market, and worse; stuff that a Western person can't fathom."

"Red market?"

"Most of the third world is worth more as bones, blood, and especially organs. Those who aren't are sold as slaves—sex, labor, or soldiers. Google 'red market.'"

I recheck O'Hare Airport to my left and right. "The poem has coordinates."

"Tell me it's not Haiti."

"Jamaica."

Susie yells: "Yes!"

I jerk the phone from my ear, recover, say, "Good news, huh?" and hold the phone away.

Susie Devereux, gunfighter, black-candle palera, says: "Fucking Christmas."

"Meet you at Anne's?"

The call goes silent.

"Susie? You there?"

"Anne was right, you are a man worth knowing. That clue's our life, Bill; keep it and you safe until I can get there and guard you proper."

"I'll feel safer if you wear the pirate outfit."

***

2:00 p.m.

I'm seven hours gone from Chicago O'Hare—thank you, Baby Jesus—buckled into a coach seat on United's flight 622 to Kingston. Did the plane change in Newark ninety minutes ago. No Chicago police warrant greeted me. Unfortunately, neither did New Jersey's Springsteen or Debbie Harry. Nor was my swashbuckling pirate girl there to protect me from the rubber airport pizza that people on the East Coast must think is pizza because it's flat and red.

Window glance.

I am, with substantial trepidation, about to remeet the West Indies. My reunion will have Anne and Susie D. in it, but will likely be 100 percent downhill from there. JOLT. United 622 bucks hard, buffeted in the first of two storm systems churning in from the Atlantic. We're over central Cuba, rolling the dice above hurricane alley—"kissing the serpent's tale," as the vodou *mambos* used to say; the same *mambos* who told me in 1986: "Never, ever come back."

Lightning rips across the windows.

United 622 flat-falls, jolts hard, then bucks higher. The cabin lights flash off-on-off. Twenty-three goddamn years; the West Indies and the Corazón Santo haven't changed. Both still kill a lot of people in September, many of them innocent. And dying down here isn't the worst thing that can happen to you.

FLASH. JOLT. FLASH.

My knuckles grip white. Sweat drips into my left eye. I'm breathing in bursts. Goddammit, why did I think I could come back?

Both eyes squeeze shut.

Because Bill fucking Owens is a suicidal idiot, running from someone else's disaster.

Just like the last time.

PORT-AU-PRINCE, HAITI

1986

Chapter 14

BILL OWENS

February 4

As the lion tamers say, "What could go wrong?"

My fellow passengers and I crowd the aisle to deplane our DC-8 from Kingston. I share my sunniest twenty-two-year-old smile. We descend rollaway stairs onto the cloudy and humid two-country Caribbean island of Hispaniola. The newbies balk at the visual— submachine guns, sunglasses, military caps—then the smell: a Detroit factory on a three-shift day.

Hispaniola is a troubled "paradise" currently awash in Colombian cocaine, DEA agents, and *Miami Vice* wannabes, although that's mostly on the Dominican Republic half. The Haiti side has a different set of troubles.

I, however, am not a party to the troubles on either side of the island, nor do I dress, talk, or look like I'm a party to those troubles. I sell Jamaican rum. Call me Bob Marley in a bottle. This is not completely clear to the raptor-eyed customs officer representing the République d'Haiti's half of the island.

On a good day, François Duvalier International Airport's customs and immigration isn't fun. And with armed rebellion already killing people in Haiti's eastern mountains, the prospects for foreign arrivals are . . . well, you can imagine. (The rebels want a Cuban-Communist utopia, not the hellish "democracy" of President-for-Life Bébé Doc Duvalier.) And had I taken the time to "imagine," I wouldn't be here with a hidden agenda. I've been on my own since I was sixteen; I know better.

The customs officer rereads my US passport a third time. His accent is French: "William Lyman Owens, born Chicago, Illinois." He looks up from behind his metal table and stares round-eyed, third-world authority. "This passport is counterfeit. You are a drug trafficker. Here to finance the rebels."

"No. No. No. See, right there." I point my most confident fingertip at previous Haiti stamps and visas, all legitimate. "I come here all the time. For Myers's Rum. From Jamaica. I live in Kingston, see? Moved from London. It's on the other pages."

I don't mention the reason for the move—East London's twin-brother crime bosses Ronnie and Reggie Kray want to kill me for refusing to dope horses they'd bet against. I point to my Myers's order book, then to the Myers's Rum bottles that the uniformed officers have removed from my suitcase. All the customs people have added pistols to their light-blue uniforms in the seven weeks since my last trip.

The officer growls: "Why are you here?"

"To sell rum. Like always. I have a meeting with our new distributor; he's waiting at the Oloffson, the hotel. You can call."

He barks Haitian Kreyol, Haiti's slave-era patois of African and sugar-plantation French. A junior officer steps up, takes my passport, and disappears into the airport's noise and confusion. I will myself to not think about Carel Roos, Rhodesian mercenary. *Business meeting. Business meeting. Business meeting.* That's why I'm here.

Sweat beads on my forehead. Carel once told me a good operator could smell a revolution coming. He'd been part of several in Africa and mentioned the smell again last week when he called me in Kingston to make me this offer.

STOP. You're here for legitimate business, rum *business, same as always.*

I glance beyond my interrogation table into the open-air terminal that I haven't been allowed to enter. Would be bad if Haiti's already-rattled authorities have a record of Carel's call to me. *Swallow.* Very, very bad.

Straight ahead in the terminal, watching me from either side of a dirty-tile support column, are two black men in ratty sport coats, porkpie hats, and sunglasses. Pistol grips are prominent in their belts. They are freelance street militia. President-for-Life Bébé Doc Duvalier's Volontaires de la Sécurité Nationale. Successors to his dead father's horror show Tontons Macoutes. Same show; different name. To whom the Volontaires will be loyal in the coming weeks is up for grabs.

The junior customs officer with my passport struts past the Volontaires without comment and back into the interrogation area. He hands my passport to his boss, who explains nothing, points me to repack my suitcase and pass into the République d'Haiti.

"Thanks." I accept my passport, stuff my suitcase, wishing I'd been sent back to the plane. My decision to muck about in Carel's world felt a lot less ominous on the phone.

Behind their mirrored sunglasses, the two Volontaires bend their necks like tree snakes do when they intend to interdict your path. I've had previous encounters with Volontaires and look down to shuffle my documents, pretending I'm foreign-white oblivious to the rebellion tension vibrating off the walls.

Outside, under François Duvalier International Airport's porte cochere, it's ten degrees hotter. My shirt collar steams to my neck.

Tense soldiers stand the outdoor arrival area. Bayonets glare in the sunlight. Armored concrete checkpoints block any vehicle's approach to, or exit from, the terminal.

Per Carel's instructions, I make a mental note of locations, equipment, and personnel. Under the porte cochere, I switch hands on my Samsonite suitcase and sidestep through soldiers who make no effort to create a lane for passengers and luggage.

At the curb, I catch the eye of a private-taxi driver, then slide in the back of his bedraggled '71 Ford Fairlane.

"*S'il vous plaît*; Hotel Oloffson." A heart wrapped in thorns hangs from his mirror, a "graven image" of the Corazón Santo.

We inch up to the exit checkpoint. My driver's brown hand drops part of the fare he will earn into the ranking soldier's palm. The soldier stares at me too long, then bends and stares inside the taxi. Still looking at me, the soldier makes a gesture behind his back that I can't see.

Another soldier raises the rusted-white pipe barrier and allows us through. The Fairlane coughs forward past two stalled or abandoned Fiats, then out onto the Mais Gate road.

My driver checks the soldiers in his mirror, then me.

My heart rate drops to 150.

We turn right, burrowing through clouds of black flies breeding in the mud fields between us and Cité Simone-Cité Soleil—according to Kingston TV and radio, the most dangerous ghetto/city on earth.

At the first roundabout, we turn left to skirt the angry crush of Port-au-Prince. I'm sweating lots more than usual and now smell as strong as my driver and his taxi. He, like everyone who sets foot in this country, is wary all the time. The constant menace cooks a peculiar smell, stronger now with Rebelyon coming. The locals call the smell "poor man's perfume"—the Duvaliers' thirty years of night terror and murder mixed with the local staple of pepper & pig-fat rice. The tropics cooks it all into an unmistakable fear-sweat that's hard to wash off your skin and out of your clothes.

Traffic should be clear this time of day, but isn't. Patrols of faded green uniforms walk the road's shoulders; more soldiers than last month; more military trucks and jeeps, a lot more. I make the mental notes for Carel.

Bébé Doc's not stupid, nor deaf. He's tortured Haiti for fifteen years to remain the president. Bébé Doc's heard the screams on his street corners, and he's heard the faraway rumbles in Washington, DC, and maybe most threatening, in Miami, where his successor, Luckner Cambronne, "the Vampire of the Caribbean," is waiting in exile. Bébé Doc's grip on his generals is unknowable, but his cunning is a matter of record.

My Fairlane passes the never-completed racetrack. I didn't have to ask the driver to take the long way that avoids Cité Simone-Cité Soleil. When the Rebelyon starts—whether Castro is at its heart like

President Reagan says or not—Cité Soleil will likely be ground zero, then spread too fast to contain to everywhere there's poverty, and in Haiti, that's everywhere.

We dodge potholes on an all-weather road south out of the malaria valley, then begin to climb toward the mountains. My meeting is with Myers's Rum's new distributor. His predecessor was a Frenchman who had trouble paying his taxes, then had trouble staying alive. The meeting is up-mountain in Pétion-Ville, a suburb with breezes, bougainvillea, and a natural barrier to the squalor and desperation below.

My taxi serpentines higher into the flamboyant red trees. The soldiers and personnel carriers begin to thin, as does the stench of the sun-scorched, rusted-tin ghettos and open sewers.

At 1,200 feet, we approach tall cut-stone walls topped with jagged glass, then the massive iron gate of l'Habitation Leclerc, an estate once owned by Napoleon Bonaparte's sister. In the 1970s it was converted to a decadent resort and casino. I never got past the gate when it was still running, but in there was the Hippopotamus Disco, moved down brick by brick from New York City, along with Mick Jagger, Iggy Pop, and the crème d'Studio 54.

Now the whole estate is empty. There wasn't enough dope and Barbancourt Rhum for the pretty people to fade Bébé Doc's escalating horror show—

Screech. I bounce face-first into the front-seat headrest.

Four of Bébé Doc's Volontaires block the road, pistols in hand. To their left is a mutilated, naked black man propped up at the l'Habitation Leclerc gate, an emaciated dead dog in his lap. The sign strung to the man's neck reads *"Mangeur de chiens."*

The taxi driver freezes his eyes forward but whispers a translation, "Eater of dogs. A traitor. Loyal to the Americans, the coup they plan."

Two of the Volontaires approach the driver's side of our taxi. My driver goes motionless, both hands on his steering wheel. A pistol barrel raps my door.

Bending into my open window, a black face with cheap mirrored sunglasses peers in, then says: "Documents."

I have no choice, and hand my passport through. He speaks Kreyol at my driver. The driver reaches to open his door. A pistol barrel slams though the open window, breaks the driver's nose, and splashes his windshield red. The gun wags in my face. "Not him. You. Get out."

My heart rate ramps back to 150. I open my door, push my feet out onto the rough concrete, then stand with both hands up.

"Your money." The gunman extends the hand that already has my passport and visa.

"I'm here to see General Peguero." I point uphill toward the Hotel Oloffson. "We have business."

General Peguero is our new distributor, a friend of the Myers family, some say on our payroll already.

"Peguero is a traitor. You are CIA, here to kill President Bébé Doc." The gunman throws my passport into the road. "Tonight you can sleep with General Peguero's head."

Motion behind me. I spin. Everything goes black.

***

SLAP. "You were part of Operation Urgent Fury, yes? President Reagan's invasion of Grenada. You impersonated a student there at the medical school."

"No. No." Blood spray and saliva punctuate my words. "I was in college." Pant, cough, dungeon air. "I told you, at Oxford in London; just a couple of years ago." My eyes can't focus. "You can check."

Four hands clamp me in the chair. In my face is the same round-eyed, round-faced black man who's been interrogating me since midnight. His name is Kolonèl Idamante. I don't know if he's Haitian Army or Volontaires, or somehow both. Sweat drips onto his wire-rim glasses; he removes them, cleans each lens with a handkerchief.

"We have checked, Monsieur Owens; we are aware of who visits the République. Again, your age is twenty-two, but you appear older. You are an American, but you are here."

I blink to focus and can't. Kolonèl Idamante replaces his glasses, then stands with his zipper near my shredded lips. His long black fingers knead a leather sap. He swings; the blow knocks me out of the chair. Lights blink out and on. Pain radiates in my jaw, ear, and neck. The floor tastes like vomit. A boot stomps on my back; my chest flattens on the concrete. Another boot mashes my neck and cheek flat. Blood bubbles from my mouth. Blurry boot toes and laces are all I see.

"So very strange, Monsieur Owens. One day you are a 'game theory' and 'literature' student at Oxford University in England, the next day you are in the République d'Haiti . . . selling rum for Jamaicans." Fingers stroke the top of my head. "Why would an American leave America for university? America has many universities."

The boot on my neck presses harder.

"Scholarship"—cough, spit—"four years ago; when I was a freshman. I'm working for Myers's now, in Kingston." Pant; spit blood and concrete dirt. "Moved from Chicago to London; for school. Got job . . . been in Kingston two years."

"No. No. No, Monsieur Owens."

"Myers's salesman; come to Haiti all the time, for Myers's. No America, not since high school."

Kolonèl Idamante squats so our eyes can make contact. He flips my passport again, smudging at the stamps with his long thumb and polished nail. "Yes, I see that you have been to the République nine times this year and last. You are with the CIA, yes? The 'Game Theory Department'? Here to assist in President Reagan's coup d'état?"

"No. Not."

"But you know of the coup d'état. The vampire Cambronne returns."

"Don't know anyone. Not like that. I work for Myers's, that's all. Honest."

"Lies do not help. You have been many times to Odricks Corner, Virginia?" A boot slams my wrist and Kolonèl Idamante attaches pliers to my thumb. "In Miami, you work for the vampire Cambronne. You wish to make Reagan's puppet our new president. Anything to stop a Rebelyon that aligns Haiti with Cuba. Admit this and prison for you will be easier."

"Never *been* to Miami. Don't know Cambronne."

The pliers crush my thumb. I scream, writhe on the floor, rip my hand away, and lose the nail. "Goddamn, man!" I scrunch away holding my hand.

Two Volontaires point pistols at me.

"Monsieur Owens. Oxford informs us that you do not finish university; you become embroiled with a bad element and are forced to leave England quickly. This is a lie as well, yes? The CIA recruited you, brought you to the West Indies to stop the communists and help sell CIA cocaine. This is the truth."

I squeeze at the pain in my hand. "No. Wrong." Flies buzz the blood on my face and hand. "I was a bookie's apprentice"—pant, cough—"for horses; part-time on weekends; legal there. Ronnie Kray—twins, the Krays, gangsters—Ronnie Kray wanted me to dope horses; I wouldn't. A friend, fellow student helped me get out; got me the job at Myers's."

Two black men jerk me up from the floor and slam me back in the chair. Rubber cords loop around my shoulders, waist, and feet.

Kolonèl Idamante sets a chair across from me and sits. His boot slides a doctor's valise between us. To my left, a chain is hoisted through a hook in the ceiling.

"No. C'mon, man, don't . . . don't."

"Yes, I know of the Krays. I am a professional policeman; I also studied in London, and in Paris." Kolonèl Idamante opens the doctor's valise. "Who was this *student* who could save you from a London crime syndicate?"

"Anne Bonny. Her family's from Ireland and Jamaica. She arranged it."

"Anne Bonny . . . a girl, by herself."

"Her boyfriend helped her, with the Krays, not Jamaica. He was a Selous Scout in Rhodesia."

Kolonèl Idamante sits back in his chair. His lips form a small, tight smile under his glasses.

Shit. Shit. Shit. Shouldn't have said Selous Scout. Be a rum salesman. Not a spy. Gulp. Swallow. Focus goddammit; you cannot be a spy.

Five pairs of white eyes are looking at me from the dark of medieval stone-basement jail . . . for doing amateur recon; for college friends and a good cause. Get paid, big adventure—

"Selous Scouts." Kolonèl Idamante's smile widens. He reaches inside the valise. One hand extracts a saw and he shows it to me. The other hand rises between us. He extends one finger and says: "Rhodesia's Selous Scouts were *counter*revolutionaries." Kolonèl Idamante adds a second finger and says: "Jungle fighters," then a third finger: "Mass murderers of black men, even by African standards. They have no country now. Are they the surrogates you and the CIA employ to kill my president? Before my president can accept Cuba's support and appease the Rebelyon in our mountains?"

"No! Carel was with Anne. After the war in Rhodesia, he came to university, that's all. I hardly knew him; don't even know his last name. Coincidence—"

"No, Mr. Owens. In Haiti, we cannot abide coincidence. We are awash in the meddling of others. Our citizens die in the streets for causes they do not understand. All to achieve your CIA's goals for America's benefit. You are an American; we will show you what awaits the vampire and his surrogates."

More men enter the room. They leer at me and grab their balls. Two drop their pants as the others unbuckle their belts. The first one steps toward me. The others begin some kind of screech, guttural, then high-pitched—

"You will learn to like black men . . . as your women do."

"No! GODDAMMIT, no!"

***

Thursday?

I'm curled in the corner. Hurts to breathe. *Blink.* One eye half-focuses. Sewer stench. Loud voices echo somewhere in the dinge. Maggots crawl the stone floor past my fingers. Haiti will not kill me; I can take . . . more, stay curled up—my tongue licks at dried blood; two fingers touch at the swelling. I can take it; I can.

My mom says, "William?"

My dad died in a hole like this. No, he died at the Y on Chicago Avenue, and it was whiskey, not soldiers. No, these aren't soldiers, these are night howlers. With no pants and loud white teeth. Dry swallow—pain shoots from ear to neck. Cringe. Ragged breath. Eye shut, then open. Blur . . . shadows . . . outside my iron bars.

I curl up tight. Eye closed. My head and heart pound. I push into the wall. Rusted hinges creak. *Don't be here—*

"William."

Blink. The tall, thin shape standing inside my cell door doesn't have his pants down; doesn't hit me or stink. Blink. He's blurry and white, in a white suit and plantation hat. *White devil; the fucking devil.* All of me scrunches deeper into the corner. Both hands shake up and out to stop him—

Formal European accent. "William, can you stand?"

Two shapes laugh behind him and squeeze at their balls. *"Orevwa, masisi."* Bye-bye, faggot.

"William." The white man extends a hand. "Can you walk?"

"Wh . . . what d'you want?"

"To take you home. Can you walk?"

Blink. "Not going to hell. I didn't do anything."

"We must leave, William. *Now.*"

The shapes behind the white man have their dicks out . . . or maybe pistols. The tallest leans toward me and purses his lips into a kiss, says, *"Ou gen SIDA."*

The white man forces/helps me up. Pain shoots down my legs, knees, back. Dry heave. The white man grabs my waist. "William, we must walk. Now." His arm tightens around my waist. We straighten; he shuffles us past the blacks.

Wet, ugly Kreyol voice and another kiss. *"Ou gen SIDA."*

"No; I'm not a spy."

The white man shuffles me toward stone stairs and what might be sunlight above. "He said you have AIDS, their gift from the devil to America."

***

Friday

My bed; my room; the Hotel Oloffson. Both hands tremble on the cotton bedsheets; the painkillers are working fine on the rest of me. A brownish doctor strips latex gloves above his scuffed leather valise, then tells me my condition has improved since I was brought here last night "from the prison at Fort Dimanche."

All things considered, he says, the beatings and assaults should have killed me. He does not know if I have AIDS. He does not know if the men who raped me had AIDS, but he suspects that many people in Haiti are infected. From what he understands, the virus is transmitted by blood and body fluids. The doctor shrugs narrow shoulders. "Unfortunately, there is ample evidence you have been subjected to large amounts of both."

My head turns away against the headboard. Swollen fingers hide my face, then pat shredded lips I can't feel. I want to quit hearing the night howlers laughing and grunting, not feel their dirty hands in my hair; dirty cocks in my face. I want to be angry, make rage bury the weakness and disgust. AIDS is a gay man's death sentence.

"I could get checked somewhere?"

"No, not under present conditions. Since your arrival to me last night, the streets of Port-au-Prince are crowded with gunfire. The fighting will become worse before it becomes better." My doctor glances across the room to the white man who brought me here, then back. "President Duvalier has fled the island. The Rebelyon comes now, Communist rebels, your CIA, the Haitian army—"

"Monsieur Docteur." The white man waves his hand to enforce the interruption, his European accent more pronounced. *"Merci.* I will explain . . . in time."

My good eye still won't focus.

The doctor hands me a bottle of blue pills and a small bottle of cooking oil. "Eat no solid food. If you must defecate, prior to defecation, one hour, take one tablet for pain; a half hour prior, sip the oil. Should the blood continue in your stool after seven days, I will come here; it is too dangerous for you to come to my clinic."

He glances at the white man again, then back, "If you can be gone from Haiti—and my advice is that you are gone immediately—go to a hospital and be checked. You are badly damaged by the ra—" The doctor stops before he says *rapes,* tips his hat, and leaves.

The white man says, "Carel Roos wishes to speak with you."

I force my feet off the bed, have to use both hands to balance against dizziness, then wince into sharp pain in my abdomen and rectum. I'm wearing new underwear I didn't own yesterday. The cheap cotton covers parts of me that I don't want to look at again. I wrap a towel around my bruised waist, wobble to the verandah's tall louvered doors, take a breath that hurts, and lean for balance. Behind the hotel, the mountains that split the Dominican Republic from Haiti rise nine thousand feet and block the sky. "Never heard of him."

"Nor have I. But he wishes to speak with you. Now."

I limp to the hallway door, open it, don't see a hallway full of green uniforms or Volontaires waiting to haul me back to prison.

"By telephone, from my office. It is more private."

If calling Carel is truly where we're going, then Carel already knows what happened, and so does Anne Bonny, and I don't want anyone to ever know what happened, what those . . . did to me, made me do, over and over.

"William? If you would dress . . ."

Dressing is hard. Meeting people's eyes will be harder; they'll want to know what happened. No, they'll *know* what happened to happy-go-lucky Bill, handshake for everyone, let me carry that package, ma'am.

I squint into the tall mahogany mirror—

Whoa, shit, Elephant Man.

The white man and I exit the Oloffson via a servants' stairway. At the bottom, I trail him into the tall palms, fronds motionless in heavy air. His Citroën sedan is spotless; feels like a Hemingway ambulance, not a kidnap car.

We drive through my painkiller fog, then through a manned iron gate set in the old bluestone walls of a Frenchman's plantation. The white man's great house is not where we go.

His office is a separate building; one blurry room built of newer wood, not stone. The room is breezy and square under a high, peaked wood ceiling. Louvered hurricane shutters filter sunlight and humidity. The white walls are empty. I smell flowers I can't see, not rapists. The white man points me to his desk chair, dials his desk phone, speaks French, hangs up, and waits for it to ring.

I listen under the hum of a ceiling fan's rattan blades, then lean back in the man's desk chair, the doctor's painkillers beginning to wear thin.

The phone rings; the white man answers, listens, then hands me the receiver. The Rhodesian Afrikaner accent in my ear is emotionless. "Are you there, Bill?" This transatlantic call has none of the static it should have in a country whose phones *never* work. The clarity makes Carel's precise questions worse. "What did you tell the kaffers in the prison? Each question, each answer, each assault."

My good hand covers my face. "Have you told Anne . . . what happened . . . to me?"

"No." Pause, no static. "Word for word, Bill; moment by moment—what do the kaffers know of our plans?"

I detail the questions I was asked, my answers, the beatings but not the rapes, and the one mistake, the Selous Scout reference.

"That's the whole of it?"

"Yeah."

Silence, then Carel says: "When we all swam at Brighton, you asked after my scars. I told you about Rhodesia, what the kaffer does in the bush. So I know the warders did more; know you told the warders more; I would have."

"No. You wouldn't tell the guards shit. And I didn't; don't ask me why or how, but I didn't."

"Hiding from what they did, what you did to stay alive, will not change what you told."

"I told you the only slip: Selous Scout. That's it. If you don't want to believe me, don't come."

Silence. "Have you done the recon, the boats?"

"Just the airport and the outer road." My teeth gnash at the pain in my side. "But I will . . . 'cause I said I would. If you're still coming."

"Can you still complete the job as paid?"

"I've stayed at the hotel nine times; know the hotel and grounds already. Arranging the backup and decoy boats will be harder, but I'll get it done if the captains I know haven't run."

Silence while Carel considers his options, my veracity. "The one mistake, Bill, you're certain? Willing to bet your life, and Anne's as well?"

I look at my knees, covered by scuffed pants that the hotel washed, knees that knelt in front of one . . . after another. Tears dribble out of my eyes. "Don't know what I want, Carel. Just wanna go home."

"You might want to get even."

My eyes shut. "Don't think I'm up to it."

"That's good, Bill. Revenge is expensive even when you're thinking clear. And you won't be for a while."

"Don't want Anne to get hurt."

"Good and proper, Bill." In Afrikaans, Carel adds, "Then the Ncome River it is, *mi boer bru*; to Dracula's castle." The connection quits.

I blur-focus the white man's office, then recradle his phone, a line that has to be secure or Carel Roos would never have spoken a word on it. The white man in his white suit reappears. He walks past me in his desk chair and sits opposite his desk. His long, thin legs cross at the knee. He doesn't speak.

"How'd you get me out?"

"Friends in the government."

"General Peguero?"

"General Peguero was executed last evening."

Blink. Swallow. Semi-focus. "You and Carel are . . . friends?"

"I know no one named Carel." The white man has no discernible accent beyond European, and it sounds learned.

"You don't know Carel, but you know what he's doing."

The man's hands fold together, patrician, calm and comfortable, no jewelry. He says, "A young woman in the UK called your employer in Kingston. Likely concerned about the Rebelyon and the peripheral matters at hand, although this is not for me to say. Your superiors at Fred L. Myers & Sons said you were here but not communicating as you should. Parties contacted me; I determined that you had arrived our airport but not your hotel. From there"—he opens both palms—"I found you at Fort Dimanche."

"But you know about Carel and—" I don't make another suicide amateur mistake; don't say Anne's name or Luckner Cambronne's. "But you know about Carel."

Headshake. "Again, William, in Haiti, there is no such man."

***

Saturday

Forty-eight hours and I'm "better," other than the blood on the sheets and headaches that make it hard to hear and see. I'm living on pain-killers and cooking oil; on fear-sweat and terror jolts that now seem commonplace. The combination has improved me sufficiently that I have completed Carel's recon, the small part that could still be done by someone in my condition.

Haiti has not improved. Down-mountain, Port-au-Prince has begun to burn, scenting the air with ash and oily rubber. This is the anarchy twilight—the descent into "the wild" as Carel Roos calls it, the reshuffling of the deck before the organized carnage of a three-way civil war begins. By now, Carel and his team are in-country, en route to the Grand Oloffson through Haiti's mounting ethereal madness, undoubtedly bringing a special kind of hell with them.

Anne may have already arrived at François Duvalier International Airport. And will have to survive far worse scrutiny than I did five days ago. Carel, and whoever he brings with him, will enter Haiti illegally, I'm guessing by car, over the mountains from the Dominican Republic. Carel's mission isn't to help the CIA put Luckner Cambronne in the president's chair, that much I do know. Carel's mission is to effect a kidnap of Cambronne that couldn't be done in America, then take Cambronne to the west coast of South Africa. And hang him.

Carel's target is not to be taken lightly; on that the vodou houngans and mambos are not full of shit. When Luckner Cambronne was in power, he terrorized, kidnapped, and murdered the Haiti peasants to the point that the survivors believe he is a monster unscalable in Western culture until you confront the devil. They say Cambronne murdered thirty thousand of his own countrymen, harvested their blood, sold their cadavers for anatomy classes and prime chunks of their flesh to restaurants.

Carel's employer would likely agree, but for different reasons. Although I don't know the employer's name, I do know he's Rhodesian, the father of two students kidnapped and murdered in Haiti fifteen years ago. Anne described the father as a "million-hectare backvelder, a war-hardened, fire-breathing Calvinist rooted deep in the colonial era."

Fifteen years ago, the father paid a massive ransom for his children. Three days before the transfer was to happen, Haiti's then president, Papa Doc Duvalier, died. Haiti fell apart. Cambronne and his Tontons Macoutes "lost" the children, then lost control of the country to the army and Bébé Doc, Duvalier's psychotic son.

Rather than face Bébé Doc's firing squads, Cambronne fled to the USA on a US military jet. Our president Nixon kept Cambronne safe, using him as Nixon's—and now Reagan's—War-on-Drugs, anti-Communist dictator-in-waiting should Bébé Doc get too twisted (which he did), or fall into Fidel Castro's embrace.

According to Anne, the Rhodesian Afrikaner father did not retire in his grief; he prayed to his Calvinist God for a righteous man's vengeance. When this vengeance was repeatedly refused in Washington, DC, then snuffed in a failed Miami gunfight, then snuffed again when Cambronne's household domestic workers were uncovered as agents of the Rhodesian father, the father began sending money and emissaries in support of Haiti's always boiling insurrections.

The father knew some of Washington's plans, was certain that if Bébé Doc fell out of favor, Luckner Cambronne would be the CIA's choice for control of the country. To do so, Cambronne would have to leave his protection in Miami. And then, for a brief window, while Cambronne incited the citizens and re-formed his army of murderous Tontons Macoutes, the vampire would be vulnerable.

Noise in the hall.

I grab the sharp dinner knife that I kept from room service. The door knock is followed by a voice announcing in Kreyol-accented English that I have a guest from the BBC.

I open my hallway door to a stunning Irish woman and a porter. Anne Cormac Bonny is the taller of the two, wearing a Balmoral regimental beret, BBC News T-shirt, and confidence she earned on the Falls Road in Belfast.

She tips the porter, adding her devastating smile, avoids looking at me a second time or my knife, and walks to my floor-to-ceiling verandah doors. A hint of her de la Renta perfume trails her, just like it did in London.

I shut the hallway door, double lock it, pocket the knife, then follow to the verandah.

Anne Bonny concentrates on the growing fires that dot the malaria valley below and the waterfront far beyond. Her eyes cut to the nearest threat, the torches dancing in the overgrown breadfruit, pine, and flamboyant trees at l'Habitation Leclerc, close enough that she can smell the pitch tar. Anne can't see the freelance killers and rapists going tribal, but I don't have to tell her that's who's there picking sides, preparing for the slaughter when the control-of-the-country presidential negotiations fail and the Castro-CIA three-way civil war cooks off with the rebels.

Anne strips the beret, stays focused outside on the torches, then pulls her long red hair back to her shoulders and asks, "Our Dracula is there?" Her Irish accent is cool and measured. She's neither nervous nor relaxed. When she turns to me, her emerald eyes flash. Anne's seen badly beaten men before, but she can't quite hide her reaction.

The best joke I can make is, "Elephant Man?"

Anne studies me, but it's not for the two years since we last saw each other. Carel told her; he must have. Shame burns through the narcotics and heats my face. Anne Bonny is twenty years old, two years younger than me, but big-time older in experience, the reincarnation of her never-hanged pirate great-great-great-grandmother. Anne touches the bandages on my swollen forehead.

She says, "Bébé Doc arrived Paris all the dazzler on a plane provided by your USA. UPI says he brought $500 million dollars with him. Can you imagine?" Anne smooths patches of my hair into better order. "Assumin', Bill, you can imagine anything beyond pain and the tablets."

"I'm all right, tougher than I look."

She smiles *the smile*. "And did ya do Carel's lookin' about?"

"Best I could . . . the rest I had to get secondhand; people I work with who have family all over the island. Not as good as seeing it, but . . . it's already so bad out there . . ."

"Our Dracula?"

"Landed last night." I point down to l'Habitation Leclerc. "Torches are for him."

Anne turns back from the torches, uses both hands to stroke my neck and shoulders. "Are you up to the remainder, Mr. Bill?"

"Hope so. Would kinda like to go home."

Anne searches my face from girlfriend distance, looking for the rapes and beatings. "Are you steamin' mad, Bill? Behind that libertine smile you're known for?" She pats my shoulders. "Best we keep any new temper in your shoes or we'll all be dead."

Pride tries for bold-hero boyfriend material, but I can't get there. "Did the recon; haven't heard back on the boats yet."

"But are you *up* to it, Bill? Say no if it's no, and I'll do Carel's boats myself."

I uncork a bottle of Barbancourt Reserve du Domaine with a bandaged hand, take a sip, and hand it to her. Anne sips, keeping her eyes on mine. "Then we best be on with it. There's the storm comin' . . . from the east *and* the west."

Carel's plan will be the "storm from the west," meaning he's not arriving how I'd guessed. But he will arrive: simple, violent, and direct. I ask, "What's the plan?"

Anne looks back out the window, then back to me. She weighs my condition, my reliability, and my unfortunate need to know, then explains:

"I entered the country as a BBC war correspondent, engaged to you," she shows me the engagement ring and a BBC lanyard ID. "Stayin' here at the Oloffson, in this room. Tomorrow, I interview Luckner Cambronne for the BBC. He and I have the history. The bugger asked my sister and I to his room when we were but schoolgirls in uniform." Anne holds her hand four feet off the floor. "Was at a Kingston polo match where he was a guest of the high lord ministers and their ladies. The actress Maureen O'Hara was his preferred, on hand that day shootin' a movie in Kingston she was, but the glorious one would have none of him. During tomorrow's interview, I'll be Mr. Cambronne's Maureen, light his famous libido, use that thirst for Irish redheads to parlay him into a tryst right there." She points to my bed.

"Jesus, Anne, you *are* fucking nuts."

She smiles. "A man's weakness is what I am. During our tryst, I'll spike Mr. Cambronne with a syringe. Carel and his Scouts will kill Cambronne's guards, place our Dracula naked in a bag like the gunnysacks his Tontons Macoutes bogeymen use, then drive to a port on the south coast."

"Driving through a three-way civil war?" I grab the bottle and drink.

Anne smiles and avoids educating me. "Carel is known for his planning."

"The guys with Carel are all Selous Scouts?"

She nods. "They'll remove Cambronne from the island in a twin-engine fishing boat, cross the Corazón Santo to Port Royal. Requires six to eight hours if the sea stays favorable. From there, Cambronne sails to the hangman in Afrika." Anne air-washes her hands. "Done."

The plan sounds too simple to work.

Anne reads my skepticism. "There are no better than the Scouts. Carel and his mates are infamous for infiltrating rebel camps."

She's got a point. One of the stories I remember was at a place in Mozambique called Nyadzonya Pungwe. The white Scouts marched in, pretending to be prisoners of their black comrades. Eighty-four Scouts total, including Carel Roos. When it was over, they'd killed almost a thousand.

Anne reaches for the Barbancourt bottle, no smile, only resolve. "Best you and I be ready. My man Carel is as proficient a hunter-killer as walks Afrika. He's not sayin' so, but I can tell he's got a bad feelin' about this one."

KINGSTON, JAMAICA

NOW

Chapter 15

BILL OWENS

Sunday

United 622 from Newark skirts Jamaica's spectacular Blue Mountains, then banks to land mid-harbor on a completely unprotected landfill airstrip with water on three sides. I weathered the jolts and lightning and white-knuckle miles over Cuba by trying to handicap Eddie O'Hare—lawyer, horseplayer/poet—and his treasure.

The bad news is that even though I can read a *Racing Form* backward in three languages, I couldn't handicap Eddie O'Hare's poems. Poems I'm certain Mr. O'Hare wrote to protect himself should he be killed, or kidnapped and tortured for the gold's location, forcing his kidnappers through a minefield that'd he'd never have to walk, and all others would.

And if *I* can't figure the *starting gate*, let alone the finish line in this race, then there's better than a fifty-fifty chance this treasure hunt is about something else other than treasure. And *that*, given the players on all sides, would be a construct I probably can't survive.

But then, I probably can't survive the Haitians and Loef Brummel either.

Kingston's landing strip is ten feet above sea level; probably half that by tonight when the storms land. For the fiftieth time, we jolt hard left, then right. The college kid sweating in the middle seat next to me goes rigid, his eyes shut, both hands death-gripped on the armrest. Marlboros pop out of his pocket and onto my lap.

I nudge his hand using his cigarette pack. "Don't worry, I fly this route every week. Trust me, odds are twenty to one these cigarettes will kill you. A plane crash, even down here, is twenty *thousand* to one."

The kid nods an inch, doesn't grip for his cigarettes, and doesn't open his eyes. Our Boeing 737 jolts again; people gasp. Lightning rips far to the east. The cabin PA announces: "We have completed our preliminary approach into Kingston and will be landing shortly."

The storm wall is on the other side of the plane. My window is Jamaica's south coast lit in the odd half-light of inbound weather. Over the wing, directly across Kingston Harbour from the airport, are Eddie O'Hare's coordinates for $26 million in gold. I squint for the waterfront downtown. The pilot banks a final time and the wing blocks where a giant **X** marks the spot should be floating. That's how it would be in the Hardy Boys / Nancy Drew mysteries, so that's how it should be for me. Probably no room for Anne Bonny and Susie Devereux, though, not in a Hardy Boys adventure.

United 622 hits the runway hard. Three overhead bins snap open. The plane shudders, swerves, and the engines roar. Our speed quits; the engines cut . . . and we don't slide into the bay. The cabin lights blink on. The college kid next to me opens his eyes and sucks a breath.

I smile at him. "See? Just like I said. Get yourself a piña colada at Redbones; ask Enola Williams to take you to the all-night dance in Rae Town; party like Bob Marley sent you the invitation."

The kid doesn't ask for his Marlboros and I don't offer them; Marlboros and bad judgment killed my mom when she was forty-six. I repack the Eddie O'Hare poems, map, and photos, then deplane into Kingston's Norman Manley International Airport and my reunion with Herself: Anne Cormac Bonny, siren, sorceress.

Been twenty-three years. *This time*, though, our three-way will include my new Bond-girl girlfriend instead of a Rhodesian mercenary. I smooth my wrinkled, stinky reunion outfit that might be overlooked if Brad Pitt had it on.

Walking shiny linoleum toward immigration, the modern version of Norman Manley International Airport is a surprise. It wasn't spotless or modern last time I was here. The steel-and-glass architecture feels like a real airport, not a matchstick rebuild waiting for the next hurricane.

Up ahead, two hundred passengers stand in the immigration and customs queues. Only one intake crew is on duty. God bless tropical time. I smooth "wanted fugitive" out of my madras jacket and join the queue, then feign interest in one of the TV monitors and their real-time weather maps.

The Atlantic Ocean is a spider cloud of hurricane possibilities.

Blue-uniformed security people watch us. None seem interested; neither do the three immigration officers behind their podiums. I have unpleasant history here, but twenty-three years is half a lifetime in many parts of the West Indies. My heart rate increases anyway. The officer who will process me is a large woman in her forties, properly fatigued in the late afternoon and unmotivated by the crush.

After twenty minutes in line, she waves me up. I present my passport and the white immigration card, using my hand without the name on the palm. She smells like the ocean, matches my face to my photograph, then checks her computer. "The reason for your visit to Jamaica?"

"Vacation."

"You have been to Jamaica before, Mr. Owens?"

"Nope. Looking forward to it."

Her round face turns from the screen to me. "No?"

"First time."

"This is your passport?"

"Yeah. A reissue; I lost the last one years and years ago."

She stares at her computer screen, shakes it with her palm, then slaps the monitor's side. She frowns, looks to her right for a supervisor, mumbles a complaint in patois, and waits.

A male supervisor appears, gestures toward the long lines behind me, and tells my immigration officer to get on with it.

She turns back to me. "When did you work for Myers's Rum?"

"Me? Never. Never been here before."

She scowls an otherwise unlined face, slaps her computer again, and looks for her missing supervisor. "Your hotel?"

"Eggy's Bohemian, Treasure Beach."

She checks her computer screen again, shrugs, then stamps my passport so softly the ink is unreadable. Her tired, overworked exhale is audible as she hands the blue booklet back; her voice robotic: "Any change in your location, please contact immigration with your new hotel. Welcome to Jamaica."

I smile. She's already looking past me. I weave through the crowded baggage-collection area to the customs line. The customs officer sleepy-eyes my immigration card: "What items have you to declare?" The suit-and-tie official next to him cranes around my shoulder to the baggage carousel and three Jamaicans yelling at each other.

"None." Smile.

He waves me through into a throng of waiting black faces. I scan them for kidnappers and Haitian gunmen, politely snake between shoulders and hips and dreads to the terminal's exit doors, don't look back, and step outside:

Heat blast and humidity. *Jesus.*

But the pre-storm twilight is soft and pastel, fragrant and floral like two decades ago. Beyond the arrivals' drive aisle, royal palms rise out of the pink-and-white bougainvillea. The palms have wind in them from the Atlantic front we just skirted. I look left, then right for Anne Bonny and our reunion. No Anne; no stand-in sirens or pirate girls; no armed guards for the clues I'm carrying to $26 million in gold.

Anne or armed people from her crew should be here.

The Anne-Bill reunion might be a college fantasy, but the Haitians at Nick & Nora's weren't. To my left, the tourists who were on the flight crush at the curb for the three taxis there with the required red PPV plate. Probably not a good idea to be here when immigration's computers reboot. I break for the taxi line at the domestic terminal and call Loef Brummel while I walk.

He answers, "Where are you?"

"Trying to find your money. Had it won at Arlington, but Earle Fires invented a foul the stewards gave him."

"So I heard. Where's my money?"

"I'm trying something else. Dave's dead; Barlow's probably dead, and unless I get lucky, so am I. Paying you is important, but so we're clear, this isn't my debt; I don't give a fuck what you say or who you say it to, this is between the fuckups who work with you and Dave."

"'Cause you disappear, the debt ain't goin' away."

"If I'm alive in seventy-two hours, I'll be in touch."

I button off. Waiting alone at the domestic terminal is an AMC Gremlin gypsy cab freshly painted with green latex paint. One headlight is on. I bend to the driver's window with $20 US. "Take me to town?" Town would be away from the storm.

"No problem, mon."

The Gremlin's door clanks when I open it. The back seat smells like fabric softener.

We bend around the airport drive under courtesy lights beginning to cloud with bugs as the pre-storm dark overtakes the south coast. At the first roundabout, I touch his shoulder. "Make it the Sazerac Bar."

My driver adjusts his rearview mirror and fixes me with focused brown eyes. He wants to make the easy left into Kingston proper and the rest of Jamaica, not the looping right out onto the Palisadoes, a sandspit road Jamaicans don't trust and probably shouldn't. The Palisadoes is "seawall harbor protection" that also pretends to be a road. This "seawall protection" is compacted silt, a total of twelve inches above sea level. One good earthquake—and they have biggies down here—and this seawall/road either liquefies or drops to the bottom of the ocean from beginning to end.

But if luck is with you, and drowning isn't to be your fate, then the Palisadoes will connect you to an island, the once-fortified pirate capital of Port Royal.

Jamaicans have a centuries-old, almost genetic fear of Port Royal, and not without reason. In 1692, God dropped half the pirate-island city into a fiery ocean chasm, literally swallowing 80 percent of the residents, buildings, and all the ships in the harbor. Paintings and stories depict the initial survivors buried alive to their necks at God's new shoreline, packs of hungry dogs eating at their heads.

Not long after the 1692 earthquake, the remaining pirates and their descendants "repented." Seeing God's hand in their continuing brushes with cataclysm, the pirates traded outright piracy for privateer status with the British Empire—the residents of Port Royal could still be pirates, but licensed with letters of marque and reprisal as long as the prizes they took were enemies of the British Crown.

Unfortunately, the anticipated end to God's wrath against Port Royal didn't happen. So, various disasters later, the locals abandoned piracy/privateering in favor of "black gold," the slave trade. God didn't see selling slaves as a behavioral improvement and continued to destroy the city. But the pirates' descendants were nothing if not tenacious. The price for that tenacity has been repeated earthquakes, catastrophic fires, and a wave or two of disease on the scale of Europe's Black Death.

Fast forward into the mid-1980s when I was selling rum: The men and women of Port Royal had become *fishermen*. Translated from 1980s speak: contrabanders trafficking cocaine. Like their forefathers, the 1980s cocaine pirates of Port Royal didn't like strangers. Hence, I didn't visit.

Our Gremlin slows approaching the dead end of the Palisadoes. Our one headlight splashes an unwelcoming headland of high, garish rock. My driver says, "Gallows Point. Where dey hang the pirates."

Like most everyone in Kingston, I've seen pictures, but that's it.

My driver cold-eyes the cut-stone colonial fortress built atop the headland, what would be the last connected landmass between here and Cartagena. He says, "Lotta men from here died bad on these rocks."

Above us, orange light flickers inside narrow windows. Wind rustles the palm fronds.

Gosh, how fitting. We've arrived at Anne Cormac Bonny's family heirloom, the Sazerac Bar.

My driver clears his throat and semi-whispers, "Respect, mon, this no place a stranger wanna be."

"Hear that. What's your name?"

"Delroy." He shakes his head. "We leavin' now."

"Wait. I gotta go in. If you can wait, I can pay."

Delroy eyes the Sazerac, obviously familiar with its ownership and history. "No, mon. Mos def, me leavin' here."

I pat his shoulder with a second US twenty. "Just stay in the car, leave the engine running, anything gets weird—you're gone."

He frowns. "Gone to sufferation."

I exit Delroy's Gremlin and climb twenty-one granite treads to a gusty, wet verandah naked to the storm and windward ocean. The verandah is a slippery checkerboard of oversize green-and-black tiles wet with salt spray and marked with a stamp of some kind. I can make out "Mariana, Queen of Spain, 1655." Alone in the wind and spray, the storm feels lots closer. Probably because it is.

Between me and the Sazerac's open doorway are six wood tables, all made from heavy ship-plank. The doorway is flanked by two fifty-five-gallon drums burning scrub wood that smells like charcoal. The drums glow, each perforated with the shape of a Christian cross.

There should be guards here or lookouts—unless Susie's bad guys got here first.

My loyal taxi drives away.

Deep breath. All . . . righty . . . then. I step past the barrels.

Inside, the Sazerac is ten degrees cooler and would be called medieval if we were in Ireland or Scotland. Two steps down to the right, under a heavy-timbered low ceiling, is a twelve-foot gleaming bar with one kerosene bowl-candle at each end. The two candles throw more orange glow than light. Behind the nearest glow is a jet-black barmaid cutting fruit I can smell. Her white eyes focus on me and her knife stops cutting. She's wearing Jamaica's traditional madras plaid, and I'm quite sure, armed with a modern semiautomatic pistol.

Behind my shoulder I hear: "Respect, mon."

Nodding at me from a leeward window is a twenty-four-inch electric-blue parrot. To the parrot's left, lit with hanging ship lanterns, is a life-size oil painting bolted into the stone wall—two women armed with flintlock pistols and cutlass.

The bartender says, "Anne Bonny and Mary Read. Be the only known portrait, painted 1700-something in Charleston, America. Artist Eric Meyer."

I step closer. Anne's resemblance to her pirate-queen namesake is stunning, a bit scary.

"Ah-rite," says the parrot.

I turn back to the barmaid and step down to the bar. "Hi. I'm Bill Owens, friend of Anne's from America. She was supposed to pick me up at the airport."

The barmaid eyes me; her hands and knife no longer visible.

I inhale to add *happy*—

The arched-stone doorway I just walked through darkens. Four black shapes file in. I can't make out anything but their size and eyes. I fast-glance the bar to grab the fruit knife; I'm not going to Haiti.

The eight eyes give me a long inspection. The largest shape steps forward into the orange glow: six two, 250, shaved head, one earring, one large hand visible.

"What be your business here?"

"Anne Bonny."

"Uh-huh. The minister send you? Ministers don't hang us no more in Port Royal." A pistol emerges from behind his back. "I send you back to Babylon in a bucket."

The barmaid two-hands a pistol at my ear.

"BeBe!" A woman ducks in under the low wooden beam, jumps the stairs, and lands on both feet between the big man's pistol and me.

Five foot seven, black boots and pants, a pistol grip visible against her naked stomach, and a boatneck shirt that doesn't hide muscled arms. The very best part is hair so red you'd swear it was burning.

"Bill!" Anne Bonny hugs me with both arms. "A fine, handsome man you are." She smells like cinnamon, pulls back, kisses me full on the mouth, then stiff-arms from my shoulders. "Did ya bring my Susie and all our breadcrumbs?"

My eyes jump between Anne and the men behind her, the big one, BeBe, in particular. "Not feeling the love, Anne. Missed you at the airport."

"Aye, Bill, wanted desperate to be there, dressed and did my hair for it, don'chya see, but we've had a bit of trouble since we talked." She smiles *the smile.* Girl's in her forties and still has it, both barrels. Her eyes are emeralds.

"Anne Bonny!" screams from the dark. "Be gon from here! This minute! You goin' to the gallows at Tower Street, you don."

The three men behind BeBe have parted to either side of the doorway. A solid, curvy girl with dark-cinnamon skin stands backlit by the drum fires outside. She's too young to be Siri. Whoever she is, she's naked from the waist up, midtwenties, long perfect dreads, and pointing a silver cross like it's a gun. "Anne Bonny be jailed and hanged for murder! Two hours' time!"

Anne raises her voice but doesn't turn. "Sistah, be gone, now."

"Sistah" glares at the back of Anne's head and doesn't move. Sistah's muscles are tight; her nipples hard. Candlelight glints off her cross.

I fake a smile for Anne. "Jamaica wants to hang you?"

"Somewhat of a new development." Anne rebuilds the smile into a grin. "Grand to see you, William. Grand." She kisses me again, slower, keeping the grin on her lips and her hips pressed to mine. Sistah jumps down the stairs to us.

Up close, Sistah shocks me backward. She has white birthmarks that surround both eyes and cover one cheek. I've seen those marks before.

She says: "Radio Kingston sayin' Anne Bonny been convicted; for killing dead a Gordon House MP." Sistah wedges in, her muscled shoulder and dreads pushing me back. Her lips stop at Anne's cheek. "Say Anne Bonny feed him to the crocodiles by Black River, Treasure Beach. Say Babylon gonna hang Anne Bonny at Tower Street under the old law."

Babylon used to be slang for all things corrupt-government. A Gordon House MP is a "minister," a member of parliament.

Anne doesn't move, blink, or turn. "Bill, do you have our breadcrumbs?"

My eyes bounce from Anne to Sistah and back. I lie. "Half."

Anne loses part of the grin. "Half'll kill us, Bill. The trail's full of tricks and traps. Susie said you found Astor Argyle and the second bottle; is she wrong?"

"Lotta unhappy people in here, Anne."

Anne leans around Sistah's dreads and tells my ear: "Our Dave Grossfeld's dead with barbed wire beat into his head; both eyes carved out, feet and hands cut off. That's Petwo Vodou if ya ne remember, the bad, bitter-loa kind practiced up in Souvenance."

Sistah rams her chest against Anne's shoulder and shouts: "Anne Bonny, you be gon with all that! Babylon comin' *now*! They hang you *today*!"

Anne grabs Sistah and hugs her chest-to-chest, the crucifix wedged between them. She whispers past Sistah's ear to me, "They *sayin'* Grossfeld had the second bottle and lost it to his killers."

"*They'd* be wrong. Dave didn't have the bottle at five a.m. this morning. When I saw it."

Anne grins. "Have to be sure, Bill. Clever-certain. The Corazón Santo is a livin' thing, and already feels us comin'."

"Whoa. Never said I was going anywhere but here."

"Won't be us deciding. Our man Dave dying how he did was no accident. Our adversaries are marking their trail. I know you're not forgettin' the Oloffson. Luckner Cambronne's girl in my bed was big, big Petwo Vodou."

Sistah screams, rips out of Anne's arms with Anne's pistol in her left hand. "*You* the white man!" Sistah jams the pistol at my face. "*Who* murder de Baby!"

Flash and roar pound off the walls. Anne rips the smoking pistol out of Sistah's hand, locks Sistah's arm, then shoves her to BeBe. BeBe crushes Sistah to his chest with both giant arms.

Anne shouts, "Take Sistah to her medicine, then the boat till she recovers herself."

Sistah screams: "I know you, white man! You murder de Baby! Murder de Rebelyon!" Her round eyes blaze in the birthmarks. A wide, ugly hangman's scar circles her neck. BeBe lifts Sistah off the ground, turns, and carries her through the men.

Anne inhales to speak.

I shove my hand in her face. "What the fuck was that?"

"You know what it was."

"Bullshit." I rub my ears. "Your girl's a fucking psycho—"

"And I'd say she's not. Vodou is poor-people politics. Don't be laughin' because it don't belong to white people."

"Do I look like I'm laughing?"

Anne gently pulls my hand down. "Petwo true believers are God-driven; she's a formidable religion in the provinces—if that's where this adventure's goin'." Anne belts her pistol, hesitates, then twists her hand like a noose at her neck. "A Rebelyon gurl Sistah was. Advocated the violent overthrow of Haiti's church and state and paid for it dearly.

"But the Christian rope couldn't kill her. That makes her a saint in Haiti's dark arts. As do her birthmarks." Anne looks over her shoulder, then back. "Remember?"

Frown. Goddamn right I remember.

"Sistah's decidedly more accomplished than she's actin'. A good use in Haiti, for a number of true believers' reasons we'll hope not to encounter, situations our girl Siri and a mountain full of rebels can ne handle."

"Listen to me, okay? I'm not going to Haiti. Got it? Bill Owens is not going to Haiti."

Sistah screams French Kreyol outside.

I look at the door. "She's your girlfriend?"

"Sistah's a family matter to me you'll not encounter again."

I scan the Sazerac for more psycho apparitions behind the three men who haven't left. "And Susie Devereux?"

Anne waves the three men and the bartender out. "Bill and I will have a moment, thank you," then turns back to me. She waits till we're alone, then answers.

"Susie booked a nonstop that should've beat you here. It landed without her. Her phone rings but doesn't answer."

"Susie saved my ass in Chicago. I mean stone-cold saved me from another round in Haiti. We gotta help her."

"Aye, only way now is gettin' on her gold's trail. Susie'll find us if she's still on her own. If not, and she's alive, whoever has her will do the findin'." Anne cants her head. "Talk to me, Bill."

"And what would our deal be . . . on the trail?"

"Full share, twenty-five percent. Susie, me, Siri, and you."

"Siri's the revolutionary? Florent Dusson-Siri?"

"Florent's another reason we might survive Haiti. Do you have our breadcrumbs, Bill?"

Inhale. Exhale. No reason to keep telling her I'm not going to Haiti. "Yup. I do. Better still, the second bottle has coordinates, in Kingston, straight across the bay. The old frigate docks downtown."

Anne grins. Her emerald eyes sparkle; she turns, jumps stairs to the door, and shouts toward the water: "Tell BeBe to finish loadin' both boats." She points across Kingston's five-mile bay. "Have 'em to the Rodney's Arms at sundown, ready to run," then turns back to me.

"Best we have a look at your coordinates and find our Susie; be on with the talkin' and the doin' . . . *wherever* that leads us."

"Those coordinates are in town. Your psycho girlfriend seems to think they want to *hang* you in town."

"Aye, William, is it a picnic you came for? Or a grand adventure with the girl whose knickers you fancy?"

Nope, not much has changed. "Could I see them now? Just in case they hang us both?"

"Hang us?" Anne thumbs down the waistband of her pants an inch and leers. "Do ya not remember who you were standin' with when the whole of Haiti wanted your head, and my Carel did as well?"

"Kinda hard to forget that."

"Aye. And did I step aside when conditions said it'd be prudent? Conditions of your own makin'."

"Nope, you didn't; you said, 'We sail together; we finish together.'"

"Then that's our plan, William. And it'll be satin sheets for all of us, not a gallows."

Chapter 16

BILL OWENS

Sunday

The lights of Kingston begin to glitter in the odd twilight. Anne Bonny and I shrink lower in the sticky back seat of a rumbling, rackety Land Rover. Her man BeBe is driving. On his lap is an open-bolt MAC-10 submachine gun and four magazines. I have Anne's pistol. She has a Belgian FN pistol-grip shotgun and her own MAC-10. On our left, Kingston Harbour is calm. The radio says the storm front has veered north as hoped. The bad news is the storm behind it, already a tropical storm that NOAA has named Lana. How big and how bad Lana will get is too early to tell.

On our right, the *how bad* is well defined. The Tower Street Penitentiary is a brick-and-stone nightmare *on the outside*. Peter Tosh, Bob Marley's guitar player, once said Tower Street on the inside was as low as mankind could descend on the mother island, and Peter was from Trench Town.

Anne's knee touches mine. She says, "My gallows is inside the main yard; being special-built brand-new. Ministers intend to make a show of me."

"Jesus, what'd you do?"

She winks and pats my knee. "Defended myself." Her hand stays on my thigh.

Traffic slows as we pass under Tower Street's twenty-foot walls and gun turrets. Any police roadblock or army stop will be a full-auto gunfight.

"In case you're who they hang first, could you fill in the blanks? Susie said you fell into this before she did?"

Anne squeezes my thigh. "Five, six years back, Barlow needed a partner down here, someone who knew their way around. Barlow went to your Dave Grossfeld and his fishin' connections; Dave came up empty, then came to me. Piccard and the Gryphon came in later as the expedition's bankers." Pause. "So you know, Cranston Piccard is the CIA rogue who got you out of Dimanche prison."

I lean away so I can see Anne's face. "The guy . . . in the white suit?"

Anne nods. "Piccard and Barlow are the same tribe. Ex-CIA fixers, professional lads who keep the world safe for democracy when there's a profit to be made. None of us knew Barlow had gone to Piccard for the money—and Piccard to the Gryphon—until it was too late. Our only way out of the 'debt' the Gryphon decided he was owed was to find the gold." Anne bites her teeth. "Didn't work out. For Susie in particular."

"Susie didn't say what's in your file."

"A lot. But not enough." Anne shows three handwritten pages. "Eddie O'Hare's notes." She shuffles the handwritten pages to a typewritten page. "Susie's synopsis." Anne paraphrases the notes in her hands: "In 1931, O'Hare was approached by two murderers he was already defendin'. They couldn't pay their legal bills but didn't want to die in America's electric chair using a lawyer who couldn't reach 'an accommodation' with a Chicago magistrate. Without explainin' how they'd come by the Haiti gold, the killers said they had it—$500,000 worth. That's back when $375 would buy a new Ford Model A. But owning the gold carried serious penalties—a guaranteed military-court execution for the missin' Marines of the ghost ship USS *Machias*. Then there's the gold's location."

BeBe says, "Duck."

Anne ducks behind the seat, cuts to a police car speeding past in the other direction, then continues. "O'Hare's clients offered him the gold for $100,000."

The Land Rover bumps, then slows. BeBe says, "Traffic stop."

Anne folds the file under her MAC-10 and tells BeBe, "G'wan through. Calm as you go." She ducks lower below the seat and pulls me with her. BeBe weaves through the traffic stop using both of the road's shoulders, patting his arm out his window like it's okay that he's in a hurry.

No sirens chase us. Anne pushes the file at me. "Read the rest. I'll be watching behind us."

I sit up, look behind us, then read what remains of Susie's synopsis: "In August 1931, Eddie O'Hare bonds out the least dangerous of his two killer-clients and goes with him to Santiago de Cuba, near Guantanamo. There, O'Hare sees, weighs, and verifies the Banque Nationale gold."

I look at Anne. "Holy shit, it *is* real."

Anne taps the file. "Read."

Susie's synopsis continues: "O'Hare calls Capone. Against his accountant Jake Guzik's advice, Capone agrees to finance O'Hare's $100K purchase. O'Hare buys the gold at twenty cents on the dollar, but prior to O'Hare's return to Chicago, O'Hare cuts a side deal with Remi Péralte to rob Capone. O'Hare knows Capone is just days away from being indicted by the Feds because O'Hare is the Fed's snitch."

I blurt: "Our coordinates came from a dead Péralte in Chicago. Who's Remi Péralte?"

Anne says, "Half brother to Haitian hero Charlemagne Péralte. Charlemagne died in 1919 fighting for Haiti's independence from the USA. Fifteen years later, Remi's the perfect local partner for an American like O'Hare. Remi can operate in the Corazón Santo and anywhere in Haiti proper. So, at some point during the years Capone's in Alcatraz, 1934 to '38, we think O'Hare used Remi's connections down here to move the gold from Cuba to"—Anne frowns big—"*somewhere* the map and coordinates you brought us will hopefully lead."

"What happened to Remi?" I stop Anne before she answers, and tell her: "Once the gold was hidden, O'Hare killed Remi Péralte like a good tomb-builder would, then returned to the US to wait for the gold's problems to wear off."

"Aye."

The rest of the story doesn't require me to read it. "But Eddie O'Hare, being an egotistical asshole, even by crooked-lawyer standards, makes a crucial miscalculation, given that he's just put America's most powerful gangster in Alcatraz. He miscalculates how long the gold's 'purification' process will take versus how long he has left in this life."

"And there you have it, William."

I finish the story. "But one miscalculation doesn't mean Eddie's completely stupid. He would've worried that his days were numbered or at least open to discussion. So he creates this series of 'artful' clues and traps that only his poetic self can unravel; life insurance, should the wolf come to the door or his own memory fail."

Anne nods.

"Is his death poem in here? The one the cops found in his pocket when he was murdered outside Sportsman's?"

"Aye."

I rifle the file. Although I've never seen it, the poem is part of Sportsman's-Chicago gangland lore, likely written years after the poems Eddie stuffed in the Barbancourt bottles. I find it and read out loud:

> The clock of life is wound but once
> And no man has the power
> To tell just when the hands will stop
> At late or early hour.
> Now is the only time you own.
> Live, love, toil with a will.
> Place no faith in time.
> For the clock may soon be still.

In the front seat, BeBe says, "Police ahead. You say it's the water behind the market?" His wide-set eyes stare at me from the mirror.

"Take Ocean Boulevard. Where the ruined frigates were back in the '80s."

"Know it." He turns.

Just past downtown, I tell BeBe, "Pull off where the boulevard turns back inland into the city."

BeBe drives five blocks of the only modern high-rises in Kingston, bends inland with the boulevard, steers a few yards, and stops. I peek for police, see none, and sit up.

Across the road is Google Earth's satellite image of Eddie O'Hare's coordinates.

No **X** floats ten feet offshore; must be why I couldn't see it from the plane. The **X** would lie among the sixteen rotted pier pylons. Where you'd dock a boat or boats. That could move. Like the ones that were here twenty-three years ago when I was here.

Anne motions me to give her the file, then refocuses on the new pages I brought from Chicago. "Have a look at your spot, Bill, do your puzzlin' magic, but nothing more. Péralte and O'Hare left us the riddles and traps, deadly every one of 'em. I'll be there shortly."

My "puzzlin' magic" is just inductive reasoning—bottom-up logic that allows for the possibility that the conclusion you reach is false, even if all of the premises are true (the opposite of Sherlock Holmes; Sherlock would have died of a broken heart at the racetrack).

I get out with BeBe and walk to the water. He covers his MAC with a towel. Up close, the water is muck and flotsam and shallow enough to wade neck-deep. Three young boys are in the water. Eddie O'Hare's clue hasn't killed them. That's good, but likely means that whatever trap was here caught someone else a long time ago. The only thing that could still be here from the 1930s would be concrete. Concrete buried so deep that a hurricane couldn't suck it up and toss it across the road. And how many hurricanes have come through here in the last seventy to eighty years? Twenty? Fifty?

I glance the pylons; all sixteen have survived long enough to rot. That's a good sign.

But Eddie O'Hare's not burying a clue for life insurance, a failing memory, or his heirs, then *hoping* the clue stays there, even for a year or two.

Okay . . . what if the clue is a boat that sits at the dock the pylons supported? Some kinda special boat that eight decades ago in the 1930s wanted to be next to downtown?

Gambling boat? Hookers, musicians, et cetera? Like the SS *Rex*, the converted four-master casino boat that anchored off Santa Monica, California, long enough for Cary Grant to play the owner in *Mr. Lucky*?

BeBe's standing next to me. I ask him.

He shrugs, thinks about it. "Maybe way back, them Rae Town people fish from here." He frowns, shakes his head. "Nah, dock too short. Maybe a longboat fishing the Pedro Bank for the queen conch. Thirty miles out, long time ago before us born . . . could be."

I got nothing. Zip.

BeBe points west toward the gantry cranes in Kingston Harbour. "Before the harbor get big like she is now, this foreshore all sand and fishermen canoes from end to end. After that come the ganja and cocaine." BeBe points north beyond downtown. "Dudus Coke and the Shower Posse come down here, make all the rag-a-bag yardies fish somewhere else."

"Can you get those boys to dive? See what's on the bottom?"

"Why bwoys? Afraid the crabs get you?"

"Actually, yeah."

"Every bwoy on these beaches can dive. Say what you want."

I point the three kids to generally where Google Earth said the coordinates were. "You get $10 US to dive, but be careful. And another $50 US if you find something I want."

BeBe glances up the road. "Been a time since I was here. Used to come as a punk, look for treasure on them old brigantine wrecks. The *Becca*, the *Falmouth*, the *Primrose*. Took the wood into town for the charcoal burners."

Punk used to mean "youngster," not asshole, not that I intend to confirm either.

Anne approaches from the Land Rover. She's wearing sunglasses, hiding her hair under a Rasta tam, and laughing at me. She mimics BeBe's Jamaican accent. "Where you been born, bwoy?"

"Chicago. We don't have five hundred years of history."

"The mail ship HMS *Primrose*. Queen mother of the island." Anne wags the file. "Before Jamaica had her roads, the *Prim* sailed the mail and supplies up and down the coast to the small towns, the forts, and fisherman camps."

I can visualize Eddie O'Hare and a ship, sort of. "Where's she now?"

Anne shakes her head in disbelief, like we're talking about the *Mayflower.* "Aye, Bill, don'chya see it?"

"Enlighten me."

"She's in Spanish Town."

I stare.

Anne says, "Jamaica's first capital? Where they hanged Calico Jack? My great-gran's consort?"

"When did they move her?"

"*Parts* of her were saved and moved. Must've been the '20s. She's a monument now, on Eagle House hill."

Hmm . . . Eddie O'Hare, lawyer-poet being poetic: the coordinates are here, but without the history you're "dead in the water"? I'm too embarrassed to say that out loud, so I don't. I wave the diver boys up to us and hand BeBe $50. "Please pay our divers; we're going to Spanish Town."

From the murky water, the boy points at Anne in disguise. "You Anne Bonny, the hot steppa runnin' from Babylon."

BeBe tells the boy that talk like that will kill him, then looks at Anne. She's pulling a new pistol from her waistband and checking the road we'll take.

Shit. Now I remember Spanish Town.

Chapter 17

BILL OWENS

BeBe drives us into Spanish Town from the south, avoiding stalled cars, hordes of rainbow-dressed, market-day pedestrians; higglers selling everything from rebottled water to salvation; and two police roadblocks—probably the sporadic car-document-and-dope checks that pretend to be control of the roads.

Ten blocks from the HMS *Primrose*'s supposed resting place, another roadblock forces us off the road and into a housing scheme, what the Jamaicans call a housing edition.

Anne grips the MAC-10 on her lap. "Not where we want to be. A few streets up we'll be facin' the first of Spanish Town's sixteen garrison communities, headquarters of the One Order gang."

"What's a 'garrison community'?"

"Same as she sounds—fortified private enclaves that used to be neighborhoods. 'Political' gangs run 'em now. They answer to the larger drug gangs, the posses. After you left in the '80s, the MPs from both our political parties used the posses and garrisons to win elections but still had control of 'em. Now, the posses run the country—Dudus Coke and the Shower Posse in particular—and it's the members of parliament who do what they're told."

BeBe stares through the windshield, reading the terrain and traffic.

Anne says, "Maybe we walk up from behind Eagle House hill."

BeBe doesn't answer. I pull the pistol I've been given and ask Anne how far.

"Half mile, three-quarters. No whites, though, not alone, maybe not even with BeBe."

I point at the clues. "No choice. We have to go."

BeBe throws an arm over the seat top. "I got a bad feelin' about dis fuckery we intendin'. Best we get to the boat and gone."

Anne glances east toward a tropical storm we can't see yet, then me, then the papers, then BeBe. "My gallows at Tower Street sounds better, does it? Or fishing the Pedro Bank for a livin'?" She winks at BeBe. "G'wan, now, time's a wastin'.'"

BeBe studies Anne, then turns and studies the loud, busy street market beyond his windshield. Something he sees, or thinks, puts his foot on the gas and we speed through the first intersection and don't stop until the hill at Eagle House.

The half-mile walk is uphill in the nubby grass and takes fifteen minutes. Trash is burning somewhere upwind. The stern of the HMS *Primrose* is the monument. The grass around it hasn't been cut in months, maybe years. Scorched piles of blackened wood dot the low hill. Crab shells, plastic bottles, and used condoms make up most of the debris.

Anne glances back a hundred yards toward BeBe and our car blocking the road, then does a slow 180. I walk to the stern of the *Primrose*, inspect the hull for something carved in the wood . . . something that undoubtedly would've been painted over a hundred times in seventy or eighty years—Jamaicans *love* paint, paint their houses twice a year if they can afford it.

I step back and try to take in the whole picture, the angles, the brass plaque affixed to a giant coral chunk, then the five guys watching Anne and me from a hundred feet away. My pistol's in my hand. Anne steps between me and the five men watching us, says "Hurry up," and pulls the towel off her MAC.

I walk to the plaque, read the HMS *Primrose* history. The last line reads:

This Jamaica national land donated and maintained in
honor of the Sephardim of St. Jago de la Vega, Hunts
Bay.

Blink, slight turn toward the ocean. I point, ask Anne, "That's
Hunts Bay, right?"

She nods, refocuses on the five men, says, "A back bay. Every year
when the big weather begins, Hunts Bay fills up with whatever the
Kingston sewers can't hold. Breeds clouds of mosquitoes. She separates Spanish Town from Caymanas Park Racetrack—your alma mater
during your Myers's days. Squint, and you'll see her as well."

I squint at the plaque instead, read "Sephardim" out loud.

Sephardim rings a bell. Back in my Myers's days, I worked with
Spanish Jews who are, or were, the descendants of Sephardic Jews
expelled from Spain and Portugal. They attended Synagogue Shaare
Shalom, around the corner on Duke Street from Myers's.

Anne points at the "St. Jago de la Vega" on the plaque. "That's the
original name of Spanish Town."

I squeeze the pistol grip, try to see what Eddie O'Hare saw, not
the five garrison gangsters deciding how best to circle an armed white
woman and her idiot tourist boyfriend.

Hmm . . . local Spanish Town Jews donate, then maintain this
"national" land. In honor of Jews from *Hunts Bay.*

Except no one can live in Hunts Bay.

Hmm.

Donate?

Maintain?

The Jewish congregations my mausoleum company works with
back in Chicago make a big deal about protecting and maintaining
old Jewish cemeteries and their residents. Dave got us a bunch of that
business.

If the Hunts Bay reference meant a Jewish *cemetery*—my lips curl
at both corners—a Jew could be 'from' there. And it would be a great
place to bury something you didn't want to lose. Lots better than the
boat dock or this spot.

"Bingo." I slap at Anne's shoulder. "I *am* handicapper of the year.
Tell me there's a cemetery at Hunts Bay."

"Aye. Old, though. Way, way older than what we're lookin' for."

"If you can get us past our friends there on the hill, I'd like to pay my respects. I do believe our lawyer Eddie O'Hare may have left our birthday present there."

Anne doesn't bite.

I explain.

She kisses me on the cheek. "What lovely man you are. Susie and I may have to fight over you." Anne shows the MAC and its magazine to the garrison gangsters. They hold their ground. She tells me: "Show your pistol but don't aim her. Just walk me to the car like we're courtin' on the Falls Road."

"We're courting?"

Big grin. "A lad as smart as you ought to have children."

***

Finding Hunts Bay Cemetery is on its fourth stop-and-ask even though Anne and BeBe "know" where it is. We're stopped out front of the crumbling Apostolic Assembly Church. The church's cross is half the size of a far newer JLP banner (Jamaica Labor Party) hanging above the front door. The rail-thin preacher talking to me says he can provide directions but wants to talk first, while the white-and-blue police cars drive by. He thinks I should know that he's well informed on Jews, that there are two hundred Jews living in Jamaica, but there used to be many more.

"Really? Gosh. And where's the cemetery?"

He smiles his white-stubble beard at Anne disguised in the Land Rover and points. "The Jews at Port Royal, they were merchants and pirates, same as all the peoples out there. But burying-wise, the Jews was different, didn't use the ocean; used to row their dead four miles across the harbor and back bay; carry them a hundred yards to that low hill." He smiles at Anne again.

I dig for a small donation to his church. "And where was that?"

"Better I show you."

***

We follow the preacher's dented Yugo. His last turn is onto a rutted red-dirt lane long forgotten by the JLP government. The lane leads to an open, scrubby five-acre wasteland that fronts the bay between two heavy industrial neighbors. Eight hundred yards south of us the sky is dominated by giant sky spiders, the seventeen-story gantry cranes of Kingston Harbour.

Anne smiles the smile and says, "Hunts Bay Cemetery," then slaps my thigh like we've arrived at Woodstock just as the fences come down.

From the car, I scan the storm-dimmed twilight and finally see the graves, uneven rows of mostly sunken gray slabs. BeBe backs the Land Rover to a spot with a clear view of the graves and the red-dirt road in. Anne and I keep our weapons and step out.

Mosquitoes buzz and promise malaria.

Anne and I walk into the rows of grave slabs—bluestone, marble, and limestone—some dating from the 1600s. Several are engraved with elaborate skulls and crossbones. Maybe three hundred graves total, some on raised brick bases that haven't partially sunk. I smile manly confidence at Anne and wish I knew what I was looking for.

I point her at the stones and step into the next row. "Read the names out loud as you walk past. I'll do the same. If one means something to you, say so."

Anne drones through the rows: "Lindo . . . Sangster . . . De Silva . . ."

So do I: "Marish . . . Babb . . . Magnus . . ."

Nope. None means anything to a treasure hunt. She stares at me for *Now what?*

Okay, I build mausoleums. Weight matters. Foundations. Start with that. Except I'm in a swamp where weight and foundations would have to be kept to a minimum.

Okay, maybe weight's not it.

Be present; be Eddie O'Hare when he was here. Eddie's right here sometime between 1934 and late 1938. Mosquitoes, lowland swamp, and heat. Eddie is a Christian lawyer from St. Louis and Chicago, not a Jew—why's he here? He's into dog racing and horses, walking right here, hiding 1,650 pounds of gold stolen from a Sicilian gangster. Has to weigh as much as ten caskets. Weight has to matter—

"Look out!" I grab for Anne's arm.

She rocks forward, rigid on her toes, then back to her heels, MAC-10 in both hands, staring at the parched grass in front of us; then the dirt between the slabs. Our feet have stopped just short of a booby trap that isn't there. I say, "Sorry."

Anne fisheyes me.

"Lemme see the file."

She hands me the file from her waistband. I pull the page from the Barbancourt bottle I recovered at Zelda Calhoun's house. Below the Kingston coordinates that sent us to this cemetery are two lines I've read fifty times.

> Fear the feds; fear the sky;
> fear the pencilmen; who never die."

I read the last words on the page out loud:

> Fear the feds; fear the sky;
> fear the pencilmen; who never die.

Eddie's life insurance policy can't just say it? Has to be cute?

The nearest grave is inscribed, but it's in Portuguese and Hebrew. Couldn't be Spanish, or God forbid, English. I do a 360 in the sticky heat and shadows, swearing at Eddie and his Haitian accomplice—

No, Remi Péralte wouldn't be here; this is reverse engineering, a minefield trail made *after* the gold had been relocated. Remi's already dead, Capone in prison . . . I look at Anne, then the sky: "'Fear the feds' I get, but why 'fear the sky'?"

Anne checks the sky, the distant storm in the east. She says, "Hurricane? Demons? Locusts? Rain? Flood?"

The back bay to the harbor is four hundred away . . . and drains a bunch of Kingston's overflow. I turn slowly toward the nearest tree line . . . whose trunks disappear below the grade we're standing. Walking toward the trees, a deep, dry reddish ravine becomes visible . . . a big drainage channel that probably carries a bunch of water when it rains. From the *sky*. 'Fear the sky'?

The ravine's edge is exposed rock. There are more gravestones over here, these planted into and above the rock, not in the softer, easier-to-dig lowland. I kneel, looking for a booby trap I can't see. Try to translate the first granite-slab engraving, can't, and neither can Google in a "no bars" neighborhood.

"You're a pirate, can you read Portuguese or Hebrew?"

"Gaelic." Anne refits red hair back under her Rasta tam.

From my knees I stare at the slab. Why can't I read Hebrew? Just for today? I stand, step up on the slab, and 360 again: Lowland cemetery in half-light shadows, bugs everywhere, heat. What am I missing?

Anne walks to the end of the row, stands on the last stone. She reads the name, steps onto the next stone and reads them all as she walks back to me:

"DeCohen . . . Levy . . . Guzik . . . Codner—"

"What?"

"Codner."

"Before that."

Anne walks back one grave. "Guzik."

I step to her. Right there between her shoes is a name with bagsful of poetic justice for Eddie O'Hare, aspiring poet/pirate. Carved into marble hundreds of years ago that will never die:

GUZIK.

I reread Eddie O'Hare's warning out loud:

Fear the feds; fear the sky;
fear the pencilmen; who never die.

Eddie O'Hare thinks like a handicapper. I'm starting to like Eddie O'Hare, crooked lawyer, murderer aside.

"What?" Anne looks between her shoes where I'm pointing. "Have you found it, Bill?"

"Eddie O'Hare had one sworn enemy in Al Capone's Outfit, a man who sensed that Eddie O'Hare was a liar and a cheat—Capone's *pencil-man*, Jewish accountant Jake 'Greasy Thumb' Guzik."

Anne grins big, then steps off the grave. "And be soft with your inspection, Bill. In our adventure, this'll be where the grave defiler dies."

***

Moving the slab will require help that my good friend the preacher is now hiring off Spanish Town Road at $10 US per man. While the preacher hunts for grave robbers, Anne stands guard and I check the slab, then the exposed casing and brick foundations every way I know how for trip wires or contact points.

Nope. Nothing.

"Think we're good . . . unless it's some kind of spring-loaded detonator from the inside. But why do that? If Eddie put the gold inside, then he'd have to open it someday as well."

"Aye," says Anne, "but the Egyptians were famous for death traps on their hiding places and so were the pirates from here to Cartagena. Sent slaves in first to take the blast."

***

Of our six young grave robbers, Lorenzo appears the strongest. Nice-looking kid; might have been a college student or a soccer player had he grown up with schoolbooks instead of garrison communities and drug posses. Lorenzo has a lengthy iron bar and looks at Anne longer than I would if I were him.

Anne makes sure the boys also see her MAC and the pistol in her belt—robbing us won't be less work than grave-robbing, assuming we all don't die in Eddie O'Hare's trap.

I wave for the bar. "Lemme see that."

Lorenzo hands it to me.

"Stand back."

All six move back. Anne shakes her head, then moves back as well.

I take the iron bar, poise it at the top slab's edge, say "Flyers rule," and wedge it in—

A booby trap doesn't kill me.

I exhale big, wedge deeper, and lean into the bar as a lever. Lorenzo jumps over to help. The slab moves four inches off the low walls—

EXPLOSION.

I land on my ass; so does Lorenzo. His pants are on fire. I jump on him, put out the flames, roll off and away.

The grave doesn't explode again. The now-cracked slab that saved us is scorched black and three-quarters off the grave.

Crouched, Anne 360s her MAC around the cemetery's borders. "In you go, Bill. Don't let good sense hold ya back."

"Wasn't that you who said step soft?"

She nods east. "Dark's comin'. We'll not want to be here."

I kneel at the open grave, point Lorenzo back to his mates. "You all get your $10 if you hang around to put the slab back." I sniff, smell nothing but the explosion, visually sift the dust, rags, and human bones. If the gold is here, it will be underneath.

I nervous into the brick-lined hole. Between my feet I find a skull . . . stringy hair . . . long whitish bones . . . bits of bone . . . glass—*a bottle.* Of Barbancourt Rhum. The bottle is light and dusty in my hand, sealed with ruby-red wax. Something rattles inside. I cut the wax with a bone shard, twist out the cork, and pour a long corked glass tube into my palm.

Decanted, the tube contains linen stationery and a sliver of gold ingot stamped with a US Mint serial number. "We've got gold. And somewhere else to go—"

Click.

I look up at Anne. Her finger's tight on the MAC's trigger. I let the bottle settle back into the chalky dust. "You're robbing me?"

"No." Her eyes are slits and focused elsewhere. "I'm shootin' the garrison bwoys your preacher hired." Anne's MAC is leveled across the grave above my head.

She yells, "I'm the better shot, bwoys! Stand down, or I'll stack the lot of ya in this hole. Mama never find ya."

I pull my pistol and stand up in the grave.

Lorenzo and our laborers are gone. Four gunmen and the preacher aim handguns at Anne. The preacher shouts: "Radio say you a convicted woman! A hundred thousand $J on your head for murderin' a JLP minister. Better price than removing ten crocodiles." He waves a cell phone with one hand; shakes a revolver at Anne with the other. "Drop that gun, woman! Police comin' now."

Anne steadies, knees bent, MAC aimed at the four gunmen. "I'd be Anne Bonny herself." She strips the Rasta tam, the red hair wild at her shoulders. "Don't you bwoys get killed followin' this git. G'wan home." Over her shoulder she yells: "BeBe! Babylon on the wire!"

The four gunmen shout patois, grab their balls, and threaten with their guns. A rank breeze blows in off Hunts Bay. The foul air mixes with the fermenting trash and poverty of Spanish Town, a good reason for these fellows to believe a gunfight with Anne Bonny is worth the risk.

BeBe's out of the Rover.

Three. Two. One—

"Don't!" I yell at the garrison bwoys.

The preacher and his garrison bwoys fire first. Anne empties the MAC. BeBe empties his. The roar lasts two seconds. Sixty rounds total.

Four Jamaicans are sprawled; one running away. Anne slaps another 30-round magazine, racks the bolt, but doesn't fire. She runs to the preacher sprawled between two graves, pulls her pistol, and screams in his face, "Ya fuckin' jammy bastard!" She fires twice into his chest, then five times over the head of the man running away. "Ya think I'd walk to the gallows?!" She fires again. "Goddamn ya!"

BeBe runs for the Land Rover. Anne and I race behind him and dive in the back. He guns it up the red dirt. Sirens wail from both directions.

We hit the main road, skid-turn onto another, then onto a water-front causeway. BeBe loops a container terminal, makes it all the way around and onto a narrow bridge that separates the bay from the main harbor. My heart pounds; cars and trucks whiz past. The last of the causeway dumps us onto a shorefront road. BeBe stays on the gas, slams the brakes at the Rodney's Arms pub, then ducks us down behind a line of fishing shacks that separate Rodney's Arms from the beach and Kingston's twenty-square-mile harbor.

Our vehicle skids onto the sand.

Fifteen feet offshore, Anne's two gleaming jet-black contraband boats bob at anchor, a 43-foot Donzi ZR and a 48-foot Sea Ray Sundancer with a flying bridge. The three black men I met earlier at her Sazerac Bar stand on the dirty beach, all armed, eyeing the road we just raced.

Anne tells one: "Sundown, take the Rover south to Dream Beach; hide it; Captain BeBe pick you up now." She circles her hand above her head. "In the boats! Babylon comin'."

BeBe wades out fast to the deep-V Donzi. On her stern is: "*Esmeralda*, Port Royal, Jamaica."

Anne tells me to follow her out to the Sea Ray. BeBe climbs aboard the Donzi and fires the engines. Anne and I climb aboard the *Sazerac Star.*

Sistah—who tried to shoot me earlier today—rises from the deck. She's wearing a T-shirt now and holding a live chicken by its feet. She watches me board the *Sazerac Star,* then drops down into the main cabin.

Anne fires the engines and yells me up to the bridge. I climb the chrome ladder, grab Anne's MAC-10 off the seat next to her, then strap in for the run across the harbor to the ocean. Anne slams both throttles. My neck snaps back; she shouts over the engines: "If we make the ocean, they'll not follow us into a hurricane."

I focus east where we're pointed. "Lana's a hurricane?"

The wind keeps most of the engine roar and all the smell behind us. "Up to a Cat 1 and buildin'." Anne chins at a screen next to the throttles. "She's out there, due east eight hundred miles of Hispaniola. We're built for wind and water. If we hole up somewhere proper in the next thirty-six hours, it'll be rough but likely won't sink us."

"Likely?" I twist to see if soldiers or police have reached the beach.

So does Anne; she winces apology. "Unfortunate back there. Dudus and the posse dons got these gang bwoys crazy." She eyes me for bullet damage I don't have, then refocuses forward. "Might be we could run north for Cuba, the hurricane hole at Punta Barlovento."

"Our treasure hunt's killing a lot of people."

"Aye. Maybe our Susie, God bless her; and us, too, if our luck doesn't hold. Our adversaries don't worry blood; they'll be bold with it. Try Susie's phone."

I hit redial on "Rugby Gurl." It rings, but no answer.

Anne frowns. "Susie's a good one." She knocks the wood wheel with the heel of her hand. "But Piccard and the Gryphon are . . . a lot."

She bends around and yells to the deck, "Taller! Get on the glasses; track us any police boats comin'!"

I re-glance the coastline behind us, then out east into the enormous harbor we have to escape, then back to Anne. Three days ago I was some version of normal.

Wind blows through Anne's red hair. One scarlet fingernail pokes the new piece of stationery death-gripped in my hand. "There's nothing we can do for Susie that she can't do for herself. If she didn't think she could hold the best of it, there's no way they'd take her alive." Anne checks her mirror for Jamaican police boats. "But if somehow the bastards did take her, then the gold's her only chance. What's our new bottle's news?"

I read from the stationery aloud:

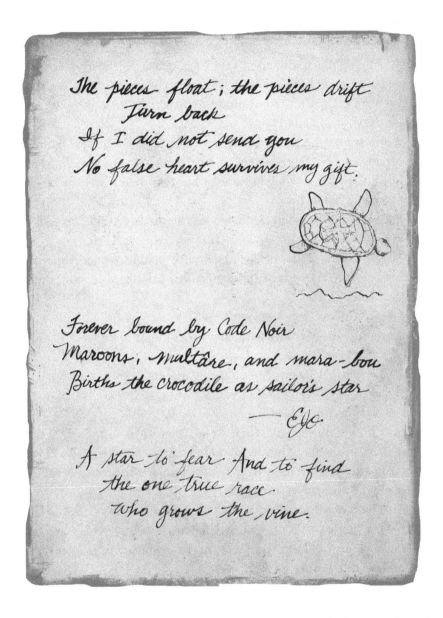

The pieces float; the pieces drift
    Turn back
If I did not send you
No false heart survives my gift.

Forever bound by Code Noir
Maroons, multâre, and mara-bou
Births the crocodile as sailor's star

        — EJc.

A star to fear And to find
    the one true race.
    Who grows the vine.

Beneath the word *gift* is a small drawing that might be a turtle and a carefully drawn squiggly line below it. The turtle's flippers sort of resemble compass points. If they are, and the top of the page is north, then the turtle's "head" points east-southeast. The turtle's shell bears an insignia of some type, part relic-style cross, part . . . animal shape?

The *Sazerac Star* knifes east. I steady against the hull's concussions.

Anne says, "We'll make the open ocean between Drunken Man's Cay and Hellshire Bay. Waves will double."

Staring at the stationery, I say: "If it matters, the cross could be crossed coffin nails, the old kind. I saw a cross made out of 'em at the Field Museum in Chicago, a pirate exhibit, the slave ship *Whydah*. Vodou uses coffin nails, right?"

Anne traces the turtle shape with her fingernail, then the head, then the wavy line. Her eyes cut to me, then away. She frowns, shakes her head, then shouts down to one of her two men who came aboard with us, "Get Sistah."

I stare at the drawing but don't see the message that Anne seems to see.

Sistah climbs to the bridge and stands behind Anne. Anne pulls her between us. "We gone from Kingston, gurl, like you want. But we goin' to Haiti."

Sistah stiffens, then recovers.

Anne squeezes Sistah's hand and says, "I have to know. Will Sistah keep hold of herself?"

"Why Ayiti? Why now? With *this* white man?"

Anne shows Sistah the slice of US Mint gold ingot. "The best treasure of all time. The fabled Banque Nationale gold."

Sistah fixes on the gold, then Anne, then turns to me. "This time, white man, you will not kill Ayiti's Rebelyon; my country will kill you."

Anne turns Sistah away from me. "G'wan down, now. Tell Taller to bring me the charts for Tortuga."

Sistah climbs down. Anne says, "She'll bear watchin'. Should leave her behind, her past loyalties and memories being what they are, but I can't. Babylon would imprison her; maybe give her my gallows. I'd be honor bound to set her free."

"Don't take me to Haiti, Anne. I'm not kidding. Not gonna happen."

"Ya think *I* want to go?" Anne waves me off. "Not to Haiti, just close." She taps the turtle drawing beneath *gift*.

Taller's oversize hands precede him up the ladder. A red kerchief is tied to his thick neck under a scarred chin, badly sewn lip, and two gold teeth. He hands Anne a roll of charts. "Sistah say it's Haiti?"

Anne nods.

"Fuckery it is. Anne Bonny got no friends in Haiti." Taller looks at me. "And Sistah says your white man got the goddamn devil waitin' on 'im there."

"Aye, Taller." Anne gives him the smile. "But she's *our* fuckery and the devil don' scare us."

Taller frowns hard like he wants to argue, thinks better of it, and climbs down.

Anne loses the smile and unrolls a chart of Haiti's north coast across her instruments. She points at a tiny island shaped like the turtle in Eddie's drawing and says, "Tortuga; first buccaneer capital of the West Indies." She smiles. "Not Haiti. Read the poem again."

I mantra *Not Haiti*. Try to visualize Eddie O'Hare sitting somewhere drafting his poem. Our boat pounds the water.

Anne notices, says: "Second verse—"

Forever bound by Code Noir
Maroons, multâre, and mara-bou
Births the crocodile as sailor's star

"'Maroons' in Jamaica and Cuba were runaway slaves. 'Code Noir' were the slave regulations that governed them." She points at *crocodile* in the same verse, reads aloud:

"'Births the crocodile as sailor's star.' *Caiman* are Haiti's crocodiles." Anne drags her finger two inches east-southeast across the Tortuga Channel to where the well-drawn turtle's head might point, then stops on mainland Haiti near the port city of Cap-Haïtien and says, "Bois Caïman is here," like I'm supposed to know.

I don't.

"Bois Caïman is where Haiti's historic slave Rebelyon began. Where vodou houngan Dutty Boukman and mambo Cécile Fatiman made their pact with the devil for the freedom they'd win; sold the souls of Haiti for a thousand years. Year of our Lord, 1791."

I refocus on the poem's second verse, speculate: "'Sailor's star' could mean 'navigation'—like it's what we want to follow."

"Read that last verse." Anne pats at the poem.

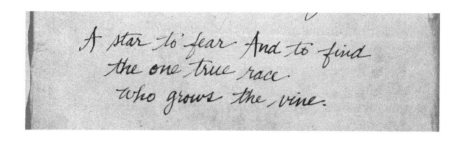

I do.

Anne cuts to me for help. "So maybe it's the 'sailor's star' we're supposed to follow? Find her at Bois Caïman?"

I frown at her theory. "You said Bois Caïman is in Haiti. I'm not going to Haiti."

OPEN OCEAN

Chapter 18

BILL OWENS

Every minute of the last hour the open ocean has beat the shit out of me. I go below to collapse on the day bunk, hoping me and my Flyers talisman can sleep. My good friend Sistah and her live chicken are on the floor, wedged into the galley's far corner.

Sistah waits till I'm prone, then pulls a knife I didn't know she had. She decapitates the chicken; squeezes its neck to paint a blood circle on the floor around her—

I bolt off the bunk, climb up and out to the aft deck. Sistah probably hasn't read *Moby Dick*, but I have. She's doing the dreadlocks-Corazón-Santo version of Queequeg-the-harpooner building his own coffin.

I curl up between the fifty-five-gallon drums of high-octane gas. The smell will add to the rat dreams of where this "adventure" is headed. Sleep is doze-then-jolt, the precursor to night terrors; then gory flashes of Susie Devereux in the hands of the monster she feared most.

Sleep is obviously not the way to go. I climb back to Anne on the bridge.

***

All night, the *Sazerac Star* and the *Esmeralda* roar northeast. Anne points me at the Southern Cross, low in the night sky, then smiles like that should mean something good. In the brief moments when Anne's satellite phone gets a signal, Susie never answers. Sistah stays below in her blood circle.

Guantanamo Bay's lights flicker twenty miles to port.

Ten minutes later, we pick up a series of lights. Anne says: "Gunboats. Cuban. We're on the outer edge of their territorial waters."

The gunboats close to three hundred feet on the port side. For two hours we race under the stars, Anne running full-throttle. She's trying for the Windward Passage, a fifty-mile strait that separates the eastern tip of Cuba from Hispaniola.

Anne points down the ladder. "Decision time. Grab us two life jackets. Cubans don't care that we're fugitives from Jamaica, but if they decide we're pirates, they'll sink us rather than let us go."

Near Cuba's eastern tip, both gunboats veer into us, preparing to shoot. The lead boat draws so close I can see the sailors manning a deck gun. It veers again, this time hard to port, and away. The second boat does the same. Anne says, "Their radio's broadcastin' same news as ours."

"Huh?"

Anne nods dead ahead into a sunrise that should be on our bow, but isn't.

Anne doesn't relax as Cuba disappears to our left. The maritime warnings over her radio are saying Hurricane Lana has grown to a Cat 3. She's out there behind the black, six hundred miles east and closing.

I try to remember the words to "On the Good Ship Lollipop" but can't. Anne's radio continues to crackle with official warnings—everything afloat should be somewhere else, then for the fifth time, rebroadcasts our boats' descriptions and Jamaica's bounty offer.

I glance blue ocean for the white whale. There won't be a non-Communist port in the Caribbean that can't ID us when we hole up from the hurricane.

"We made her, the Windward Passage." Anne pats her chest twice, then stretches both arms to point port and starboard. "That last bit of Cuba we just ran is twenty miles to port. Haiti's north coast and Tortuga is twenty miles to starboard. Landfall in ninety minutes."

She tries Susie again, can't get a signal, then touches the phone to her chin and looks at the sky. "Tell me where you are, Susie." Anne punch-dials another call, tells me, "Tryin' Siri." Anne gets a signal, but no answer. She calls Susie again, gets no answer, shuts her eyes, and says, "I'm comin'. Tell me where you are."

Thunder rumbles over the boat. Anne's eyes snap open.

Our radio updates the hurricane: Lana has slowed down. Anne chins dead ahead into a surreal, backlit horizon of gray and black. "I'd say we have forty-eight hours before we need to be elsewhere."

"Is forty-eight hours enough?"

"Maybe. Storm's good cover, though. Cat 3 or better hittin' a ragamuffin island like Haiti, and at high tide?" Anne shakes her head. "Won't be us the authorities are worried about."

"Which authorities would that be?"

Anne locks eyes with me. She blows out a breath, grabs her radio mic, and call-signs for Captain BeBe. He answers. Anne tells him to change course, recradles the mic, and yells down for Taller to take the *Star*'s wheel. Taller climbs to the fly bridge and takes over. Anne points me off the bridge to the main cabin.

Down below, Sistah sits cross-legged in her blood circle, eyes closed, unaffected by the hull's constant crashes and the smell of death. Someone has added a heavy Spanish crucifix to her lap. Anne counts the tablets in Sistah's medicine bottle, then grabs the chart of Haiti's north coast and a bottle of rum. She slides into a bench seat behind a fixed table and waves me to join her.

Sistah doesn't look up as I pass. If she still has her knife, it's not out. I take the bench seat facing her. Anne rubs tired eyes, spreads the chart on the mess table, holds it down with her elbows, then drinks from the rum bottle. "Would ya like the good news first, or the bad?"

"If we can survive the bad news, let's go with the good."

"Survivin'll be difficult, Bill." Pause. "We're goin' to Haiti. I'm sorry, but that's the whole of it."

"Gosh. I'm shocked."

"So we best discuss who's waiting for us. I need to know you understand the ramifications, all of 'em."

"Now I *am* shocked."

"Your clear thinkin' under fire will be . . ." Anne licks her lips. "Cranston Piccard is a lot of people's nightmare, but he'd be Christmas compared to the Gryphon." She swigs from the bottle. "Some of Haiti's ministers and police say the Gryphon's a myth, like they say the red market is a myth, but they know different—"

"Susie mentioned the red market. That shit's true? Why the rebels called Cambronne 'the vampire'?"

Anne nods. "Back in the 1970s, before AIDS was identified, Haiti's blood was in demand for its concentration of antibodies. US hospital corporations paid a premium and imported all that was available. The Gryphon was the Luckner Cambronne lieutenant who saw the market, built Cambronne his blood farm to increase the supply."

"Blood farm?"

"Hospitals—one in Cap-Haïtien, one in Port-au-Prince. A ferry truck would come through Cité Soleil and Cap-Haïtien every day. The poor and desperate would be collected to sell their blood. When the US demand would spike the price above the supply, the Gryphon would kill the donor, say he died by accident, take *all* his blood and sell the body separate. Estimates guess he and Cambronne drained thirty thousand . . . to death."

"Jesus." The visual gags me. "And you think we're gonna trap this monster?"

Anne wince-nods, then places her fingernail on the chart at Haiti's far northeast border. "Ever been into Fort Liberté Bay? The Mangrove Coast? *Monde perdu?*"

I shrink into the bench.

Back in the '80s, the Mangrove Coast was called *monde perdu*, "the lost world"—an impenetrable warren of brackish mangrove swamp fed by one river and cut off by steep mountain cliffs; nothing there but malaria and crocodiles. And monster myths. When the Haitians in the cities said "Gone to the groves," they meant the devil had taken a person, and bullshit myth or not, the person never came back.

Anne takes another drink from the bottle, weighs our sliver of gold ingot. "For a dollar less than $26 million, I'd turn us to Cartagena and take our chances that Lana doesn't catch us open-ocean."

"Nobody's that scary."

"A big reader, ya were at Oxford, Bill. *Heart of Darkness, Frankenstein*?" Anne's green eyes narrow. "At best—and we're a far distance from *best*—the Gryphon's a pirate, a Corazón Santo warlord, like the Somali warlords in east Africa who pushed the US army back to Bill Clinton's desk—except much, much stronger. The Haitians believe the Gryphon has God and the devil in his pockets. If I had to guess, he's landing almost half as much cocaine as Carlos Lehder did when Carlos was *the* man. The Gryphon's sending his to Mexico, not the US direct. People who'd know guess five tons every month. That buys a lot of power on a third-world island." Anne's fingers close around the ingot until her knuckles whiten. "And at worst, the Gryphon's proof demons can take a man, infect him . . . just like the Bible thumpers say. We'll not survive a meetin' with him on his home ground, nor anywhere else without a trap in place."

Demons and Haiti is not a concept that requires a salesman. And no one wants to hear their pirate captain quote the Bible out of fear. Anne was once a dramatic Irish lass, and I mention that possibility.

She finds a half-smile but her eyes harden. "Remember our balcony that night in '86 when the Tontons Macoutes were dancin' in the fires? Celebrating Cambronne's return to lead the fight? The Gryphon has him a thousand of those night howlers, bartered for out of the prisons, recruited from the street gangs and garbage heaps." The half-smile quits. "Men and boys like the ones who had you in Fort Dimanche. Has 'em up in those mangrove swamps, armed to the teeth, white-out crazy on bloodroot and cocaine, capable of behavior no Somali warlord would sanction."

I glance at Anne's white knuckles, then Sistah on the floor in her blood circle. White and blood seem to be a theme here. Sistah looks up, chin elevated, the rope scar wide and shiny. She wants her country and its latest Rebelyon to kill me.

The waves shake Anne and me sideways. She puts two fingernails on the chart. "We're goin' *here*; the Gryphon's somewhere *here*." Her fingernails are a grand total of one inch apart. "The UN has six thousand troops in Haiti but they don't go into Fort Liberté Bay or the other two reef cuts that lead up into the Gryphon's bayou river. Five years ago, your DEA crossed the DR border at the Rio Masacre with fifty DR special operators. Sixty men total boarded boats at Fort Liberté.

Not one boat or one man came back." Anne eyes Sistah. "And the fifty thousand Ida rebels who are about to put Haiti to flame, as fierce committed as they are, don't go near the Gryphon either."

Sistah blinks just once.

I fake the best smile I can. "Look on the bright side, Eddie O'Hare's treasure doesn't have a volcano."

Anne cocks her head backward toward the bow and the cloud wall dead ahead. "A volcano, this boat might could outrun. I've just done the numbers, Bill. Outrunning our hurricane will take more gas than the *Sazerac* can carry."

"Do not fucking say that."

"At some point, Lana will add speed . . . and she's comin' dead at us."

I palm my face. "If I was a believer, I'd say we're cursed."

"Aye." Anne reaches to touch Sistah in her blood circle. "The whole of the country's cursed, if ya ne remember."

Glare. "I remember. No god-fearing tent shouter can have black heathens outfight a white professional army without help from hell."

Anne smooths at Sistah's dreads, both finding comfort in the touch. "Aye. As impossible as it was, Haiti's slaves outfought the French *and* the Spanish armies. Took thirteen years. Created the first black people's republic in the history of the world." Anne's eyes pay Sistah respect, then cut to me. "And the slaves' patron, Bill? Who all sides say the devil birthed that night in Bois Caïman to lead the slaves first revolt?"

Anne reaches across the table and turns over my gun hand, holding it open. Her thumb presses the **Ezili** carved across the lifeline in my palm. "The Black Madonna, Ezili Dantor." Anne's fingers roll my palm up tight in hers. "You and I killed her bloodline's daughter. Year of our Lord, 1986."

***

Pétion-ville, Haiti
1986

My high-ceilinged room at the Hotel Oloffson has six blurry people in it—Carel Roos, three Selous Scouts, Anne Bonny, and what's left of me. Anne has just returned from her "BBC" interview with "the vampire" Luckner Cambronne. She says the interview went as expected but doesn't elaborate, walks to the bathroom, and shuts the door behind her.

Thirty minutes later she opens the bathroom door in a robe, toweling her hair. Anne looks across my bed to Carel cleaning an Uzi next to a Ka-Bar fighting knife. She says, "Not even a small chance you'll take Cambronne. Either you kill him for half your contract or die tryin' to get him out alive for the full amount."

Carel answers with a smile. His accent is fluid Afrikaner and matches the three Scouts in the chairs behind him checking their weapons. "Mind ya, now, Anne of the islands." Carel's smile broadens. "This is your professional opinion?"

Anne hardens her tone. "*Mentallers*, Carel, Tontons Macoutes. Every one of 'em armed with CIA-delivered AKs, tarted up in chicken blood, and screamin' high on cocaine." Anne points out my tall, open verandah doors. "And even if we trap Cambronne in this room and escape his Tontons, you yourself said the peninsula highway was already a bunny-fuck when you came in."

"We've passed worse. Afrika—"

"No, Carel, Haiti may look like Afrika, but she's different here, the regular army's strong. They'll take control of the ports. But the roads and cities—where *we* have to be—they'll leave to the rebels and Cambronne's Tontons to fight over. Castro's Communists have supplied the rebels well, probably just as good as the CIA has supplied Cambronne's Tontons." Anne nods to me. "Bill's local people done their jobs and we best listen—they say there's no gettin' out east to the DR either. By the time we're on the mountain road to the east, Cambronne's Tontons will've barricaded it against the rebels. I see it as it is; we should've stayed in England—but since we didn't, you and your mates settle for half: kill Cambronne, take his head, then trek south for Jacmel on the coast. It's the only direction we'll survive. We make the coast, grab a boat when this three-way war is full-on, then run open-ocean for Jamaica."

Carel smiles at me and mimics Anne's Irish accent. "She's a pirate, that one."

Anne moves in to Carel's face. "Cambronne wants me to be with him and his girlfriend. She's a child, ten or twelve; she'll come here before him, she and I'll cozy up, call him, say we can't wait. Cambronne will take a break from the war he's startin', come up the back stairs to this bed"—Anne's hands tie an air bow on her plan—"and it's over."

Carel's still smiling. "Sounds like you miss the kaffer. Maybe you'd want some time with him and his little *stekkie* first?"

The Scouts laugh. Anne darkens. "Pleased to let the big man fuck me *again*. So you and your mates can watch."

The room goes silent, a vote on how seriously Carel's world-class killers take Anne Bonny, her temper, and her willingness to act on it.

Carel turns to me. "Haiti's your part of the world. Anne's as well, arsehole that it is. Is our *esteemed* pirate lady spot-on?"

I nod my weak neck and swollen head an inch. "Cambronne's Tontons Macoutes are psycho; carve that in stone. Can't say how well armed or how many, but the CIA has plenty of money." Blink. I refocus, dizzy. "But even if Cambronne has ten thousand down there, they'll be outnumbered fifty to one by Haiti's citizens . . . once the killing starts for real in Port-au-Prince. Yesterday's terrified citizens are today's rebels, and they *hate* the Tontons *and* the army."

"Well armed, they are? The citizen rebels?"

My hand steadies me against the louvered door. "If Castro supplied the rebels with even half what the CIA gave Cambronne's Tontons, it'll be a bloodbath. Everybody above ground will be somebody's target."

One of Carel's Scouts nods to my foggy assessment and says, "Lebanon."

"If you say so. But for sure, Anne's right about any escape plan. The path south I showed you on the map will get worse the closer we get to the lake, but the path *does* skirt the worst of the mountains. And you guys are jungle guys. From the south side of the lake you might could veer east through to the DR."

Anne waves her hand. "Nobody's goin' uphill or on a 'path' to the DR. Bill ain't thinkin' straight."

Carel turns back to me. "What about our boat to Jamaica? The seventy kph contrabander you said we could hire on the south coast? Your kaffer's there waiting?"

"Whoa." I push both hands between me and Carel's Ka-Bar knife, stumble, and use Anne for balance. "You told me to find out but *not* make a plan. Once the shooting and machetes start, it'll be civil war every mile in every direction."

Anne says, "Sailin' from the south coast can work, *if* we can get there. We grab this hotel's assistant manager—Bill says his family 'fishes' there out of Jacmel; the cocaine trade. We avoid the mudslides and floods that Bill's already mentioned on mountain road, get down to the family's dock, and sail west.

"After we clear Haiti's peninsula, it's two hundred miles of open water to Port Royal." Anne winks. "Run out of gas, tiny bit of motor trouble, and we're adrift, waitin' for whatever God sends us."

Carel turns to the Scouts. "Take this kaffer's head? On delivery, we'll only get half pay, less our upfront money. But the cocaine here is mealie-cheap; we could pool what money we have on us, plus what we take from the kaffer, buy cocaine here or ganja in Jamaica; we could come out near the same when our boat docks in Afrika."

They look at each other and nod. Carel turns to Anne, "Call your little girl."

"Don't have to, she's downstairs in the bar. With five of Cambronne's Tontons."

Carel tells his Scouts to take their positions. "Once Cambronne's in this room, we go hot." Carel hands me a 9 mm pistol that I don't know how to use and shows me the safety. "Cambronne's bodyguards expect you to be here somewhere. Go down to the bar where they can see you. Stay there till you hear gunfire up here, then get back to us fast. Shoot whoever's in the way. But not until you hear gunfire up here. Can you do that?" Carel looks into my one hooded eye. "Do you understand me, Bill?"

"Up the stairs. Shoot whoever I have to."

Carel says it again, "Do not stay in the bar. There's a bomb there. Run up the stairs *after* the shooting starts."

"Shoot whoever I have to." The gun feels like a lump of metal in my hand.

"*After* we start up here." Carel turns to his Scouts, says, "Howzit, laaities?"

All three punch their thumbs.

Carel points at the ceiling, says to Anne, "We'll be the rats in the attic. Make us proud."

***

Downstairs, the lobby is full of Tontons Macoutes who watch me into the bar, then climb the stairs to prepare my "bride-to-be's" room for her three-way tryst with their boss, Luckner Cambronne. I gentle onto a barstool and do not look at the young girl as she climbs the stairs.

The bartender arrives. He's new, but professional, asks what he might make for me.

"A double, Myers's dark. Bring me two." I don't look in the mirror. The barstool hurts. I stand and waddle-walk to the windows, stare into the nothing for so long that my knees begin to ache.

Two more black men enter the bar but stay at the far end. They are Tonton rapist prison guards; one is my AIDS goodbye from Fort Dimanche—he grins and blows me a kiss as he cups his balls and laughs with his friend.

I shuffle back to the bar, sit in spite of the pain, and don't look in the mirror.

My rum is there, as are several flies that found it unprotected. I shoo the flies and drink. The 9 mm digs into my spine under my shirt. The Tontons laugh again. They chop out two lines of cocaine on the bar, telling the bartender what happened to me, why I waddle like a woman and look like a dog.

My head pounds under the bandages. I tap my glass on the bar to remind the bartender. He disengages with the rapists, walks to me and asks what I'd like.

"The rum I ordered. Another one. Please."

He doesn't acknowledge our previous conversation and waits for me to release the glass. The rapists laugh. The one I recognize snorts his line of blow, wipes at his nose, then walks halfway to me and stops. He steps away from the bar, leering, as if to admire my ass, then tells the bartender he'll pay for my drink.

The bartender tries not to smile but can't help it. He brings me my second double. I drink all the dark rum in the glass, set it down, then stand off the stool. My left hand grabs the bar for balance.

The bartender smiles. The rapists laugh. Like they did at the prison.

I glance at the blurry stairs that lead to my "bride-to-be" being raped by a gorilla on our wedding night.

Again.

The men notice and say something in Kreyol that they think is funny. They don't waste the energy to tell me I won't be allowed to stumble upstairs while their boss is doing to Anne what they did to me.

I regrip the bar.

The nearest rapist smiles and flicks his tongue.

Flies re-form on my glass.

My feet shuffle the curve of the bar toward the laugher. The Tontons watch me, unconcerned. One Tonton motions me to turn around, show him my ass. If I'm nice, he'll have me again.

I draw the 9 mm from the back of my pants, thumb down the safety, and without hurry or adrenaline, raise the pistol and shoot him in the face.

LOUD. The backbar mirror splashes red; brain matter splatters the bartender. The second rapist backs away. I shoot him in the chest. He bounces off the wall; I fire again; he pancakes back on the wall, then slides to the floor. The 9 mm I'm holding stays level on the wall where the rapist used to be, my finger tight on the trigger.

A third man runs in from the lobby, gun in hand.

I turn and fire. The bullet hits him in the neck and he careens onto the stairs. My ears are ringing. I walk toward him, shoot him again, step over, and mount the first tread.

The stairs are blurry and slow. I use the railing. Slow-motion fog world lasts until the final tread. My foot lands; I turn into the hallway and full-auto gunfire explodes from every direction. One knee buckles. Bullets rip the wall above me. Fog world goes blood mist and cordite.

Carel leaps through the mist, jumps over splattered black bodies, kicks a gun away, and shoots a Tonton whose leg is vibrating on the wood floor. A figure appears at the doorway behind me. Over my shoulder, Carel fires twice into the cordite smoke, spins, races down the hallway away from me, and fires again.

I stand and stumble through my room's splintered, open door, and—

Blood spatter everywhere. Shell casings; cordite smoke. Pocked walls and chewed shutters.

A large black man is naked, slumped half off the bed, and shot to pieces. Two of Carel's Scouts stand the room's center, both bleeding, their submachine guns smoking. Four Tonton bodies and their weapons litter the floor. The bed sheets are sticky red; Anne is in the bed. Her eyes roll to white and she falls off onto the floor. Cambronne's teenage girlfriend wide-eyes me from the pillows. She's not a teenager, more like ten or eleven. Her eyes are birthmarked white and stay on me as her left hand sneaks toward . . . a pistol ruffled in the sheets.

"Gun!" I shoot her twice in the chest. She bounces into the headboard.

Carel's Scouts fire into the bed, wall, and floor. I duck shell casings and plaster debris. One Scout staggers into the wall, heaving for air his lungs can't breathe. His eyes roll; he struggles his Uzi up under his chin, hesitates, and pulls the trigger. His head splatters the wall and ceiling.

The other Scout squeezes at arterial blood pumping from his neck and chest. He falls to sitting, says, "Take the kaffer's head."

Carel enters the bedroom with the last Scout behind him. Back-to-back, they fire a waist-high full-auto line through three walls of the room. Carel grabs Anne half-naked from the floor, jerks her to standing, and out to the hallway.

The unwounded Scout shoves me out into the hall, but stays behind with the Scout bleeding out from the neck wound. I hear *"Pamwe chete,"* then a gunshot.

Footsteps pound up the front stairs. Carel detonates his bomb. The explosion splinters the stairs and shudders us all into the walls. The unwounded Scout runs out of the bedroom with a bag in one hand, Uzi in the other, chokes on bomb-dust cloud, and shoves me toward Carel and the back stairs. Carel counts to three, then detonates another bomb Anne planted in the lobby.

The four of us fly down the back stairs, jump a second set of dead Tontons, and scramble into a waiting truck, our bloody faces and hands lit by the fires and screams we leave behind.

Gunfire explodes; bullets rip our truck.

After two miles, the truck's engine succumbs to the bullets. Anne scrambles into clothes and boots from the truck and we bolt into the bramble and thatch. Carel and the surviving Scout bracket Anne and me in a serpentine column. For three hours we trek down-mountain through trampled vegetation and vibrating urban jungle. Sporadic gunfire echoes on the roads and deep in the tin-shanty mazes we skirt. In the distance, fires glow across the sprawl of Port-au-Prince. My legs continue to cramp and buckle. Carel says commandeering a vehicle inside the city limits isn't worth the risk with no hostage to transport.

Finally, we reach the last ridge on the southwestern outskirts of Port-au-Prince. Carel stops our column; I collapse against the rusted shell of a stripped car and slide to the ground. My one good eye still has some focus. I rub my left thigh, then the right, then both hips. My insides gurgle, feel like mush.

Below us, a brightly colored, overturned tap-tap bus belches smoke, then flame. Voices shout Kreyol. Bodies and shadows scurry in every direction. The black smoke rolls into the street. Beyond the smoke, deep in the distance, the Port-au-Prince Iron Market appears to be on fire, as are both airport runways farther north. The dark is wet, smoky, suffocating; I'm dizzy, fuzzy; have trouble breathing—

The ten-year-old I shot straddles my hips, her chest pumping blood, her fingers clawing out my eyes. I bat at her face. She slaps me awake, leering into my eyes—

"Bill! Stop it." Anne says, "Get up. Walk, or Carel will shoot you."

Pant. Swallow.

Slap. Anne uses both hands to grab my collar. "Get up!"

I stumble to standing. Blood dribbles from my bandages. My balloon face is hot, my legs cramping again. "Is she dead? The girl? Did I kill her?"

Carel reaches past Anne, grabs my shirt, and jerks me square to him. "You killed us all."

Anne pushes him away but doesn't disagree.

Carel and his Scout discuss whether to commandeer a vehicle now that we're outside the city. We drop out of the jungle down to the road. Anne strips her strap T-shirt, then stands mid-road, naked from the waist up, like she's delirious. A conscripted tap-tap van stops. Carel and the Scout kill the Tonton driver and his shotgun rider. Anne helps me into the back seats, the air humid with blood. Everything goes black.

***

Bright lights flash. My hand jerks to block the glare. Carel is driving, talking to Anne. She's seated with me, behind him. Anne shakes my arm and shoulder. "Bill. We're here; Jacmel. Have to find the contrabander with our boat. Where is he?"

"Huh?" Dry swallow. "Bar Guilanno's. The hardware store in back."

"It's three a.m., Bill; where will our contrabander be at three a.m.?"

"Right. Right. The dock, with the fishermen. The harbormaster's house . . ."

Anne grips Carel's shoulder and says, "I best clean up first."

We stop just west of the harbor. Anne splashes filthy beach water on her arms and face, then mine, scrubbing away the dried blood of a ten-year-old I murdered.

I mumble, "God, I'm sorry, I—"

"*Bill.*" Anne slaps me. "Get ready."

At the Jacmel harbormaster's house, Anne tricks the contrabander captain out and into our tap-tap van. His accent is French. "No. I cannot. You are too dangerous."

Carel is cold and calm. "We go to your boat now, or you die telling me where it hides." He points to Anne. "We have our own captain."

"No. You are too late. The dawn comes; no contraband boat can leave now." He points toward a silhouette—the deep bay's outer shoreline that will be clearly visible in one hour. "My boat will need all sixty minutes just to escape our bay. By then, when we reach the maritime line, where the navy patrols, it will be sunrise. The navy will sink us."

Carel says, "Get the boat."

"No. You can only cross the maritime line in absolute dark. Tomorrow I will take you."

Pop. Pop. I look up at our tap-tap's roof. Pop. Pop. Drops of rain; it can rain down here.

Carel says, "Take us to the boat and load; we're going now or you're dying now."

***

The boat is long and open with three 150 hp outboard motors. Our captain jumps aboard with the dock rope. He makes another plea. "If we survive the bay and then the maritime line, we must sail parallel to the coast for 120 miles, until we reach the end of the peninsula and open ocean. There is little chance we sneak past all the patrol boats."

Carel says, "Go."

The captain points into the dark. "After the patrol boats would be five hours of ocean. A plane with radar and we are dead. A problem with our motors and the storm coming from the east will catch us."

Lightning drills the mountains to the east and the sky explodes. Rain sheets the Jacmel dock and boils the bay. I ask about the ropes and leather cuffs anchored into the bench seats.

The captain answers me as he casts off at gunpoint: "Tie-downs. For when we can no longer hold on."

***

The navy doesn't intercept us at the maritime line, but ten minutes past it the storm worsens, battering us from the north and east as we race west along Haiti's long Tiburon Peninsula. The dead girl says this voyage will kill me; the dead girl says it will be fair. She says her gun will find my family; she says hell is only minutes away.

At Vache Island the ocean seems to shudder, confused by energy from every direction. Open ocean slams our boat, breaking high and hard, jarring the hull and my unmended insides. The captain ties himself in and we do the same. The murdered girl doesn't; she smiles from across the bench and never takes her eyes off me. Spindrift and spray flash in the lightning.

The dead girl ties herself to me and whispers wet in my ear: *God hates you for what you did. He will want something soon. More men will rape you while you drown—*

"Bill!" My face and shoulders are jerked backward from the water, back into the boat. Anne's armlock is cinched around my neck. She ties her leg to mine, then hooks our arms before I can roll us overboard. The world goes black.

***

I wake to roar. Engines, not storm, the boat pounding into waves. A rope cinches me to the bench, another to Anne's leg. Carel and Anne bail water. Carel's last Scout is gone. My one eye adds focus. Land materializes off the bow. The captain shouts: "Jamaica; Kingston."

I look behind us at the storm wall, yell at Anne: "Downtown. The dock at Church Street. Myers's building. Will be locked down; empty."

Carel eyes the storm wall, shouts to the captain: "Church Street dock. Not Port Royal."

The captain skirts us past a blurry Lime Cay, windblown and foamy, and ducks into the bay. The waves cut by half. The captain holds his speed straight across the bay toward the spillway at Church Street.

At the concrete dock, we crawl off the boat. Downtown is deserted; usually is if a big storm's coming. The Myers's building is one block inland.

Panting, I point due west two miles and tell the captain: "The best hurricane hole is at Port Henderson—the canals there. No gas, but your boat won't sink if the storm's bad." I give him all the money I have. "Sorry; thanks."

Carel gives the captain money, shoves the boat off the dock, then strips his shirt and wraps his weapons in it. We walk/limp deep shadows to the Myers's nineteenth-century fortress of cut stone. I fumble the keys to the modern lock.

The three of us hurry inside; use a flashlight to climb the wood and stone stairs.

In my boss's palatial office, I open his verandah doors. Framed with civilization, Carel and Anne look half human, monsters from a Faustian play. Each of us grabs a Myers's bottle. I limp outside onto the bayside verandah and chug from mine, lips numb on the bottle.

Anne and Carel take turns washing Haiti into the bathroom sink. I will avoid the bathroom and its ornate framed mirror. I want to puke over the railing but can't make my stomach work.

Carel and Anne reappear, both swallow pills, then spread the weapons on my boss's teakwood desk. Carel begins cleaning the weapons. Bits of his and Anne's conversation drift out. Anne argues that ganja should wait for another day when Carel is stronger.

Carel says, "Make the call. We do the ganja," then toasts his fallen comrades—whom my actions killed.

Anne drinks to each toast. Neither she nor Carel looks at me alone on the verandah.

Carel says, "No reason to keep him. He'll have us in shackles, the first warder who asks."

Anne hugs Carel tight. "We sail together; we finish together. And that includes Bill." Anne leans away to see Carel's eyes, tells him "I mean it," then reaches for the telephone.

I keep my hands on the iron railing and look east toward the Tower Street Penitentiary and the storm approaching. Anne gave me pills in the boat, probably some type of speed, made me swallow them; that's why I'm not shivering or dead. Anne's magic will wear off.

Behind me, Anne hangs up the telephone, then walks out to me. She chugs from her bottle. Carel follows her out. Her hand with the bottle points north, uphill into the Blue Mountains. "We'll ride out the storm up there, do the ganja business, then run. C'mon, we best be goin'." Anne is exhausted, but the phone call put purpose and fear in her eyes and she makes sure I notice. "My people up-mountain already know about the Oloffson. They say that girl in my bed was a Petwo baby."

"A what?"

"A talisman to protect Cambronne. She had the white birthmarks around her eyes and the mark—the red dagger and blue bayonet."

"Sorry, I don't get—"

"She belonged to a *bokor*, Bill. Those are the bad, bitter-loa ones, woman sorcerers from the triangle above Souvenance, if you don't know your Corazón Santo. Worse, the girl was a *mambo's*"—(high priestess)—"daughter. To harm her is to insult God."

Carel laughs, then winces. His eyes harden at the pain. "In Afrika, this vodou *kak* is the *venda*, child body parts and mystics—end of the day, she's religion; just another way to mount an army." Carel sucks a mouthful of rum he has a hard time swallowing. "And it works. Saw kaffers run through AK rounds. Didn't know they were dead."

Anne frowns. "Laugh if you want, Scout, but we just birthed the Crusades in the Corazón Santo. Our friend in the white suit has our names. The Oloffson has Bill's name and this address here." Anne points at my verandah. "Every true believer the *bokor* has in Jamaica is eyes-wide-open and on the street. I'm surprised they aren't already here." Anne stares hard at Carel. "Vodou or not, now or when the storm is over, all manner of well-armed, unhappy mickers will be comin' our way."

I tilt down more rum. "What was her name?"

Anne keeps her eyes on Carel but answers me. "Best you put the baby away."

"What was her fucking name?"

Anne turns slowly, her green eyes as cold as I've ever seen them. *"Ezili."*

THE WINDWARD PASSAGE

NOW

Chapter 19

BILL OWENS

Anne and I stand the flybridge. The *Sazerac Star* crashes the waves at full throttle. We're running east in the high-water channel between Tortuga Island and Haiti's north coast. To starboard are the lights of Port-de-Paix, Haiti's main Coast Guard gunboat station on the north coast. The *Esmeralda* is fifty feet behind us. Dead ahead, somewhere in the black, is Hurricane Lana.

Anne points to Haiti's coastal lights and yells over the engines' drone: "Cubans will've notified the station. Either we're inbound for Haiti's north coast, or running the channel for the Dominican Republic."

No sirens blare from either side of the channel. We blast past the Port-de-Paix station.

For two hours, we run in the rough water into a blackish electric dawn. Just before we reach Cap-Haïtien and her large bay, Anne veers out hard to avoid the city's naval fortifications. For ten brutal minutes both our boats are naked to the open Atlantic. The wind slashes and the waves double.

Two miles past the city lights, at the far eastern rim of Cap-Haïtien's bay, BeBe and the *Esmeralda* overtake us, then veer into the wide bay. Anne follows him in.

The ocean wind and waves quit. We cut our engines, slow-motor toward deep shadows that hide the bay's southern rim a mile ahead.

On our far right, two miles west across the bay, lights twinkle Cap-Haïtien's harbor and shoreline. Anne points there. "Five hundred UN peacekeepers with their backs to this water. Five thousand Ida rebels surround 'em on the land."

"Sounds like the Alamo. They lived twenty minutes."

"Same'll be true here. UN soldiers been plundering every city they occupy. The bunch up at Leclerc was caught running a sex ring with the rebels' children."

Those stories are not new, and not just here.

Anne shows me seven fingers. "We're eight when we get Susie back. Nine if Siri stays the course." A fatal grin brightens Anne's face. "Add the police we'll have to evade as well, and that's six hundred gunmen for each one of us."

Six hundred to one, and she's grinning?

We stop short of the southern rim's shadowy mangrove thatch. Both our boats bob in the inky water. Taller shoulders an AK-47 at the trees. Anne's other gunman does the same. They're aiming at barely discernable bits of colored clothing that mark a lone anchorage. It's midmorning-storm dark. The bats and birds should be slicing the treetops, but aren't. Silhouettes of nervous cormorants and terns watch us instead. Low thunder rumbles out of the mangroves, over us, then out into the bay.

Anne squints into the mangroves. "Drums."

On the *Esmeralda*, BeBe raises binoculars. Our boat's gunmen listen to the unseen drums, their trigger fingers keeping time on milled AK receivers. I pat my pistol. Anne points east over Taller's AK barrel into a dark tree canopy that spreads in every direction.

"The Gryphon is fifty miles into the groves. The hurricane will hit him first and leave him first." Anne pivots 180 degrees west. "Bois Caïman where we're going is seven miles west, five past the city lights . . . but the road is along the picket line between the UN peacekeepers and the rebels. The UN and national police have the low ground and the city to the north, the Ida rebels have the high ground and jungle to the south."

"What about Haiti's army?"

Anne shakes her head. "Bill Clinton invaded after the last coup d'état; disbanded the army in 1994. UN's the only army now. And like I said, the rebels are rabid-mad at 'em." Anne looks at me, then Sistah. "The hurricane's winds will be the rebels' forward assault line, the great equalizer their commander's been waitin' on."

Yep, see it like a movie. The UN peacekeepers will lose 50 percent of their fighting strength to storm defense. The national police will lose 100 percent, saving themselves, their property and families. Our 600-to-1 snowball's chance improves to a mere 250 to 1—not enough to matter. But if Bois Caïman is the "sailor's star" in Eddie O'Hare's poem, then Bois Caïman is where we have to go.

Anne makes a series of hand signals to BeBe, then says to me, "Had we arrived earlier, we could've holed up the boats in there"—she points to the colored bits of cloth—"then trekked the road to take up our clues. Now, best we can do is leave the *Sazerac Star* here, and Sundown to watch her; take the *Esmeralda* up Cap-Haïtien's shantytown river far as we can." Anne points deeper south. "Down there, the river's more sewer than river, but with the water risin' . . . we'll dock, commandeer a vehicle, and make for Bois Caïman, dodge the rebels and UN, ride five miles of bad, overcrowded road."

Sistah shouts at Anne: "Kolonèl Idamante is not 'the rebels.' They are the true Ayiti—"

"What?" I choke on the name. "Who the fuck did you say?"

Anne says, "Easy, Bill."

"Did she say *Kolonèl Idamante*?"

Anne nods. Sistah bristles, her shoulders back.

"That rapist motherfucker is *here*? He's *alive*?"

Sistah growls, sets her feet—Anne pats at Sistah to calm down, then says to me: "Ida rebels are with Idamante. When the USA disbanded the army and the CIA contractors shot the officers, the kolonèl went into the mountains."

I look inland, then out to sea, try to figure how the fuck I got to this fucking moment. "He's *alive*?"

"Aye, Bill. Kolonèl Idamante *is* Haiti's Rebelyon. If he's alive three or four days from now, he'll be Haiti's new president for life."

*** *

The *Esmeralda* is moored upriver in a dark, filthy lagoon that stinks of flood and squalor. Five of us are now crammed into a sweaty, over-full tap-tap school bus, creeping a westbound road jammed with Cap-Haïtien's refugees.

Diesel exhaust billows in headlights and fills the open windows. Anne rides on Sistah's lap. Both have their hair tucked high into Rasta tams. Kerchief veils hide their faces.

On our right, armored UN vehicles and helmeted faces brace for the Rebelyon's first charge out of the trees. The UN's truck-mounted lights shine into those trees but die ten yards in. This is the picket line Anne described.

The final two miles burns an hour we don't have and stalls at the last, isolated UN-defended intersection. I've seen peacekeepers in action. The UN draws their Alamo defenders mostly from poor countries. The country gets reimbursed at $1,000 per day and pays the guy on the ground about $50 every day he's alive. Good use of third-world HR, unless you're the HR. These guys here will run if they get the opportunity. And if they can't run when Hurricane Lana fires the starter's pistol, the poor bastards won't live any longer than Davy Crockett did.

BeBe shoulders through to the front of our bus and tells the tap-tap driver to stop three hundred yards past the last intersection the UN controls.

He does. Five of us file out, run across to the rebel side of the road, and duck into the bush. Assuming Cap-Haïtien is the rebels' main target, we should be just outside the main body of the rebel force.

Sistah grabs Anne's shoulder, stops, and barks: "No."

"Aye." Anne shushes a finger to her lips. "The woods at Bois Caïman."

"No! You say plantation de Mezy."

"Quiet now, Sistah. All of this was plantation de Mezy."

"Bois Caïman is sacred ground; Anne Bonny cannot go there." Sistah jabs a finger at me. "*He* cannot go there."

Anne nods. "And we wouldn't be goin' if there were another way. But the treasure papers say we have to go." Anne points east. "There's a storm comin' and the Rebelyon with it. Sistah can lead quiet or Sistah can stay. Anne Bonny goin' to Bois Caïman."

Sistah fixes Anne with an absolute death stare.

Anne doesn't fold.

Sistah bares her teeth. "Step careful, then, white woman, and only where I go; there are traps."

I hear the safety drop on Taller's AK and BeBe's MAC. We single-file south in waist-high scrub and moonless dark. Sistah refuses a flashlight, leading us through downed fences and tree stumps. Weeds grab for my feet. Malaria buzzes our ears and eyes. Sistah stops. Our flashlights shine waist-high across a clearing we've entered. The light beams die at the surrounding logwood and tamarind forest.

Bois Caïman.

Small offerings gleam in the clearing. Little piles of small animal bones, colored glass, food tins, bits of cloth, and crosses—lots of little crosses, monuments to the devil or a slave revolt that worked.

Anne says, "And the traps, Sistah?"

Sistah glares. "I warn you not to come."

"You'll let Anne Bonny die?"

Sistah hesitates in Anne's face. "No." Sistah nods to me. *"Him."*

My fingers squeeze pistol grip and flashlight. I fan again with the flashlight and rerun the last half of this treasure clue from memory:

> *Forever bound by Code Noir*
> *Maroons, multâre, and mara-bou*
> *Births the crocodile as sailor's star*
>
> *A star to fear And to find*
> *the one true race*
> *who grows the vine.*

Sistah stays put. Four of us and our three flashlights soft-step into the clearing. My companions give me a wider berth than usual. Unfortunately, I don't know what I'm looking for—inductive reasoning being a grade below mind reading. But based upon Eddie O'Hare's style so far, I'm *guessing* the clue will somehow resemble, or incorporate, his tortoise-shell drawing.

The tortoise shell has what I've decided is a coffin-nail vodou cross. Anne is fifty-fifty on that guess. She's 100 percent that the shell drawing was Tortuga Island and that the tortoise's head and flippers pointed here.

Anne's also 100 percent that whatever's here in Bois Caïman is the "sailor's star" we're supposed to fear and to find.

I'm hoping one of us stumbles over a giant stone turtle with the inscription "Game over. Treasure here" before the shit hits the fan from five directions.

We spread out, searching amid the scrub and booby traps for thirty minutes.

Distant lightning splits the eastern sky. Hurricane Lana's thunder rumbles across us. I stumble upon a low shack of rusted tin and wood scrap. Next to the shack, my flashlight lands on a foot, connected to a leg—I jump back; the foot's connected to a body prone in the grass. Our other two light beams converge on me, then the body. A man's body. Next to him is a bottle. A long snake crawls across his leg and into the brush. I shine my light into the man's face. Old, white-haired, a few teeth.

He stirs, pats at the light, then swats and rolls over, mumbling Kreyol.

Anne steps to him and kicks lightly at his hip. In English, Anne says, "Old man, is there a stone? A tortoise? A monument to Dutty Boukman and the Rebelyon?" She kicks him lightly again.

"Ajam sdk afaaa."

"I have rhum, old man. Barbancourt."

He rolls to his side, then up to sitting, roofing his eyes against the flashlights. His hand trembles. He shouts Kreyol at Anne.

Anne interprets. "He is the keeper of the slave Rebelyon. Is paid to talk."

I belt my pistol, dig out $20 US and push the bill into his hand. "Is there a turtle? Would've been here since you were a boy."

Anne translates. The old man looks up, trying to see her behind the light, then me. His eyes are clear. No part of this guy is drunk.

Anne jumps back, stiff-arms her pistol at him, and yells to all of us: "On your guard."

The old man switches to barely decipherable French English, wants to know how I know about the turtle.

"Boukman came to me in a dream; told me that I must find his turtle."

"Why you? A white devil?"

"Because, motherfucker—" I stop mid-threat. It's not this guy's fault I'm back in Haiti. "So I could kneel and ask him what I can do for Haiti."

"You speak American." The old man straightens, more interested, probably because all Americans are rich. He glances to Anne, then me: "No turtle; you are fools."

Anne keeps her pistol on him. "Ezili Dantor is no fool." In English, Anne says to me, "Show him your lifeline. Then my hair."

I shine my light on **Ezili** carved into my palm.

The old man squints at my hand.

I shine the light on Anne's tam. She pulls it, spilling the flaming red hair.

Anne says, "Pétion-Ville, 1986. I rose from hell—Anne Bonny, just like the mambos say I did—and took the Baby." Anne turns and yells across the clearing, "Sistah!"

The old man is frozen.

Out of the dark, Sistah appears behind Anne. Anne rips off Sistah's tam and veil. Sistah glares Anne with the birthmarked eyes. Anne pulls Sistah into the old man's vision and shouts: "See? It is *I* who bring the Baby! I bring the Rebelyon back, not Idamante!"

The old man's eyes widen at Sistah's skin color and birthmarks. Both arms jerk up to cover his face and head.

"Tell me. Or tonight when I take Ayiti from the white man, I take all your family to hell with them."

Head down, the old man points into the forest. Anne's light beam follows his finger.

Sistah spits on the old man for his assistance, yelling insults in Kreyol. He ducks lower, covering his head.

Anne glances to me. "On your horse, Bill, we've wind and company comin'." She cuts to the old man, then Sistah. Anne stares hard at Sistah, but speaks to me: "And careful now, somethin' isn't as she should be."

BeBe and I slow-step toward a dirt trail that leads into the thicket.

Flashlight sweep—

Ten paces up the overgrown trail, we reach a muddy creek. I hear something and stop; BeBe stops behind me. We sweep both banks with our lights. My beam lands on two pairs of wide-set eyes in the water.

BeBe jerks me back.

My foot slips. I stumble to a knee and my light shines the ground where my next step would've been. Two inches from my knee is the exposed rim of a brick-edged pit . . . covered with *fresh* thatch.

I stand, easing backward with BeBe, his light now on the wide-set eyes in the creek.

BeBe says, "Yellows. Six to eight foot, and fast. Put your light on the crocs."

I do. He shines his light on the pit's exposed edge, steps around me, grabs a heavy stone and drops it on the pit's thatch. The thatch collapses and the stone thuds ten feet to the pit's bottom. Sharp sticks point upright.

BeBe says, "Man pit."

He finds a smaller rock and tells me to do the same. We throw them at the crocs. The crocs splash backward. We jump the man pit, run through the creek, and scramble to the top of the other bank.

I reshine my light in the creek. BeBe finds us two long branches to prod the ground ahead of where we will walk. Insects stick to our skin and buzz our lights.

After sixty feet of forest and no more man pits, we stumble upon two piles of rocks stacked into crude pyramids. Stabbed into the top of each pile is a bayonet. Both bayonet grips are wrapped with red and blue wire.

Beyond the pyramids, my light lands on a flat, three-foot, oval-shaped stone. A cross is etched into it. Around the cross is an outline of a splayed, four-legged animal.

Not a turtle; might be a pig, but the cross is unmistakable.

BeBe mumbles, "Black pig . . ."

I belt my pistol, dig out Eddie O'Hare's drawing of the turtle with the cross on it, shine my light on the drawing—

—then back to the stone. The cross matches the drawing.

BeBe says: "Black pig is what Ezili Dantor sacrifice at Bois Caïman. Use its blood to start the slave Rebelyon, kill all the white masters—1791."

I lean my light on the ground. "Grab your end; this has to be it."

BeBe doesn't move.

"C'mon, man, you're a pirate. You don't believe this vodou shit."

BeBe glances the **Ezili** carving on my hand, doesn't move.

I try to budge one end of the stone but can't, then grab one of the bayonets in the rock pyramids. The bayonet won't come out. I drop to my knees, dig with both hands under my end of the stone, and try again. Nope.

"Anne!" My hand fans insects away from my mouth and eyes. "Send some muscle up here."

No one answers. No one comes up the trail.

"Anne! You there?"

BeBe waves for Eddie O'Hare's poem. I hand the paper to him, then grab my light and shine it back down the trail for Anne.

BeBe shines his light into the thickets that surround us. "Dis fuckery gonna kill us. Sure as shit."

"Anne!" I pull my pistol. "Anne, goddammit! Are you there?"

"Comin'."

"Watch out! At the creek. There's a man pit . . . and crocodiles."

We hear movement. It's already on our side of the creek before we see a light beam, then Anne behind us, Taller with her.

She says, "Had to calm Sistah. Have we found the gold?" Anne fans away the insects. BeBe hands her the poem and drawing. She looks at him, doesn't like what she sees, then points Taller to the stone. "Be quick about it."

Taller and I dig out the stone, then move it. BeBe and Anne shine lights into the hole. The sides are bricked like the man pit. At the bottom are animal bones, a hook-blade knife . . . and a Barbancourt bottle. I lean in to reach for the bottle—

"Wait!" Anne jerks me back.

Her light slides the four walls and the bottom. She grabs a branch and moves the bottle from left to right, careful not to disturb the bones. "Okay. Just the bottle, Bill, and quickly."

I grab the bottle. It doesn't have the same wax-sealed cork as the ones we found in Chicago and Hunts Bay. I shake the bottle; it clinks. The cork loosens easily and opens with a musty pop. I pour five square-head nails and a smudged, charred page of old linen stationery into my hand. The stationery has a series of numbers in the middle—map coordinates—and a drawing of a five-pointed star.

Okay . . . five nails; five-pointed star.

Anne's chin touches my shoulder. She points at the drawing. "The 'sailor's star'? Except there'd be no need for a star to follow . . . if we're holdin' map coordinates."

"Yeah. Doesn't feel right." I match Eddie O'Hare's stationery clue that led us here. The new clue's handwriting and drawing could be a match. "Any idea where these coordinates are?"

"They'd be where we'd be going directly from here. First numbers mean it'll be Haiti for certain. Can't be exact on the remainder till we get back to the boat."

"Doesn't feel right."

Anne looks at me, then the nails and new stationery, then beyond BeBe into the trees. "You're thinkin' she's a lie, Bill? Like led Susie to the Camagüey Breaks?"

BeBe fast-scans the trees in every direction.

"Don't know." I roll the nails in my palm, then stand into a sudden chill. "Can't say for sure, but theses nails, the drawing . . . just doesn't feel 'artful' like Eddie, like a white guy from outta town."

Anne does a slow 360 with her flashlight. "Gentlemen, if we've come here in error, misread our poem"—she points her pistol back toward the road—"then the old man works for the Gryphon. The old man would have a cell phone and has used it by now."

"Shit." I squint at the paper. "Then these coordinates are where the Gryphon wants us to go. Probably got traps all over Haiti with these same buried coordinates . . . everywhere a treasure hunter might stumble . . . or be led."

Anne turns to Taller. "We go. AK on point; BeBe on the follow."

We trek back to the road. The old man's gone. We hide in a dark uphill curve and prepare to commandeer the first vehicle from the westbound exodus and turn it around toward our boats. As they say in the Boy Scout manuals, *We need to get the fuck out of here.*

Eastbound headlights. High, like a UN armored vehicle heading against traffic, back into the city. We shrink deeper into the bush. A three-truck convoy rumbles past. Heavy trucks with uniformed reinforcements.

BeBe whispers, "National police."

The UN's budget is paying the national police; and for sure those payments are making the police commanders rich. But no telling whose side the rank-and-file police will be on after the storm passes and the rebels start shooting.

Anne tells BeBe we have to grab a car.

BeBe says we can't; another driver will phone in that we hijacked the car. The first UN checkpoint will shoot us.

One hundred yards up the main road, a sweaty man tips a gas can into a rusted flatbed in his yard. The truck is packed with possessions and family. BeBe tells the startled driver that we will pay six month's wages for a fifteen-minute, two-mile ride to Cap-Haïtien, or we'll shoot him and steal his truck.

***

The family man and his truck have dropped us and gone. On foot, Anne stops our column just shy of the lagoon basin where we moored the *Esmeralda*. The sewer stench is almost unbreathable.

All five of us crouch in the dark outside the roofless scavenger shacks we left two hours ago. We can't see the *Esmeralda*. She's invisible with her black hull and decks. We can see what remains of the dock that the rising lagoon hasn't covered.

Taller aims his AK; BeBe flashes a penlight at where the dock disappears.

A small light flashes back three times.

BeBe ducks to our right to scout the mangrove bank for trap. He signals for Taller to track behind him. Sistah remains motionless with Anne and me. We aim cocked pistols at the dark.

Anne says, "Don't be taken alive."

Bugs are half the air. I breathe short with my free hand over my nose and mouth. Three minutes. No Gryphon. No gunshots.

BeBe's penlight flashes on our right.

Dead ahead, the *Esmeralda*'s engines fire.

Anne says, "Once I'm aboard, count to five, then run to me." She sprints the dock and disappears into the dark.

Sistah and I count to five, run the dock, splashing water. The gunwale's outline materializes, we jump over. BeBe and Taller do the same.

We cast off with no running lights, aiming weapons in three directions. Anne idles us into the lagoon, then into the river; she'll check the coordinates we found once we're safer.

The river is fifty feet wide now and rising. Barrel-drum fires light the shanties that cram both shores. The shanties' rusted metal roofs are stacked with bags. I ask.

BeBe says, "Human shit; nowhere but the roof to put it."

Anne skirts debris slicks bunching on the storm tide that's pushing everything inland. The stench knots my stomach and waters my eyes. Easy to forget how precious little some people have.

I borrow BeBe's penlight to reread Eddie O'Hare's papers. In a world as fucked up as this, the Gryphon setting a trap at Bois Caïman is the *good* outcome. If Bois Caïman was a fake, then there was no O'Hare clue there that's gone missing—I fucked up, misread the real clue we found in Jamaica. Simple as that.

I go with that possibility because it's the only 'truth' I might be able to handicap, then reread each sentence of the Jamaica clue.

Eyes shut, I whisper O'Hare's words out loud and listen to the words—rhymes—cadence. We were on O'Hare's trail in Jamaica; then he sent us *here*, but not to Bois Caïman? My teeth grind. The goddamn clues fit too well for Bois Caïman to be wrong.

So what's the fucking answer, *Bill*?

Voices rise and fall from both riverbanks, frightened and angry. BeBe nudges my shoulder, "Get your pistol up. River be narrow ahead. Kill anyone swimmin' who comes to the boat."

Our wake ripples layers of trash as we enter the narrows, the poverty and desperation so close I can taste it. In one day, Hurricane Lana will erase all this and wash these people out to sea. I tight-grip Eddie's papers, aim my pistol at the dark water behind us, then lean backward to the back of Anne's head. "You said the UN had a $600 million budget. What the fuck did they spend it on?"

Anne stays focused on hidden obstacles that could sink us. She whispers, "They've their own treasure; $200 million for AIDS alone on top of your six hundred; $800 million total to fight over. Idamante will be a rich man. Revolution and Rebelyon have a way of bein' the same story, different name."

On my left, Sistah rocks side to side. BeBe looks at her. I look away from my pistol barrel, toward the debris shoreline and hovels that won't be here tomorrow. "What's the Gryphon's share of the $800 million?"

Anne's Rasta tam shakes an inch. "Like I told you, the Gryphon stays separate of Babylon's business. That distance is why each new government allows him his kingdom." Anne turns her chin to her shoulder. "I'd be studyin', Bill. Talkin' won't fix where you have us."

The river's width triples to 150 feet. Anne says we're in the mouth of the Shada shantytown river. On our left, larger fires scorch-light the river's western shore. Shadows jump and dance. Anne veers away toward the opposite bank.

We pass a blind curve. UN riot lights illuminate a long perimeter of razor wire and UN vehicles behind it. Looks like a riverfront prison.

BeBe says, "Airport. Five-thousand-foot landing strip. Too short for cargo planes."

Anne says, "She's a resupply base. Supplies the UN's frontline fortifications downriver at the harbor." Anne points at the razor wire and fences. "Idamante won't come at this base from this river; he'll come from the mangrove swamp, beyond where we anchored the *Sazerac*, the same moment his rebels hit Cap-Haïtien." Anne pauses, glances at Sistah. "Siri's one of Idamante's commanders; she'll either be here or Port-au-Prince."

"That's good, isn't it? If she's here?"

Anne nods. "If she's not all caught up in Rebelyon"—Anne glances at Sistah again—"thinkin' our gold belongs to the Rebelyon's treasury."

Past the base and its lights, we spill out of the river into the bay. Anne hits the throttles. We veer hard right for the *Sazerac Star* hidden in the mangroves on the bay's east side. I belt my pistol and return to O'Hare's pages. My light shines the three poems—Chicago, Jamaica, Bois Caïman.

I shuffle the pages and shine again. The drawing on Eddie's turtle *is* the same as the etching on the pig stone.

Why do that if it's not the clue? Think, goddammit. Handicap. Inductive reasoning. Eddie O'Hare's a horseplayer speaking in poetry, but he's still a horseplayer.

> *The pieces float; the pieces drift*
> *Turn back*
> *If I did not send you*
> *No false heart survives my gift.*

Okay, that verse is a threat, not a clue. Unless . . .

Does "false heart" mean something other than the obvious? "The pieces float; the pieces drift"—shipwrecks, right?

False heart and a shipwreck?

Did someone's dishonesty or betrayal (false heart) wreck a ship in this bay? On this coast? A slave ship . . . like the *Whydah*? Anne knew of none and she's a pirate with an Oxford education.

Okay. Maybe "false heart" is a place?

I look up to my left, then right. No answers appear in the dark over Cap-Haïtien. What about "survive my gift"? What gift?

Eddie O'Hare's a shithead lawyer, a horseplayer who robbed and murdered his partners. *Gift* is your ego talking, right, Eddie? Eddie doesn't answer. I run through it a tenth time.

Forever bound by Code Noir
Maroons, multâre, and mara-bou
Births the crocodile as sailor's star

A star to fear And to find
the one true race
who grows the vine.

"Code Noir" is slavery stuff. So are "Maroons, multâre, and mara-bou."

The slaves meet at "the crocodile"—Bois Caïman. There, they "birth" the Rebelyon.

The "sailor's star" is the goddamn North Star, right?

Out loud, I say: "So you go to Bois Caïman to 'find' guidance . . . from the slaves."

Simple. *Has* to be right. Both verses are about runaway slaves and that night at Bois Caïman in 1791. And the fucking clue is there, at Bois Caïman. I know it. The bottle is a 99 percent plant, but the stone isn't. The stone is telling us something we needed to know. Just like the HMS *Primrose* plaque did, sent us from Spanish Town to the Guzik grave. A midpoint in the clue, a waystation.

Anne says, "'Code Noir,' 'Maroons, multâre, and mara-bou' are multiracial. What if 'the one true race' doesn't mean slaves—but the black race?"

Blink. Hadn't thought of that. Why would white-man Eddie O'Hare think blacks were the one true race?

"Yeah. Meaning it isn't blacks who are growing the vine." *What if Eddie's hiding his horse's workouts, showing the horse but not the speed?* I touch Anne's shoulder. "Who's the one true race, the pure one? Down here?"

Anne repeats: "'The one true race who plants the vine'? That'd be the French, God bless the sanctimonious bastards."

"Right. The slaves weren't a race, not to the French colonial masters. The slaves were farm animals."

"So it's the French who grow the vines—"

"To make what? Wine. The colonial masters lived for wine; it was their demonstrable status, *everywhere* in the world, right?"

"Aye."

"And the French planters wouldn't have allowed the slaves to *make* the wine. Slaves could've picked the grapes, but that was it."

Anne nods.

"The first line of the last verse—"

"The *A* in *And* is capitalized, like a new sentence. Read it like this: 'And to find the one true race who grows the vine.' Get it?"

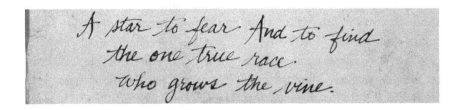

A star to fear. And to find the one true race. Who grows the vine.

Anne shrugs, trying to see it. "We're supposed to find . . . *the French?*"

Her words hit me like a train:

Plant the vine.
Harvest the grapes.
Make the wine.

"We're supposed to find a fucking winery." I hug Anne from behind. "The Jamaica clue wants us to sail past Tortuga to the sailor's star at Bois Caïman, just like we did. From there, the star would point us to 'the one true race who grows the vine.' That's it. The 'star' is the pig stone we found. The stop we made *wasn't* bullshit. The bottle was planted. For sure, the bottle was planted. And if the pig stone wasn't replaced with a fake—"

"Oh, I'm guessin' she's real."

I visualize the stone with the splayed pig outline and the cross inside. "What direction was the pig stone pointing?"

Sistah turns 180 to me, full in my face.

I lean back, checking Sistah's hands—she has a cell phone, no knife, so I keep talking. "C'mon, Anne; see it? Boukman rallied the slaves to Bois Caïman to start the Rebelyon, right?"

"Aye."

"The slaves had to come from French plantations, right? Close by, right?"

Anne nods.

"All of the plantations would've made wine, or tried. The Bois Caïman pig stone pointed to the plantation we want. There'll be a wine cellar. A safe place for Eddie to bury his gold. See?"

I'm so happy I want to dance—

Anne doesn't hug me off my feet. She squints at the tree-line silhouette we're approaching, then nails the engines into reverse. Sistah and I slam forward into Anne.

Anne roars us backward into the dark. Her boat planes; Anne slows; we stop one hundred feet farther out from the mangroves.

Taller and the other gunman level their AKs back on the trees. BeBe sweeps a high-power light on the tree thatch to the left of the moored *Sazerac Star*, then the trees to the right, then focuses on the *Sazerac Star*'s deck.

The extra gasoline drums are gone. What remains of Sundown, the man Anne left behind, is naked, stretched across the cabin door in an X, no feet, no hands, bloody holes for eyes.

"Jesus." I pull my pistol.

BeBe cuts the light and whispers patois. Taller and the other gunman set down their AKs and slip over the side. Sistah is rigid, eyes straight ahead, cell phone still in one hand, her knife now in the other.

Ten minutes pass in sweaty, dark silence. Sundown would've talked, told whoever cut him up everything he could in the almost three hours we've been gone.

A light blinks from the *Sazerac Star*.

BeBe waits, then blinks a light back.

Engines fire in the mangroves, but no running lights. The engine noise rumbles out of the mangroves toward us. BeBe and I aim at the sounds. The engine rumble increases until the *Sazerac Star*'s stern begins to silhouette off our port bow, then slow-motors past us into the dark.

Anne keeps pace in reverse. A mile deeper into the bay, we're broadside to the *Sazerac* and stop. BeBe eyes the crucified body stretched across the cabin door, then tells Taller and the other gunman to cut down Sundown.

They do. BeBe hops off the *Esmeralda* onto the *Sazerac Star*, pistol in one hand, marine flashlight in the other, and begins to search. Taller and the other gunman aim their AKs at the mangroves they can no longer see.

From our bridge, Anne watches the search, one hand on the *Esmeralda*'s throttles, her pistol in the other. Sistah remains stone-still, eyes on the mangroves, her left hand gripping and regripping her cell phone.

BeBe checks the bloody pockets of Sundown, then reaches across the water to hand Anne something. She accepts the object, stares at it, glances at me, then slides the object into her pocket.

BeBe cuts his light. Only his eyes and silhouette are visible. He says, "They gone through everythin'; tore it up lookin' for somethin'." He nods at me and Eddie's papers, then fans one finger at Anne. "Piccard and the Gryphon done this. Boat worth too much for anyone else to leave behind."

Anne says, "Aye."

BeBe says, "Goin' below. See to it that everything cook-and-curry."

"Careful, BeBe. The Gryphon *wants* us to have our boat back. Likely we don't want her." Anne eases the *Esmeralda* ten feet away from the *Sazerac Star*. She turns to me. "Keep your pistol on the starboard water. Crocodile or man, anything swimmin', you shoot it."

I squint for threat but can barely see past my hand.

BeBe splashes his light through the *Sazerac Star*'s cabin. Our engines bubble salt water. Gasoline fumes linger in the humidity.

BeBe yells, "Popper!" Then climbs through the main cabin's doorway way too fast for it to be good.

Anne hits him with her light. BeBe blinks at the glare and stumbles, both hands gingerly cradling a metal canister—a military-type explosive connected to a cell phone. "Gryphon gon' ransom us on dis boat for the maps on yours." BeBe raises the bomb to throw it over the Sazerac's other side. He slips on the deck in Sundown's blood.

Blinding white light.

Roar and concussion blow me over the side and the *Esmeralda*'s black hull halfway into the air. It crashes down, slides over, and buries me underwater.

Gasp. Claw. Choke. I explode to the surface. Suck for air and flail my arms to stay there. Twenty feet away, the *Sazerac Star* is flames to the waterline. A hand grabs me from behind.

Anne shouts: "Bill! In the boat!"

I suck more air and scramble up the ladder. Sistah is prone in the bow, fanning a marine light across the water. No survivors flail in the beam. Anne yells, "BeBe! Taller! Lon!"

No answer.

Anne yells the names again, sees no one in the water, and pounds the wheel. "God*damn*!" She hits the throttles and leaps the *Esmeralda* past the flames into the night.

Chapter 20

BILL OWENS

We're mid-bay on the *Esmeralda*. Pieces of Anne's friends dot the water. Smoldering debris and burning oil carbonizes the air. Three survivors total—Anne, Sistah, and me. My heart rate's still at 150. Anne has one hand on the throttles, the other squeezing the grip of a .45.

Her face can't hide the emotion. She looks away, forces herself to focus, then back. "We've not enough fuel to outrun the storm. Worse, there's nowhere to hide where the Gryphon won't overrun us. I've tried Siri four times since we left Jamaica and get no answer. Either we chance a dock raid in Cap-Haïtien for two fuel drums that'll at least allow us to run *with* the storm, or we hunt Susie and the gold now, with what we have, and bear the consequences."

"I'm right, Anne; the gold's in a winery."

Sistah, armed only with her phone, spits over the side.

Anne extends her hand to me. "I'll have the poems and coordinates from Bois Caïman. Keep your eyes on the water. He's out there."

I pass Anne the papers, keep my pistol and eyes on the water. Anne maps the coordinates, exhales deep, spreads the remaining papers between us, glances at the lights of Cap-Haïtien dead ahead, then back to the last poem. Anne rereads the verses, then asks me to handicap Eddie O'Hare and the winery again.

I do. When I finish, she nods. "Could be ya have it."

"What about the coordinates?"

Anne shakes her head. "Only a fool like Dave Grossfeld would go where they lead."

Sistah points with her cell phone. "Before Boukman birth Rebelyon at Bois Caïman was Messiah Mackandal. Mackandal kill six thousand white men, women, and children." Her eyes add pride. "Back then, de Mezy sugar own Messiah Mackandal and all the land roun' Bois Caïman. One plantation, no wine there, no wine cellar."

I look sideways at Sistah. "They were *French* for chrissake."

Anne balks. "Sistah born in Haiti, was a nun in Haiti, and fought Rebelyon in Haiti."

"Your girlfriend's got some issues with what she knows and what she doesn't." I make a small medicine bottle with my thumb and finger. A medicine bottle that burned with the *Sazerac Star.* "Among other things."

Anne snorts hard to clear her eyes and nose, then squints at the poem. "Don't recall another plantation, but there could've been another, or several, in three hundred years. Only way to know is in town." Anne glances at Sistah. "To check the records."

Sistah thinks about it, then nods, suddenly with the program.

None of this feels right. "Where are the records?"

Anne shrugs and looks at Sistah.

"Town square."

I look at the lights on shore. Not too bad from here. Up close, Cap-Haïtien will be mayhem. "Which direction did the pig stone point?"

Anne says, "West."

"Is there anything remotely like a winery west of Bois Caïman now? A big plantation house?"

Sistah doesn't answer.

I look to Anne. "Where was the de Mezy plantation? Must've been big if Sistah's right and they were the only sugar plantation for miles."

Sistah stares. Anne nudges her for an answer. Sistah says, "Town. The records will say."

Nobody in their right mind wants to go to town, but now *town* is Sistah's answer for everything. I glance at Anne but she doesn't seem hinky about it.

"Screw *town*. Anyone who lived here should know where the biggest plantation house in the area was." I nod at Sistah. "Including her."

Anne gathers Sistah into her arms, hugging Sistah's back to her chest. "If Sistah says she doesn't know, she doesn't know."

Sistah glares at me. "If de Mezy keep a plantation house, it stand in the breezes on Mountain Morne Rouge. G'wan. Find it there. Find the national police too. If the police there camped strong, they kill you for comin'."

Anne nods. "Hadn't thought of that. National police have to bivouac somewhere so it at least *appears* they intend to participate. Could be high ground anywhere. No way to tell till we get near."

Sistah leans out of Anne's arms and closer to my face. "And if the police gon, Mackandal's spirit kill you for comin' jus' like he kill all the owners of de Mezy." Smile. "Unless Idamante take you off the road first and bwoy-fuck you. Again."

Anne jerks Sistah back and spins the two of them toward the bow. I stare at the back of their heads . . . and don't aim my pistol.

Anne tells the dark, "Sistah's just mad at things. Sundown, BeBe, Taller, and Lon were her family. And good men they were." Anne turns to face me, keeping Sistah behind her. "Can ya turn that pistol for me?"

I notice my pistol is now aimed at Sistah. My hand agrees to lower the pistol.

"Good. We've a hard, difficult decision to make." Anne favors me with a small portion of *the smile*, then a plan.

I listen, then repeat her plan in the worst tone I can muster: "*You want me and that psycho to go ashore . . . together?* Not you and her, *me and her?*"

Anne nods.

"I'll grant you that a redheaded white woman with a bounty on her head might attract unwanted attention, but I'm not going *anywhere* with your unmedicated psycho girlfriend. She can tell me where the records are and I'll find a way to get to them on my own. If that doesn't work for you, get your best disguise ready and I'll be here when you get back."

"Bill, you don't speak the Kreyol. You're not black. And you don't know the city. Any trouble at all—and there's bound to be some, given all the circumstances comin' at the country—you'll go mad hatter, start shootin' *like you did at the Oloffson*, and we'll all be lost."

"And her being with me is gonna change that? Jesus, she'll *start* it. Rebelyon-religion meltdown is her bread and butter."

Sistah sits the gunwale, silent and calm, no hint of meltdown.

Anne says, "Come up with a better plan and we'll do her."

Exhale. City glance. Pitch-black bay glance—scary, scary shit in every direction. Clues glance. Anne's right. If I'm going to solve this puzzle with the resources available, admitting what's actually available is the next step. "Okay." I focus on Anne's emerald eyes, hoping they blind me like they always did. "Make me a believer."

***

Anne points Sistah to the *Esmeralda*'s bow to test the anchor.

I climb off the stern into the inflatable dinghy. Anne's at the motor, whispers, her lips on my ear, "At the square, keep Sistah away from the cathedral. She was sick with it once."

"What?"

"Where they hung her. After accusing the bishop—"

Sistah returns from the bow and drops into the dinghy. She coils the mooring rope at her feet, looks before she sits, and says, "The poem maps?"

Anne cocks her head a slow inch, then answers, "Stayin' on the *Esmeralda*."

I push off. Anne motors us toward the city's seawall outside the main harbor.

Closer in, the lights begin to define Cap-Haïtien's industrial harbor. Bits of sound echo out onto the water—muffled music, engines, fear.

Lightning crackles behind us to the east. Sweat beads my forehead. The air's heavy. My mouth's dry, my skin black with lamp tar.

The sounds from shore loom louder, echoing across the water in disjointed screeches of mankind and machinery. Anne points left to the seawalls of the main harbor, lit by a battery of riot lights like the airfield on the river was. Armored UN trucks and blue-helmeted soldiers line the harbor's outer seawalls.

Farthest from us, a stacked container ship is docked in the harbor at the main pier. One hundred feet of concrete separates the ship's bow from a splash-lit fence lined with spirals of razor wire on top and at the bottom. UN soldiers defend their side.

Outside the fence is Cap-Haïtien's jammed waterfront boulevard. One thousand kaleidoscope-colored Haitians shout and crush, hoping for a way onto the ship. Some wave large white flags at the UN soldiers. Some brandish machetes.

I've seen CNN video of overloaded boats from Haiti capsized in the Florida Straits. If a thousand people pile on the deck of that container ship and Hurricane Lana comes through the harbor . . . What the fuck are these Haitians thinking? I look inland for conditions that must be worse than an open deck in a hurricane, then at Anne. She's shaking her head, either for them or for all of us.

The outer harbor's lights and UN fortifications fade on our left. Dead ahead, the city's outline materializes and seems to shiver in the gloom. A crumbling seawall defends this section of the waterfront's boulevard and the three- and four-story colonial façades above it. The air smells and tastes like a barn fire where horses died.

Anne points us at a barren outcrop fronted by riprap. Anne asks Sistah.

Sistah says, "A park, the day lot for donkeys, for the ladies who bring their goods to the Iron Market."

One hundred yards out, Anne makes a slow pass on the park. The park is a triangle and slopes downward from the boulevard above. Drum fires splash orange light. Shapes in the park shrink and tower in the shadows. Panicked, frightened shapes. Angry and drunken shapes, shapes that could, and would, swamp a dinghy with a motor in seconds.

Anne has Sistah test-call the cell phone Anne will keep. International would be hopeless, but on-island might work another day if it works now. On the third try, Anne's phone rings. Anne reads her screen, then drops her phone back into a waterproof pouch hanging from her neck. She reaches for the outboard's throttle, then stops and stares ashore, listening, trying to read something she can't quite hear or see, mumbling to herself: "Aye, Gran Anne, it's dark water we sail. The witchin' hour's upon us."

Anne keeps her hand on the throttle but adds no gas. I look for the threat but can barely see the water except for patches of oil that reflect the light. Anne finally gives in and points the dinghy southwest. Her voice sharpens. "Eight blocks from the park to the square. Pick up a bottle, but don't look drunk. Follow Sistah." Anne grabs my wrist, stares hard at me, and mouths, *"No cathedral."*

I nod an inch.

Anne hesitates a last time, then swings the dinghy hard left toward the riprap on the park's far north side and runs us in fast.

Garbage-and-debris slicks ring the riprap. Sistah jumps first. Her fingers grab the rocks but can't hold their edges; she fights for purchase.

I jump and pancake against the riprap. The rocks are slimy and stink of human waste. All of me grips tight, pulling my face to the rocks. Flame shadows crackle above my head. Kreyol voices shout. Cinders fall on my shoulders, the char mixing with the bay's stench. Four feet away, Sistah is spidered across the rocks. I grab higher. Four pulls, face in the stink, and I'm to the top.

Blink. Focus. Reset the pistol in my belt.

Sistah climbs up and over, crouches near me, quick-reads the park while tying a kerchief across her nose and face. Like the "new her" on the boat, "meltdown" is no longer part of her act. She coils, then sprints into the park's loud voices, barrel fires, and shadows. I follow, head down, bumping through shapes and shadows to the park's edge.

Overloaded tap-tap buses cram the boulevard. Tailpipes spew diesel and unmuffled roar. Hordes of people crush in every direction and no direction. Bright clothes, black faces, a goddamn street carnival of drunks and thugs . . . and rag people with baskets and—

A loudspeaker blares in Kreyol. It's a PA, mounted on top of a gray UN armored personnel carrier trapped in the bus traffic.

Sistah jumps into the boulevard between the buses, edging, shouldering, head down, hands up, and finally across into the city. She looks left, then right. Open sewer runs at the curb. Half-naked kids play in the offal. I run through the traffic and push her forward out of the light.

The street is a river of sweaty people, arms above their heads; black faces, white eyes. Hands grip Sistah's shoulders and mine. A man grabs at Sistah's dreads; her knife slashes and he screams. We push and shove. Fistfights erupt to our left. Glint of her knife. Men yelling. Urine. Sweat. Red paint is stenciled on the buildings:

Idamante!
Rebelyon!

Sistah veers left onto a lettered street. Hundreds of sandals and shoes kick up spalled-concrete dust that will soon be rivers of mud. The dust stings my eyes and lungs. Coughing, we fight through the first block. Sistah turns right at the corner of a shuttered building and onto a numbered street. Freshly painted **Idamante!** drips on both sides of the building. Crowds crush toward us. We hop from doorway to doorway, then left onto another lettered street sloshed with foul water. Sistah pushes through the crowd, farther and farther until the narrow street bursts into the open.

The square.

Two blocks long on each side, and packed with . . . revelers?

Bright-colored clothes roil like boiling gumbo. Music pounds from powerful speakers hidden by the huge crowd. Sistah adds posture, eyes locked on the white colonial edifice that dominates the square from two blocks away—has to be the Cathedral Notre Dame. Skunk weed and sweat is all I can smell. Black faces shout; bodies mosh tribal; faces drink from plastic bags.

Radio crackle. Foreign voice. Military.

I spin away. My feet tangle with an old man and woman crouched on the pavement against the wall. Six UN soldiers push between Sistah and me, rifles ready. I jump from the sidewalk into the roiling square. The revelers swallow me. I slice left, then right, push through crowd, find a spot, and look back.

The six UN soldiers in the square are outnumbered one hundred to one.

Sistah is coming toward me and away from the cathedral. Ten revelers bang me into a statue, a tall figure splashed in red and caped with a white sheet. Five Haiti national police burst through the revelers, club two with rifle butts, and rip the sheet off the statue. I stumble away, slide deeper into the square, and am banged into a lone iron column. It has an iron plaque at eye level: "Place d'Armes, 2001."

Blink. *2001?* I look down. Underneath the roiling boots and sandals and bare feet is smooth concrete and cobblestones.

All new.

New, like rebuilt. *Broke and starving, so the government tore down the buildings and rebuilt the square?* I do a frantic 360. All new. Whatever buildings were here for plantation records aren't here now. Sistah pops through the revelers and stops four feet away, seemingly unthreatened by the mayhem.

I shout over the bedlam: "Your records building is gone. Right?"

Sistah scans over the heads that surround us.

"The square's all new. We have a plan B for the history of plantations?"

"Messiah Mackandal's death stone is not new." She zigzags into the mosh.

"Wait, goddammit!" A large white flag tied to a bamboo pole unfurls between us. Stamped in red is: **Idamante!** and an outline of the rapist's face. I'm twenty feet behind Sistah, skirmishing through Haitians wild-eyed on *end-of-the-world* coming at them from three directions.

The music quits when I get past the flag. A man's voice exhorts the crowd in Kreyol. I look up to a high stage. A national police commander is centered on the stage behind a pole microphone. He's backed by twenty helmeted commandos with automatic rifles. Sistah keeps moving. I catch three of the commander's Kreyol phrases, which translate to "white man," "white woman," and "money or reward."

The crowd pays no attention. Two more **Idamante!** flags unfurl, and the crowd roars approval.

"RE-BEL-YON!"

"RE-BEL-YON!"

Eight commandos leap off the stage and fight toward the flags.

Sistah stops mid-square at a lone palm tree, just south of a wall built of PA speakers. She opens her cell phone like she's answering a call, speaks, and disconnects.

An old woman sits against the lone palm tree on dirt inside a formal stone border. Sistah yells at the old woman in Kreyol, then French. The music starts again and the old woman shrinks. She's gaunt and rickety. When I help her up, she's apologizing. The old woman blinks leathery eyelids at my English and my accent, then extends a frail hand.

I scoop all my coins and fill her palm. My lamp-tar disguise smears on her skin. She squints and tries to figure the stain.

Sistah shoos the old woman, demanding she make room for the patriots.

The old woman hobbles over the low stone border, clutching my coins to her chest.

Under the palm tree, Sistah points at the headstone of slave-leader/sorcerer François Mackandal: "Here. The French devils burn Mackandal at the stake."

"Okay."

Sistah looks above the crowd, then squares up toward the turrets of Notre Dame.

I bang her arm. "Plantation records."

Sistah turns just her head. "Your Susie Devereux is here."

"Where?"

"Susie Devereux has the answer." Sistah points her knife at me. "She is here. The records are here."

I step back and bounce off gyrating bodies. "Where, goddammit?"

"There. The Christian house. Susie Devereux has always been there."

"Bullshit. Susie isn't here and neither are the plantation records." My hand cocks to defend against the knife. "Gimme your phone. We're going to plan B."

"The records *and* Susie Devereux. I know where they are—" Sistah shows me her phone but doesn't give it to me. "Same as you knew the winery." She backs into the crowd; the mosh swallows her. She turns and bolts toward the cathedral's main doors.

A fight starts behind me. I'm shoved hard, trip, and land face-first on Mackandal's oval-shaped gravestone. It has a cross carved into it. A hand bats my head. I jump up into a circle of dangerous faces, features aged by poverty and AIDS. I shove through before the faces can decide I'm a target.

Sistah's white T-shirt and dreads flash in the crowd. She's almost to the street that fronts the cathedral. On her left, two armored UN trucks roll into the square, their lights flashing, PAs blaring Kreyol to disperse the crowd.

I look at the night sky for Hurricane Lana, can't tell how much time we have, then look back for Sistah and our only phone.

Lightning cracks loud across the eastern sky to my left, then in front of me above the cathedral. The revelers jolt. Thunder hammers the square. I step back out of the UN trucks' path. Sistah's already at the cathedral's doors. She's on her cell, feet planted, facing the square.

On my right, five women push through to the street. Serious-looking women, not revelers. I duck to a knee. One isn't a woman, it's the old man from Bois Caïman. He's speaking fast, pointing at Sistah but not moving toward her. Gotta be the Gryphon's crew.

On my left are six national police in riot helmets and gear. They sieve through the crowd and re-form into a phalanx, rifles at port arms, all but one looking at Sistah and the cathedral's doors. He has a finger in his ear, talking to a radio.

Five more national police join the formation.

I glance right to the Gryphon's crew. One woman pulls a pistol from her pants and a second pistol from her shirt.

The eleven police and the four women are fifty feet apart in the crowd. Sistah is between them. She closes her cell phone. One of the tall cathedral doors cracks open behind her. A bloody pig bursts through, slit down its back, squealing as it slips and slides on the cobblestones. Sistah strikes at the pig as it passes. She sees me and stops. We lock eyes; she disappears inside.

The police stop on their side of the cathedral entry. The armed women emerge from the crowd on the opposite side. All four of the women now have pistols in both hands.

Three. Two. One—

The women stiff-arm eight pistols and fire them all. Five of the eleven policemen buck sideways or down; three run; three fire automatic rifles. Sixty rounds spray the women and the crowd. I drop. People scream and ring backward.

Both armored UN trucks lurch into reverse. They roll backward through the square toward the gunfight at the front of the cathedral.

Three of the women are down; the fourth and the old man run west toward the edge of the cathedral. One of the last three policemen is still alive, on a knee, rifle at his feet, dazed in the cordite haze. Revelers sprawl the plaza, dead or dying. Blood runs the cobblestones.

I stand up as the nearest UN truck passes and run beside it. The driver veers toward the cathedral's main doors. I angle off toward a low white wall just to the right of the main doors. The wall is topped with bars but has an open gate and I race through.

A uniformed guard crouches inside and stays crouched as I run past him. We're in a courtyard, a cloister. No lights. Has to be a door into the cathedral? There, on the left, a heavy door . . . would be to the cathedral's nave. Gunfire explodes in the square. I duck.

The nave door opens a crack.

I rush it, slam through, bounce sideways and into cool candlelit shadows. A nun is sprawled on the floor . . . like maybe the door just knocked her down. She struggles to make her knees and aim a pistol. Footfalls echo in the side aisle. I duck into a pew, draw my pistol, and crawl toward the center aisle.

From behind, cold metal slams into my neck. *"Estope! Rete!"*

I spin, am knocked down, scramble up and into the center aisle—a boot kicks the pistol out of my hand. I make my feet. A rifle butt pounds into my chest, bounces me off a pew's end. I land on the stone floor, a boot slams between my shoulders: "No move! No move!"

I fight to stand; body weight lands on my back. Boots crowd my face and shoulders. Can't move; hot breath on my neck. Through the boots, I can see more men . . . ragged green fatigues. Red armbands.

Rebels. At least fifty.

A pig squeals. Sistah's at a side altar. She yells in Kreyol. More boots rush toward me.

Black hands wrench my armpits. A bar is rammed between my biceps and back. Hands and bar hoist me to standing. I kick a rebel in the balls, am jerked backward, and both arms are roped tight to the bar. Fast fingers cinch my wrists with leather. A rifle slams my shin. Pain rockets my hip. The black hands stink of jungle.

A woman screams. It's Sistah at the altar, screaming at another woman.

Well-armed men pull them apart. A tall woman in crisp fatigues steps into the argument. She points at me, then shouts Kreyol at Sistah.

The cathedral goes silent.

The tall woman radiates military presence. She hugs Sistah once, barks orders at the two men, then walks down the cathedral's center aisle toward me. A .45 is strapped to her leg, four magazines on her belt. Behind her, Sistah strips her T-shirt and pants, and pulls on rebel fatigues, then a nun's habit over them.

My eyes squeeze shut. *You fucking idiot.* Eyes open. The main-altar crucifix towers over Sistah and the men. The fear rush is so strong my knees buckle.

Dimanche. Again.

Chapter 21

BILL OWENS

Die standing. No dicks. No demons. *Die standing.* My head's foggy. Hard to think. I'm leg-cuffed to a chair, trussed with the rod, my face flattened on a heavy wooden table.

Dish candles light military belt buckles and fatigues that ring the table. Kreyol voices echo everywhere in the cathedral. Six belt buckles leave the table.

Hands jerk my shoulders up and backward.

Blink, stare, scan. This is the cathedral's sacristy. Game time. *Die standing. Die standing.*

A black Hispanic mulatta is seated across from me, staring. A hand missing a finger removes her beret. She says, "*Possibly,* I can help you."

Die standing. No dicks. No demons. No—

"I *said* . . . possibly, I can help you."

Show her your teeth. Rapists and demons respect teeth. *Die standing.* "Okay. Good. Shoot that psycho bitch with the birthmarks."

Her eyes harden under straight hair cut short for the bush. Commander's stars glint on the collar of her fatigues. She says, "In two hours, the hurricane's outer bands will reach Ayiti." The accent is educated bland. A long scar carves down her forehead across the left eyebrow and half the cheek. "The People's Liberation Front will attack

Le Cap. By dawn, we will control the airport, the harbor, the square—
all of Cap-Haïtien will be ours. The UN forces will fight a retreat to
higher ground—west up the main road. We will allow their retreat as
far as the Highway 1 bridge before Cercaville. There, the surviving UN
forces will be trapped, captured, and ransomed to their multinational
leaders, or they will be executed for war crimes. By noon tomorrow the
entire north coast will belong to Idamante's PLF—People's Liberation
Front."

I play stupid, blurt: "You're Idamante?"

"I am Commander Florent Dusson-Siri—"

"The Witches of Eastwick Siri? Anne's partner? *Hello?* I'm a friend
of Anne's. And Susie. Susie's MIA; we're trying to find her."

Commander Siri speaks Kreyol to whatever rapist she has behind
me. Footfalls echo in the sacristy; a door slams.

Oh my God. Blood rush; prison Christmas.

"The gold you seek belongs to the people of Haiti. Lead us to it and
Idamante will guarantee your safety."

"You heard me? Anne Bonny? Susie Devereux?"

Commander Siri draws her .45 and places it on the table, pointed
at me. "We know from Sistah's call that the gold—or clues to its
whereabouts—is at the de Mezy plantation house, the wine cellar. In
Idamante's PLF, we have many local soldiers from the Nord-Est prov-
ince; all of them know the plantation ruins well. Some knew of the
wine cellar and were able to enter it. For years, they know it as the local
mambo's root cellar."

Anne and Susie don't seem to matter, but gold does. My chances to
die standing have gone from zero to fifty-fifty. I replay Sistah's act since
we found the gold ingot in Jamaica, Sistah telling us: "Go here; don't go
there." Sistah "lost" at Bois Caïman, no doubt on her cell phone, then
on her phone again in the square.

Plain as fucking day—Sistah went patriot, delivered Anne, me, and
our treasure hunt to the Rebelyon.

Commander Siri glances her watch, yells Kreyol at the closed door.

A rebel opens the door and brings Commander Siri an old
Barbancourt bottle. She accepts it, sets it on the table between us.
"From the de Mezy wine cellar. My compliments; you are an excellent
reader of American treasure maps." She removes the seal and shakes

out a glass tube. "Unknown to Sistah, there was a trap. Two of our comrades were killed." From the tube, Commander Siri unrolls parchment papers. She shows them to me in the candlelight. She says, "I have never been to America. And would not understand the nuance of these words. But because you are a very lucky man, you do."

"I'm lucky? Tied to a fucking stake, surrounded by tomorrow's dead heroes?"

She waves again, then sits back. The same rebel who brought the bottle steps into the shadows, returns with a long, heavy iron pipe. Shackles hang from the pipe high and low.

Commander Siri says, "*This*, Mr. Owens, would be a proper *stake*. Similar to the one used on Messiah Mackandal when the French burned him alive." She waves for the stake to be planted next to me . . . like I'm being measured.

"The *bokors* and *mambos* say you and the pirate Anne Bonny murdered the Baby. Stopped the 1986 Rebelyon. The Baby was the loa child. It was she who had forced Bébé Doc from the palace. She would pick the Rebelyon's leader and Haiti would be saved."

The rebel with the stake coughs. Not a man, a woman.

I say, "The Anne Bonny you played rugby with—"

"But because of you, Haiti falls into agony for another twenty-three years. Your palm bears the proof of your crime." Commander Siri shrugs small. "So, yes, you are lucky. If you could not read American treasure maps, you would already be burning at your stake. The fire would be kept low. And last for hours."

Her threat produces an odd vibe instead of more fear. It's not just the commander's reluctance to acknowledge Anne Bonny and Susie as partners, or the tone being used, but the length of her preamble. This woman is a professional soldier, minutes away from lighting up her part of a revolution. But she's taking a long time to get to the point.

Basically, the point should be: *Decipher the map or we make your worst fears come true.* Her style isn't gruff, it's as smooth as her skin where she isn't scarred. She's explaining, taking me into her confidence, building trust. Like an interrogator would. A professional. Like Susie Devereux.

I say, "Sistah said Idamante's rebels have Susie Devereux. You remember Susie, right? From Guantanamo Bay, maybe? Rugby before that? You, Susie, and Anne in Glasgow? Susie and I are sweethearts. She's in serious trouble; needs our help or she's gonna die. Badly."

Commander Siri doesn't bite on Susie either. "The gold, Mr. Owens."

A man and two women are led past the sacristy door. All three are handcuffed; all wear church vestments. The man wears the high hat of a bishop. I glance to the altar at Sistah watching the bishop pass.

Commander Siri says, "Shortly, we will hang all three as collaborators. From the balcony overlooking the square. Are you ready to read the Barbancourt papers?"

"No. Can't concentrate trussed up like one of your magic pigs."

Commander Siri's eyes narrow just enough that I notice, then she smiles. Under the scar, three teeth in her upper jaw are missing. "Haiti fights for her fair opportunity to flourish. I wish us all luck, Mr. Owens; all of us will need it."

She stands, palms her .45, tells the rebel holding the stake to tie my waist to the chair, then cut me loose of the truss. When I'm resecured, she holsters her .45 and opens two bottles of warm Prestige beer. She passes one to me along with the papers. My hands are free; the rest of me is not. The beer bottle isn't a gun, but smashed it could cut my wrist to the bone. I'm almost giddy.

Eddie O'Hare's two-dead wine-cellar ode reads:

Go over the mountains of the Moon
Down the Valley of the Shadow,
Ride, boldly ride,
The shade replied —
"If you seek for El Dorado."
—ESO

But in the wind eat the herb.
Only they avoid the Slaughter
Beyond the cape, Fish the shallows
For they swim in freedoms tomorrows,
—EAO

Drink your fill The pirate's will
Trust only the vintner
And his hare contraire
Never the shade
nor his fille fille de joie."

The first verse is a stanza from Edgar Allan Poe's "El Dorado." A poem about a knight hunting for a treasure he can never find. At Oxford, we decided Poe's poem meant 'live life to the fullest,' because it's the trip on the rainbow that's the treasure . . . not the pot o' gold that even the leprechauns never find.

I sit back; my neck bumps into a pistol barrel. Did Eddie O'Hare, shithead lawyer, run this entire game as a life lesson? Did he just kill me and every other sucker who chased his treasure . . . so he can be philosophical to the one schmuck who gets this far?

No way. A lawyer's ego needs a bigger audience.

And lawyers don't have life-lesson genetic code. And for sure, horseplayers don't. The long-shot/riddle/handicapping-puzzle/pot-of-gold is why they get up in the morning.

Long, slow exhale. I glance through my eyebrows; Commander Siri hasn't moved. I can feel the rebel behind me but can't see her or her weapon. Back to the poem.

Go over the mountains of the Moon
Down the Valley of the Shadow,
Ride, boldly ride,
The shade replied—
"If you seek for El Dorado"
—EJO

But in the wind eat the herb.
Only they avoid the slaughter
Beyond the cape, Fish the shallows.
For they swim in freedoms tomorrows.
—EJO

Drink your fill The pirates will
Trust only the vintner
And his hare contraire
Never the shade
nor his fille fille de joie."

Shade is repeated in the Poe stanza and the last verse. A shade could be a ghost or black person.

The shade is telling us to "ride, boldly ride . . . if you seek for El Dorado." Okay, pretty straightforward—a ghost or a black person is telling us to hunt the gold.

But if you skip to the last verse, we're told don't trust the shade.
Hmm. So why talk about the shade at all?
Maybe try the second verse.

But in the wind eat the herb.
Only they avoid the slaughter
Beyond the cape, Fish the shallows
For they swim in freedom's tomorrows.

No idea. My head hurts.
Try O'Hare's last verse again.

Drink your fill The pirates will
Trust only the vintner
And his hare contraire
Never the shade
nor his fille fille de joie.

Don't trust the "shade" or his *"fille de joie."*

Fille de joie could mean "a woman of pleasure." Or it could be a filly that you like in a race. Either way, it could be O'Hare deep into his raconteur persona suggesting that you should "ride, boldly ride."

Eye rub. Maybe look at the big picture? Eddie O'Hare's new clue was found in a rhum bottle, hidden in a French plantation that owned both of the slave-rebellion leaders, Mackandal and Boukman. It was in a wine cellar. The plantation's owner the de Mezy sugar company. Rhum is made from sugar.

"Well?"

I look up at Commander Siri. "You think this is simple?"

"I think it must be." She nods backward to the window behind her. Tree branches scrape and slash the window. "We lack the time for difficult."

"Bring me Susie Devereux, if you have her. Put us on a safe ship with Anne Bonny, and I'll get smarter."

Commander Siri sips her beer. "Would the other photos and papers assist you?"

Shit. I glance for Anne's trusty sidekick, Sistah.

Commander Siri finishes her sip and sets the brown bottle down. "We took the *Esmeralda* before we took you."

I nod at all things femme fatale; those movies in the '50s didn't lie. "Yeah. The photos and papers would be good. Anne too. She helped me get this far."

"Anne Bonny is necessary?"

"Her *and* Susie Devereux. Need 'em both if you want the gold."

Commander Siri smiles. "There are worse ways to die, Mr. Owens. I understand you have history with mon kolonèl."

Heat prickles my neck. "Wanna watch, huh? Like that kinda sport? Like your fucking *nigger piece-of-shit* kolonèl?"

Her lips go tight. She speaks Kreyol to the woman rebel behind me, who in turn yells into the cathedral nave. Commander Siri sips her beer again.

"I am born in Cuba"—she pronounces it "Cooba"—"on my mother's side, the direct descendant of Cap-Haïtien slaves. The white French planters here"—she draws her .45 and raps the table with the barrel—"bought members of my mother's family. The French planters sailed them to Cuba during the last days of Boukman's Rebelyon. My mother's people were *braceros* who cut the cane that their French owners introduced in Guantanamo and Baracoa. My mother's people were slaves, Mr. Owens, and we remained slaves to the USA's United Fruit and others until Fidel rode into Havana on January 8, 1959."

Exhale. I dial it back a little, nod out the door at the rebels. "Castro trained you?"

"He did; as did others in Eastern Europe. And Africa, where the 'niggers' successfully dethroned their colonial masters. Everywhere and always, slave-rebels—*niggers who fight*—are the people's answer to capitalism."

She reads me as I try to rein in some serious fucking poison.

"Do you wish to help the *people*, Mr. Owens?"

"Depends. Like you say, I have history with your kolonèl. Probably kill that motherfucker dead if we ever go face to face. Again."

"Your interrogation by Kolonèl Idamante is minor compared to America's transgressions in this hemisphere. Your revered secretary of state, John Foster Dulles, and his brother, Allen, director of the CIA, were both major stockholders in United Fruit *during* their tenures in high political office. Did you know that, Mr. Owens? Imagine their conflict of interest, the thousands of 'niggers' and *braceros* who died under the assaults of America's military, including two of my brothers, all to enhance the profits of United Fruit and the Dulles brothers. Imagine why Kolonèl Idamante might investigate that you were CIA."

"*Investigate* isn't what your fucking kolonèl did—"

Commotion at the door. Two large rebels bring Anne Bonny through the arched doorway. Her clothes are torn. She's cut, bloody, and smells of seawater but walking under her own power. Two rebels seat her at the end of the table and handcuff her to the chair. Anne winces but bites it back. The rebels give their commander a bag from the *Esmeralda*. Commander Siri checks the bag for weapons, then pushes it to me.

I ask Anne, "You okay?"

Anne checks the room. "Never better."

I shake Eddie O'Hare's new pages at her. "Right where I said they'd be."

"A good man you are, Bill."

"Not like your chicken-blood girlfriend who can't remember whose side she's on. No, Sistah's valuable. Gotta have her with us."

Anne looks at Commander Siri. "The day's ne ended yet."

I nod out the door at Sistah. "Hers has, if I get to her."

"And the papers, Bill." Anne is still staring at Commander Siri, who's staring back. "Do they tell us anything?"

"Maybe." I read Anne the three verses, then push the page to her place at the table. She cranes her neck to read, reads again, then sits back.

"Poe. Thought we'd be done with his misery at Oxford."

"Guess not. Anything in there that jumps out at you?"

Anne refocuses on Siri and asks, "What deal do ya make?"

Siri says, *"Deal?"*

"Bill and I will keep a big piece of the gold if we find it. If we don't find it, you get none." Anne nods at me. "We lack time to negotiate and so do you, *Florent.*"

"We have Susie Devereux."

Anne sits back. "Do ya now? Present her, then. She'd be the tailor's breakfast, even all blood and bandages."

Commander Siri's jaw clamps. The sacristy vibes away from survival negotiation and into ghetto street dance. Anne and Siri stare, like two alpha females with boyfriend history. Siri mimics Anne's accent. "Are ya comfortable, Anne Bonny, handcuffed to yer chair."

"I'm down four friends and two boats; close to a million dollars. I'll not be sent home empty-handed."

"Home?" Commander Siri drops the accent. "I understand Jamaica will pay to hang you."

Anne shrugs, then nods toward the door and Sistah beyond. "Seems Sistah has returned to your Rebelyon. You could thank me for not leavin' your former girlfriend to my rope."

My eyes tennis-match between Anne and Siri. I can't help a fatal laugh. "Susie and I are gonna die in girl-bar catfight because you and Anne stole each other's *girlfriend*?"

Anne stares three hundred years of pirate blood at Siri and her .45. "No, Bill, you'll not be dyin', not if we can figure the poem. Treasure hunters with those talents are worth $26 million dollars. And you,

Commander Florent Dusson, bring Susie in before she never forgives you."

The window behind Siri shatters. Half the candles blow out. Glass splatters the table and Eddie O'Hare's poem. I grab for the .45. Siri jerks it back and levels the barrel dead-center on my chest. Wind shrieks through the window. The three of us freeze. Hurricane Lana—the other absent femme fatale—has taken her seat at the table.

***

The sacristy's window patch has held for an hour. Commander Siri returns, stepping through the door without Susie Devereux. Two hard-looking black rebels follow.

Anne says, "Our Susie?"

Commander Siri points one rebel toward Anne. "Convince me that you can find the gold, or you, Susie, and your man have consumed all the protection I can give you. There are those outside who believe it is time for the plantation owners to hang with the clerics."

Anne smiles. "I believe Bill and I have her figured, at least what can be figured from inside a dark cathedral." Anne nods at the candles on the table. "Does Idamante allow his hero commanders a map to go with his fine uniforms and heroic speech makin'?"

Siri frowns. "That mouth has always kept you close to the gallows."

"And the pretty boys and girls as well. The map, Commander? Or do you cut me loose and I draw you a picture?"

A rain-soaked rebel rushes past the sacristy's door guard and shoves a field radio at Commander Siri. She turns her back, already talking, and walks to the far corner under the patched window. Siri's arm twists her watch close enough to read. She covers the phone and in English asks the rebel, "Is Sistah ready?"

The rebel touches his ear, confused. Commander Siri repeats her question in Kreyol. He answers *"Wi,"* making a fist at his neck like a hangman's knot.

"Sistah may hang her bishop, but not the nuns. Tie Sistah's mask tight." Siri swears at herself, then repeats her orders in Kreyol.

The rebel hurries out.

Siri wags her phone at Anne. "Four hours ago, Lana drowned San Juan. Just now, she makes landfall at Punta Cana, DR; Category 3, winds above one fifteen. Waves at twenty feet. The storm will slow over land, slower still over the mountains. Lana will be here full-force in ten hours or less."

Anne says. "Winds that high'll drown your army too. Your messiah, Kolonèl Idamante, won't be—"

Siri waves Anne off and focuses on me. "Explain the poem or Idamante's PLF hangs Anne Bonny next."

I say, "Where's Susie?"

Siri tells the rebel behind me. "Hang him instead."

"Wait a goddamn minute. I can't get us to the gold without a boat and a pirate captain. And Susie."

"There are other boats and captains."

Anne says, "That's enough, Bill." She nods to Siri. "Bring us a good map of this coast and we'll explain some. Although you'll not be glad of it."

Siri reaches behind her for a military satchel and drops it on the table. In it, she finds a map of Hispaniola's north coast, spreads it on the table, then anchors the map with four candles. Her glance at Anne is no longer anger and banter. "Where is the gold?"

Anne nods to me. I read Siri the first verse, the stanza copied from the Poe poem—

> *Go over the Mountains of the Moon,*
> *Down the Valley of the Shadow—*

—then offer a blind guess about what it means to this treasure hunt because Anne and I don't know.

"'Mountains of the Moon' are Haiti's easternmost mountains— moonrise is always east.

"'Valley of the Shadow' is Psalm 23—the valley of the shadow of death. That's what we decided at Oxford. O'Hare's using Poe to foreshadow the second verse, the heart of the clue."

"Aye," says Anne and continues with what we *do* know. "The second verse reads as the 1937 Parsley Massacre—where the 'shadow of death' occurred. You'll see her plain. O'Hare's telescoping us to our treasure. Show her, Bill."

I use Siri's coastal map of Hispaniola to draw the rest of the island with my fingertip, then slice the image in half.

Anne says, "The Dominican Republic half is the *windward* side of the island. On that side, Dominicans see themselves as European. On our side, Haitians see themselves as African. The Rio Dajabón separates the races. In 1937 the Dominicans wanted to 'cleanse' their sainted country of Haitian *braceros* come to work the cane. President Trujillo sent army murder squads to the Rio Dajabón. The Dominicans showed every black worker a parsley sprig. Any black who answered *pèsi* in Kreyol instead of *perejil* in Spanish was slaughtered. Killed twenty thousand Haitians in five days."

Siri cranes to see if any of that is in the second verse.

But in the wind eat the herb.
Only they avoid the slaughter

She reads the first two lines out loud:

But in the wind eat the herb.
Only they avoid the slaughter

Anne continues. "O'Hare's 'in the wind' translates to 'windward.' Haiti's eastern border is the river where 'they avoid the slaughter.'"

Siri touches Rio Dajabón on the map. "My aunt and two uncles were among the murdered." She looks up at Anne and me: "And the westernmost boundary would be?"

From the Rio Dajabón I push my finger west through five miles of swamp and jungle into a hidden inland bay in the mangroves. The bay is labeled Fort Liberté Bay and Freedom Bay.

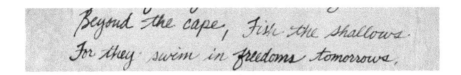

I read Siri the final two lines of the verse:

Beyond the cape, fish the shallows
For they swim in freedom's tomorrows.

I tap the bay's western edge. "'Cape' is the city of Cap-Haïtien. If you go 'beyond' the city to the 'shallows' to swim in freedom's tomorrows, you're in Fort Liberté Bay." I grin at my fabulousness. "After that—"

"After that," Anne interrupts, "Ms. Florent Dusson-Siri will be makin' our deal or she'll be goin' to the groves alone."

Siri turns the poem to her. One fingertip traces the last line of the verse. Out loud, she says: "'Swim in freedom' in the bay at Fort Liberté. But *where* in the bay?"

Anne chins at the other rebels in the room. "And that's why you need a pirate captain, dearie. Not a rebel you have standin' will go into the groves beyond that bay."

Siri hardens, focuses on the poem. "And this last verse? It says the groves?"

Anne shrugs. "What deal do you make?"

"Your life. And his. And Susie's."

Anne shakes her head. "I'll not face the devil in the next life *and* this one. Look at your men; battle-tested, livin' in the jungle—not a one will get on that boat."

Siri keeps her eyes level and hard. "Then you'll hang with the bishop."

"I'll not go near where this adventure's leadin' for less than the lion's share. And only now because I need the money. Facing the devil on his home ground will likely kill us all in ways only Satan himself knows. And you know that's not a lie."

Siri turns to me. The pretty half of Commander Siri's face isn't pretty anymore. "And you? Your price to work with the 'niggers'?"

"My understanding is we split four ways—you, me, Susie, and Anne."

Anne and Siri forget I'm in the room and begin to argue in earnest. They threaten each other with the past, present, and future. Our three guards remain with us, uneasy on their feet, eyes searching the shadows. Siri calls for a noose.

It arrives and she throws it on the table.

Anne calls her a "mindless fuckin' harlot" and tells Siri they'll *both* be dead by the end of today.

Finally, a deal is made: Anne and I get our freedom and forty percent; Siri and the Rebelyon get sixty. Siri will provision Anne's boat with the arms and tools I need to chase Eddie O'Hare's clue. Siri tells a guard to untie Anne. Siri keeps her .45 cocked. The look on her face is not comforting.

I do another tennis-match between them. "What about Susie?"

Anne shakes her head small, either that Susie's no longer important (no way) or it's a subject we shouldn't press given the recent exchanges with our captor.

I nod at Siri and her beret. "We're gonna bet on your Che Guevara? Your last revolutionary—Sistah-the-beloved—proved a little iffy."

Anne cuts to Siri and adds soothing apology to her tone. "Siri's one of the very few on the planet whose word I'd trust. Read her the last verse."

"Sorry, not good enough. You guys have a habit of leaving each other by the side of the road."

Anne lowers her chin, but keeps the soothing tone. "Read us the verse, Bill. We've a plane to catch."

"Not till you two tell me—"

Anne shouts me down, eyes blazing. "Read the bloody verse, Bill, then explain the goddamn thing."

I ease back, cuffed to a chair in a fucking she-wolf three-way where your dick stopped mattering right after you picked up the dinner check.

Anne taps the narrow entrance from the ocean into the five miles of Fort Liberté Bay, says, "Three hundred years ago, like now, this channel was too shallow for the deep-hulled ships from England and Spain to navigate. Pirates like my gran used the channel to escape into a treacherous five-mile bay, now called Fort Liberté." Anne runs her finger into the bay, veers to the right to a small island. "The only island in the bay was said to have a freshwater well. The 'Isle of Souls,' Ile Bayau."

I glance at both she-wolves, then the verse.

*Drink your fill The pirates will
Trust only the vintner
And his hare contraire.
Never the shade
nor his fille fille de joie."*

I do a big inhale, and read out loud as instructed:

Drink your fill The pirates will—

"Not about rhum like you'd think," I say. "It's about *fresh water* in the middle of a saltwater sea. Like Anne said."

Siri frowns. "But the island now . . ."

Anne explains for me. "The myths say the island's a *boutique osseuse*. Nothing to do with us. It's the well we want."

Anne and Siri's expressions don't look like *boutique osseuse* is nothing.

Anne is all about pirate history and continues: "The well was likely dug sometime in the 1600s, forty or fifty years *before* Fort Labouque and the Batterie de l'Anse were built at the mouth of the channel to keep the pirates from using it."

Siri says, "Wrong. Labouque is not pirates. Labouque is a religious prison."

Anne says, "Splittin' hairs, dearie."

Siri barks, "'Hairs' may be the difference between goin' to the groves, and facing what waits there, or going where the gold actually *is*." Siri turns to me. "Labouque was a criminal sanatorium, Ayiti's monument to black-on-black slavery. No connection to pirates—Anne Bonny's ancestors or any others."

Anne says, "You're lost in the Rebelyon glory, *Florent*. We've no time for the myth buildin'."

"And I've no time for another Anne Bonny 'adventure' that has me rescuing us, *again*. Fort Labouque was converted to a prison by Emperor Faustin the First, a black puppet ruler whose sole contribution to Haiti was devising the faux French Haitian nobility. If those facts fit these clues, then—"

"If you'd stop preachin' Rebelyon, you'd see it."

Siri refocuses on me. "Why the island and the well? This is the gold?"

"Not the best spot for it, but could be it." I tap the next line—

Trust only the vintner

—read it out loud:

Trust only the vintner—

"We're thinking 'the vintner' is the guy who dug the well. I think there's another clue inside the well, not the gold. Maybe a brick with a mark on it . . ."

Siri says, "There were marks, images in the clues we took from the *Esmeralda*."

She motions at the files. I point her to O'Hare's drawing found in Jamaica.

Siri inspects the "tortoise" drawing of Tortuga.

I say, "There was an image like it at Bois Caïman, too, cut into a stone that pointed to de Mezy. And one in the Cap-Haïtien square that's supposed to be—"

"Mackandal's mark." Siri traces the cross. "His death stone from Port-au-Prince. Mackandal spoke fluent French and Arabic, but made a mark instead of a signature. The slaves used his mark to mark trails and trees, the houses of the planters to be killed." She points at the latest Barbancourt bottle. "In the de Mezy wine cellar, the *mambo* pointed us to the brick with Mackandal's mark."

"When was he born?"

Siri says, "Early 1700s."

I look at Anne, ask: "The well was dug in the 1600s?"

She nods. I say, "Fits perfect. *If* Mackandal's mark is in the well, it would've been put there long *after* the well was complete. By Eddie O'Hare and his crew . . . before Eddie killed them all."

Siri nods again, leans back, says, "The first verse—the Poe stanza— you don't know what it means, do you?"

I glance Anne. She says, "The well's where we're supposed to go."

"Two verses out of three's a start." I nod at the window patch. "And we need to . . . start."

Siri listens to the wind. "Anne made it clear that not understanding *all of it* will kill us."

"Yeah. And so will everything else in your fucking country."

THE RED MARKET

HAITI

Chapter 22

SUSIE DEVEREUX

The last time he had me here I tried to kill myself. Tried hard, real hard. His iron gibbet is cold on my naked skin. His drugs cloud my eyes, but not enough to kill my memories. The room's smell is sweet, sharp, and pungent; one of his signatures, unmistakable, burned into my nightmares. Two days ago, my pistol jammed in Chicago. If not, I'd be in the ether, possibly a different hell, anticipating a less horrifying outcome.

The gibbet fixes my field of vision rigid, straight ahead at a four-by-four glass pane, into an air-conditioned, antiseptic room. The glass separates where I am from where I will go next. That room has a tilt operating table, bright lights, and instrument trays. His room is part of a modern germ-free facility amid the jungle rot—an operating theater in his red-market "hospital."

I have escaped him once and outfought his kidnappers three times. My best hope now is to be "harvested" for my organs. Harvesting means my death will be quick—an overdose of Heparin, then kidneys, heart, lungs, liver, intestines, tendons, ligaments, and skin. My parts have far more value when the organs aren't damaged. Torture destroys the value. If he decides that money matters more than pride. If this horror palace hasn't driven him completely insane.

Noise. A door behind my cage. A rush of humid air.

They're coming. He's coming.

Two men in lab coats move past my metal cage and into the operating room. Both secure masks over their nose and mouth, then rubber aprons, then gloves. One begins to arrange surgical instruments on the trays. Neither look through the window at me.

A pungent odor sours my side of the glass. My skin hives. A cane clicks on the floor. I squint for a reflection in the glass; can't see what I know is behind me—

Breath on my neck. Warm, measured. The inhale is nasal, sniffing my skin. I jam forward into the gibbet's bars. The warm breath creeps down my spine; stops at my waist. Two fingertips touch; I jolt—

The door again: humid air; voices. A naked black man is rolled past my gibbet and into the operating room. He pleads in Kreyol. Only his head can move. His eyes are wide and white. The door closes. One of the lab coats wipes the man's chest and abdomen with an antiseptic, shaves a four-inch strip from chest to pelvis, then injects the man's arm. The other lab coat lifts the autopsy saw.

The black man's mouth gapes in a final scream. They begin to harvest him before he's dead. My eyes crush shut.

"There, there . . ." The voice behind me is French-accented and calm: "Our donor suffers only a moment." Silence, breathing. "We will do nine today . . . Then, Susan, I will do you. Slowly. Just you and me."

The voice trails off as it walks past on my left and into the operating room. His shirt and pants are European; his head small, the neck narrow and long and too thin to fill his collar. His movements are measured, calm; regal because God has no authority here.

With his back to me, the Gryphon dips a small finger in the harvest's blood, turns, rubs a red cross on the window, then places his nose almost on the glass. His breath clouds the small cross. The fingertips of his left hand lean his cane against the window, then gently knead at my breast through the glass. Behind the hand, his eyes are hooded, sunken; his butterscotch skin scarred from cysts and boils, old and new—the source of the soured-perfumed odor that still lingers on my skin. The face frames a distended mouth and a practiced, gray-lipped smile.

Demons are real.

I am naked in a cage.

In my nightmares, he eats parts of me while I am still alive.

Chapter 23

BILL OWENS

Muffled gunfire rips outside the sacristy's window patch. I'm still inside, still leg-cuffed to the chair. Anne's broken fingernail is on Cap-Haïtien to show where we are. She traces the route we're about to take—pushing her fingernail east along the north coast of Haiti for twenty miles, fifteen of which will be open ocean—then stops at the narrow channel that cuts inland like a tunnel, into the five-mile Fort Liberté Bay.

"Beginning here, at the channel's entry, then halfway around the bay's east rim are a series of purpose-built fortifications. The French garrisoned them to defend their colony's interior. Five forts total, not four."

Anne shoves her hand at Siri to stop whatever Siri intends to say, then continues.

"The fifth fort, the original Dimanche, is inland, not on the bay, buried in a hundred square miles of mangrove wren." Anne taps an unmarked spot deep in the mangroves south of the bay. "*This* Dimanche is a fortified sixteenth-century French Corsican monastery that sank in the earthquake of 1762."

"Wait a minute." I point her at the island in the center of the bay. "We're going to the island, right?"

Anne doesn't move her finger from the monastery spot. "Susie's alive. And that monastery is where she is. The Gryphon has her."

Commander Siri tosses a thin glassine packet on the table. "Piccard's people delivered it yesterday. He and the Gryphon want the gold; all of it. If not, Susie dies in the gibbets, then the rest of us, all our families, all our friends, wherever they hide."

The packet has a two-inch square, a rose tattoo on thick parchment.

Anne plants her right foot onto the table, then points at the rose tattoo on her ankle. "That was on Susie's ankle. From the Rugby World Cup in '94."

Wind slaps at the patched window.

Anne and Siri cut to the sound of Hurricane Lana closing in. Siri tells the guard behind me to uncuff my leg.

Anne continues, "Part of the myth—why Siri's rebels will face UN cannon and hurricanes but not the Gryphon—is the devil lifted the monastery out of the sea in 1986 and gave it to the Gryphon in return for his services. Haiti has a history of earthquakes. Big ones that do odd things. If the original Dimanche *has* risen, then it makes sense that it could be the Gryphon's stronghold."

I stand to make sure I'm free. "You guys don't believe that devil bullshit."

"Remember where you are, Bill. It's ne what *we* believe that matters."

"Swell. Why tell me?"

"Because knowing may keep you alive and sane, readin' Eddie O'Hare's clues."

Anne and Siri prep to leave.

Outside the cathedral, the crowd erupts. Siri cuts to the sacristy doorway as a rebel rushes through. He gushes Kreyol. Siri answers, then shouts orders at a woman rebel rushing in. The woman skids-stops, turns, and runs back into the nave.

Siri says, "Sistah is on the balcony preparing to hang her bishop. And the nuns. Blacken your faces and hands; my adjutant will bring you fatigues. We leave for the boat dock in five minutes." Siri rushes out, presumably to save the nuns and raise the curtain on the Rebelyon blood theater she and Sistah are producing.

Anne grabs her fatigues and throws me mine. The fatigues don't fit, but the caps are wearable, as are the red armbands. Anne uses gun oil to blacken her skin. Gonna be ugly out there on the square when the UN forces get sucked in; lots of gunfire from lots of directions. All to see who owns a city that might not last till lunchtime.

Siri returns, her face hard and purposed. "We go."

And we do, taking a rear passage out of the cathedral compound onto a street that skirts the square's eastern edge. The air tastes like burning rubber. Sporadic gunfire bangs and pops in the crowd. Asylum voices shriek and chant:

"IDA-MAN-TE!"

"IDA-MAN-TE!"

In the square, four UN vehicles are on fire. Six UN soldiers are sprawled at the tires. A thousand black faces press toward the front balcony of Cathedral Notre Dame. **Idamante!** flags and banners are now everywhere. Hands and arms jab weapons at the sky. Bodies of national police litter the cobblestones, their boots and weapons gone.

"IDA-MAN-TE!"

"IDA-MAN-TE!"

Gunmen bristle along the cathedral's rooftop and turrets. Between the turrets, a white **Idamante!** banner unfurls down to the balcony. In front of the banner, Sistah, dressed as a nun and backed by five rebels, faces the jeering crowd. Two of the rebels push the bishop forward and cinch a noose to his neck. He's naked other than his tall miter hat.

Anne stops to look. Siri grabs her arm to keep moving, and Anne jerks it back. Anne's glare is full murder. "You killed Sistah, allowin' her up there."

"Sistah's a Rebelyon gurl; she chose Ayiti's freedom no matter the cost."

On the balcony, Sistah raises a saber two-handed and yells a mix of French and Kreyol: "The devil is no more!" She wheels and buries the saber in the bishop's stomach. The rebels push him off the balcony. He falls ten feet, then jolts at the bottom of his rope. His feet swing next to the two UN soldiers already hanging above the cathedral's main doors.

The crowd roars. Sistah strips the nun's habit to her rebel fatigues, then the bandanna from her face. The birthmarks radiate bold across her eyes.

The crowd is stunned silent.

A woman yells: "The marks! Ezili Dantor! Ezili Dantor!" She falls to her knees. Hundreds more follow.

Sistah produces another saber and jabs the sky. "Ezili brings you the storm! Ezili brings you *FREEDOM*! Ezili brings you IDAMANTE!" The crowd roars.

Sistah kicks a hacked black pig's head off the balcony. The head knocks the bishop aside and splatters on the cobblestones beneath him. Sistah yells, "RE-BEL-YON!"

"REBELYON!"

"REBELYON!"

Mobs of people surge in from the outer streets toward the square. Anne, Susie, and I knife through against the flow and to the boulevard.

At the seawall, the boulevard is still jammed with tap-taps and would-be refugees. Harbor water blows over the wall and splatters buses. Four hours ago, the harbor was calm enough for our dinghy. Siri points left, away from the main harbor and the mobbed UN container ship. We run the loud diesel-choked boulevard until the pavement crosses over a small canal and the boulevard becomes "the Carenage."

A sheltered cove docks the *Esmeralda*. Four ferocious-looking men and women in civilian clothes guard her, each with an AK-47. Siri speaks to one man; they sync their watches, then test their radios. Anne jumps aboard, fires the *Esmeralda*'s engines, checks the gauges, and waves for us to follow.

On the deck are three more AKs, a box of magazines, two pistols, three marine flashlights, and a short-handled military hatchet. There's also what looks like a box of hand grenades. One of the women rebels hands me a heavy coil of rope as I step aboard. Another rebel hands Siri a pulley.

Anne yells over the noise, "Buckle in tight," and points toward the loud pitch-dark ocean we can't see. A high white line materializes in the black. Spindrift? Three seconds later the shore lights reflect the eight-foot wave underneath the white line. The wave crashes into the seawall and splatters us and our shore guards.

Anne shakes off the foam and yells over shoulder, "Cast off. She'll only be gettin' worse."

***

We're outside Cap-Haïtien's protected bay, running blind on instruments through open ocean. Anne, Siri, and I are buckled in three-across behind the *Esmeralda*'s windshield. Anne yells over the constant collisions and engine roar. "Wind's gustin' forty; be three times that when Lana crosses the mountains, so loud you won't hear it."

Siri shouts, "Four miles more and we'll be at the channel into Fort Liberté Bay. Batterie de l'Anse and Prison Labouque guard the channel mouth. The fortress is deserted, but the Gryphon's night-howler lookouts control her."

"Huh?"

Siri shouts back, "When the Gryphon's pirates take a large prize in the Windward Passage or a yacht from the Turks and Caicos, they bring the boat and its occupants through the channel, then back west past the 'Isle of Souls' and into the deep-water section of the mangroves."

We crash waves for another three miles that seem like a hundred. A glow in the black—off the starboard bow—becomes three dim lights.

Siri yells, "Prison Labouque. The lights are the Gryphon's; he expects traffic."

"Us?"

"No one else would be out. Before you landed, all of Haiti knew you two were coming."

Anne yells, "Not just us. The Gryphon draws any ship in distress to this coast. Attacks 'em in his channel; hard to maneuver. Bad weather is good huntin'." She points one hand at the weapons. "Cinch in tight. Get those AKs up and ready. We'll go in dark, hug the west side, try to stay off the rocks."

I reach for an AK; a wave pounds me back into my seat. "You know this channel, right?"

"No. But on the east side they'll board us. Use nets to foul the props."

I squint at fortress lights high up on the east side.

Anne points us to the AKs. "Should we foul, don't be taken off this boat alive."

The lights at Prison Labouque get brighter. We fight another five minutes of pounding ocean, then Anne yells: "Ready!"

Heart rate pounds my chest. Siri and I lift the AKs, safeties off, fingers on the receivers, our seat belts the only things holding us on the seat. Anne points at the lights of the cannon battery that fronts the fort. "We're downwind of the fort. If the Gryphon has no one on the west side—" Anne veers the *Esmeralda* hard right and into the channel. "Shit! I'm too far east—"

Lightning rips through the black. "Look out!"

Medieval battlements tower over us, high, black, and terrifying. Thunder hammers just as the waves cut by half. The *Esmeralda*'s stern bucks high, caught in a following sea. Anne jams the throttles. Lightning strikes the medieval battlements, then leaps the length of the fortress wall.

Anne spins the wheel hard right. Siri and I whiplash like dolls. We re-aim our AKs at the fort. Any closer and the props will foul in the pirates' nets. The following sea grabs us again before we can foul. We slide broadside, deep into the channel. Anne yells: "Dig, ya maggots!" and spins left.

Behind us, the channel's mouth has been splash-lit with marine lights. Siri and I jerk the AKs to the lights—

"There!" Anne jabs her hand west at the opposite shoreline. "To starboard!"

The channel has narrowed. Siri is already unbuckled and aiming over my head. I'm frozen to port, transfixed by the prison's battlements and the lightning. The following sea fishtails us. Anne fights to mid-channel and yells, "Gettin' wider!"

Both shorelines fade to dark. The water calms.

Anne snakes the *Esmeralda* through a mile of black, staring only at her gauges. Dead ahead, dim lights glow in the hidden bay. I punch Anne's shoulder. She looks up, then far ahead at the lights. "Fort Liberté, what's left of the town. South rim of the bay. About a mile."

Siri says: "UN landed Spanish Marines there, could not hold it against the Gryphon's pirates. Pulled out to support Cap-Haïtien against the Rebelyon."

The wind picks up from our left. Anne says, "We're into the bay." She veers the *Esmeralda* ninety degrees to the right, away from the distant lights. "Our island's dead ahead. Maybe a half mile. She's mid-bay; I'll circle her once. We'll anchor alee, swim in."

I pull out Eddie O'Hare's poem, hold it under the gauge lights.

Drink your fill The pirates will

That's the well.

Trust only the vintner
And his hare contraire

It's the vintner's well. We can trust him.

We can also trust the vintner's 'hare contraire.' No idea what that is. Maybe that's the marked brick we're hoping is inside the well—Mackandal's mark, a turtle, or a *contrarian* rabbit.

The last two lines of the verse are:

Never the shade
nor his fille fille de joie."

Don't trust either one. Like I'll somehow meet them inside the well? And have to decide?

A windblown tree line silhouettes in the dark—the island. Anne veers left and begins to circle from thirty feet out. Wind muffles our engines. Siri and I aim AKs, squinting at the island's mangroves. Anne slows the boat and tells Siri, "Ready the anchor."

Anne squints off the port bow at the barely visible shoreline, then stops the engines. "Drop anchor. Leave your pistols on the boat. Take the rope, pulley, the AKs, and the lights." Anne touches her pistol to her head, eyes cold and hard. "No prisoners; them or us. The Gryphon doesn't get us. We shoot each other."

Siri and Anne hit fists and we go over the side.

The water's warm and to our shoulders. We wade in toward shore on the island's leeward side, AKs overhead, aimed at the island's outline. I'm in the lead and stop in knee-deep water. The beach is a five-foot ribbon of sand, then rocks, then mangroves.

Behind me, Anne and Siri split ten feet apart. Anne shines her flashlight into the trees. We wade north, parallel to the beach. Anne's light tracks the shoreline's sand, rocks, roots, and trees. The light lands on an opening in the trees.

Anne waves me in toward the opening, then cuts her light.

I rehoist the rope coil around my shoulders, grip my light tight under the AK's barrel, and crouch-step out of the water onto the beach and into the opening, finger tight on the trigger.

The opening is five feet wide and walled with dense mangrove thatch . . . like walking inside a snake. The path is soft sand and rises as I go deeper inland. Insects cloud my light beam. Partial footprints appear in the sand.

I stop, try to listen for something other than wind. The path is too wide for wild pigs or big lizards. It was man-made—for carrying water from a well. Anchor alee out of the waves and wind, carry empty barrels in, cart the full barrels back down a wide path. I turn to tell Anne we got lucky.

Anne's not there. Nor is Siri.

I duck, cut the light, and listen. The dense thatch blocks the wind. A light blinds me.

Anne yells "Don't!" before I can fire. Her light quits. She scrambles to me, then whispers: "The trail splits, we took the fork. Firepit. Rhum bottles, fish bones. Been used, recently."

I start back up the path, light and AK aimed at . . . The path turns; my light hits an inverted metal cross nailed into deadwood barricading the path. I shine behind the cross to a sandy clearing. It stinks of rotten eggs. The clearing has . . . seats?

Anne reaches my shoulder. "See anything?"

Headshake.

She sniffs. "Sulfur. Cut your light."

I do. Everything shrinks to my skin. Anne tells my ear, "Walk careful to the cross, then in behind it five more paces. Listen for two minutes, then turn on your light and shine a circle."

Bait.

Hell with it, one of us has to. I take four blind steps to the cross, feel my way in behind it, then count five more paces into the dark and stop; nothing but claustrophobic black. The rotten-egg stench hurts my eyes. Pirates could be right next to me, their tongues out . . . Insects buzz. The wind has quit. I shut my eyes; try to listen; try not to shit in my pants. Two minutes pass.

I flip on the light and begin the 360—only mangrove trunks appear in the narrow beam, then more mangroves, sand, then plastic drums labeled "H2SO4." Beyond it, a huge vat, then large hog-wire cages and long tables made of scrap wood, then scarecrows—ragged, stained clothes draped on stakes.

Anne's and Siri's lights flash on. I stumble backward. The lights fan the crude equipment, then quit.

"Bill." Anne's voice is next to me. "Cut your light."

I point it at the ground. Siri steps to my other side, AK tight to her shoulder. She toes at the burned wood under the vat, speaks Kreyol to the scarecrows, then looks up into the trees and the black-dark bay beyond. "All these years, the Gryphon's *boutique osseuse* is true."

I aim my AK one-handed. *"Boutique osseuse?"*

"Bone shop." Anne's light scans the perimeter. Over her gun barrel, she whispers, "Beggars disappear from Cap-Haïtien, AIDS people, and the dead from the graveyards. Complete skeleton brings $1,000 in the med schools of Europe and America."

"This island's a red-market *rendering* plant?"

"Aye. AIDS made blood from Haiti worthless. Captives and the infected go into this bay staked in these hog-wire cages. Fish and crabs feed on 'em until the body is loose bones and mush. Boil the skeletons, add acid, or lay 'em out in the sun, bleach 'em up to medical white, rinse in fresh water from our well."

My light shines on another path. "There, to the left of the tables." I point into the trees and a way out of a human rendering plant. "I'll take point. Warn me this time if you two sidetrack." Deep breath. I step out of the stench. The path stays five feet wide and leads higher. My cheek sweats against the AK, finger on the trigger, flashlight under the barrel. My toe catches on a root. No prisoners. Shoot anything that moves—

Shape in the path.

I fire. Three AK rounds splinter the trees. No shape in the path, only shadows. Tired eyes. The path curves hard left. I cut the light and duck into the sandy curve. No attack. I remain ducked and flick on the light. The path leads higher, mangroves on both sides, roots and rocks to trip over.

Uphill, the path narrows to four feet, then three, then . . . ends?

No, just overgrown.

I continue through the scrub, twisting sideways. Trees rip my shirt. Roots grab at my feet. The trees thatch tighter into a woven wall. My toe stubs again; I lose the light. The flashlight lands, shining on . . .

A pile of bricks? Ship's ballast bricks? Long ago they were the pavers used for New World streets. I grab the light and splash a tight 360. Trees and scrub block the beam. More ballast bricks are in the sand; could be a trail to—*There.* The bricks form a square . . . hole? The ninety-degree corners of a high brick rim? Holy shit. The well.

"Up here! I found it."

Lights bounce through the mangroves. Anne and Siri snake through the thatch into the small sandy clearing. We shine our lights into the well. Three-foot square. Old ballast bricks down all four sides. No bottom. I drop the rope coil, wipe sweat, and ask: "Who's going?"

Siri says, "I am the lightest."

Anne and I agree without hesitation.

"But I am not going."

I hate the whole fucking concept of a water-well tubular-torture chamber, but I'm not staying on a human-slaughterhouse island a minute longer than necessary. "Hack down a tree, make a crossbeam for the pulley. I'll go."

Anne pulls the military hatchet and attacks a six-inch mangrove. I run the rope through the pulley. Doesn't fit. Won't fit. "*Fuck.* Cut two mangroves; the pulley doesn't work."

We make a loop-seat rig I've had to make on construction sites, anchor the rope in nearby trees, test it, then coil it over Anne's crossbeams. Good to go. Anne hands me a Ka-Bar knife and takes my AK. I weave my belt through the flashlight's grip, then rebuckle and glance at Siri. I'm guessing she doesn't trust me anything like Anne trusts her. And I have to trust them both.

I climb into the loop, wedge my back against a corner of the well and my ruined Top-Siders against the opposite corner. "Gimme six feet."

They do. I crab down the well until the rope tightens and stops. Test . . . a little weight . . . a little more . . . all my weight. The crossbeams creak. Total dark wherever my light beam isn't, like floating over an abyss that wants to eat you.

Six feet into the well, I shine my light beam across ballast bricks, moss, dirt, spider webs.

Nothing looks like a clue. "Drop me to twelve."

The rope slackens. I descend deeper, feet and back tight to the walls. The air begins to stale. I shine the flashlight above my right foot on the new section of wall twelve feet down the well. Nope. Then the new section above my left foot. Nope.

I slowly switch sides of the shaft, bracing my way around until I can shine the light on the two walls my back was pressed against. Nothing there either.

"Anne." My voice echoes.

"Aye."

"More rope. Ten feet this time."

The rope slackens a third time. I crab down until the rope stops me at twenty-two feet deep. It feels like a thousand. What air there is smells like a mausoleum we're inside to repair. I shine to inspect the wall above my right shoe and repeat Eddie O'Hare's first stanza. The one he copied from Poe that I can't figure. My voice sounds dead:

> *Go over the Mountains of the Moon,*
> *Down the Valley of the Shadow,*
> *Ride, boldly ride,*
> *The shade replied—*
> *If you seek for El Dorado.*

Maybe I wasn't grabbing straws back at the cathedral; maybe the well *is* our "Valley of the Shadow."

I shine the light a foot below my right shoe at twenty-three feet.

Nope. Next wall, under my left shoe. Nope. Wait—one of the stones has a mark. A cross? I lean with the light as close as I can. The mark is a cross, but the oval isn't there. Trap?

I brace around the shaft while shining the light at twenty-three feet. No other marks. No trip wires.

Okay. In theory, I *am* supposed to be in the well. I *am* supposed to trust the vintner—the well-builder. I *am* supposed to be looking for the 'hare contraire'—the turtle, a rabbit, Mackandal's mark. What I'm *not* supposed to do is trust the 'shade' or the *'fille de joie.'* And it's the shade who is telling me to go down the "Valley of the Shadow" . . . to take the Psalm 23 trip.

Twenty-three. Hmm.

I shine the light on the ballast brick placed at precisely twenty-three feet. I know it's twenty-three feet because I counted the ballast bricks on my way down. Let's say the brick is the trap. What would the trap be? This isn't a King Tut movie with a Hollywood budget. Did Eddie O'Hare's guy plant a spear on a truck spring? A WWI grenade? That's possible—would've been a bunch of US ordnance here when Eddie O'Hare was. A grenade in the face would be messy.

Okay. We won't trust the shade and his "twenty-three." I shine all four walls ten feet above me. Nothing. Then the cross again. I pull the Ka-Bar and lean toward the brick. The cross is upside down. None of the other crosses in Eddie's drawings were upside down. Swallow. I bend back and sheath the knife.

"Gimme six feet."

The rope slackens. I shimmy down to twenty-eight feet. The air is almost too thin to breathe, but not too thin to see a ballast brick with the turtle/Mackandal mark at twenty-eight feet. I yell "Found it!" and pull the knife to dig it out. And stop.

Are we sure? Grenade in the face?

I stare at the mark. Twenty-three feet had big meaning; does twenty-eight?

I replay Eddie O'Hare's poem, don't see a 'twenty-eight,' hold my breath, and chisel out the ballast brick.

It doesn't explode. Exhale. Something's in the hole—

The light quits above me. Anne yells down the well, "Cut your light."

I do. The three-by-three shaft goes black. I freeze. All of me tries to hear. Sweat dribbles my face. Someone is on the island. Anne saw or felt someone. My legs ache. Slowly, I trust the rope seat with all my weight. It holds . . . then jolts.

I jam my feet and back into the bricks just before the seat goes slack. The rope above me falls straight down and smashes me in the head and legs. Mackandal's ballast brick slips out of my hand, falls into the silent dark. A splash echoes. I stare straight up for the light beam that will ID me. Listen for the voices. My only escape is a fall to the bottom. Dry swallow. Heart rate in my neck. Down there below me, in the three-by-three walls, my night terrors wait.

Chapter 24

BILL OWENS

No light beam. No voices. Can't see my hands. Or my feet. I untangle from the weight of the rope. It falls . . . then splashes.

Dry swallow.

I reach into Mackandal's hole. A bottle? Grab the neck and pull. Can't see it, but can slide it into my ripped shirt. Using my feet and back I wriggle higher against the walls, climb three feet of the twenty-eight, and stop. Whatever spooked Anne was bad or she wouldn't have dumped the rope.

AK flashes and full-auto gunfire erupt above the well.

Then stops. One, one thousand. Two, one thousand. Three, one thousand—

The AKs roar again.

No flashes. Not as loud. I wedge up the wall, pressing and pushing, keeping constant pressure with my legs and back. My leg muscles ache.

Shouts. *Men's* voices.

I freeze, wait for their light to shine down twenty feet. Drowning will be better. I death-grip the knife; try to see faces but can't. No flashlight beams shine down the well. The voices fade. Push, press; my thigh muscles burn, want to cramp. Ten feet. *Don't fucking cramp. Don't slip. Don't slide.* Five feet to the top. You can do this—

Voices—Not voices, *one* voice, and it's singing, demented, high and shrill. But not immediately above the well.

My right thigh cramps.

I pound at the cramp; bite down on the scream, pound the cramp, wedge higher, then higher, make the well's lip, hear nothing, and crawl over onto the sand.

Both hands claw into the leg cramp.

No one attacks. I bite my scream silent. Blood drips down my chin.

Somewhere in the trees, the voice screeches singsong Tontons Macoutes, then slips into a work-song cadence. A light flickers fifty feet down the path, brightens into a glow.

I regrip the Ka-Bar, suck air; wipe my eyes; search dark and shadows for Anne or Siri; listen for more rapists crawling through the trees. My heart pounds. And keeps pounding for five minutes. One voice, the Tonton, is all I hear. Alone? Or the only rapist making noise? A guard left behind? A lookout? One of the Gryphon's pirate Tontons . . . has to be. Must've come in from the prison we passed at the channel's mouth. If the pirate's alone, the others didn't leave him here to die. Maybe he has a boat. For sure he'll have a gun. I pat sand for my AK. It's not where I leaned it. The work song stops.

My free hand pats more sand and dark for the AK. No brass casings in the sand—the flashes and gunfire weren't up here, that's why the Gryphon's pirates didn't look in the well. The night-howler screeching starts again. Siri wouldn't die easily. Anne would fight hand-to-hand to the death. If either woman were alive, the screeching piece of shit below wouldn't be.

Pat, pat—no AK.

I do have the knife, and surprise. And this rapist, night-howler Tonton Macoute pirate piece of shit doesn't know I'm here. I stand, knee-lift each leg to make sure they work, then crouch through the mangroves onto the path. Wind gusts cover my approach.

In the clearing with the sulfur stench, a Tonton faces a small fire that he's sheltered from the wind. Three pirate bodies are sprawled where they must've died in the fight with Anne and Siri. The rhum bottle in the Tonton's left hand is three-quarters full. His multiple shirts are an odd mix of color and shape, and he wears an Ida rebel cap backward. I make him five eight, 140, shorter and lighter than me. His face is painted ash white. A boning knife extends from his right hand. No pants; he's naked from the waist down.

He turns toward my tree cover like he hears something. As he turns, a shape silhouettes behind him in the flickering shadows. Lifeless. Naked. A woman posed, submissive, sexual. The breath catches in my throat. Anne Bonny or Florent Dusson-Siri. His boning knife glints. A red flash streaks from the trees. The Tonton turns; Anne Bonny buries a knife in his stomach. He screams; she pancakes with him to the sand, shoulder-rolls off his chest to her feet, then on top of him again before he can move, twisting her knife and stripping his.

From the trees, I shout, "Anne!"

She spins on her haunches, knives in both hands, and realizes it's me before she lunges. The fire glows her. She's soaking wet, a wound across her cheek and forehead.

I step out of the trees, knife at my side. "You okay?"

Anne jumps to the Tonton's AK, checks the magazine full, half-racks the bolt, curls her finger on the trigger, and waves me to her side of the fire.

She says, "Miscreants thought they'd have their way before they delivered me; thought me too beaten to kill them at sea." She stoops, checks Siri's dead from three gunshots to the chest, cups Siri's head with both hands, kisses her once, and whispers, "A beauty you are, Florent, and it's a first day in heaven you're having." Anne flattens Siri's legs, covers what she can, and points me up the path toward the well. "Did ya find it?"

"Bottle's in my shirt."

"A good man ya are, William. We've the *Esmeralda* and our arms. We'll bring our dying pirate to the beach, then Siri to the boat, drop her in the bay so these maggots can't have her. The Gryphon's small boats will be comin' back straightaway."

"Why? Let the fucking rapist die here."

"Move, Bill; we need him where we're going."

I use the Tonton's belt to pull him up. He screams and struggles. Anne jumps into the Tonton's painted face, her knife point buried under his chin.

"The Gryphon has my friend." Anne's eyes are green murder. "You and I, Tonton, will be gettin' her back."

***

We've buried Siri in the bay's waves. The Tonton who raped her in death is faceup on the bloody deck of the *Esmeralda*, hands tied behind him. If the wound Anne punched in his side is left untreated, it will likely kill him in a day, maybe less, and every one of those hours will be excruciating as his insides go septic.

Anne sails us without lights. We're pointed away from the storm and away from the break in the mangroves where the Tonton says we will find the Gryphon's hidden bayou channel. She slows, then turns the *Esmeralda*'s bow back into the waves blowing in, and says, "We'll need the gold to trade for Susie. Do we have it?"

"Don't know." I pull the Barbancourt bottle from the transom locker where I secured it. The bottle rattles. I open the seal. No vial; a key, an odd one. Nothing else. I shine the flashlight in the bottle—empty. Just the key. The head of the key isn't flat, it's a translucent amber glass bowl. I look up, blinking. The Tonton is staring at me.

Anne says, "Keep the light below the gunwale." She opens the first aid kit to put her face back together.

I kneel on the deck, look at the key. Bits of debris blow past my head.

An amber bowl?

Why a bowl key?

"Meaning a bowl *is* the key? The gold is in a bowl?" Have to be a ginormous bowl for 1,650 pounds—

A canyon? No, too big. A pool, like a swimming pool?

Yeah, could be that. Probably not many pools in Haiti in the 1930s. Did Eddie O'Hare pick one of the few, hide the gold, then fill it in? And figure no one would notice?

Would have to be an estate he owned or controlled . . . that no one in the last eighty years has decided needs a pool—

A bay wave bucks the boat; the Tonton groans. Anne says, "Florent Dusson-Siri," and kicks him in the jaw.

I say, "Sorry about Siri."

Anne nods, patching her face.

My left hand hefts the empty bottle of Barbancourt.

No vial, just a key. And a face-painted Tonton Macoute from my night terrors. *Quit looking at him.* Naked from the waist down. *Not part of the clue. Concentrate on the clue—the clue, Boss, the clue.* Fantasy-fucking-Island.

Eddie O'Hare's key plays in my fingers.

Okay, what about the key itself? Where would Eddie get a key with a translucent amber bowl on the end of it? A nice one at that. Sort of primitive, but almost jewelry?

Lots of artists in Haiti.

US-type key? Could be, but so what?

Would fit a US lock.

And . . . I fumble the key again. The key and the lock it fits are probably too *general* to be a clue written in the 1930s.

Meaning the clue is the translucent amber bowl? Exhale. Face rub.

Anne looks down her shoulder. "Can you figure it?"

"Not yet."

"What about the bottle? Anything on the label?"

I roll the Barbancourt bottle and look at the label, the image of Napoleon's sister, Pauline Bonaparte, and her husband, General Charles Leclerc. I say what I know out loud: "I was Barbancourt's main competitor when I was with Myers's. Big story, Barbancourt. Great rhum. Cool family, two families actually—three if you count the niece, Jane. She started her own brand *and* a family war."

Anne grabs at straws. "Does a *key* 'fit' that? Family or a family war?"

Hmm. "Don't see it. Maybe just *family*? Like *key to the family*?"

Anne says, "O'Hare's taken with Barbancourt; used it in every clue. Is it the rhum itself?"

Blink. Could be. Every clue since Astor Argyle has been in a Barbancourt bottle.

Gotta mean something, doesn't it? I shine the light tighter on the label, thinking out loud: "These bottles would've been hard to come by during Prohibition. Hell, any time. The Reserve du Domaine—even back when I was here—was just for family and friends, never enough to sell."

I re-look the label, read each line for a *bowl* or *key* reference.

"This is the best Barbancourt made. I drank with the owners a couple of times in Castle Barbancourt and never saw this vintage . . . and Eddie's O'Hare's got at least five of 'em?"

Squint. Headache. Saltwater wind. The Tonton rapist motherfucker is staring at me.

"What, motherfucker? You want me to shoot you? That what you said?"

"*Bill*. Get hold of yourself. Concentrate."

I sit back on my heels, allow the water, dark, and wind to slap me with survival.

Anne says, "So the clue is family? Or the rhum? What's grand about the Barbancourts that matters to us? To O'Hare?"

Maybe Anne's right. To have all these bottles, O'Hare must've been a friend of the family in the 1920s or '30s, principally the Gardère family, a Haiti and rhum dynasty that could rival the Ewings of TV's *Dallas*. I squeeze my eyes shut to recall what I can.

"Madame Gardère-Barbancourt was the founder's wife. They had no children. Her husband, Dupré Barbancourt, died first, and she passed the company on to her nephew Paul Gardère, whose sons probably still own it.

"In my day, the distillery was near Damien, moved up there after World War Two from Port-au-Prince. Jean Gardère ran it. I drank with him in the Oloffson's bar. Saw a nasty argument between him and the niece, Jane Barbancourt-Linge."

Anne says, "So? O'Hare knew them? How? Where?"

I reinspect the vintage, the label—Reserve du Domaine.

Domaine, like 'house'?

Reserve of the house. Is this Poe again? *The Fall of the House of Usher*?

"The family battle started when Jane built her own distillery right after World War Two, the same time that Jean Gardère moved the original Barbancourt distillery out of Port-au-Prince to Damien. Jean built a basic farm/factory out there, but no great house.

"But Jane, Jane built a *castle*. Used the foundation of an old fuel depot or pipeline. An addition actually to the original castle . . . that would've been there when Eddie O'Hare was around." Blink, wonder. "And Jane threw lavish parties. I was a guest at two of them in the '80s, toured Castle Barbancourt four or five times, the cellar, the tasting room, the balcony . . . old casks for chairs, chandeliers made from bottles. She had bottles everywhere—in the walls, even the floors."

Anne says, "Bottles like O'Hare's bottles?"

I nod. "Uh-huh . . . same color too." I look at the key. "Same amber color as the glass bowl on the end of this key."

Anne restarts at the beginning, quotes me: "Meaning a bowl *is* the key? Our gold's in a bowl? Where's Castle Barbancourt?"

"On a mountain, southwest of Pétion-Ville, in La Boule—"

Anne shouts: "La Boules is French for a game: 'the bowls.'"

"Eddie's a game guy . . . That's it!" If I weren't sitting, I'd fall down. "This key will open a vault somewhere in Castle Barbancourt. The vault will have twenty-six thousand ounces of gold. Holy shit. I should've been a treasure hunter."

Anne frowns. "Pétion-Ville is one hundred miles south, over mountains, through a three-way civil war we won't survive, then mangrove swamps we won't survive. Then we do it again, backward, to trade for Susie."

"I just hit the pick-six for us. Can I enjoy that for a minute?"

"Are you sure?"

"Am I *sure*?" Horseplayer-happy melts to reality. "I'm in Haiti, surrounded by a revolution, facing an inbound hurricane. No, I'm not *sure*."

"Then the only way is to get Susie first."

"But you said—"

"We convince the Gryphon we *know* where the gold is. Use his plane—that we know he has for his cocaine and red-market business— he flies Susie and us *above* the Rebelyon, *away* from the hurricane, and to Castle Barbancourt."

"But you said there's no way to face him without the gold—"

"Susie Devereux's my friend." Anne pats her bandage to her face. "We sail together; we finish together."

"And that magically changes—"

"If ya'd rather not, then you're on your own and the best luck to ya."

I look at my options in the water, dark, and wind.

Anne says, "We've been to the brink before, William, and made it back."

Pause.

Anne's right. And the "before" was me who'd needed the saving, on the Oloffson's road, then in the boat, and finally from Carel's gun. I'd laugh if I could. For three years, I drank the demons back into the dark. I stare at Anne; no way they're taking her alive, she just proved that. And I owe Susie for Chicago or it'd be me in the mangroves.

I glance the Tonton. "If these cannibals grab us, you kill me. That's the deal."

"Aye, Bill. No prisoners. Them or us."

Twenty-six million in win tickets. Life in the world-loves-me lane. Headshake; exhale. I hear the dumbest guy I know say, "Fuck it, then; let's go get our Bond girl."

Chapter 25

BILL OWENS

Mid-bay, hugging the southern rim.

Anne's hands grip the *Esmeralda*'s wheel and throttles. Mine sweat on the AK I hold at port arms. All around us, Fort Liberté Bay is three-foot waves blowing west. We slice through, backtracking east. Wind peppers us with bits of debris in the starless dark. The Tonton is prone on the deck. He told Anne this is the way "to the woman in the cage."

I try not to visualize that or the Gryphon's boats hunting us in the bay, focus instead on the clues, on what I can remember of Castle Barbancourt's interior—the walls, windows, terraces, paintings, furniture. The amber key is safe in my sock. We have to figure the gold's location in the castle, or at least a compelling lie, to buy Susie's life. And ours.

In fantasy world, happy-ever-after will go like this:

We make Anne's deal with the Gryphon—trade him a share of the treasure for Susie and a fast way for his crew, and us, to reach it. We beat the hurricane, find the gold, and don't die when the Gryphon tries to murder us. Hammer Film makes the movie: Christopher Lee as the Gryphon, lots of T&A. It premieres in London; the Krays are dead, so I can attend; we all live happy ever after. What could go wrong?

Anne interrupts. "So, we're inside Castle Barbancourt, walk me to our treasure."

I edge closer to her ear, my eyes on the Tonton, and put the Barbancourt bottle under her dim instrument lights. "Try this: In the castle, there's a life-size painting of this image"—I tap the bottle's label—"Napoleon's sister, and her husband, Leclerc. Same pose and clothes."

Anne looks . . . begins a grin . . . says, "Our *fille de joie.*'"

"That's what I'm thinking. O'Hare's last clue before the key warned us to never trust 'the shade' nor his *'fille de joie.'* We figured *fille* could mean a prostitute or a whore."

"And Pauline Bonaparte was a whore. Assumin' what our Oxford professors taught was so."

"And her husband was—"

"Napoleon sent Pauline's husband to Haiti to put down the Rebelyon and ensure slavery, the two things all these clues contain." Anne grins wider, building the theory. "But Haiti kills Leclerc. Yellow fever."

"Right. And that makes him our ghost or 'shade.'"

Anne kisses me. "What'll we name our children? Even if she's a darlin' girl, I'll call her Bill."

"Picture this: Off the castle's main entry, in the old, old section, there's two opposing stairwells that curve down to the cellar, where all the bottles and casks are. In the stairwell to the right is the life-size painting. I've been to the cellar, I'm positive that's where the key will fit into . . . something. We go past, or to, that painting, but we're not supposed to trust them. Together, Pauline and Leclerc are—"

"A shear."

"Huh?"

"Expect a *shear* if we're finally close to the gold. If O'Hare were forced to lead in a captor, a shear would kill the captor, not O'Hare. And you say *don't* trust 'em."

"Yeah; but I don't see the shear in the clue—"

"That'd be the point of it."

"Great, you're the pirate; I'm the handicapper. When we get to the painting, maybe we don't look behind it, don't touch it; maybe it points somewhere. Beyond it at the bottom of the stairs, there's a heavy cellar door; maybe go through it, then look for something that O'Hare would connect with slavery or Rebelyon, or the water well, or racehorses, or a turtle—a door or a wall, another painting, something."

Anne's grin fades.

"No. Trust me. We'll know it when we see it. Doesn't have to be big, but it could be. The key will fit a lock. The key's amber. The lock could be covered by an amber bottle—"

Rumble ahead. Somewhere in the dark, louder than the wind.

Anne cuts our engines, kills the instrument lights. Wind shoves us backward.

I jump on the Tonton's back and arm-choke his neck. "Not a sound."

Ahead on our right, the mangroves begin to glow. The rumble becomes roar. Running lights leap out of the mangroves and into the bay.

Two smaller sets of lights follow, loud but slower, definitely not canoes. The three boats race toward the slaughterhouse island.

Anne says, "Count ten, then fan your light fast to starboard."

I face-plant the bent Tonton, grab a light, and splash the mangroves on our right, now only six feet away. Just ahead is the opening that belched the pirate boats. It's black dark and fifteen feet wide with mangroves thatched across the top.

Anne wipes at her mouth, then sets her shoulders. "Through that hole, there's no mercy and no turnin' back."

We eye each other for a way to back down.

A way to run for the gold and let Susie twist.

Anne Cormac Bonny has a fault or two, but she's who you'd want on the other end of your promises when the wolf's at the door. She makes the sign of the cross on her chest, winks at me, waits for a break in the waves, and knifes us in.

Chapter 26

BILL OWENS

Branches scrape the *Esmeralda* as we squeeze through the mangrove hole. The air and water go dead calm. I fan my light. It's a main-bayou channel, forty feet wide, steamy and fetid, roofed by a thousand years of tall mangroves tangled together. No satellite camera could penetrate that canopy, and no UN naval ship could sail under it. Any attack would have to come up this bayou in a convoy of nothing bigger than fifty-footers . . . and hope the guns they carry would be enough.

Everything is eerie still. Like we've been swallowed. Anne glides the *Esmeralda* upriver. Five minutes become twenty in the flat, pungent water and heavy air, then sixty. Then another sixty.

Three hundred feet ahead, the black dark thins to deep gray. Dim lights appear, one to port, one to starboard. I squint. My finger tightens on the AK's trigger.

Anne has one hand on the throttles, one on the wheel.

As we pass, the source on both sides becomes five small lanterns, one after the other. Each lantern glows four feet above the water in the chest cavity of a cloth-and-straw manikin chained to a mangrove trunk. All ten are impaled on pikes and topped with oversize dolls' heads.

Insects cloud the lanterns and dolls' heads. My jaw clamps. The heads aren't *dolls*—

Lights behind us. Loud engines and running fast.

Anne gets past the pike lights, hugs the black hull of the *Esmeralda* into the mangroves, then says, "Don't shoot. When I toss the bottle, hit 'em with the light."

I press my foot on the Tonton's neck. "Not a fucking sound."

Two small boats motor past; same running lights we saw exit this bayou two hours ago. Behind them, higher, brighter lights follow mid-channel. The bigger boat is ten feet off our port side when Anne tosses the empty Barbancourt bottle onto their deck.

I spin the marine light and fire it.

Four men jerk toward the light, shading their eyes.

Anne shouts: "From the island well! We know where the gold is!"

The big boat's engines reverse. The two smaller boats in front veer to turn back.

Anne shouts: "Tell your boats to go on!"

A voice from the big boat yells a command in Kreyol. The small boats keep turning into a full 360 and slow-motor farther up the bayou. I shine the light on them—both have drums of high-octane avgas strung on the deck—then shine my light back to the big boat. All three are loaded for long, ultra-fast pursuits.

Anne says, "Tell the Gryphon I have his gold. We trade for the white woman in the cage."

The black man standing at the big boat's wheel wears bright-red pants, a pistol belt, and no shirt. His long hair is straight and dyed white. He answers with a French Caribbean accent: "I am Captain Fan-tom Chimere. You have the gold aboard?"

"We know where the gold is. Twenty-six million dollars."

"For this you want the white woman?"

"Go tell him."

The captain shakes his ropy white hair off his neck. "No, *mon ami*, you mus' come."

"The woman. Brought to this boat. Or no gold."

The Tonton under my foot yells in Kreyol. I stomp him silent. The captain of the big boat laughs. "He say whites fight over the gold. Gon' kill the other."

Anne shouts: "Then no gold for the Gryphon. He sells your kidneys, serves the rest of you for dinner."

The captain laughs and palms his heart. *"Kalm, mon ami. Kalm."*

Out of the dark, the silhouette of a boat rushes at our bow. I two-hand the AK and empty the magazine. So does Anne. The bayou goes white-light concussion, blows me backward off my feet, and showers the *Esmeralda*'s windscreen and Anne behind it.

I fumble for another AK magazine, jam it, rack the bolt, and roll up to my knees.

Burning mangrove branches light the bayou, char the air. No boarders rush from the big boat. It hasn't moved. Men aim rifles at us.

Anne shouts: "We die, your boss gets nothing!"

"Kalm, mon ami. Be kalm."

I jump over the Tonton to our starboard gunwale that's up against the mangroves. My feet hit a wooden box, the grenades. I grab one, pull the pin, throw the grenade over the big boat into the mangroves behind them, and shout: "Grenade!"

The explosion showers the pirate captain with water and tree shards.

I yell, "Get the fuck back! Next one's in your boat!"

Anne shines a light on the water between our boats, then up-bayou for the remaining small boat. "Get me the woman in the cage, or we all die here."

Captain Fan-tom Chimere shakes his head.

I aim the AK at his chest.

The captain raises his hands and shows us a radio. "I call now." He pulls the radio to his mouth. Static drifts across the water, not voices.

Anne whispers, "They'll not bring Susie here."

"What do we do?"

The captain quits the radio and chins inland. "Up; go to the Gryphon. He decides."

I yell down the AK's barrel: "Fuck you. *I* decide. The woman, or I put a bullet in your chest."

Slow headshake.

Anne tells me, "Plan B," then shouts across the dark: "If we die, the gold dies. Lead us in."

I lean the AK against the far gunwale, grab the two grenades, stand, and tell the pirates: "Shine a light over here." A beam splashes me. I spread my arms, holding the grenades so the pirates can't see that the pins are still in. "US government issue, M67. I just pulled the pins. Somebody grabs for me, or my hands get tired, no gold."

The light stays on me. The captain speaks Kreyol and the light quits.

I shout: "We got a hurricane coming. And *maybe* we have to go to Port-au-Prince for the gold. The Gryphon can make that happen. But all three white people have to go."

The light splashes me again. "Where?"

I show him the grenades. "My hands are getting tired. Lotta money at stake."

"Port-au-Prince is far."

"Bullshit. You have an airstrip. Somewhere. And at least one or two hangars for your planes."

"*Non.*"

"You're moving blow by the ton, right? And red-market body parts. The Colombians fly it in; you steal boats out there in the passage, pack 'em full of dope, package the crews you kill into red-market pieces, and it's off to Mexico or America. Get a fucking plane ready, asshole; get us on it, and we'll go get the gold."

Lightning flashes above the tree canopy.

The captain thinks about it. "We see the Gryphon. He take you to Port-au-Prince. But if you lie, better to swim naked with the crocodiles."

Anne shouts: "Storm's comin', Cap. Lead us in."

The captain's big boat throttles up, and we fall in behind. Anne tells me over her shoulder, "Get all the grenades and the extra magazines up here. Our plan B is all or nothing."

Ahead of us, the big boat's running lights splash the mangroves on both sides and above. Three miles in, two bayous converge into ours at a sharp Y. At the vertex of the Y, a large tube-like cage hangs from a pike. The cage is man-size and conical.

Anne says, "Gibbet."

This gibbet's empty. A large vulture of some kind sits the top, eyeing us as we pass. He wouldn't be sitting there if the cage were always empty. I picture the vulture eating, then glance at a new oily stench to starboard, in the trees we're passing close enough to touch.

"Whoa. Shit."

Perched in the stench are vultures feeding on three bodies crammed into gibbets. The faces are forward, mouths torn ragged and eyes gone. I stumble sideways and bump the Tonton. He's standing and rips my AK out of my hands. I bang him backward into the gunwale, grab the AK, and he backflips over the side.

Anne shouts, "Goddammit! We needed him."

Past the three gibbets and vultures, lanterns glow in the trees, hung every twenty-five feet. Between the lanterns, we slow-pass more gibbets, each with a corpse, two with what might be bloody Arab keffiyehs hanging from partially exposed skulls. And more vultures, maybe twenty. They line the trees, flexing their wings, soundless, watching.

Captain Fan-tom's running lights bend left to port. The bayou narrows under a much lower ceiling of thatched mangroves.

Anne ducks, rotating her head to check for pirates above us in the branches.

We finish the low ceiling, then pop out and veer hard to starboard into a large bowl-shaped bulge on both sides of the bayou channel. The right side is strung with naked electric lights in the mangroves. Under the lights is a medieval cut-stone seawall.

The seawall rises three feet out of the water and fronts the right side of the bayou for eighty feet. It continues until it bends into a blind turn clogged with anchored pirate boats and canoes.

Back at the seawall's midpoint, a short dock juts into the bayou.

Eight iron pikes angle out over the water. Gibbets hang from the pikes. Fifty Tontons line the dock, seawall, and the anchored boats, all armed, all silent, wearing clothes of every imaginable type. The women are naked to the waist, painted with inverted red crosses from neck to belly. Some have chalk-white eye sockets and foreheads . . . masks that resemble Sistah's birthmarks.

Captain Fan-tom fans his boat so his stern is to the anchored boats and his bow faces ours from the other side of the short dock.

Lightning cracks to the east.

I rocket back to 1986, sling the AK, hook one grenade to my shirt pocket, and pull the pin on the other. "Not raping me."

"Bill! Goddammit." Anne's voice. "Don't kill us! Plan B. Plan B."

"*Kalm, mon ami.*"

Tontons pump weapons overhead; painted mouths shriek and howl. Gunfire explodes into the mangrove thatch.

I snap backward and stumble. "Not raping me."

Anne shouts, "Grenade!"

My hand still has a grenade but no lever.

I throw. Anne rams the throttles. The bayou explodes. We crash into the jutted dock, slide its length into the seawall, then bounce back into the bayou, bow still facing the shrieking Tontons on the seawall.

The Tontons rush to board us. Anne reverses the throttles. I rip the other grenade off my shirt and grab a .45 sliding on the seat.

"Goddamn, Bill."

Fifty against two. Every Tonton weapon aimed at us. "No fucking way. We can't go in there. Not raping me."

"They'll not let us leave."

I raise the grenade. "Not raping me."

"Don't!" Anne kicks at me but keeps hold of the wheel and throttles. "Susie's in there! We're here for *her.*"

Jolt. Howling savages everywhere; rifles in our faces. Anne yells over the windscreen at the Tontons. "Tell the Gryphon it's *plata o plomo*, bombs or treasure—"

"Ahoy, the *Esmeralda.*"

I wheel with the .45. Astern are three boats. Two are gunboats and Tontons aiming automatic weapons. The middle boat is a pontoon, roofed and lit with lanterns. The pontoon boat has a table with a soiled tablecloth and two chairs. A rail-thin white man in a white suit sits in one chair, a white woman in dirty pants and shirt in the other. The woman's face is down on the table, her hair long and dark. Her arms and legs are chained to hooks on the deck. She has a square bandage on her ankle.

The white man's hands are folded on the table next to an enormous glass jar. He says, "My compliments, Mr. Owens." His fingers uncurl and remove papers from a file. "These poems are, for the most part, indecipherable. But fate has smiled upon us, brought you and I and Miss Bonny together again." He turns the jar.

Inside is Dave Grossfeld's head.

The white man is Cranston Piccard, the CIA conduit who pulled me out of prison twenty-three years ago. Even seen through lantern light at this distance, his twenty-three years have been some kind of hell.

Anne says, "Hold tight, Bill. Hold tight." She's focused forward at the rifles on the seawall.

Behind us, Piccard drums his fingers on the jar. "Your associate David was dishonest. But you are not. You have the gold as promised?"

"Not raping me."

"Bill!"

I snap to Anne's voice. "Yeah."

Piccard smiles. "The gold, Mr. Owens?"

"Yeah." Pant, blink. "Found a map in the well. Memorized it, then burned it."

Piccard frowns. "Memory has a way of muddling any endeavor. Trading for a memory is risky business."

"Right." Pant, blink. I focus on Piccard. "Not trading shit if you can't put Susie Devereux on this boat."

Piccard looks to his right. "And here she is."

Anne yells without looking back, "Susie, it's Anne. Say something."

The woman who might be Susie doesn't move or speak.

I thumb-cock the .45 to make sure it fires when I'm shot, then cock my arm with the grenade. "Tell Susie to say something or I'm gonna throw this grenade at you."

"Ms. Devereux has nothing to say. She and Miss Bonny betrayed me. And they will betray you." Piccard's fingers stroke near the scars on the woman's wrist. "We have much to arrange, you and I, and little time before the storm."

"Put her on the fucking boat. If you need the Gryphon's permission, get it. My hand's getting tired."

"I am merely the Gryphon's humble associate, his liaison in certain delicate international situations, and his occasional guest."

"Give us Susie," Anne yells over her shoulder. "We all go to Port-au-Prince—on a plane you'll find in the next ten minutes. Bill will bring his grenade."

I add, "Or you fuck with us here, and I kill us all."

Piccard shakes his head. "Ms. Devereux is not the issue. Your ability to produce the gold is the matter before the court. Possibly, you feel the red dots on your head? Marksmen with sniper rifles. Should the marksmen—quite on their own—decide you intend to throw your grenade, they will pop your head like a watermelon."

A flash of red crosses my left eye. My head probably glows with red dots. I say, "We die; no treasure."

Piccard shrugs. "There is always tomorrow."

"I'm worth $26 million *today*." I lean into the gunwale and steady with the .45. "You don't want us; you want the gold. But to get it, you, or someone you pick, is getting in that plane that I know you have, then flying us to Port-au-Prince." Pause. "I know that, and you know that. So quit fucking around and let's go."

Piccard says, "The plane you speak of is a twin-engine, but small; the only plane that has not been relocated from the storm." He reaches for the woman—

She jerks upright, psych-ward rigid, nowhere to go. She's Susie.

Piccard says, "Your plane cannot hold everyone and make it safely to the capital."

Anne shouts, "You know who we are. We sail together; we finish together. Susie dies; this adventure's over."

"No, not for all of us." Piccard leans back in his chair.

I yell, "Even the goddamn devil needs money to run his army. These pirates in your boats, and behind me on the wall, all of 'em get a share of my treasure. More money than they'll ever see any other way."

Anne shouts the pirate's code: "No prey, no pay."

"All of 'em speak some kind of English; the ones who don't burn in the fireball will know you bluffed away $26 million when the sniper drops me." I suck a big breath and shout over my shoulder. "Twenty-six million dollars! In gold. That's what we pay for the white woman. Twenty-six million dollars!"

Piccard smiles across the murk between us. "Dimanche is not a true pirate camp, Mr. Owens; like your previous Dimanche was not a true prison. The men who surround you here have given their *souls*, not their signatures. Their father *owns* them."

Piccard calls out two names in Kreyol.

Nothing happens on the two boats in front of me. I glance fast toward the seawall.

A black woman in a nun's habit leads a stoop-shouldered boy through the Tontons and out onto the dock. The boy has been in a nasty accident; the doctors saved his life but not his appearance. The woman has a machete in her belt. Piccard says, "The boy is Kleeford. Notice his posture, his lack of . . . shape. Haiti has many."

I cut back to Susie. Piccard switches to Kreyol, soft and caressing.

Anne shouts: "No. Don't . . ."

I look back before I can stop. The nun draws the machete from her belt, grips the machete with both hands, raises it to her shoulder—

"Jesus Christ, don't—"

Another black woman steps out. She's my size and might be wearing a mask. Her hands stop the machete arm mid-arc. She yells angry, educated English across the bayou at Piccard.

I cut back to him and Susie and the pirates in the boats to my left and right.

Piccard answers softly, but with an edge this time. "Madame Tafat, you are beyond your bounds."

I hear Anne say, "The goddamn devil . . ."

My eyes cut back to the dock. Five men have gang-wrestled the large woman to the dock. The nun swings the machete.

Piccard speaks softly again.

The nun scoops the headless body and retreats inland through the line. Kleeford's head lies on the dock by the large woman who tried to stop it. The night terrors that tried to kill me charge across the water.

I dump the grenade's pin and turn back to Piccard. The pin tinkles on the *Esmeralda*'s deck. New plan B: I will now raise the armed grenade, let the marksmen focus on it, then fire my .45 at Piccard's white suit until they drop me. It'll all work out like it's supposed to.

Anne shouts, "No!" then whispers: "Bill. Don't. He'll give us what we want."

"This place's gotta die."

"It will. Please. Let me get the gold. We'll arm the rebels, send Siri's planes in here. Gasoline barrel bombs. Please."

I look over my shoulder to the dock, then back to Susie on the pontoon boat.

Anne yells over me to Piccard: "I believe we've taken this bit o' theater as far as it'll go. Bill here's been a bit unstable and I fear he's nearin' the edge. If you'd look closely, you'll see it clear, knowin' you're a fine judge of crazy. Bill has the answers *and* he's ready to die. As much as I'd prefer it otherwise, the choice is yours. Not ours."

"Well said, and not a surprise considering your breeding." Piccard looks at Susie, then back to Anne. "Thankfully, I have experience in trades made under duress. Mr. Owens will tell me the gold's general location in Port-au-Prince. Two of the Gryphon's men will accompany you and Ms. Devereux to the gold; Mr. Owens will remain behind—"

"None of us stay behind."

Piccard continues as if Anne hadn't declined. "When you and Ms. Devereux are safely on the plane, call Mr. Owens; he will then relinquish his grenade. When you land at the gold's general location, you will call again. Mr. Owens will direct you and the Gryphon's representatives to the gold. When the Gryphon's representatives have our share of the gold, we will release Mr. Owens."

Anne says, "Cell phone in a hurricane?"

"Yes. You will find a way, if there is one."

"And the split is?"

Piccard smiles. "The three of you will keep one million each."

"I'm down a million in boats and three friends. A million won't do it."

Lightning crackles across the sky. Thunder hammers right behind it.

"A pity, yes, but as you said, Anne, it requires an abundance of capital to run a thousand-man camp."

"Dope, skeletons, and body parts doesn't turn a wee profit?"

"Cocaine, unfortunately, is in substantial oversupply. Flesh and bone, in all its varying forms, remains profitable"—Piccard nods inland—"but not without substantial costs."

"So the Gryphon has to steal from me?"

"Would you care to discuss it in the monastery? I can arrange it."

Anne doesn't answer.

"As I thought." Piccard points at me. "On to the arrangements, Mr. Owens."

"What?" My lips are mouthing every Flyers mantra I know. "Not arranging shit till Susie's on this boat."

Piccard looks at Susie again. Three red dots dance on her chest. "As you wish. I will step off with my companions." Piccard motions a Tonton to board, then stands, walks to the pontoon's railing, and is helped aboard a gunboat.

The Tonton unlocks all but one of Susie's arm and leg restraints, then jumps back aboard his gunboat. Both gunboats back away from Susie's pontoon boat and block the bayou's exit.

Piccard says, "The key for her final lock is on the ring in the ignition, out of her reach."

Anne reverses the *Esmeralda* toward the pontoon boat. "Careful, Bill. No tellin' what Susie's seen of late. And don't tell her Siri's dead."

I drop the hammer on the .45, pull the bowl key from my sock, sidestep to Anne, and wrap her arm with my hand. "Take this."

She does, then pulls us broadside to the pontoon boat. I jump onto its deck.

Susie's eyes are straight down at the table. She doesn't speak. Her hands are fists, the knuckles bloody and scabbed.

"It's me, Bill Owens. Say something."

Her posture stays rigid. She smells like triage—blood, antiseptic, dirt. I grab the keys from the ignition. Unlock her last restraint.

"Can you travel?"

Susie bends only her neck. Her eyes lock mine and shock me backward. Susie starts to say something but doesn't.

"Did you hear what Piccard said? We can get out."

Susie nods an inch. Her lips peel across bloody teeth.

Anne says, "C'mon, Susie, stand up, get aboard; only the here and now. Get aboard and we'll be gone."

Susie doesn't move. I reach for her. She jolts.

"Easy." I pat the air between us with the grenade. "We're leaving. You gotta get aboard Anne's boat."

Susie breathes through her teeth. She stands, unsteady, swivels her head to the Tontons, then fixes on Piccard, and says, "Give me the grenade."

Anne shouts, "No! We'll not have that, Susie. Get aboard."

Susie swivels her head to me and holds out her hand. The red dots dance on her chest.

I say, "Happy to, but we gotta get aboard first. I'm gonna do that now; you follow me."

Piccard is twenty feet away. He says, "Not until you've told me the gold's location. It will be where my pilot flies and nowhere else."

"Pétion-Ville, then Boutiliers, or maybe Fort Jacques."

Piccard grins. "The observatory." Then shakes one finger. "No, not built until 1981. Fort Jacques."

I cut to Susie. "The train's leaving. Only way you get to kill this asshole is get aboard the *Esmeralda*."

Susie stares at Piccard, then me, then steps between us like she might dive in the water to get at him.

"Don't, goddammit. We came a long way to save you."

Anne's voice behind me: "Sail together; finish together."

Susie stops. Eyes narrow, teeth bit, she tells Piccard: "Cyril and Tommy are waiting," then climbs over the *Esmeralda*'s black gunwale.

I step to follow and the red dots dance on my chest. Piccard says, "Stop. Stand down, Mr. Owens, or we will put you down."

I stop mid-step, change sweaty hands with the grenade, and cut to Anne. She cants her head at the entrance to Monastery Dimanche. "Stayin' here with Piccard wouldn't be a future I'd choose."

"Abso-fucking-lutely. Plan B. Tell me how we make that happen."

"Can't say as I know. If you can scoot a bit closer, dive aboard and we'll see how the chips fall."

Piccard's gunboat reverses its engines and adds distance from my grenade. He shouts: "Dead or alive, Mr. Owens stays. If your women do not betray us a second time, all will be well."

Anne eyes our situation, palms her pistol, but doesn't change her offer. "If it were me, William, I'd rather die out here."

"No shit." I suck a big breath and squeeze the grenade. The red dots feel like bullets that have already hit. "Work some magic. Don't think the dive will work."

Susie rams a fresh magazine into my AK and racks the bolt. Anne shouts at me loud enough for Piccard to hear, "Susie's gonna shoot Piccard. You dive when she fires."

Piccard says, "Unnecessary. We want only the gold. You all have a way to survive. Mr. Owens will trust us—we will trust you."

Susie shoulders the AK, says: "In the water, Bill—"

Bullets rake the pontoon deck between us. I block shards from my face. *Fight or flee*—both are suicide. Heart rate at five hundred . . . I stutter-step, do suicide's *moment of clarity*, and don't dive.

My hand shows Susie the grenade. "Can do it right now, out here. Or inside the monastery—three seconds and it's over either way. Might as well run the fucking race."

Susie glances me; so does Anne.

"Find the gold; we all live happy ever after. Flyers win the Stanley Cup."

Susie shouts, "No! Nobody goes back in there."

"I hear you. I surely fucking do. But my way's the only decent bet on the board that doesn't guarantee we're dead. Keep your shit together, I'll try to do the same. You and Anne get us the last furlong, and we're in the hall of fame."

Anne shouts, "Five years, Susie. Don't kill us. We've got the bastards beat and a man willin' to buy us the bullets."

Susie's eyes cut to me.

"My turn," I say. "Hate it all fucking day, but it couldn't be any plainer. Anne saved me from a Port-au-Prince prison. You saved me in Chicago or these bastards would already have me." I show her the grenade. "I got this. Go get us the gold."

MONASTERY DIMANCHE

Chapter 27

BILL OWENS

I'm on the seawall dock, surrounded. Fifty face-painted Tontons split to make a narrow path for Piccard and me. They stink of jungle. Sweat drenches my face, arms, and hands. Five gunmen separate from the others. They walk with Piccard and me onto a wide cobbled carriage-way, toward a hole in the tree line. Two Tontons with torches front the dark hole.

This would be the monks' once-palatial entry to Monastery Dimanche, now overgrown by a living rib cage of dense strangler vines slick with swamp rot.

The torchmen lead us in. The carriageway worms through the vines and fetid air, then dips and rises through a watery tidal pit, and finally ends at tall rusted iron gates. Roots and leech trails crawl the cut-stone gateway and battlements. The gates are held open by eight hollow-eyed Tontons wearing sleeveless, tattered sport coats and bright pants of different colors. Each Tonton is armed with an AK-47 and belted machete. Wood smoke rises from somewhere behind them.

My M67 grenade is my business card, rosary, and exit visa. The grenade is a one-pound baseball-shaped death machine that will kill everyone within fifteen feet of me, but most importantly, it will kill me.

Piccard waves me to follow him through the gates. My feet move but not forward. If Anne's correct, three centuries ago Monastery Dimanche was sucked under the ocean by an earthquake. But now it's here, resurrected. A ghost ship of stone. My fingers ache around the grenade. Night terrors crawl my neck. This would be a real good spot to call it a lifetime.

***

Cranston Piccard and I sit fifteen feet apart in flickering candlelight. We're at opposite ends of a long granite-slab table that might have been an altar in this low-ceilinged hall. Burned incense masks the stink of jungle. Every sound we make echoes once.

Two black women stand behind Piccard. The walls around us are thick and heavy, too heavy for swamp ground. The cut-stone blocks reek of colonial hubris, slave ships, and slave labor. And madness. Centuries of cruelty, obedience, and penance that madmen committed to forge the one true way. Terrible things have happened here, beyond what horrors Siri understood about the other forts, things I can feel on my skin but could never explain.

To Piccard's right are four large square openings cut through the stone wall. The openings overlook a courtyard paved in ship's ballast and surrounded by mangroves that intertwine in odd, tortured roils. A deep firepit burns at the courtyard's center. Flames flicker above the pit's lip, and the mangroves rattle in the wind. Faces balloon forward from behind the tangled branches, then recede.

Piccard studies me with pig eyes. His face is gaunt, yellowish; his neck a thin tube. His trademark white suit is soiled in places; one cuff is frayed. He points a finger that is mostly bone at a high shelf that runs the length of the wall above the openings, and says, "The monastery's entire complement of French Corsican monks drowned in the earthquake. As did the slave children the good friars were in Haiti to save. The children's skulls line the ledge above you." He waits for me to look, then lifts a bottle of Barbancourt. "Another, Mr. Owens? Keep that hand steady?"

I glance at the grenade. "I was drinking Barbancourt the night you fucked us at the Oloffson Hotel. Anne says you're CIA. Were you doing CIA business that night? Or your own?"

The black woman standing to Piccard's right grips the Barbancourt bottle, brings it to my end of the table, and fills my glass. She's feminine in her movements, but large like a man. And her face is wrong, sort of . . . H. G. Wells and *The Island of Dr. Moreau.*

Piccard smiles. "Ah, the Oloffson. By now, the remaining Witches of Eastwick are near there in Pétion-Ville. Should they betray our arrangement, we'll know shortly."

I stare at the black woman, then Piccard. "If Susie betrayed you once like you said, why would twice be a surprise?"

He nods his narrow neck. "Susie was not her name when I first worked with her . . . at Sheberghan, then Abu Ghraib, and Guantanamo."

"You and Susie *worked* together? Doing what?"

"The king's business, Mr. Owens. The waging of the Western way."

I flash on the gibbets, the rags I thought could be keffiyehs. "You're not saying 'detainees' from those camps were sent *here*?"

"My, is that indignation for our monastery? There is a network of 'heres' across the globe—Egypt, Uzbekistan, Djibouti, Haiti, Poland among them—that the high-minded *choose* not to see. 'Extraordinary rendition' is the operative term, when used by the dignified men who authorize such responses. Men who keep Main Street safe."

"Those are keffiyehs in the gibbets?"

Small smile. "Look closely next time, you will see what the new arrivals are shown before they are questioned." He points at a Koran up on the shelf with the skulls. "Allah's swordsmen and videotape for the infidel; gibbets and water for the jihadist."

"Interrogation is a *business*? You gotta be kidding me."

"*Information* is a business, like flesh and bone is a business. And always has been."

I rub the grenade hand. My arm aches. "That was Barlow's part; how you and him know each other?"

"Know? What man really knows another? Mr. Barlow was a pirate operating on the 'civilized' side of the sphere, as I often do. His brethren have lawbooks, briefcases, and robes, but then the good men of

Spain wore robes for the Inquisition. As did the devout friars who buried countless slaves to put this elegant roof above our heads."

I sip the rhum.

"Mr. Barlow was greedy and it bettered him, a man of hubris who did not travel sufficiently to know his own limitations." Piccard exhales, then adds a thin-lipped frown. "And as a consequence of Barlow's actions, you and I now have the problems Messieurs Barlow and Grossfeld created instead of opportunities."

"Incinerate this place. That's a fucking opportunity."

Piccard leans back in his chair. "Not that I believe you are educated beyond the two years at Oxford, but why not Washington and her cherry-blossom ICBMs? Moscow and Tel Aviv? Do they not wreak sufficient havoc among the disenfranchised? Or the Vatican with her high hats and lowered pants? Or Mecca, for that matter, and her promises of virgins for defense of the faith? Select but one from my list and they produce far more suffering than the Gryphon."

"You're okay because you're not *as* bad?"

Piccard smiles. "An educated man sees the world for what it is. The purest geography has no humans present whatsoever. Wherever humans breed, they stain the landscape. You would do what? Kill the evil Gryphon and the world falls back into balance. Nonsense." Piccard shrugs. "But it has been this way since the Christ walked the earth. Kill the goat so the sheep of the same hoof might fatten in the sunlight."

I glance at a row of gleaming surgical instruments arranged between us on our stone table, instruments meant for me if I ever give up the grenade. A little truth serum, a scalpel . . . "You *beheaded* a retarded kid on the dock. How the fuck do you justify that in your stained fucking landscape?"

"I do not." Piccard sips the rhum. "Nor do I justify your murder of the emissaries we dispatched to Chicago. The strong eat the weak, though in the first world, *eat* is a figurative term."

"I hope God's real, I really fucking do. And I hope Susie and Anne smoke your pilots, buy a DC-3 full of napalm with my share of the gold, and light up this shithole while I'm still here to enjoy it."

Piccard speaks Kreyol over his shoulder to the dark, then returns to me. "Dangerous women, I grant you, but not so potent that they nullify our advantages. If the gold is there, we will have it."

A black woman enters and places papers on the table. She, like the first black woman, combines feminine movements, a man's size, and . . . what? Bad surgery?

Piccard says, "Speaking of the gold, are you prepared to discuss the maps and their meanings?"

"Sure."

"Let us begin with the Isle of Souls."

"Sorry. The map from the well is the only map I *can't* talk about."

Piccard looks at me, then points at the instruments and speaks Kreyol.

The woman brings him the scalpel, then leaves.

"I asked her to bring us five of the *special* children. Like your 'Flyers.' I will remove their eyes instead of yours."

"Touch one more. Just one. I kill us all. Better for them than here."

Piccard squints, confused. "Have you seen Cité Simone-Cité Soleil? The sprawling ghettos of Haiti?" He spreads his arms. "*Everyone* in this camp is better off. No matter what their role."

His cell phone rings. He answers in Kreyol, listens, then motions the black woman to him. "Ms. Devereux and Miss Bonny have deplaned in Pétion-Ville. And are now in La Boule at Castle Barbancourt, not the observatory and not Fort Jacques." Piccard shows me a smile full of yellow teeth. "I must admit I do not have your eyes for Mr. O'Hare's clues, but Jane Barbancourt's castle is a perfect location for twenty-six thousand ounces of gold."

Piccard hands the cell phone to the black woman on his left. She brings it to me—

I point her to stop five feet away and leave it on the table. I grab the phone, jump away, put it to my face, eyes on Piccard and the women. "Anne?"

Static, weak signal. "Aye. We're at Castle Barbancourt, out front. Susie started a fight in the plane when I told her about Siri, came close to killin' the copilot *and us*. She's bein' the mentaller, but we've overcome it."

"Who went on the plane with you?"

"No one we could bribe. God bless ya for gettin' us out."

"Your turn now; sorority sisters with cannons. Make it happen."
The phone goes all static, then dead. I slide it down the stone table,
scattering Piccard's surgical instruments.

Piccard looks at the phone. "You did not tell them where to look."
He smiles and nods. "Because . . ."

"We gotta go back to the well."

Piccard squints, thinks about it, then says: "The Gryphon awaits.
Please relinquish the grenade as agreed."

"Yeah, I'm gonna do that. Shove it right up his ass. And yours."

"Mr. Owens, I don't believe you understand the gravity of your
situation."

"Line up every kid here, do to them what you let Idamante do to
me, and I'm not giving up the grenade. You fucking animals had me
once; never happen again."

Piccard calls over one of the black women. She bends; he whispers;
she walks out into the courtyard.

I step farther back. "Whatever horror you're gonna pull, you're
killing your people for nothing. And there's a point where even these
maniacs will know what you are."

"They already know." Piccard points out into the courtyard. "In a
few moments five of the special children will be brought to this table.
Each child will be brought by a woman, then secured to those hooks."
He points to the wall. "Each woman will have a boning knife. One child
at a time, we will begin a vivisection until all five are open for your
inspection." Piccard smiles. "Or you may wish to be their executioner;
use your grenade to save our little ones from the knives. I'm certain
they will appreciate your humanity."

No fucking way I'm killing five children. Not gonna watch 'em dis-
sected like frogs either.

"Something further, Mr. Owens? Before the entertainment begins?
A mixer perhaps, to go with the rhum?"

Somehow, I knew it would come to this; press every button until
one works and I spill. Unfortunately, this piece of shit waited too long.

"Assuming I give a shit, what do you wanna know?"

"Everything."

"Good. Fine. We'll start at the beginning."

"No, we'll start at the end—explain the clue in the well; why we are at Castle Barbancourt?" Piccard dials his phone, waits until it answers, then lowers it. "And what, *exactly*, we can expect there."

The stone table between Piccard and me is the size and shape of a craps table. I imagine the green baize layout, all my money—every goddamn thing I will ever own—on the pass line. I look at the surgical instruments, the hooks, the balloon faces outside in the trees. Deep breath, then: "All the clues have been in bottles of Barbancourt Reserve du Domaine. The last bottle produced a key. The key has an amber bowl for a head. As in 'La Boule.' O'Hare would've used Barbancourt Castle in La Boule to store the gold, not the Gardère's building in Port-au-Prince. Someplace historic and safe from demolition but way out of the way."

"And who has this key?" Piccard picks up his phone.

"Still in the well; in the bottle, behind a ballast brick with a turtle on it at twenty-three feet. Exactly."

"You left the key where you found it."

"Yup. Sure did. Planned to go back after I rescued Anne and Susie."

"But you allowed the women to leave without the key?"

"I had to get them away from you, out of here before the storm hit. But I also had to be sure they didn't run off with the gold. They're pirates, remember? Sorority sisters, but with cannons."

Piccard narrows his eyes at my second use of *sorority sisters*. He says, "But now you have told us . . ."

"Yeah, well, I went with plan C—dice players at the foot of the cross. I'd give you the hero speech, but what's the fucking point."

I grip the Flyers talisman around my neck. The M67's lever releases in my other hand.

One, one thousand; two, one thousand—

I tell Piccard, "There's six ways to roll seven," then roll the fragmentation grenade down the stone table. "You and I just bet it all."

CASTLE BARBANCOURT

Chapter 28

SUSIE DEVEREUX

The battered versions of Anne and I approach the castle, herded up the road by two heavily armed Tontons who stink of the Gryphon's paradise. I spit blood downwind and shield my eyes from wind debris. The wind didn't kill us flying in here, but it had built sufficiently to kill the Gryphon's pilot when he tried to leave.

Anne glances me. Most of me still vibrates. I mantra what kept me alive since Chicago, what will kill these motherfuckers behind us.

At the castle's entrance, fourteen frightened locals crowd the archway, unable to break through the massive Moorish doors to safety. One Tonton fires a burst from his AK, raking the doors. The locals scatter.

Anne and I stop at the iron-and-wood doors, turn and face the Tontons.

One curses his dead phone. The other gunpoints Anne away from me, eyeing me for more violence they know is coming. It's clear they got no new intel from Piccard on where the gold is. Bill died without giving it up.

Hurricane Lana is 80 percent of the sky behind the Tontons, and she will be on us all before long. The scarier of the two says, "Next time you make trouble, I shoot you; fuck you while you die."

I eye him back, the blood dry on his forehead and nose from my headbutt and teeth. *Maybe* he shoots me; but without the info Bill promised to provide Piccard, this miscreant can *talk* rape and murder, but if he kills me, their "treasure map" chances drop by 50 percent; kill Anne too, and they have zero.

All they can *really* do is to escort us to the castle, torture us into producing the gold—if we can—then execute whatever orders Piccard and the Gryphon gave for our limited future.

Anne touches my arm.

I recoil; both Tontons jump back, fingers tight on their triggers.

Anne keeps her eyes me. "Easy, girl, our day's comin'."

The Tontons motion us away from the doors, then fire twenty AK rounds into the lock panel. The metal and wood splinters. They kick the doors, but they don't open. One Tonton tries the shredded lock-set on the left-hand door. It opens; Anne and I are motioned through. Both Tontons follow. The doors shut behind us.

The one who thinks he's going to fuck me says, "The gold. Now."

I step toward an open area with descending stone stairways on either side. "Then what? I let you shoot me? Fuck you."

This time Anne doesn't feed me *calm*.

The Tonton says, "Which one of you wishes to live? I shoot the other."

Anne and I both say: "Fuck you."

He levels the AK at me. Anne shouts, "Wait! The gold's down there." She points down the stairs to the right.

The Tonton cranes down the stairs. At the bottom of the first turn, built into the wall, is the life-size painting of Pauline Bonaparte and General Leclerc that Bill said would be there. I pretend to start for the stairs. The Tonton rifle-butts me in the kidney. I block part of the blow; pain buckles my knees; I land on the stone floor, ball fetal.

One Tonton steps over me. He descends the stone stairs, past the painting, and disappears into the curve. I push up to my knees, glance at Anne, and say, "Dumbass missed the painting."

The Tonton still with us levels his AK at me and shouts Kreyol down the stairs. The other Tonton reappears, leans his AK against the wall, pulls a fixed-blade knife, then pries at the painting. He pries until he can wedge in the knife's blade to the hilt, then pounds the hilt with his hand. The wall explodes. Stone fragments and razor dust blow up and out of the stairwell. I land on my back. So do Anne and the Tonton.

Smoke, dust, echoes.

I roll, cough smoke, try to focus; Anne leaps on top of the Tonton. She pounds his face with one hand, her other arm limp and bloody. He wrestles her off and braces to stand.

Anne lunges again, clawing at his eyes. I land on his legs, rip his pistol out of his belt, ram it into his chest, fire twice, scream "Die, motherfucker!" and fire the pistol empty into the stairwell smoke.

Anne staggers off the Tonton. I grab his AK, butt-stroke his blinking eyes, pound his face again, jerk the AK to my shoulder, 360 the room—

Anne's arm is a mangled mess.

"You're hit."

Anne clamps her arm to her hip and staggers against a wall. "Never . . . better." She sucks smoky air, coughs, wipes her eyes, and says, "Dial her back, Susie. Need you thinkin' clear."

I uncurl my finger off the AK's trigger; feel my lips cover my teeth, hear my mouth panting.

Anne says, "Our man William, God bless 'im, saved us a second time. We run his clue now and fast. Only way Piccard and the Gryphon will trade for him."

The Tonton's phone is by my foot. I grab it and hit redial to ransom Bill. "No signal."

Anne staggers.

I wrap my arm around her bloody waist. "We gotta doctor you."

"A sat phone, Susie." Anne sags against me. "With a signal. Has to be one in this castle somewhere. Doctor me, then call the Gryphon, say we're already holdin' the gold—"

I finish her sentence: "Then, gold or no, we bait that fucking monster to his last red-market dinner."

Chapter 29

BILL OWENS

Run. Mangrove branches slap my face; both hands block what I can. Muck sucks at my shoes and swallows one leg to the knee.

Wind howls above the trees. Behind me is smoke and flames. Fifteen feet of thick stone table saved me. If I'm hurt, I don't know how bad.

Voices yell; flashlight beams sweep high and low.

I trip, fall onto odd, dry ground. Lights fan the trees. I jump up, run, smash into a ragged ridgeline, leap up and grab a crag I think I can see, claw higher on rock.

Lighting cracks above the trees. Lights splash me and the rock. Voices shout. Hands claw me off the ridge. I spin, smash a face, kick another, bite. Rifle butts club me to the ground. Boots stomp my chest.

I roll blind, make a knee, and—

***

My eyes blink open. It's dark but not black. The sound of torrential rain pounds everywhere, but I don't get wet. Wind screams through the cracks of stone walls. The massive structure that surrounds me seems to shake. I'm seated, naked, skin on stone, shivering.

They have me.

THE GRYPHON

Chapter 30

BILL OWENS

They have me.

Wall chains and rusted manacles cuff both wrists. Adrenaline widens my eyes, pounds my chest. This will be medieval bad.

A shape approaches me from the deep shadows. He checks me, then the wall chains, then grabs my hair to bend my neck. Eyes check my eyes. Animal stink and vomit breath coat my face. Behind the eyes, a door creaks.

Light spills but doesn't reach us at the back wall. A misshapen shadow steps into the low doorway, killing most of the light. The hand holding my hair releases. The eyes and body disappear. No words are spoken. The door closes. A lone ray of light remains.

A cane clicks on the stone, followed by hard-soled shoes. An old-world French-aristocrat accent speaks from the dark above me: "Our time, and yours in particular, is limited." The voice seems to sit. "May I suggest we use it wisely."

My eyes water from a strong sour and antiseptic odor. I cough at the taste.

Two hands appear in the narrow light.

I startle backward into the wall.

The hands are the sour smell. The fingers are curled atop a cane. Atop the hands, a light-brown face settles into the light. Boils and cysts cover the skin. Tinted glasses hide the eyes. The nose is piggish; the mouth opens and the tongue touches left, then right, then recedes. "My proposition." The voice is steady, practiced, false in its calm: "Deliver my gold; I will deliver one hundred innocents from their blood-farm confinements. The UN hospitals will suffer a loss in supply, but they will make do. The innocents are suitable for your rescue; we keep them soft, in living crates, much like your veal merchants keep their calves. After the hurricane passes, they will be put aboard a boat with a qualified captain and sailed to the destination you name. You may make hockey players of them all."

The cell door opens wide. Dim light spills across me, but not him. Ten children are led in. All appear . . . awestruck or confused, retarded. None speaks.

"Or. After we have told you each of their names, histories, and hopes for a life outside their crates, you will watch them die in this room, one at a time. Their bodies will share this room with you until no space remains. The door will be sealed. We will leave you to your thoughts and the rats' appetites."

"Twenty-six million," I murmur. "That's what I have."

"What you *have* is a moral dilemma, to save . . . someone."

"No, no, I have $26 million. A man's gotta make a lot moves, take a lot of risk, to make that much money. Money I can give you."

His hand produces a syringe. "So we understand from your women. They called from inside the Castle Barbancourt. Susie Devereux has proposed an exchange to save you. This means she does not have the gold. For if the gold were in her possession, she would leave you to your fate." The syringe glints between us. "The water well on the 'Isle of Souls' held a bomb, but then you know that. The Castle Barbancourt was the same, and you knew that as well. Perhaps there is no gold, only bombs."

"I lied to Piccard; Anne and Susie have the key. Probably already found whatever Eddie O'Hare left at Castle Barbancourt. If it wasn't $26 million in gold—and you don't know *for sure* that it wasn't—then it was a clue. I can handicap the clue, they can't. And you can't. Take Susie's deal; take me to them at the castle."

"Your decision on the children?"

"Wait, goddammit!"

The brown face slams into mine. My head bangs stone and my eyes jam shut. His breath is rancid and hot on my cheeks. Lips peel on my skin. Teeth click. He's gonna bite me, rip part of face and neck away.

Through my teeth I say, "Twenty-six million."

His lips move to my ear. "When the time comes, and it will come very soon, you will save yourself."

A knock on the closed cell door.

Someone speaks urgent Kreyol from the other side.

The lips tell my ear, "A matter requires my attention." The lips ease back. The cane clicks on the stone floor, and the hard soles move away. The door creaks. My eyes snap open; dim light paints a wedge on the floor. The door doesn't close.

Dust falls on my skin.

From the mortar joints? Jesus, Lana's wind must be—The wall shakes against my back. A flashlight comes through the door; the figure holding the light is backlit, a large disfigured woman—the black woman with educated English who was wrestled down on the dock. She snatches my chain lock like she wants to open it.

A Tonton comes in behind her. The large woman shouts in Kreyol; the Tonton balks, shakes his head, then goes for his gun. Her hand flashes a knife that buries in the Tonton's chest. Blood gushes. She stabs and stabs until he slides down the wall.

Standing over him, she wipes her hands, belts the knife, strips his keys, sucks a breath, and says: "I am Tafat." Her left hand keys the lock on my chain. "His boots, take them. Hurry-hurry."

She smells of soap, not rot, throws me my clothes tied in a roll by a red armband. "We join the rebels. Put the armband in your pocket until we are clear of here."

The room shivers floor-to-ceiling and knocks me back a step. "*Damn.* Gotta be a monster to do that."

"Soon, some or all of Dimanche will drown. The Gryphon saves what he can. We must beat him into the groves." She points at my hand. "Messiah Mackandal brings Ezili Dantor. Ayiti will be free again."

Tafat checks the hall. Two black women with backpacks crouch there. Both are world-class not pretty, armed with knives and AK-47s.

Tafat shoos the ten children out over two bodies who moments ago were their captors, speaking soft Kreyol and pointing.

I dress, and Tafat waves for me to follow. Behind the two black women are two more dead Tontons. I look for another way—see none, and run with the women to the left, then right, then through a maze of passages and rooms and more passages and finally outside.

Into a gale.

We stop running and duck under a roofed courtyard open on three sides. Everything is drowning in rain and dark. One woman yells in my ear: "A trail—your escape was near it—difficult, but can be passed." She stinks of sweat and bayou. Tafat grabs my arm and we run into the howl.

And keep running.

***

Every step for the last hour has been battered in rain and wind, and I'm so fucking happy I could run all night.

Tafat stops us in the trees, short of a road that's half water. Panting, she says, "The Gryphon's hunters will lose no time to the rising water. This is the slave road to Valliere; we must take it." She points at my biceps. "Put on the band." She adjusts the knife she used to kill my guard, then unhooks a flashlight from her web belt. "We must make the mountains, then the high rivers, then to Idamante in Port-au-Prince."

"Idamante?" I tie the red armband. "How far to him?"

Tafat eyes me for fight or flee. "Far." She points north toward Cap-Haïtien. "Idamante's PLF surrounds Le Cap, but the UN fights harder there than anticipated. The Gryphon is between us and any Idamante assistance."

Tafat speaks Kreyol to the two women. They raise their AKs at the road. She flashes her flashlight twice into the torrential rain.

Up the road, two hundred feet east, a light blinks once. Then again. Then again.

Tafat flashes once.

My "rescuers" must know about the gold and want it for the Rebelyon. Headlights appear; a small truck splashes up. Two canoe shapes are painted on the driver's door. A shredded red T-shirt snaps and pops on his antenna. Tafat's comrades toss their backpacks in the truck bed and jump in.

I point at the pair of canoes painted on the truck's doors. "We're taking the rivers? In those?"

Tafat says, "You do not fully understand what is behind us, or you would be pleased to die in the river."

I glance back into the mangroves and lightning. Tafat and I pile in the cab. The driver is young and scared and smells it. He wipes at his cracked windshield, grinds gears, and we lurch south on the rutted road, away from the Gryphon but toward the rivers and eventually Idamante.

I mumble, "Another day, another Dracula; got 'em on every corner."

Wind and rain buffet the old truck. We try to hug the mountain's craggy face. For two hours, we crawl higher through the storm, into the mountains and away from the Gryphon. Lightning splits the dark. Canyons and fissures flash on alternating sides. Our driver's chin stays crammed above the steering wheel.

Three thousand feet above the Gryphon's monastery, we exit the truck at a riverfront shed. Our truck disappears. We collect two canoes.

The river charging past my feet is loud and frothy, already Class 3 whitewater if it's a nickel. Tafat yells that she will steer my canoe; says she has experience in the rivers, then hurries us to a cut in the bank.

Our truck's brake lights and headlights blink in the trees as it snakes down the road we just drove. Tafat points me to the front bench of the canoe and yells instructions in my ear: "On your knees, not the bench; remain low. Bang the rocks with your paddle. No roll." She wheels her finger. "Roll, we drown."

I look at the road the Gryphon's hunters are surely on, then at canoes built for adventure tourists, kids insane enough to come to Haiti in the first place. I could survive this; it could happen.

Tafat's two comrades go first. They're gone in a blink. Three, two, one . . . and probably already dead.

Tafat and I climb into our canoe. The hull vibrates like it's up against a belt sander. She shoves us from the bank cut, and the river sweeps us away.

The current's fast; visibility is close to zero. Every fifty feet, white-water hammers us from six directions. I slam my paddle at rocks after we've crashed them. The canoe tries to roll left, then right, but somehow doesn't. River and rain try to drown us but can't. After an eternity of whitewater, we beach on a muddy ledge, crawl out, and collapse.

The wind and rain feel like they've tripled. The two female Tontons are there, alive. They speak Kreyol to Tafat, then stand, and wave me to my feet.

Tafat yells in my ear, "Caves. Downriver twenty miles."

"More river?"

Nod. "In the caves, we survive the hurricane. And the Gryphon."

We hoist the canoes over our heads and begin the portage to another river entry. The canoe is heavy but shields the wind and rain, a trade against the hammering echo that's constant and deafening. We'll never see or hear an attack coming. Tree branches scrape the canoe and my forearms. I focus toward my feet, invisible in the mud. Any kind of leg injury and that'll be it.

Lightning cracks. It snapshots a black-and-white river three feet away screaming past on our left. We drop the canoes at an entry point, then huddle under the trees. The women talk to each other's ears, check their weapons. Tafat shouts in my ear: "No roll; roll, we drown."

The two women put in first; then Tafat and I. Whirlpools spin us dizzy. We careen through stark whitewater canyons flash-lit in lightning. Lana's outer bands howl. We crash and rocket but don't roll, don't drown, and finally crawl out of a heart-pounding 8 mm horror show onto another muddy bank sheltered by toppled boulders, and collapse again.

Tafat pants, pulls her pistol, and yells: "Here we meet our truck. The Gryphon's reach is long, even in a hurricane. Be prepared to fight."

I flex my fingers, try to make them work. "Gimme a gun."

She doesn't. No truck arrives.

We carry the canoes higher, then crawl into a deep cave, its mouth shielded from the hurricane. The women pull the canoes in with us, explaining that we will hide behind them.

At the back wall, we sit and shiver against one another. The woman on my right pulls a small light stick out of her pack and pops it. The cave illuminates to a dim, eerie green. Hurricane Lana roars outside. Lightning flashes at the mouth. The cave's depth kills much of the roar.

The women discuss something in Kreyol. Their tone is sharp, clipped with anger and fear, but uses an educated diction that I noticed back at the road. All three wear the red armbands. Tafat's two comrades eat food from one of the packs, curl up with their AKs, and pass out. My hands are cramped and shaking. We've been running eight hours. I'm beat to shit and hungry.

Tafat hands me dried fish from the second pack. I devour it, lean back, and try to calm down. Tafat eats hers more slowly. I nod at her two comrades. "Question?"

Tafat spits fish bones. If she had sunglasses and a porkpie hat, she'd be 100 percent night howler. But after eight hours together, cheating death six feet apart, she *seems* different. I say, "You look crazy. You live and work at ground zero for crazy. But you don't sound crazy. And you're damn good in the river. I don't get it."

No reaction.

Her face is a mess, a combination of high and low cheekbones, thin and full lips. Swollen, but not, like someone beat seven shades of shit out of her and she never recovered. She continues not to answer, a pair of white eyes in the dim green of the light stick.

I lean toward her. "Whatever you know about me, we both know I'm not going to Kolonèl Idamante. Before we get out of that last river, if I can't run, I'm killing all three of you."

Blank face. "I know you will try."

"Try? Like you said, roll the boat, we both drown. I'd rather drown."

She nods. "Yes. There are worse deaths than drowning."

No shit. But drowning isn't a childhood aspiration either. "Up in Chicago, on Saturday, four shooters tried to kidnap me. They're from here?"

Tafat's chin rises.

"There was a similarity to you, two of them . . ."

"I was their English teacher." Tafat pushes off the cave wall, crawls over the canoes to the edge of the cave's protection, unzips her pants, and pisses an arc downwind. She zips the pants and returns. Seated, she says, "The similarity you search for is born a man."

I look like I don't quite get it, because I don't.

"Some of us are the 'third sex,' common in Southeast Asia, Polynesia, and India, although each call us by different names."

"The *third* sex? Why here? I mean, with Piccard?"

"Not Piccard. In poor countries, people are a commodity. In all their forms, alive and dead. Men and boys in the prisons, in the street. Women, children, are sold to brokers to be slaves, 'servants' for the rich. In Haiti this is called *restaveks*. Others are kidnapped from families who would not sell, then sold by the Tontons Macoutes to the Gryphon. Some of his children become soldiers, Tontons, as they do in Africa and Mexico. The ways of the pirate are all they will know.

"Others, those deemed more valuable, are given hormones and education, schooled in the ways of India and Pakistan's *hijras* and the *fa'afafine* of Samoa. If we show promise in those years, we undergo surgical procedures. Those of us who do well in the surgeries, and who do not grow too large, are groomed with great attention until twelve or thirteen, then sold or gifted as companions and entertainers for the wealthy and powerful . . . in those markets where such gifts foster closer relationships. A profitable business with a thousand years of history."

"No shit, that's for real? A guy told me about it in Morocco thirty years ago. I thought he was drunk."

Tafat blinks her unlevel eyes. "How American you are. The world does not operate on wealthy Western standards. The world operates on famine and murder. Extreme conditions create extreme responses. I, we—the failed Exquisites"—she nods to her comrades—"are but one of those responses."

"But you're still here, not in the Middle East, North Africa, or Eastern Europe."

"My surgeries were unsuccessful." She shrugs wide shoulders. "The surgeon, then at Dimanche, had his own problems. As a result, I was not attractive and grew too large to be valuable as an Exquisite." She pulls up her shirt and shines a penlight on what might be a small raised *E* intertwined with a cross under her left arm.

I squint to see—has to be the brand Lieutenant Waz described on two of the dead shooters at Nick & Nora's. I refocus on Tafat's botched face. "Sorry if I offended you."

She shrugs again. "I understood you were an educated man."

I laugh. "Piccard tell you that?"

"Devereux."

"How bad was it for her?"

"This time, or the last?"

Swallow. Maybe I don't want to know. "Susie and Piccard had some kind of CIA history. How's she figure with the Gryphon?"

Tafat thinks about it. "The Gryphon is empire, nothing more; built upon the same principles that colonized much of the world." Tafat thumbs a vein in her arm. "The early red market for Haitian blood was not the Gryphon's or Luckner Cambronne's invention, it was yours, as is the market in rendition, cocaine, kidneys, and bones. The rich harvest the poor. East to west. Europe and America call it capitalism."

"Marx and Lenin. If we don't drown, you'll make a good rebel."

"No. Here, it is Mackandal and Boukman. And yes, all failed Exquisites will make good rebels, as will much of Ayiti. And soon."

"What's it like, being an Exquisite?"

Tafat looks away into the canoes and the storm beyond. "If we fail in the transition but can rise to teacher, interrogator, assassin, courier, or ship captain, we gain access to the Gryphon's *haut monde* or his Praetorian Guard and, to some extent, flourish."

"Except you stole me from him for the Rebelyon."

"As captains, couriers, or assassins, we see the outside world when others do not. Some failed Exquisites begin to hate what we are, what we are part of." Tafat glances at her comrades. "Some do not, like those who hunt us now. They lack my experience and education. Their loyalty is what you saw on the dock."

"The dock wasn't third-world bona fides; it was Jim Jones."

Tafat shrugs. *"All* the Gryphon's products are for *export."*

"Export or not, it looks like slavery and murder."

"Yes, and slavery and murder are underneath your brightest lights and softest sheets; the clothes you wear; the fruit you eat; the organs you buy; and the covert intelligence you solicit to defend it all."

"And your Kolonèl Idamante's different? He's gonna fix all that?"

"Fix? *Fix* is a Western concept taught in movie houses. Go to sleep. We have more river ahead. Should our truck come, it will be when the hurricane's eye is upon us."

"We're gonna do the last lap *in the eye* of a hurricane? You gotta be shitting me."

Tafat pulls the AK barrel up between her legs and leans into the cave wall. "I wish Ayiti to be free. Of *all* her demons. For that I will take the chance. And so will you."

***

Silence—the absence of muffled roar—shocks me awake.

Tafat is standing, wiping sleep from her misshapen eyes. She toes the boot soles of her comrades. They jolt awake. She says to me, "If the truck survived, it comes now from a farm close by. We must get the canoes to the road."

Beyond the canoes, the cave's mouth is bathed in an ethereal moonlight . . . like we're down the rabbit hole with Alice. No wind; no rain; no birds; no insects. Dead silent; strange beyond what I can describe. I crawl out with Tafat and the first canoe, set it down, and stand into—

Holy shit.

The trees are snapped and shredded, half of them flat in every direction. The ground is naked rock. The air is odorless, absolutely still. I peek over the deep canyon's ledge. Far below us, whitewater crashes over and through the boulders, current that would make matchsticks of a battleship. The river we're headed to has got to be better or we're DOA from *go*.

To our west, the sky is infinity black. That would be the storm wall that just passed. To the east, the sky is stars and a crescent moon. Some number of miles *farther* east is the other side of the eye wall: Cat 3 winds, 111 miles per hour or worse. The eye could be ten miles wide or it could be a hundred. If it's ten miles, Tafat says we have one hour.

Truck engine. We all duck back from the road. The women aim their AKs. The truck stops at the canoes. One headlight works; the windshield is shattered; looks like from bullets, not hurricane. A palsied black man stumbles out, blood splashed across his pale-yellow shirt and face. He was frail before he was shot and drops before he can speak.

Tafat runs to him. The women rush the truck. The smell of gasoline is strong; probably a bullet in the tank. I wave for a flashlight and crawl underneath.

High in the tank are two holes. If we go uphill not down, we shouldn't lose much fuel. I crawl out to tell Tafat. All three are pointing AKs at the road.

Tafat says, "Our driver is dead. The Gryphon is close. Possibly ten minutes."

Her comrades load the canoes in the truck bed, climb in, and aim their AKs. Tafat and I jump in the cab. She jams gears and we lunge forward. The truck reeks of blood. I ask how far.

She leans at the windshield to see. "Twenty miles. Over the four-thousand-foot ridge above Ca Elie. The eye must last or we will perish."

I squint through the shattered glass, squeezing my hands together to stop the tremble. "Cool, something new."

The road higher isn't a road, it's a path through debris from far away, and over and around downed trees. Much of this will be airborne again seconds after the eye passes. The storm that did this was no Category 3.

***

We make it to our stretch of the river before the Gryphon can cut us off. The river is a jet stream of white foam. To the east, the stars are still visible, but the moon is fading. Either the moon's natural arc or the storm is walling it off.

Tafat pulls rope from the truck, cuts three long pieces, and tosses them to each of us. "Tie yourselves in." She points at her comrades and stays with English. "I will put you in the river. Good luck."

I drag our canoe to the water, climb in to my knees, and tie myself to the bench the way the women are doing. Tafat pushes them in. The river catapults them forward. Thirty feet of gush and they're pitched airborne. The canoe cants sideways, tips to roll, and they're gone, rolling into the dark. That fast, and it's over.

Tafat stares at the probable death scene, anguish on her misshapen face, then asks me if I'm ready. *"Prêt?"*

Maybe her comrades lived twenty seconds. I look at the road the Gryphon is on, push my knees as far under the front bench as they'll go, then hunker down for the launch. Tafat climbs in. We touch water, but just the top. Instantly we bang left, fly, bang right, fly, crash, splash,

slide, skid, fly . . . smash back into foam, twist, don't spin, sail high into
a bank, slam back down, airborne again. Nonstop, breathless, white-
knuckle death.

***

A lifetime later we end in a pile. I drag Tafat out of the water.

The pieces of our smashed canoe float off into Lake Azuéi. Tafat
gurgles and rolls to her stomach. I pound on her back until she spits all
the water, then roll her back over and give her mouth-to-mouth until
she breathes.

She coughs, fights to her side, and screams as her legs move. I pant
till I can breathe, wipe water from my face, and touch parts of me for
pain. I stand, fall, and stand again and stare at the roar of whitewater
dumping into the lake. To the east, we still have stars but very few.

Tafat bends to sit up, touches her legs, and falls back, panting.
"Broken."

Her pants are bloody bags of broken bones.

From her back she points west. "The eye passes. Travels . . . for
now . . . where we must travel."

I look at her shattered body, then her uneven eyes, the pain in her
face, then the pistol in her hand. Her other hand reaches inside her
shirt and strips a Velcro strap. She tosses the strap to me. On it is a flat
rectangular box. She says, "Susie Devereux . . . has a tracking chip . . .
unlikely she is aware. Turn the switch on."

The switch is in a press-plate in the box's narrow side. A tiny red
light pops on. Then blinks once.

"Frequency will increase . . . with proximity. A green light . . .
within five hundred meters."

"The Gryphon has one of these?"

"Many."

"Is there a road to La Boule from here?"

Tafat's eyes roll white. She sucks several breaths, then forces herself up to her elbows. "No." She nods at the lake. "Follow our bank to
Fond Parisien, the bottom of the lake; Highway 8. My mother's family
is there, in the shacks. Give them this." She snaps a chain off her neck,
a small queen-conch shell with two silver rods through it. "Tell them

I grew strong. That I am with the Rebelyon. They will take you to La Boule."

"They know about . . . ?"

"I was stolen at age six; our last time together. Ask for the Pendelane family, the women masons." She strips her armband and tosses it to me. "Dirty your face and hands."

I strap the Velcro around my chest, then cup muck and smear my face and hands.

Tafat pants, swallows, and says, "Slavery is slavery. Ayiti deserves her freedom from the world's thirst." Her features contort against the pain. "Remember this when you divide Ayiti's spoils. Slaves gave you your life."

"I can do that." We stare for a second. "For what it's worth, thanks."

"Slaves saved you. Remember." She extends her hand, palm up. "Give me your hand." She points at the **Ezili** carving, and that's the hand I offer. Her grip is strong. She releases, then transfers the pistol to the hand that just shook mine and points me back.

"Take this when I am done." She thumb-cocks the hammer, then raises the barrel to her temple. Her eyes blink twice. She mouths the word *"Liberté"* and pulls the trigger.

The gunshot slams her flat.

I flinch and stumble; the .45's echo bounces twice, then stops. Absolute stillness.

Tafat's blood rivers between the wet stones toward the lake. I look away, then kneel at her hip, unwrap her fingers from the pistol grip, check the magazine, touch her arm *thanks*, stand, and begin to run.

***

At sea level and no longer sheltered by the forests and mountains, the world inside Lana's eye is postapocalyptic Armageddon times ten, the ground thatched with leveled trees stripped of bark; naked rock that used to be sandy lake beach.

I'm the last man alive, running through gray half-light. My feet hitting the rocks are the only sounds. The air's harder to breathe, like there's somehow less of it.

Pant, jump rocks, *pant*.

This final arc of lakefront at its bottom is the same as the top where I started, except now I'm farther from the mountain and can see the east wall of the eye that's chasing me.

Pant, jump rocks, *pant*.

The wall is black with streaks of gray, rotating counterclockwise. It will be the second attack on an already-decimated battlefield.

Up ahead is . . . a road? Concrete-block walls? Must be Tafat's shacks. The roofs are gone.

I stop way short; catch my breath before approaching. Tafat's .45 is cocked behind my leg.

The first shack is small, fifteen by fifteen, and the same as the entire row. Four walls: no windows, no roof. Bits of debris—a pot lid, part of a picture frame, a doll. A can of Spam that I peel and wolf down.

I check the remaining buildings. Not a person, car, or chicken. All gone . . . and not a sound. Part of a road sign is buried in the shack's concrete wall like a knife: "Fond Parisien." Above the door the name "Pendelane" is chiseled the way a professional would do it.

I lay Tafat's queen-conch necklace on the windowsill and tell the walls, *"Liberté,"* think better of it, and scratch *"Liberté!* Tafat Pendelane 2009" into the wall.

Out front, the road east—toward the mountains and possible safety in the Dominican Republic—is now a death sentence into the approaching eye wall's towering black. At my feet, part of another twisted sign reads "Port-au-Prince 42 km."

I have two choices: run the gauntlet until I run into whoever's still alive on this road—UN troops, rebels, the Gryphon—or get sucked into the sky right here like Tafat's people just did.

I take a last deep breath, belt Tafat's .45 in the small of my back, and start running.

If Hurricane Lana is moving at ten miles per hour, the eye will advance one mile every six minutes; lots faster than I can run. I switch on Susie's chip tracker and it blinks red, but just once. It feels strangely wonderful that a light is lit in Armageddon World.

A rumble behind me—low and ugly. The rumble gains volume. Really loud now, a roar—

A rocket shoots past. I stumble and fall.

Motorcycle.

Brake light. The bike slows, turns with its headlight on, and comes back at me. Fast.

I draw the .45. The rider screech-stops, slides his back tire in a 180, and waves me aboard. I run to an old Triumph Bonneville, belt the .45, hop on, find the pegs, and stomach-hug the driver's leather jacket. He smells like motor oil and roars west down the centerline.

Again and again the rider brakes hard and swerves, passing through and around and over the remains of small decimated villages and larger towns. A few ragged people are out. They seem dazed and seriously afraid, focused on the rotating black wall marching toward them.

We make fifteen miles of bad road that buys me an hour. I can now see the rotating black sky ahead of us in the west. The rider stops at an intersection with three partial walls standing on one corner. Part of one wall reads: "Croix-des-Bouquets." I sold rum here in the 1980s.

The rider points a black finger at himself, then north. "Highway 303, three kilometers."

Going north on 303 toward Port-au-Prince will hand me to whatever's left of Idamante after he finishes his dance with the hurricane. I point south and tell the rider's helmet, "Pétion-Ville, La Boule."

He shakes his head.

I raise the .45 from the small of my back . . . but can't do it, can't steal his bike and leave him here to die. Like he could've left me back at the lake; where I'd already be a ragdoll in the wind. I step off the back of the bike and say, "Thanks."

He looks down his shoulder at me and the gun, then twists the throttle and screams north.

Across the road from the three partial walls is another wall, this one with a window hole. Painted above the hole is "Digner 2 km" and an arrow pointing south. We had a Myers's customer in Digner, an outpost on the Mad River, where the adventure travelers would put in. Maybe one of Haiti's five new governments since that time has built a bridge.

If I go there and Haiti *didn't* build a bridge, I'll be trapped on low, open ground—

Fuck it. My feet start running.

I make the outskirts of Digner, spent and limping.

Just ahead is its crossroads. A three-hundred-yard walk down the cross street will be the Mad River crossing that everyone used in the dry season. If God loves me, I can get across the river on the new bridge.

I trot to the river. God votes: No bridge.

From bank to bank, the river is five hundred feet of roaring white-water and debris. Around me, Lana's rotating black eye wall is the entire sky in every direction. My stomach blinks red. I undo one more shirt button and look at the box in the Velcro strap. The light's dark . . . but it *did* blink; it still works.

I'm within ten miles of the castle . . . *So move, asshole.*

I jog south along the granite riverbank. Up ahead will be my old Myers's customer, an ex-Aussie football player named Rohan Gittens with the wrong attitude when it was shut-up-and-smile polite time. Zero chance he's still there.

But the jutting riverfront headland is. So is a roofless concrete building with no sign. Five boat bows are smashed into the tight natural harbor, looking like catfish on a stringer. Down close, the river's so loud it sounds like a stock-car race.

At the backside of Rohan's building is a thirty-foot steel pole. The pole is planted in a partially exposed granite pit filled with concrete. Six one-inch-thick support cables anchor the pole into the high granite crag.

My eyes follow a cable across the Mad River: *Zip line.* Adventure-camp stop. In the rainy season the crazies probably raft the Mad River out of the mountains, stop here for beers, then finish with a zip line across the river.

Damn straight. Just like I'm gonna do.

At the top of the pole, the pulley and its handgrips are still on the line. But how I get to the top of the pole is gone.

Inside the building, I find an eight-foot length of rope.

Back at the pole, I tuck the rope through my belt loops, tie the rope around the pole like a logger would, then do the lumberjack-hunch up the pole. It's lots harder than it looks. The rope doesn't break. Takes fifteen minutes. And most of my strength.

At the top—thirty feet off the ground—the fucking pulley is wire-knotted to the cable. I fight the pulley loose, grab the grips, and semi-test with one hand.

Seems okay. *Seems okay?* I check the sky that wants to kill me, then the river, strip the lumberjack rope, shut my eyes, and lock-in a horror vision of my final dance with either the Gryphon or the hurricane.

I shout: "Flyers rule!" and make my feet push off the pole.

Forty feet of air separates me from whitewater screaming downhill toward Port-au-Prince. The zip line's fast. My hands don't hurt until halfway. Half a destroyed house and roof careens out of the river's bend. The roof peak is higher than the zip line.

No, don't fucking do that—

My hands and forearms cramp. Foam splashes me from ankles to face. The bank is ninety feet away. My stomach blinks red; gigantic roof fills the sky—

"Shiiiiit!" The roof hits the cable just behind me. It snaps. I slingshot the last ten feet above the water and tumble hard onto the rocks.

I roll, screaming at the cramps, jam one foot between my hands to pry them loose of the grips and pulley.

Gunfire cracks on my side of the river's roar.

I roll farther behind a snapped tree stump, force my goddamn hands flat, then scan for gunmen. There are no armed crews who will be friendly to me, white-boy colonial master. I need pirate girls and a fortified basement. Everything else in this goddamn country wants to kill me. I plunge my hands into mud thrown up by the Mad River, smear my face black, and start running.

Chapter 31

BILL OWENS

A mile behind me, Lana's rotating eye wall reaches the far bank of the river. Her roar is the soundtrack now. I'm running away, uphill on a paved road. Debris and uprooted trees cover the scraped foundations of used-to-be shanties. Some dwellings still stand, walled compounds that have hurricane shutters.

I make my legs pump faster. The ruined shanties give way to open land that might have been farm. Five dazed goats huddle nose to nose in a ditch. Two horses wander in an odd circle, see me, and bolt. Part of a tractor is crushed into a flattened concrete building. A dog underneath the tractor watches me run past and doesn't rise from his stomach. My eyes probably look like his.

The road climbs higher. On my right is a long concrete building, the paint scoured on two sides. A black man under a wide-brim planter's hat grips a rifle out front.

I stop, pant bent over, then walk toward him.

He shoulders the rifle to a dirty white shirt and aims at my chest.

"No. I'm a tourist. Canadian." I point east. "Was at Lake Azuéi."

His finger curls on the trigger.

"Whoa. Easy. I have to get to La Boule. Can you help me? Before . . ."
I point at Lana rotating all around us.

Headshake behind the rifle.

I don't show him the armband; he has things to protect. "C'mon, man. I have money." I pull out US bills.

He half fans the rifle barrel toward the road, then back at my chest to help me move on.

I remember the pistol and walk toward him waving the money. *Gunshot.* I land hard, and stay there. He's done this before or I'd be dead.

A curvy middle-aged woman runs out of the concrete building behind him, yelling angry soprano Kreyol until she reaches his shoulder, stays in his face, then turns to me. "American?"

My hand cinches up my pants as I stand, then drifts to the pistol under my shirt in the small of my back. "Canadian. Toronto."

Her face is round, dotted with moles; she speaks Tafat's educated English. "Pétion-Ville is under siege by the rebels. Extensive fighting. New fighting. You cannot go there."

"Trying to get to La Boule, up above to the south. My wife and kids are at Castle Barbancourt."

The round face hesitates. "You are friends of Bertie Linge?"

"Yeah. Good friends. From Canada." I do a fast recall. "Knew his mother, Jane Barbancourt. We buy Bertie's Rhum Vieux Labbe."

The man keeps his aggressive stance but lowers the rifle. The woman shouts at him and points inside. "There is little time, but I will take you the five kilometers. Around back, hurry. There is a good bridge in Berthe to the south. Avoids the city center." She points again, this time at oily black clouds over Port-au-Prince. She says, "The refinery and fuel tanks. Either the hurricane or the rebels." She sighs. "I will bring the car."

Her car is a shiny new Peugeot. She hands me a wet cloth to wash my face, pops the trunk, and says, "In the boot."

***

The Peugeot bounces me against the boot's metal lid. Tafat's .45 is in my hand. Hope when the boot lid pops we're at Castle Barbancourt, not Idamante's headquarters. The tracker blinks red in the blackness. Susie's at the castle, has to be. She and Anne are alive. Another blink.

We'll all live happy ever after. Be a goddamn shame if I had to eat this pistol instead.

Gunfire. The car swerves, bangs me into the lid, then left, right, and into the lid again. We add speed, brake hard, and jump a curb or downed tree.

Horn. Brakes. Jolt-stop.

The Peugeot's dark trunk illuminates to dim green and stays green. *Susie's here.*

I aim the pistol at the trunk lid—fifty-fifty Idamante has her and the castle—I cover the green light on my chest, hold my breath. The lid pops. My driver startles backward from the pistol.

Voices—commotion—

Two bandaged white faces aim .45s inside the trunk—Susie Devereux and Anne Bonny. One of Susie's eyes is black. Anne's left arm is in a sling duct-taped across her naked stomach. Susie's face softens. "Oh my God."

Anne says, "I'll be damned. Grand it is to see you, Bill."

Holy shit. I made it.

Susie belts her .45. She and my driver help me out of the car. Susie and Anne have AKs slung over their shoulders, hair tied back in bandannas like the pirate movies, boat shorts and boots they must have found inside Castle Barbancourt's shot-up main doors.

Susie hugs me with both arms. She smells like soap and rhum and has an open bottle of Barbancourt in her left hand. Anne hugs us both with one arm and kisses me on the mouth. She tastes like rhum and fresh bananas.

I tell the Haitian woman: "Thank you. Swear to God, if I'm alive next week—"

She accepts the US bills I offer, jumps in her car, races back toward her husband and hopefully safety from the black eye wall rotating around us.

Grinning in disbelief, Anne says, "Never thought, not for a minute, I'd see you again. God bless ya again, Bill, for savin' this adventure."

Susie's lips part and her head shakes once. "No matter what happens from here, I want you to know—" She chokes, sniffs, and semi-whispers: "Thanks. What you did—Thanks." Her hand with the rhum bottle and one arm pull me to her, soft against her breasts.

She feels as good as I'd imagined. My smile crinkles the remaining mud-cake on my face. I tell her, "I'm a really good dancer."

Susie keeps hold of me.

"Piccard's dead. Fed him the grenade."

She pushes me to arm's length. "You're sure?"

"Saw half his head on the floor."

Susie rocks to her heels. Anne steadies her. "Took a long time, dearie, but you got 'im."

Susie hugs me again, her lips at my ear, says something so soft I can't hear it, and squeezes hard, like the Flyers do when their emotions won't translate into words.

Anne says, "And the Gryphon?"

Susie lets go to look at me.

"No, but Monastery Dimanche was shaking bad and the water was rising fast." I show them the tracking device. "Susie got a tracking chip on her."

Susie drops her rhum bottle and starts to strip. Anne stops her, points her .45 high at Lana closing fast from two directions, and says, "Best be movin' inside. She'll happen so fast, ya won't know she took ya." Anne turns to me and chins at the castle. "We've a bit of a problem inside."

I laugh; rib pain winces me. "*Shit*. Get me inside to the cellar; I'll face any dragon you can produce."

They look at each other.

We all limp fast toward Castle Barbancourt's main doors. Lana's wind kicks up the gravel and blows Susie's bandanna off her hair. Churn builds toward howl. This place should be packed with locals hoping to ride out the storm—

I grab Susie's shoulder. "Did we find it? The gold?"

She has to yell: "Sort of."

***

Inside the castle, Susie and I jam the main doors shut against the wind and lashing gravel. Anne points me left, down into the cellar. Castle Barbancourt should be full of Haitians, but it's empty. And smells like it's on fire. Anne points again.

The stairs to the right are scorched and splattered with blood and debris . . . similar to how Susie and Anne look, other than their clean clothes. A shredded jacket and charred hat from one of the Gryphon's Tontons is piled in the first turn.

I ask, "O'Hare's shear blew you guys up too?"

"Aye." She points down the stairs to the left but doesn't go. "Feel the heat?"

Now that she mentions it, yeah.

Susie points again. "Why there's no one else here."

We walk down the steps; the air at each tread is warmer than the last. At the bottom of the stairs, the arched cellar doors are jammed open under their collapsed arch that now rests atop them. Not the type of support that will last long.

We scoot through. Instantly it's a brick-walled pizza oven. In front of me is a jagged fissure where the floor used to be. The fissure separates us from the main cellar, where I'm guessing we have to go. I look down into the fissure, way down into a glow . . . that could be the old fuel depot storage tanks. The fissure zigzags across the cellar floor to the cliffside wall. The wall is gone above the fissure, cleaved open ten feet wide. Between the fissure's gaping sides, I can see all the way across the valley to the stark white cliffs of La Boule Blanche. Empty concrete trestles stairstep across the valley.

The floor shudders.

Lana hits the castle, this time with her eastern eye wall. The jagged opening in the cellar wall goes black. The howl increases one hundredfold. Both hands jam over my ears. All the air is sucked out of the cellar like a 747's window breaking. My shirt rips open; I teeter at the fissure's edge, grab for handhold—

Two hands claw me back, then farther back and through the arched doors. We crowd into a small room lit with candles and two lanterns. Susie shuts the door behind me.

The roar muffles to a train's rumble.

Susie says, "Best we can figure, the new part of this castle was built over a pipeline or fuel reservoir." She points out toward the valley and the concrete trestles we can't see. "The hurricane ripped it up and it exploded. Most of the fire gushed into the valley, but what didn't fractured the castle's foundation where the new meets the old."

"Good guess. Fuel depot is exactly what's underneath here, originally built during World War One, I think."

Anne points Susie at my chest, the Velcro strap, box, and green light. Susie strips her boots, socks, and boat shorts and begins to search.

Anne says, "You were dead-right about the painting—Pauline Bonaparte and General Leclerc blew one Tonton to fragments. We dispatched the other, called Piccard, then Susie and I looked everywhere for what the key fit. It wasn't in the wall."

Susie, in her T-shirt and panties, is an athletic woman with centerfold body parts. She says, "Can't find the chip," and pulls her T-shirt over her head. Her back is to me, a mass of welts that run to her waist, under her panties, and down her legs.

"Jesus." I reach—

She flinches, but not as bad as before.

"Let me look; maybe they cut it into you." I hold the candle up to her back. A number of cuts and small lumps dot the long welts. She would've been unconscious not to remember surgery. I hold the candle close to a severely swollen bluish lump beneath Susie's right shoulder blade. "Does your right shoulder feel any worse than the rest of you?"

"Maybe. Feels like my ankle."

Anne looks close at Susie's back, then pushes once with her index finger. "That hurt?"

Susie spins. "Goddammit!"

Anne nods. "Be my pleasure to remove your transmitter." Anne pulls a knife she probably took off one of the Tontons. "Hands on the table, dearie. Like you've your usual line of boys behind you."

Susie's eyes narrow.

"Sorry. Just puttin' your focus elsewhere." Anne pours rhum across the blade. "Your hands? On the table."

Susie grabs the table's sides, grits her teeth, and says, "Do it."

Anne cuts out a dime-size divot and the chip with it. Susie collapses to her elbows. I rip part of the shirt and soak it in rhum. "This is gonna hurt. A lot."

I press the cloth to the wound. She screams. I duct-tape it to her back. Anne says, "Pretty as a picture, you are," then slaps Susie's shoulder and jumps back. Susie spins and I bear-hug her—most of her naked against me—until she calms.

Anne grins. "For trying to kill us in the plane."

Susie says, "Let go."

"You're sure? I'm a really good dancer."

Susie's eyes are six inches below mine but look like they mean it. I hand her the T-shirt, eyes reluctantly staying with hers, then say, "Could we talk about the key? We're sitting on a burning fuel depot, on a cliff, in a Category 3 hurricane."

Susie says, "Lana's a 4, for certain, maybe a 5," then cringes as she tugs the T-shirt over her shoulders.

I point at the ceiling. "Swell. If we're still here fifteen minutes after this thing passes, the Gryphon will be out front to retrieve his chip."

Anne says, "Aye, clock's tickin', but the bastard's still gotta beat war and weather to get here."

Susie reaches past me for the bloody chunk of her back and the chip buried in it. The chip is tiny. She holds it up close to her face, says "State of the art," then turns to me. "I figured the key."

"No shit?"

"In the floor, not the wall. The key fit an impression in one of the floor bricks. We pried it up; underneath was a three-inch pipe cemented into the rock with a bottle inside. Not a bottle of Barbancourt." Broken smile, like the first time we met. "A bottle of Myers's."

"Myers's? This rotten, fucking lawyer just ran us through the hell of Haiti, taught us all about sugarcane, slavery, and rebellion, but we're going back to Jamaica?"

"In the Myers's bottle"—Susie leans back and stops—"was another vial."

I wave for her to continue. She doesn't. I say, "What, goddammit?" I look to Anne. She grimaces.

Susie says, "Lana's front wall hit and we lost our light; the explosion was right after. We scrambled, the foundation caved in, and we haven't been able to get back across." Susie shows me the bowl key. "The clue's still on the other side. Someone, whose legs are still good, has to long-jump the fissure."

I look at both of them. "Definitely a woman's job. Rugby's about running. You guys are perfect."

Both show me the gashed-and-battered versions of shapely legs.

"I just ran a marathon, okay? Slept five hours in a previous life. Had a can of Spam. But somehow I'm the right man for the job?"

Anne grins. "A woman needs a man."

"A woman can't remember what the clue said?"

"Only read half. And you wouldn't be jumping if we could."

Exhale. I stand, tear a strip off my shirt to make earplugs. Susie does the same and hands Anne a strip to wad into her ears. I wad mine, grab one lantern, mouth "Stay put," and open the door.

Leading with the lantern, I step to the collapsed arched doors. Hurricane winds roar outside the castle's breached walls. I duck through the doors, walk to the edge of the fissure. Oven hot. The narrowest point in the fissure will be a ten-foot jump. Getting a run at it will be . . . creative.

To my right, rain churns past the jagged opening in the cliffside wall. Susie and Anne appear between it and my shoulders. They don't look confident. Susie stomps the chip, then kicks it into the fissure. I point us all back to the room.

Inside, we all pull our earplugs. I say, "Here's the plan: you two *all-star rugby players* stand at the fissure's edge. Hang both lanterns out over the fissure so I can see some of both sides. I'll run from the collapsed entry, do a Carl Lewis. If I make it, you *carefully* toss me one lantern. I find the clue, we ride off into the sunset."

Anne nods. "Full scholarship at Oxford. Never doubted you a minute."

"I didn't graduate; you did; probably why I'm the one jumping." I point at the lantern: "I'll need your matches."

Anne hands me matches. I wipe sweat out of my eyes, wad in the earplugs, and reach for the door. Susie slaps my ass and shouts in my ear: "*Girls* jump twenty feet in the Olympics."

"My favorite stripper song is 'Gloria,' the U2 version."

"Soon as you're back."

I walk out to the collapsed entry arch. The ear wads stop half the howl. Susie and Anne continue with the lanterns to the fissure's edge. At the fissure's edge, I drop to both knees, squint down into the heat, palm-sweep where my foot will plant for the leap, then consider the ten-foot *chasm* I have to jump.

I crawl back to the entry using both forearms to sweep clean my approach path. I stand, turn, take long, measured strides back to the fissure.

Five strides. *Okay.* I swivel my sweaty back to the fissure, nervous heels at its edge.

I long-stride back to the starting line. *Shit, we got this—Carl Lewis could* cha-cha *ten feet.*

Deep breath. I turn again, glance to my right at the hurricane churning outside, then wave *ready.*

Susie and Anne hoist their lanterns. Susie gives the thumbs-up.

I bolt—right, left, right, left, right, toes at the edge, LEAP—airborne, airborne, airborne, crash-land into furniture, and grab.

Made it. I check my pants. No stain. Dry as a bone.

I wobble-walk to my edge of the fissure and wave for the light.

Anne and Susie are applauding in the bad light and muffled roar. One lantern arcs over the heat blast. I catch it with both hands; the kerosene doesn't spill and set me on fire. Santa Anita's Trevor Denman says we're five lengths ahead on a speed-favoring day going into the turn.

I mantra: Girls do yoga at this temperature; I can do treasure.

The Myers's bottle, clue, and vial are where Susie said she dropped them. I roll the clue into the vial, seal it into the bottle, walk back to my side of the fissure, show Anne and Susie the bottle, and make a throwing motion.

Susie nods. She has the two hands.

I set the lantern down at the fissure's edge. Then toss the bottle.

Susie catches it with both hands and her chest. Anne extends the lantern for my jump.

I pace off six long strides. Pace it a second time. Wipe sweat so I can see . . . turn and start running . . . sixth stride, edge, LEAP—airborne, airborne, airborne—land, crash, and roll.

Fuck you, white men can't jump!

Susie helps me up. The three of us stagger out of the oven, through the collapsed entry, and back into the room with the door.

The candles are still lit; room's probably 120 degrees but feels like a freezer. Anne chugs water. We pull the ear wads. Susie hands me her bottle and wipes at my face while I drink.

Anne says, "Didn't know you could do that."

"Should see me moonwalk."

Anne opens the Myers's bottle one-handed, pours out the vial, and opens it. Susie grabs the stationery and reads.

"The treasure travels from bank to bank,
Where the frigates sail and sink,
Her Majesty is the season; La Vibora the reason,
The shade is there, me thinks."
— EJG.

"Soldiers, slaves and sailors, all have drowned under the weight, the end is the end, circles the friend, and like all thieves, death is your fate."

Anne says, "Lemme see." Susie hands her the stationery. Anne reads, blinks once, reads again, then hands it to me.

Susie says, "'La Vibora' means 'the serpent' or 'viper.'"

Anne shakes her head. "Ah, you're a pretty thing, but it's the island history that wins the boys at this dance."

Susie rolls her eyes.

Anne continues. "La Vibora is the Spanish name for the Pedro Bank." She taps the first line—

"The treasure travels from bank to bank,

—adds, "That's our poet O'Hare sayin' the gold went from the Bank of Haiti to the Pedro Bank. The Pedro's off Jamaica's south coast, forty miles of wicked reefs, three hundred shipwrecks, bad weather, and pirates."

Makes sense. I say, "BeBe mentioned the Pedro Bank when we were in Kingston at the old ships' coordinates. Said it was used by the queen-conch fishermen." I show Anne the clue:

Her Majesty is the season; La Vibora the reason,

"Ah," says Anne. "Makes sense now. 'Her Majesty' is the queen conch the fisherman hunt, seasonal weather permittin'."

I smile. "You're getting good at this."

"And we'll have to be if the Pedro Bank is where we're goin'. In the bank's reefs, there's a string of small cays, two of 'em for the fishermen and the prostitutes who service 'em. One for a Jamaica Defence Force station I avoid regular, and an officially-not-there station for the US Marshals Service."

"That's it for locations?"

"There's one more named cay on the bank: Southwest Cay, called Bird Cay by some. Now she's a government-protected home to hundreds of frigate birds."

"Frigate?" I tap 'frigate' in the verse:

Where the frigates sail and sink.

Anne leans back, seriously surprised. She smiles the smile all the way to its limits.

I say, "'Frigates' that 'sail and sink' isn't ships; it's birds—"

Susie shouts: "The gold's on Bird Cay!"

Anne nods. "But she's thirty-five acres . . ." Anne rereads the clue, looks at us, rebuilds the smile, and says, "They also call Bird Cay *One Tree Cay* because . . ."

I clap. "Yowzah!" Point at her. "Because it has only one tree."

Susie points at the clue—

The "shade is there, me thinks."

—shouts, "For *shade*, me thinks!"

"Holy shit, **X** marks the spot." I high-five Susie. We do a three-way happy dance.

Susie swigs rhum, asks, "How high is Bird Cay?"

Anne shrugs. "Ten feet, maybe fifteen."

"And the waves out there now—" Susie holds the bottle over her head. "Thirty footers, twenty for sure. Our island's under water."

"Aye, she'll be a bit damp till the storm recedes." Anne unrolls a Haiti map and flattens it over O'Hare's stationery. "And with a bit of luck, we'll be puttin' to sea to test those waves." Anne points at Haiti's Highway 101 snaking into mountains that separate Castle Barbancourt from the ocean to the south. "Our best bet is south through the peaks, then down to Marigot at the water. Twenty-five miles of mountain cut if the narrows aren't washed out."

"I was on the roads coming here; we don't want to do roads. Take the plane."

"Wind crashed it on takeoff. Into the mountain after the pilot dropped us with the two Tontons."

I say, "Any road we take, we're in the Rebelyon. And the Gryphon's on our heels."

Anne locates the castle on the map. "Idamante's fightin' to the north of us, just down the hill from Pétion-Ville. If we can make it to the south coast at Marigot, we drive the coast road west and grab the first boat that'll sail." Anne points at an island near the southwestern tip of the country. "We take that boat to here, just before the open ocean that leads to Jamaica, the big island in Ferret Bay. It's a deep-water harbor, protected, a hurricane hole Henry Morgan used. I've used it. Big boats will be there, boats we can take to the Pedro Bank."

Susie shakes her head. "Won't work. A Cat 3 or worse would've wrecked every boat on the south coast that didn't run. We'll be on that road naked to the rebels and the Gryphon."

Anne thinks about it. "A plane *would* be better."

Susie says, "Have to be a seaplane. And the pilot would have to be insane."

"Kayak Jim Jordan."

Both women look at me.

"Rum Cay. Hotel Boblo. You know him, Susie."

Susie laughs. "Jim Jordan's crazy, that's a fact."

"He flew me to Cuba looking for you. You found a sat phone in this castle, right? That's how you called the Gryphon. We call Kayak Jim, you offer him money and naked pictures for his bar, he flies down behind the hurricane. Piece of cake."

Both women laugh.

"No shit, I mean it."

Susie and Anne stare at each other, shrug, and Susie says, "Can't hurt." She pulls a sat phone from a bag on the floor. "Probably won't work again until the storm passes."

I try. The phone is live but has no signal. "Plan B?"

Anne gathers her gear. "Don't be here when the Gryphon arrives."

I step between her and the door to suicide. "Ease up a minute. There's a hurricane out there. I know we're not going out in that. And I know we're not walking into the mountains. And I know the Gryphon is coming. So, ah, if you're packing to leave, which one of you has our gassed-up magic Cadillac in her pocket?"

Susie jingles car keys. "The car the Tontons carjacked from the air-strip manager. We wedged it in under the castle for a rainy day."

Anne points toward the stairs. "Best be movin'. Every minute we're not here after the storm passes is another minute ahead of the Gryphon. Call your Kayak Jim from the car. If we reach him, he's our way off the island. If not—"

"We do something else." Susie pats her AK-47, reaches for the door, looks us both over, and adds, "Piccard's dead. We're gonna win. It's our turn."

I press up from the table to stand but can't feel it on my hands; can't feel my arm . . . cold all over . . . can't see very well. At all—

Chapter 32

BILL OWENS

Evergreen freshener? Blink . . . awake? Engine running in a parked car—back seat . . . I'm looking past a head at . . . ocean? Susie's head?

Wooden boats are piled on a beach. Beat-to-shit black people. *Oh shit, police.* With AKs. Susie's in the driver's seat. I ask the back of her neck, "Where are we?"

"Get down." Susie's hand has a cocked pistol in it and reaches over the seat to push me lower. "Be cool. We're a half mile above Marigot. Anne's talking to the police."

"What happened?"

"You passed out at the castle. We thought you were dead; let you sleep. When Lana cleared, we loaded you in the car and took backroads to the 101. The mountains were wicked, almost wet my pants twice." Susie checks the rearview mirror. "Lana's finished with Haiti; looks like she veered north toward Cuba. We've got an alley to Jamaica. Been trying Kayak Jim. No luck."

"Gimme the sat phone."

She drops it into the back seat. I wipe sweat out of my eyes and dial. Kayak Jim answers on the second ring, like he's been waiting all his life for a call. "Hello? Hello?"

"Jim, this is Jon Eig. You remember—"

"Which one?"

"The one with Anne Bonny and Susie Devereux topless on my lap. We need a fourth to share the Capone gold."

"That'd be a party."

"Not kidding. We need a ride. Three of us and 1,650 pounds of gold. You told me to call when I found it."

Static. Silence. Static. "Say again."

"Hold on, Susie Devereux wants to talk to you." I push the phone up over the seat to her behind the wheel. Susie switches hands with her pistol, grabs the phone, and holds the phone out so I can hear.

"How are you, Jim Jordan. Long time."

"*Susie?* You're alive?"

"Wearing a strapless prom dress. Anne and I need a ride to the dance. Are you interested?"

"Anne *Bonny*?"

"Herself."

Static. Silence. Different tone. "How bad is it?"

"Backside of a hurricane in the Corazón Santo. Civil war. The Gryphon. I'd say a long par five."

"Jesus. You found the gold?"

"We did. Bill did. You know him as Jon Eig."

"So I heard."

"So, Mr. Jim? Are you flying or not?"

"What would a flight like that pay? Into a civil war?"

"Naked pictures for your bar and one million in gold."

Silence. Static. "Make it two."

"That would be pictures or million?"

"Both."

"Done. Marigot, Haiti. There's a false bay a mile after the 101 turns west along the coast. Bring shovels."

"The Gryphon really in this?"

"He is."

"Wow. He's real, huh? That's, ah, genuinely awful. How close?"

"Don't know. The hurricane was hard on him, but likely not hard enough."

"CNN says the fighting's heavy in Port-au-Prince and Cap-Haïtien. Where are we going from Marigot?"

"Not far. Hurricane's already past us. I'm sure there's civil war at Jacmel, but we're well east of there, and the road between us and there is gone. Plane will need enough gas, at the very least to Jamaica. How long till you can be in the bay?"

"Three, maybe four hours *if* I can fly straight across the Inaguas. Won't know that till I'm in the air. Not exactly calm out there."

"That's why the heroes call it adventure. When you're close, call this number. If we don't answer or you don't see Herself and her red hair waving from the beach, don't put down."

"Roger that. Tell your boyfriend I'm impressed."

Before I can inflate my chest, Anne pops the passenger door, squats so she can see us but doesn't look at us or get in. Her arm's still duct-taped to her chest; red hair pouring out the back of her bandanna. "This constable blocking the road—"

Susie's .45 goes click, click in the front seat.

Anne continues, "Gave him twenty US. He's passin' us up to his captain at the next checkpoint; says the shoreline's bad-awful. Most of the road's out between there and Jacmel, like we hoped."

Susie nods. "Poor people and waterfront are never a pretty picture after one of these. At least nobody can come east at us from Jacmel." Her empty hand taps near Anne's duct-taped arm. "We got the plane. Inbound in three to four hours."

Anne cranes her head inside the window. "For true?"

From behind the seat, I say, "Put a man on the job, things happen."

"And a fine, fine man ya are, William. I take back everything Susie ever said about your gender." Anne shuts the door and walks back toward the checkpoint.

Susie says, "Get ready. No telling what this next checkpoint will be. Or how Herself will handle it. She's hurt worse than you think."

I cock my pistol as she slow-rolls our car forward and narrates what I can't see, four minutes of slow-roll, mudslide, snapped-tree narration and we stop.

Susie's voice ramps: "Anne's at the checkpoint, fifty feet up, talking to the top cop. He's pointing at our car, haggling. Three more cops now, looking Anne up and down. If I have to get out, I'll start yelling, draw them away, *then* you get out, shoot whoever isn't with the program."

Loud voices, but not Anne's.

Susie says, "Anne just waved. Better sit up; hide your .45."

I slide my hand and the .45 under my shirt. The outskirts of Marigot look like a logging camp hit by a tornado. The mountains must've channeled the wind into some kind of super funnel. What's still here is mostly wood pulp and mud.

Susie rolls us through minimal road debris and nine standing survivors on the roadside, teenage boys and grown men still dazed an hour after the storm passed.

Anne is stepping back from the roadblock and four armed men. She stops, plants her feet apart under the long legs and boat shorts, chin up, head back, a cocked pistol belted in the small of her back. She raps the passenger-side front fender as we arrive.

Susie stops the car. Anne steps to the passenger window, doesn't look in, and ice-cold, says, "Don't . . . think . . . so. Turn around; I'll walk back to the roadblock, keep 'em busy."

Susie says, "And then what?"

"Turn around."

Susie says, "Bill, pass an AK up here."

I slide one of two over the seat, grab the other one, and drop the safety. Susie lays hers across her lap, and tells Anne, "Not leaving you here. Get in the car."

Two of the four policemen shout something in Kreyol. Anne slowly raises the one hand she can. Susie kills the engine, says, "Game time." She jumps out and shoulders her AK at the four cops.

I pop the door on Anne's side, jump out with my AK. The 'cops' have shirts and hats, but the wrong pants and their gun belts don't fit.

Anne draws the pistol from her back and says, "Gentlemen, we're tourists goin' to the beach. Where we're *not* goin' is to be 'searched' or 'interrogated.' If ya have any further inclination toward either, I suggest ya draw your weapons and defend yourselves."

All four 'cops' back away.

Susie shouts "Not you" at the nearest man. "Come here."

He walks thirty feet and stops.

Susie says, "Food, water, and a roof. We have money. Not looking for trouble. Not looking for boyfriends either."

The man points west, to his left, around a blind corner.

Anne says, "Drop your gun. Have a seat on the hood. We'll kill ya first if your restaurant friends can't remember what business they're in."

***

Two hours. Humid. The flies are returning. We wait nervous in the scoured rocks and destruction at Marigot's false bay, eyes on the sky for our exit visas; eyes on the road for the Gryphon. He'll have to search the castle; probably already there. I have an AK on my lap. Anne has her pistol in hand and is unwilling to discuss her injuries. She passed out once we were set up but is now awake and wants to talk clues.

Susie has our host at the restaurant's entrance gate, his back to us, her AK pointed at him and the only way in. The Gryphon has had three hours to arrive at the castle, then "guess" that we took the only route south that was open. Essentially, we're trapped. I'm semi-surprised he isn't already here.

Anne taps Eddie O'Hare's last two clues. "Bird Cay is thirty-five acres."

"Yep, lot of sand. Gotta hope the 'shade' we can 'trust' is the shade of the tree. The shade is the map's base point."

Anne nods cautious.

I reread Eddie's last verse out loud for her:

> Soldiers, slaves and sailors,
> all have drowned under the weight,
> the end is the end,
> circles the friend,
> and like all thieves, death is your fate.

Anne says, "Drowned under the weight of what? The gold?"

"Lemme think about it. Anything else ring a bell? 'The end, circles the friend'?"

Anne shakes her head.

"Okay. Do we at least agree that we have to dig?"

Anne nods. "If the gold's there, we have to dig."

"Is there anything else on that island that's *focal* other than the one tree?"

"Nothing focal. Just crabs, birds, their eggs, and guano."

"Good. Anything different from the 1930s, when Eddie would've been there?"

Anne thinks about it. "Wasn't a designated sanctuary back then."

"Would the queen-conch fishermen from Jamaica have been using it?"

"Could. Would for certain if the fishing elsewhere had played out. Daytime only. None would lie up there at night."

"So Eddie and Remi and whoever helped them bury 1,650 pounds of gold probably did it at night?"

Anne shakes her head. "Could've been months, day or night, when no one was out there."

"And all of the diggers except Eddie O'Hare would've died there? Before he wrote his clue?"

Anne nods. "If Eddie O'Hare could drive a boat."

**

Our sat phone rings. Susie jams it to her ear. "Jim?"

She listens, circles her finger at Anne and me, then stands with some difficulty and tells the phone: "You'll have to land in close; no boats left on the coast to ferry us out. We'll wade out to you, but we're in no shape to swim."

Anne says, "Tell him not to make a pass. Come straight in, one time, and out."

Susie repeats Anne's instructions, listens, says "Ten-four," then buttons off. "Biggest plane Jim could get can fly two thousand pounds total. The three of us probably weigh four fifty; he's one sixty. Then there's the extra gas."

I scan the sky for the plane, then the road back to the castle. "*Out of here's* the priority."

Susie pats her AK. "Not stupid, Mr. Bill." She grabs her bottle of Barbancourt, turns to Anne. "Are we ready, Anne Cormac Bonny?"

Our host 'cop' jerks around to look. Anne waves him to her with her pistol, then points to a small pile of bills on the rock next to where she sits. "This money's yours." Anne aims her pistol at his chest. "So's this if you make me come back."

He nods. "Anne Bonny?"

"Aye. *I* bring Rebelyon back, not Idamante. We leave here to liberate Port-au-Prince. Take your money. Sit down till we fly away. Tomorrow, Ayiti is free."

A nervous hand grabs the money. He retreats to sit the farthest rock from her.

An engine drones above us somewhere in the bay. We scramble down the rocks to the water.

Thirty feet off the beach, a white seaplane half circles, dips a wing, and splash-lands between the long, low waves. The engines steady, spraying green ocean in three directions.

Susie, Anne, and I wade out in a line, AKs over our heads, me backward, facing the beach and the small crowd watching.

A grinning Kayak Jim Jordan pulls Anne aboard, says, "Welcome. Welcome," reaches past to pull Susie up and in, then jumps back into the pilot seat.

Susie and Anne pull me in.

Both engines rev into roar and we bounce forward on the waves. Jim shouts, "Hold on tight. Water's gonna be rough."

The plane bounces ocean, twists, dips, and we're airborne with the door still open. Anne, Susie, and I are on the floor between the seats and shovels, grinning like Christmas.

I made it out of Haiti.

We steep-climb the dead air and make two thousand feet as we pass Jacmel. Below us, the Rebelyon fighting looks like newsreels of Vietnam. Kayak Jim banks away from the fires and smoke and shouts: "Where to?"

Anne crawls up to the copilot seat, bandanna in her only free hand wiping her face and pushing red hair behind her neck. "Pedro Bank. Bird Cay. You know it?"

Jim does a thumbs-up. He looks at her, then his gauges, then her again. "No shit . . . Anne Bonny?"

"Aye. Pleased to meet ya."

Kayak Jim looks like a kid whose Cracker Jack box had a Cadillac in it. "Heard about you since the second day I was in the Bahamas."

"All true." Anne belts her pistol under her taped arm. "Can you snug this plane up to sand?"

"Maybe."

Anne points ahead of the plane. "Up ahead, the Jamaica Defence Force has a Coast Guard station just northeast of Bird Cay where we're headed. The US Marshals and DEA have a twenty-four/seven camp there as well. Got all the gadgets. They'll see this plane landin' and want to know why. Should the authorities come out, it'll be by boat, the Jamaican's JDF. We'll wanna pack up fast and make 'em think our true intentions are elsewhere."

"Okay," he says. "Once we're loaded, range depends on the weight. And how sure you wanna be that you get where you're going."

Anne scans Haiti's coastline. "We'll be needin' margin for the Gryphon as well."

Kayak Jim shakes his head. "Anyone *not* chasing you?"

"Would seem to be the full complement."

"Yeah, it would. Not sure two million was the right number." Kayak Jim banks south, then levels. "Bird Cay in forty-four minutes." Over his shoulder he shouts: "Hiya, 'Jon,' Ms. Devereux. Good to see you both. There's rum back there with the shovels."

***

Kayak Jim makes one low pass at Bird Cay's thirty-five acres of flat scrub. A mass of white birds levitates in a carpet. The island's low center is now a storm lake. The surrounding ocean is calm—a storm-churned milky blue above a ring of submerged coral shoals.

The shoals would be murder for any boat that didn't know exactly where it was going. Eddie O'Hare probably never saw the island from up here. There's one narrow channel into the beach; have to be navigated by someone who knew, and in daylight. The bow of any boat that made it in would be pointing straight at the lone tree standing on the island. No telling if our tree is the same tree that was here for Eddie O'Hare eighty years ago.

Susie says, "God's making up for his actions." She turns back from her window, smiling. "The JDF's Coast Guard station has no boats still in it; probably ran them to the mainland for cover. They'll be en route back if the storm didn't get 'em. In and out, Bill, and we'll be good."

I look up from Eddie's last clue, more than a little giddy that I'm not in Haiti. "The old in-and-out, huh?"

Susie winks, pushes me the rum bottle. "Assuming you can handle yourself after the digging."

I leer, sip the bottle that has the taste of her lips, and pass it back. "Your chances at me aren't endless; I'd take 'em while we're out here and there's no competition."

Susie does that secret girl thing where they just kind of glow.

Anne interrupts, "We'll be focusin' our energies on the gold and a fast exit."

"Fast?" I turn to Anne. "It's thirty-five *acres*. All we really know is the tree. There's nothing in the clue that says: "Shiver me timbers, ten paces, **X** marks the spot."

"Has to be fast." Susie agrees, straightens in her seat. "The Gryphon will be at Marigot by now, or soon. They'll tell him about this plane."

"So what? He can't know where we're going."

Anne says, "We passed a US-built, *Haiti*-operated radar station thirty minutes back at Tiburon on Haiti's west coast. We're already on *everyone's* radar who didn't drown."

I frown, then read the clue for the twelfth time.

We bank to land in the water. Eddie's final "trap" could easily be the shoals surrounding Bird Cay, not buried grenades. Or the trap could be both, or neither.

Anne slips out of the copilot seat and back to Susie and me. "I'm guessing we have an hour or less before the JDF or the Gryphon get here—no guarantee either are comin', but we'd be fools not to expect both. I can't dig. Jim stays with the plane." She looks at me. "Time to be special, William."

Kayak Jim puts us in the water's lone coral alley, then taxis in straight to the beach and the tree, a windblown tamarind with a few red flowers still in its half canopy.

Two battered femme-fatale pirates and I bail from the plane, Susie and me holding shovels, our AKs slung over our backs.

I look under the tree for **X** in the sand: "O'Hare's standing here with no landmarks other than this tree. If the gold is under the tree, he needs to remember which side. He's with Remi Péralte—one guy's from Haiti, one guy's from Sportsman's. So far, the entire story's been: rhum, slavery, sugar, rebellion, and horse racing."

Susie says, "Is there any left or right, front or back to rhum? Or slavery, sugar, rebellion, or horse racing?"

Hmm. "Rhum—no. Slavery—no. Sugar—no. Rebellion—maybe. Horse racing—yes, lots of 'em." I do a 360 and see nothing but the tree, bird shit, and sand. "O'Hare's the boss—let's go with horse racing. Pick words that matter to horse racing."

> "Soldiers, slaves and sailors, all have drowned under the weight, the end is the end, circles the friend, and like all thieves, death is your fate."

Weight.
End.
Circles.

> under the weight, the end is the end, circles

"'Under the weight' could be the assigned weight a horse has to carry.

"The 'end is the end' could be the finish line.

"'Circles the friend' could be the winner's circle.

"And the 'friend' is the horse who won for you."

Not bad. I don't hate that.

"So this tree is the big finish for our race. Cross the finish line, then go to the winner's circle."

Anne says, "If it's about horse racing, where's the front or back, left or right, of a winner's circle finish line?"

I visualize the finish line at Sportsman's Park.

Susie says, "What direction did the finish line run?"

"North and south. Same as Hawthorne next door." I don't explain why Chicago had two racetracks next door to each other. I ask Susie, "You're a navigator, can you mark true north?"

"If you'll hurry your ass up." She points back toward the plane. "That's north."

I face the tree from the south, where Sportsman's grandstand would be. "If the tree's the finish line, then the Sportsman's winner's circle is on the tree's right."

Anne says, "C'mon, Bill, we gotta dig."

I focus on the tree. Most of its growth is on its left side, not the winner's circle side.

A saltwater breeze gusts sand into my face. I blink against the sand. Re-look the odd tree, ask Anne: "Prevailing winds out here would be from . . ."

Anne points her AK. "Northeast trade winds."

But the tree hasn't grown on the right where the wind should have pushed it . . . instead, it flourished on the left, *into* the wind.

I ask the tree, "Why would you do that?"

Because . . .

Prior to being the best fucking treasure hunter of all time, I dug foundations all the time; I know what foundations do to root systems.

I check my two pirate girlfriends, then answer for the tree:

"You grew into the wind *because* the root growth on the leeward side had to go deeper for water." Grin. "*Because* something big was buried there that got in the way of your roots."

I mark a big **X** in the sand to the right of the tree, a "smartest guy at the track" spot I've occupied enough times that it's like some cosmic river brought me here. "Ladies and gentlemen, we have a winner."

Susie and I stack our AKs against the tree, safeties off, and start digging. We dig, and dig. And dig.

One-armed Anne walks our perimeter, AK in hand, eyes 360 all the time.

The sand's easy to dig, but it's endless and the hole continues to collapse, almost as wide as it is deep. We stop at four feet.

Anne says, "We're here too long." She looks down at me in the hole. "You're sure this is your spot?"

Frown. Pant. "Eighty years ago. Lotta sand moving since then."

Susie pants, re-grips her shovel, chugs water, and keeps digging. She's a woman possessed, outrunning an outcome I've seen in my night terrors. We sweat, dig, sweat, and dig for another ten minutes.

Susie hits rock, then I do. A natural coral pit, ten feet square.

Inside the borders of the coral, we quickly get down another three feet.

I find a skull; Susie finds a rib cage.

She pants. "Bet a hundred this is Remi Péralte." The skull has a bullet hole in the rear.

My heart beats faster. We dig faster. My shovel hits metal. I drop to my knees and slough sand. The metal's stamped "USS *Machias*," possibly the lid of a large ammunition box.

Susie says, "Oh shit."

I check for booby traps, suck a breath, hoping not to explode . . . and we pop the lid.

No explosion.

Stacked inside the metal box are twelve-inch-by-twelve-inch wooden crates, each six inches deep. Each crate is stamped "United States Mint, San Francisco." I pop the first crate.

It's divided into a grid for coins—five rows of five columns. I pull out ten gold coins from one of the twenty-five sections, then squint at the dates: "1910."

Susie's jaw drops; she extends her hand. "Gimme."

I hand her the coin.

She fingers it, flips it, and yells: "Anne! Saint-Gaudens $20 double eagles."

I pop the lids on the other crates in the top row of the ammo box. "Coins. The same. Some from 1909."

Anne yells down from the top of the hole: "How many?"

"Two-fifty in this crate. More below."

Susie the treasure hunter tells me: "The US minted six million; worth at least $3,000 a piece, probably more."

I do the math. "This *one* little wood crate is . . . seven hundred fifty thousand dollars?"

Susie grins. "C'mon, unpack 'em all up to the rim."

The little crate I'm holding weighs close to twenty pounds. We empty the metal ammo box, hauling twenty-five crates total out of the hole, then the empty ammo box that I push up and over.

Up top, Anne kneels next to the twenty-five wood crates we unpacked. She's smiling ear to ear. "Nineteen million dollars, chums. Call it $20 million with premiums." She grins as wide as her bandages will allow. "Never doubted us for a moment."

I turn to celebrate with Susie. She's at the bottom of the hole, dead silent, staring at her feet. *Fuck.* I think *Trap*, stop breathing, and say, "Don't move."

Susie doesn't move. She says, "There's another ammo box."

Anne shouts, "Careful!"

I jump down to Susie. "How rich you wanna be? Twenty mil should be plenty."

Susie's lost her grin. "Not leaving a dime for the monster to rebuild his horror show if I can't kill him. Not a fucking penny. Climb out, I'll open it alone."

"We're having kids, right?"

Susie blinks, shakes her head. "*So* glad I don't have a dick."

I point at her. "And the first night you'll wear the pirate outfit. That was the deal." I kneel, check the box's edges, and look up. "You sure?"

"Iffy on the pirate outfit till I'm put back together, but a deal's a deal."

Deep breath. "Okay. Sail together; finish together."

I pop the lid.

We don't explode. Susie and I unload another twenty-five crates up to Anne, then double-team the empty ammo box up and out. In the hole, staring at us from where the second ammo box used to be are two more ammo boxes.

When we're done unloading and not dying, there are four ammo boxes, one hundred crates total: close to $80 million in gold coins. Literally, *a ton* of money.

Susie and I climb out of the hole. Anne has already dragged the empty ammo boxes to the plane. Susie and I carry one hundred crates, two at a time, and heft them into the plane for Anne and Kayak Jim to repack.

"Weight's gonna be a problem." Kayak Jim packs crate on crate. "No one's ever gonna believe this."

Susie runs back to the tree and grabs our AKs. Jim climbs into the pilot's seat and fires the engines. Anne pulls binoculars and 360s the ocean.

Sweat-soaked, Susie and I collapse into our seats. Anne jumps in and pulls the door shut. Kayak Jim hits the throttles and we chug, heavy, into the chop.

Sweat rivers off me; my hands are shaking. I'm cold and hug my shoulders. Anne eyes the ocean, then checks her AK. Each of us has two extra twenty-round magazines and an absolute certainty we'll need them.

Kayak Jim shouts, "Feels too heavy. Where to?"

Anne shouts back, "How much gas have we got?"

"Hundred miles."

"No choice, then; has to be Jamaica direct. Put her down in the Black River; that's thirty miles from here. She'll be plenty high with the weather."

Susie cranes out her window and shouts: "Plane!"

From her window, Anne tracks the plane. "Not JDF; not US Marshals . . . gotta be the—"

I yell: "Boat!" Underneath the plane that Anne and Susie are watching is a deep V; its bow high in the water like it's coming at us fast.

Anne and Susie say, "Fuck. Jamaica Defence Force."

Chapter 33

BILL OWENS

Our plane vibrates and rattles, slogs in the waves as we try to lift off. Kayak Jim shouts, "Too heavy. Pop the door. Throw stuff out!"

Anne pops the door. The full ammunition boxes weigh five hundred pounds each. Susie and I try to move them but can't.

I say, "We pop the lids on two boxes, empty half the crates, relock the boxes, and shove two out. Maybe five hundred pounds is enough."

Susie says: *"That's twenty million dollars."*

"You can't live on sixty?"

Anne shouts: "Boat's closing."

Susie and I half empty the first ammo box, seal it, and shoulder-shove it out the door. It dives for the bottom.

The plane buzzes us again, likely a spotter for the Gryphon. The plane can track us wherever we go, but it won't be able to stop us.

Susie and I half empty the second box, seal it, shove it down the aisle to the door, and out. Our plane picks up speed but not air.

The JDF boat hasn't veered; it's coming right at us—they veer just as we lift off out of the water.

"Flyers rule!"

Anne climbs over Susie and me, drops back into the copilot seat. I crawl over wood crates to the door, pull it shut, and collapse again, shoulder to shoulder with Susie. "Treasure business is a bitch."

Susie pants, laughs. Her arm loops my neck. "Not over yet, cupcake."

Kayak Jim says, "Black River in nine minutes."

Anne yells back to Susie and me, "We'll belly in just over the harbor bridge, splash down past the last riverside dock, try not to hit any crocs, be upriver a half mile at the Broad River turn when we stop. I've people up there. If they're not flooded out, we can make the road, quarter mile east."

"And if your people are gone?"

"Plan B, William, plan B." Anne punches fists with Susie. "We're too rich and too pretty to die now."

Our plane slows. Kayak Jim yells, "Going down. Hold on."

The nose drops. The river mouth at the bridge is clogged with boats. Anne shouts: "JDF! Up, up!"

Kayak Jim pulls the stick to his chest, roars the engines, banks hard, but can't gain altitude. He quits the bank, drops the wing to level, and we fall toward the tree canopy along the river. Our belly doesn't hit the trees. We realign on the river, flying twenty feet off the water.

Jim gains enough altitude to bank north again. We do; he shouts: "Five minutes of gas, maybe ten, then we're in the ocean."

I yell, "Frenchman's Bay. Treasure Beach. Up the coast north ten miles. I know people there. Right at the water. Go there. Go."

Anne and Susie are glued to the windows. Anne says, "Only one road in and out of there. Who's it you know?"

"Captains. Contrabanders back in the day. Saw a YouTube video last year from Eggy's Bohemian Bar. Captains were in it, still alive. They can get us gas or boats. Cars, if you think that's better."

Anne shakes her head. "Can't do boats—the JDF. A car might work if we could get inland to Mandeville and change vehicles, hole up until we can get off the Rock. Except the Gryphon's plane will know we put down in Frenchman's, then track us wherever we go."

"Not if we run him out of gas."

Susie and Anne look at me.

"Gas up in Frenchman's Bay, head for the Gulf of Mexico. Guy drowns if he follows us."

"He would." Anne nods. "Even with auxiliary tanks he would." She looks at Susie.

Susie shakes her head. *"Maybe* we shake the Gryphon, but the US radar net will figure us for cocaine and force us down. No way we get the gold off the plane. It'll be ten years of court battles to get any of it back, and then only fifty-fifty."

Kayak Jim yells from the cockpit. "Is this it?"

I climb over wood crates to Jim's shoulder. "Yeah. Eggy's is dead ahead, up at the east end, this side of the crag. No shoals; they bring the boats right to the beach. Will your plane run on car gas?"

"Low altitude, cool day, no problem. Gotta be fresh, though." Jim pushes the nose down. "Where we going if we find gas?"

"Anne and Susie are working on it. Get me close to the beach. I'll get the gas."

"Hold on."

Kayak Jim banks us into the flat blue of Frenchman's Bay, hits the water west to east, and has me out and wading before the Gryphon's plane can make a second pass.

Eggy his own self is sitting out front of his bar wearing the world's largest Rasta tam and a grin that's almost as big. "Billy-mon! You come home!" He hugs me and offers the spliff in his left hand.

"Eggy, man, how you doin'? I gotta get gas. Fast, man, like yesterday."

Eggy blinks, tracks the Gryphon's plane flying too low. "Troubles?"

"Big. Babylon coming from Black River. Gotta have gas."

Eggy bends away and yells up the path. "Bernard! Billy-mon back. Him needin' airplane gas!" Eggy pulls his cell phone and starts calling.

Pete the Pirate, my trusty cab driver from my Meyers's days, who'd take me anywhere but back to Kingston, jumps off his taxi's fender, runs down the path to the soft sand, and hugs me off the ground. "Billy-mon!"

"You got gas, Pete? Need enough for that plane. And fast. Whatever you can get, we gotta be back in the air in fifteen minutes. JDF coming from Black River." I hand Pete four gold coins. "That's $12,000 US. Get me all the gas you can."

We burn twelve minutes. Almost every gas can from every car and generator in Treasure Beach is at Eggy's. Susie stands in the water at the plane's tail with an AK on her hip. Kayak Jim and Pete fill the plane's tanks. Anne's in the plane, an AK one-handed from the door.

Pete looks at Susie, hands me another can, then glances Anne and her red hair, then me.

I grin. "Yep, that's her; Herself, in person." I nod at Susie while the can empties. "But that one there . . . man, you got no idea."

Pete exhales. "You gonna be the most famous white man in JA."

The Gryphon's plane makes another pass.

Anne eyes the plane, then the far west side of the bay where the JDF boats will appear out of the glare if they tracked us from Black River. She yells at Kayak Jim: "In the plane, pilot. Fly with what we got."

***

Kayak Jim climbs us off the water with everyone in Eggy's Bohemian waving beers at us. Anne says, "Bank back north over the mountains toward Runaway Bay."

Kayak Jim shouts, "Can't. No mountains with this gas. Gotta be sea level."

Susie says, "If we can't go over the mountains, the gulf is out. Gotta go south or east."

Kayak Jim points out his windshield. "East-southeast. I'll vector us at the Grenadines. You decide where."

Anne shouts over me: "No. The Gryphon's other planes probably went there. Go due south toward Cartagena. That's another five hundred miles of open water for 'em to fly."

Susie grabs Anne's good arm. "We can't take the gold to Colombia."

Anne nods. "I know, dearie. We'd be dead before our engines stopped."

They stare. Then grin and, in unison, say: "Tania Hahn. Hotel Bellavista."

Susie shouts to Kayak Jim: "South-southwest to Isla del Maiz. Fifty miles off the Miskito Coast of Nicaragua. Come in from due east toward Managua, then hard south at the coast."

Jim does a thumbs-up.

I ask.

Susi says, "Two islands; part of Nicaragua, but not. Pirate haven in the old days. We know the Indians, the locals. It's perfect. We'll fly this asshole riding our wing into the water. His last radio call to the Gryphon will signal us as going inland into Nicaragua."

"Swell. Then what?"

Susie says, "Tania Hahn. Rugby. Defrocked FBI. Deep green-card CIA. Pirate. It's her hotel."

"Green card?"

"Independent contractor. Like me."

Anne adds, "The island has a five-thousand-foot airstrip. Commercial flights from the mainland once a day; old, old, French-made ATRs. Could carry the weight we need."

Susie nods. "Better. Tania could get us any plane we wanted. Like a jet. No questions asked. And she could pay cash for us, not gold. A Cessna Citation can land on three thousand feet. Probably get twelve hundred miles in three hours and change. Maybe Houston or New Orleans. Tania's *wired* in New Orleans."

My turn to worry. "Yeah, but customs?"

Susie says, "Have to ask her. New Orleans is kind of a CIA town— Lee Harvey Oswald, Clay Shaw, the usual suspects. Lotta dope goes through there; might be tricky."

Anne leans back against the bulkhead. "I'm wanted for political murder in Jamaica. No way I get through immigration anywhere in the US."

The tone is decidedly calm; both women are bruised, cut, bandaged, taped up, and armed to the teeth. They should sound, look, and act desperate, but don't.

I flatline a smile to the existential wisdom one acquires after many years of racetrack sure things. "Yep. Once again, I may have fallen in with bad company."

Susie fixes on the tracking plane out her window. "And this time you'll be glad of it." She looks back to me. "When that asshole's boss makes his final appearance."

I drop my chin, look at her through my eyebrows. "*Excuse me?* Final appearance? As far as this adventure's concerned, he's already done that. Hasn't he?"

***

Kayak Jim yells back to us: "Nicaragua coastline."

I check the window. "Tracking plane's still there."

Anne says, "Shit. Crapshoot now. *If* Tania's on-island, she can get us a jet . . . from somewhere. I'm sure of that. Comin' from Houston or NOLA, we're lookin' at four hours minimum *after* Tania makes the call. So, best case, we're off the island five hours after we land."

Susie checks the tracking plane that we expected to be gone, then does the math. "Haiti's what, four hours from here? Same for the nearest Grenadines?"

Anne nods. "In a jet or turbo twin—like you know he has if he's moving human transplant parts—it could be two or three."

"We'll be sitting ducks if the Gryphon knows where we landed." I climb to Kayak Jim. "How much gas do we have?"

Jim checks his gauges. "Two hundred miles. Give or take."

Anne slaps her knee with her good hand and shouts: "Costa Rica. Lake Arenal. Volcano lake. No airstrips. The Gryphon can't land anywhere near there."

Jim yells: "Arenal's the mountains. No mountains, remember? Can't trust our gas."

I stare at Jim. "You *know* Anne's volcano?"

Jim nods. "Famous. The lake below the volcano is the best windsurf spot in the hemisphere. Wind blows thirty-plus day and night."

"And we could land in that?"

"Maybe. If we had the right gas."

I look back at Anne and Susie, expecting an alternative, *survivable* option from them . . . not the thumbs-up both are giving Jim.

***

The Gryphon's plane drops off our wing at Nicaragua's Rio San Juan, heading for an airstrip we can see at the Nicaragua-Costa Rica border. Anne, Susie, and I high-five.

Anne says, "He'll be back up in thirty minutes, flying circles or outright guesses. We're a seaplane. Going to one of three places: Lake Nicaragua, Rio San Juan, or Arenal. The San Juan River would be a last resort. He'll figure us for Nicaragua first. The wind at Arenal . . . we'd be crazy."

Susie and I look at Anne, then Kayak Jim.

The brand-new plan B is a go: Land on the lake. Don't flip. Dump the gold in two hundred feet of dark water when the surfers aren't looking, get gas at a marina, fly away to safety. Somewhere. Hide there. Recover. Return when we can defend ourselves and dive deep.

My partners think this is reasonable.

What I think doesn't seem to matter.

Kayak Jim says, "Going down. Hold on."

We buckle in, dip a wing, then level out fifty feet above the lake, into the wind. The plane bucks like it's riding a corrugated roof. Jim cuts the power and drops the nose.

The pontoons hit, bounce, slide; we start to spin, don't, slice through the waves and gusts, don't get cross-winded, and don't flip over.

Kayak Jim shouts over his shoulder. "Dock dead ahead. Gas pumps and boats. Get the gas first. Make your sat call from there."

We make the dock's end and pop the door. The lake smells like sulfur. Seven surfer types shake their heads—white kids, an old guy, and a fit, leathery woman. All have hands cupped over their ears. Long blondish dreads slap one kid's face. He uses one hand to wrestle the dreads calm and shouts something Rasta-ish.

Anne leans out the door and shouts street-Kingston back.

The kid and Anne shout Rasta-hip-hop-video to each other until he does a thumbs-up. "Ja, mon! Ja, mon!"

I ask.

Anne leans back in, says: "These pumps are empty. But there's a pump up the road. They'll fill us a truck and car, drive 'em here, we siphon it in, keep 'em comin' till we're full."

Susie jumps out onto the dock with her .45 belted in her boat shorts, then separates from everyone and puts the sat phone to her ear.

All the boys do hot-for-teacher.

Anne and I jump out. I focus on the sky. Anne talks more Rasta speak to the surfer kid and watches the other people on the dock watch Susie.

Kayak Jim cuts the engine and jumps out to prep for the gas.

Susie runs back to us, stops, and points west, away. "Talked to Tania; Lana's about to hit Miami; Tania's in New Orleans." Susie pushes her and me farther away from the people on the dock. "We don't have to dump the gold. Tania said that back in the '60s and '70s the CIA had a 14-40 at Liberia—"

"A what?"

"Fourteen thousand four hundred feet. The length of the runway. Could put a full C-130 down on it; safe-supply our revolutions in El Salvador and Nicaragua. Liberia's a commercial airport now; ten-thousand-foot runway. Maybe thirty-five to forty miles from here—be a wicked drive of bad mountain road, but if we can get there, Tania's coming in on a Lear 25. Be there in four hours. Said she'll bribe the local constabulary; we load up and head for the Great Outdoors."

I want to join the party, but I knew the guys in Huey Lewis and the News back in the '80s. They had an aging Lear 25 *then*. I say, "Plane's kinda old, isn't it?"

Susie checks the sky. "Younger than you. And lots prettier."

Anne joins us, listens to Susie repeat what she told me, then says, "We'll need a truck." Anne walks to her blond Rasta pal, talks, shakes hands, and walks back to Susie and me.

"My new boyfriend Lester has a mate with a farm truck—lots of 'em around here. Told him we'd hire the truck to San Jose."

Kayak Jim walks to us, listens to the plan, shakes his head, and says, "Better we fly into Panama Bay. Your drive from here to Liberia would be a bunch safer." He winces. "But lots more eyes."

I say, "And we'd have to get back in your plane."

Anne says, "The road we'll be takin' is no picnic. Loaded heavy, bad tires . . ."

Susie spits sideways into a thirty-mile-per-hour wind and votes, "Road."

I vote, "Road."

Anne says, "Road it is." She turns to Kayak Jim. "You get 667 coins—two crates and change. Take it all with you or send 'em with us, your choice."

"What about the naked pictures?"

Anne laughs. Susie checks her condition, then Anne's with her arm duct-taped to her stomach. "Really?"

"Really."

Susie says, "We'll come see you when we've been to the hair-and-makeup trailer." She holds up her hand to stop a response. "For now, thanks. Keep your crates and get outta here before the Gryphon gets lucky and spots the plane."

"How about three full crates and I wait, let him spot me, then fly him into the clouds and take my chances?"

A full third crate would add eighty-three coins: $250,000.

Anne laughs again. "A mentaller, you are, James."

"Nah. Better pilot. You're alive, aren't you?"

Anne nods, walks to him, and kisses him on the mouth. "We'll bring a *Playboy* photographer with us. Do you proud." She waves her new boyfriend over and asks him to take a photo. He pulls a brand-new iPhone 3 that has a camera built into it, tells the four of us to scrunch together, and pops a photo. Jim scribbles him an email address.

Susie points Lester away, then tells Kayak Jim: "You know you're not going back to Rum Cay, right? The Gryphon will find you through this plane or some other way. But he'll find you. You gotta become someone else, and not in the West Indies."

Kayak Jim winks. "I'd get your gold off the plane and into your truck. Me, I've got some adjustments to make. Flew races after Vietnam, did stunt work, but not in a seaplane. Gotta grease her up a tad."

***

The road from the south side of Lake Arenal is two-lane hairpins, boulders on one side, certain death on the other, and potholes in the blind spots. Half the guardrails are gone. The sun's starting to drop, adding deep shadow stripes to the blinding glare. The good news? Arenal's volcano isn't spewing lava.

***

It takes our rented truck and *tico* driver two hours to make Highway 1, Costa Rica's version of a real road. Outside the city of Cañas, a sign points west and reads: "Liberia 43 kilometers." Scrunched against our driver, Anne says, "Change of plans. Same pay, shorter trip. Go to Liberia. The *aero-porto.*"

Our driver says, *"No comprendo."*

Susie's bouncing on my lap, hair in my face, and even with most of me beat to death, the bounces feel pretty good. Susie repeats Anne's instructions in Spanish. Our driver turns right. We can't be sure that he doesn't understand English, so we can't talk much. In Spanish, Susie asks him, "How long?"

Our driver shrugs and answers. I think he says, "One hour; a little more. The road is good, but the holes—" He points through the windshield on a sixty-mile-per-hour highway at sudden potholes that would swallow a sports car.

In English, Susie says, "One hour in Tico means two. This is the Pan-American Highway. Supposedly runs from Tierra del Fuego to Prudhoe Bay in Alaska. More concept than highway."

I have one arm around her waist. "Does it go to the airport?"

"Used to." Susie checks her watch and pulls her hair behind her neck out of my face. "Tania should be there when we get there. She said to drive all the way to the far end of the only parking lot. There's an unmanned gate to the private aviation area. She'll be at the gate with someone 'official.' They'll lead us to her plane. We'll load the crates and ammo boxes, shoot whoever won't take money, and head for happy-land."

Susie's bare neck is on my cheek. I sniff. She notices, smiles like maybe I should be thinking about survival.

Anne says, "Tania bringin' painkillers?"

Susie grins. "Bottles full."

I ask, "Her share of our boxes?"

"Five million, plus what's in the water. Includes the plane trip."

"Fine with me."

"There's a catch." Susie glances over Anne to the driver, adding: "Wait till we're outta the truck."

***

A short cherubic blonde in Ray-Ban 2140s and well-fitted jeans stands at the private aviation gate for Aeropuerto de Liberia. Next to her are three armed policemen and a dark-skinned guy in a white guayabera shirt.

I ask Susie, "Your friend, Tania, she wouldn't rob us, would she?"

Susie grips her .45, tells me to pull mine, then in Spanish, tells our driver, "Stop at the gate."

Anne says, "Don't get out, no matter what *anyone* says, till we're at the plane."

Our driver stops when the cherubic blonde pats the headlight. She walks the fender to the driver's window, glances at the bed and its covered cargo, then leans in at the window and says, "And there you are, the Witches of Eastwick." Grin. "Siri hiding under the tarp?"

Anne shakes her head. The blonde looks past Anne to Susie on my lap.

Susie says, "Died helping these two save me from that fucking monster."

The blonde frowns hard and cuts her eyes. "Sorry to hear that." She pushes her hand through the window to me. "Tania Hahn. Susie said good things about you. And that's unusual."

"Bill Owens. We ready?"

"Yeah. This ain't the kinda place a girl wants to be long." Tania points at a Lear 25 with the door steps folded out and down and the cargo bays open. "Drive."

She steps back, waits till we pass, then jogs behind our truck.

Susie, Tania, and I unload, then reload, the seventy-two remaining crates. Tania's stronger than she looks. Anne stays with our driver, keeping his eyes away from our cargo.

A Latin woman who is clearly not a flight attendant stands in the plane's door and watches the terminal. Anne pays our driver as agreed. Tania points at the Latina, says "My partner, Shelia Lopez," then does a thumbs-up at the pilot's window.

The engines fire. We board into dated luxury. Shelia Lopez has a smile on her face, an automatic pistol behind her leg, and the eyes of someone who you wouldn't want as an enemy. She greets Susie by name, hugs her, then helps Anne up without touching the duct-taped arm.

Tania follows, slaps the pilot's exposed shoulder. *"Vamanos, muchachos!"* She levers the door tight and jumps into a seat facing me. "Go. Go. Go."

The plane jolts forward, runs the taxiway too fast, and hits the runway roaring. Takeoff shoves my shoulders into my seat. The wheels clear the tarmac and we ramp into a forty-degree climb. My lungs flatten and both eyes roll halfway back. "Jesus. Your boy's not screwing around."

Cherubic smile. "Colombia. Been shot at before."

The Lear screams higher into the climb like we've got heat-seekers on our tail, then finally breaks into a bank.

Half the Gs quit. I glance at Anne across the aisle.

She says, "Nothin' in these windows."

Tania turns and shouts at the pilots: "Keep it full out. Everything we got!"

I hear "pop" and smell champagne.

Behind me, Susie hoists a foaming bottle of Dom Pérignon. "To Siri, Tommy, and Cyril." She drinks a messy chug, then shoves the bottle to Anne.

Anne chugs three swallows. "Aye, and BeBe, Taller, Sundown, and Lon. And Sistah, God rest her." Anne chugs three more. "I'll be having a tablet or two if we've any."

Tania palms a prescription vial from inside her jacket. The copilot reaches back to Tania's shoulder, pulls his headphones, and says, "Ten minutes."

Tania nods and tosses Anne the painkillers. "Go easy on 'em, we got business yet."

From behind me, Susie wraps an arm around my seat and me, grabs the bottle of Dom from Anne, and says, "And here's to you, Bill." Her arm and the bottle hug me tight to the seat. "You sent that fucking Renfield to hell for all of us. Drink the rest; you deserve it."

I take the bottle, swig it twice, then hand it to Tania. She waves it off, eyes me favorably and the compliment Susie just paid, then says, "Ten minutes, then we decide."

"Decide what?"

***

Five minutes pass.

Tania says, "Should've gotten a hospital plane. You guys look like shit."

Anne blinks. "I'm fine."

Tania looks down her nose. "Don't think I'd go with *fine*."

"See to our business. Or the extent of my scratches won't matter a'tall."

Susie takes the bottle back and chugs again. "What day is it?"

Tania says, "Tuesday. And you don't look that good either." She focuses on me. "Or you. Speaking of which, *why* are you here?"

"Well, let's see. Last Friday—five whole days ago—I was at Arlington Park wearing a well-tailored seersucker suit. Things were looking pretty good. Saturday, I met her." I nod at Susie. "Sunday, I flew to Kingston and rehooked up with Herself." I point at Anne.

Anne makes a smile.

"Anne took me on a boat ride to Haiti in a hurricane. She introduced me to Siri and the latest Haitian Rebelyon. Lots of people tried to kill us. We found Capone's gold, dodged more bad people and police, and now we're with you. I'd say we have a right to look somewhat rumpled and still be considered upstanding citizen-pirates."

Tania laughs. She looks at Susie and Anne. "He belong to either one of you?"

Susie and Anne both nod.

Tania looks as surprised as I do. She grins. "Oops. Last time these two liked the same boy . . . didn't go too well."

The Lear bends into a bank. I ask, "Where we going?"

Tania shrugs. "Up to Susie."

I turn to Susie. "You said there's a catch."

Susie nods but doesn't explain.

Tania does. "Not all of us are gonna live to spend the gold you found."

Chapter 34

BILL OWENS

Tania Hahn finishes a very short explanation.

I'm the only one in the plane who blurts, "We have to do *what?*"

Tania answers, "Kill the Gryphon." She nods at Susie. "I explained it to Susie. No way Lopez and I join this party unless he's dead. Or we are. That, and we get the $20 million Susie says you left in the water back at Bird Cay."

I choke on the bet-your-life precondition to my future; check Susie and Anne, neither of whom are rushing to take chips off the table. I return to Tania. "*You* can kill the Gryphon?"

Tania says, "Bill, my man, your two *chicas* here are formidable when they're in better shape, but they ain't me." Tania points at Shelia Lopez. "Or her." Tania's cherubic grin remains, but her message hardens a bit. "We hunt people; that's what we do. *All* we do."

"Forgive me, but I've seen the Gryphon's operation. Colonel Kurtz, *Heart of Darkness* shit. Every goddamn flesh-eater for a thousand miles, out of their goddamn minds on—"

"I know. I knew Piccard, not personally, but of him. I know the black-box interrogation business; have dropped more than one jihadist in them." She glances at Susie. "Lopez and I don't get our contracts because the Spice Girls turned them down. We're the Wicked Witches of the East, we just don't look like sisters."

Exhale. Face rub. I check Anne and Susie again for a way out that neither offers, then surrender to yet another Valkyrie trip through the roses. "Okay. It's your plane. Tell me how."

"The gold aboard this plane allows your girls to afford Shelia and me, *and* it's the center of a perfect storm; one of the very few chances to get a guy like the Gryphon out in the open. Lana hit Haiti as a Cat 5. Gotta believe the Gryphon lost ninety percent of everything he had in Haiti. No doubt he sees the gold as his insurance settlement. We'll bait him with half; Susie said $60 million. Right?"

Susie nods.

"We'll stack $30 million in gold in a 'safe' place. Susie tells him that's what will be waiting. For him, in person. She'll say she wants to see it in his eyes that he means to leave her alone. If she doesn't see it, her suicide vest kills them both; Susie's happy with either outcome."

Lopez shows Susie the vest.

"If Susie sees that he means to leave her alone, he walks away with the $30 million. Up to him."

I look at Susie again, then Anne.

Anne coughs, wipes at the blood on her chin with her gun hand, then says, "He's a mentaller, beat bad after the storm, and he's beaten Susie twice. No reason for him not to take the bait . . . if we put our hook close to his home ground."

I'm hoping *close* does not mean Haiti. "Where? Jamaica?"

Tania says, "Two choices; four minutes to decide: best for us would be Ragged Island. Lana just leveled it. Ragged's basically an abandoned salt pond mine—a hundred miles off the coast of Cuba; three hundred miles of open water from Haiti. Got an airstrip, tricky but usable. My guess is the Gryphon sends whatever boats he can squeeze through what's left of the channel and the rubble from Batterie de l'Anse and Prison Labouque. He waits till those boats are close to Ragged, flies to the boats via a seaplane he'll commandeer, then comes ashore with them full-force. That's how I'd do it. If I had the equipment."

Shelia Lopez adds, "He'll try some kind of feint so he can disable our plane on the runway. We'll be trapped. He'll kill us all."

"That's our *best* option? How do we kill him?"

Tania and Lopez trade a glance, surprised. "You mean *not* blow up Susie?"

Chapter 35

BILL OWENS

The copilot reaches back and shows Tania four fingers, a plain silver ring on all four. Tania gives him the thumbs-up, then looks at me.

I say it again: "What's the second option? The one where Susie doesn't have to die?" I glance at Susie for her to join the club.

Tania says, "M72 LAW rocket at two hundred yards. Got three aboard, French-built SARPACs. Can't use them on Ragged Island. Too flat; nowhere to hide. Has to be the vest."

"Say we use the rockets; where?"

"DR'd be best; Shelia's got DEA connections for the equipment we'd need. The Gryphon comes over the mountains from Haiti on any road that's open. Could have every night howler with him who survived the hurricane and Rebelyon; he'll like that." Tania grimaces. "We won't. So, as quality options go, I'd say option two is a *distant* second."

"And then?"

"Staying with option two?"

I cast a troubled glance at Susie. "Yeah, option two."

Tania continues. "We extricate him from the body of his army—I'm gonna guess fifty to a hundred is what he actually brings—isolate his options, show him the gold, and kill him. With a LAW we lose the gold too. He won't be expecting that."

I visualize the show, the aftermath of Tontons digging for gold fragments for the next month until the Dominicans figure it out and kill them. "Does Susie still have to meet him with the gold and vest?"

"Yup."

"But she gets away, right?"

Tania shrugs. "Maybe."

I push back in my seat. "I vote option two. And if it's that fucking bad, I say we draw straws for who wears the vest."

Susie leans forward to my shoulder. "I said I'm gonna kill him, and I am."

Anne licks her teeth, swigs the champagne. "Ours is ne a single-vote partnership. We sail together; we finish together. Them's the rules, dearie."

Susie frowns. "So says Anne Bonny?"

"Aye, Susie my dear. Tania here may think she can outfight Anne Bonny on a good day, but she'd be wrong. You'll not face that bastard alone again if I'm breathin'."

DOMINICAN REPUBLIC

Chapter 36

BILL OWENS

We're on a coffee-plantation airstrip. Shelia Lopez and our two pilots will stay inside the Lear with what remains of our life savings. Outside the cargo door, I unload a crate of 250 coins from the hold, then take the crate back inside to the cockpit.

Both pilots have Glocks in shoulder holsters and faded forearm tattoos. One squints when I show him my Flyers neck chain and say, "You look like guys who live through these adventures."

He nods. "Always the plan."

"Do me a favor? Out of this crate, you keep ten coins each for your trouble, give the remaining two thirty to Coach Kenny Rzepecki at Johnny's IceHouse in Chicago. It's for some Down syndrome kids who are gonna suffer big if this money doesn't get there ASAP. Unfortunately, I'm not certain it will if I keep it."

The copilot looks at me like he agrees with my assessment. "That redhead really Anne Bonny?"

I nod. "Port Royal. In the flesh."

"Get her to autograph the crate for me. 'To Ian Pearce.' I have a cousin in Belize City with Down syndrome. I'll get the coins to your coach."

"Thanks."

I drop down to the tarmac. Anne, Tania, and Shelia are checking our weapons. Tania waves me over. "Ever fire one of these?" She shows me one of the three LAW rockets she and Lopez have.

"Right. SOP at the racetrack."

Tania doesn't laugh. "You'll be firing one today. Pay attention; I'll show you how. Probably'll be the difference between being alive and not."

I get the three-minute course in professional M72 LAW rocket operation. The tube looks like it's been around awhile. "How old is this thing?"

Tania waves off my concern. "Works fine. French. Use 'em all the time."

Anne grins at "all the time." "He's gotta die, Bill. One of us has to get 'im."

I look at the name carved on my palm. "There may be something to this vodou shit after all."

Anne says, "Before the shooting starts, Tania thinks she can secure our side of the field, but even if she does, there'll be snipers on ya from the Gryphon's side. Find a ridge. Let 'em see ya high up there, but not the rocket. When Susie and I make our move, don't hesitate; light him up."

"Gee, simple as that?"

"Aye. Him or us; couldn't be simpler."

I walk to Susie. She's on the other side of the plane, cinching her C-4 suicide vest. I stop in front of her. "No offense, but I don't see why the hook has to be baited this way."

Susie stares, then smiles small and shrugs.

"We were gonna have the kids, the pirate outfit, some laughs. You know, boy-girl stuff, but bigger, maybe. Right?"

Susie finishes cinching the vest, steps close enough to kiss me lightly on the mouth, and does. Her fingers hook into my belt. "And if we're alive tomorrow and you're in the mood, that's what we'll do. This movie can end more than one way, sugar."

"Meaning the vest is fake?"

"Nope. But it's not plan A." Pause. Tone drop. "His hands won't touch me again. And I'm all done running."

I pull my Flyers talisman over my head and hand it to her. "I haven't been anywhere without this in a long, long time. It's real, you need to believe that."

Susie loops the chain over her head, kisses it, then me on the lips again. "Flyers rule." She turns her back to me, pulls a knife from her belt.

I watch her carve "Cyril" into her left forearm, then "Tommy" into her right.

***

We're deployed. Sweat rivers my face. The air tastes like stomach bile. Below me is a three-hundred-foot-wide crater that I've been told is a dead volcano's eroded caldera. Maybe 150 feet deep, like a Roman gladiator colosseum dug into the rock.

I'm alone on the caldera's east rim, purposely in plain sight, surrounded at my back and shoulders by thin jungle that Hurricane Lana shredded yesterday. My LAW rocket is hidden fifteen feet away, armed and ready to fire.

Tania and her LAW rocket are somewhere on the north rim to my right, but I can't see her.

Directly across from me on the west rim are thirty Tontons gunmen. Some are aiming at me. Some scan the north and south rims for targets. Most are aiming at Susie and Anne on the caldera's floor.

Susie and Anne drove down from the south rim in a Jeep via a steep, narrow ramp of partially collapsed crater wall. Even though the crater is round, Tania called it a "kill box."

In my head, I hear Arlington's bugler: "Post time."

On the caldera's floor, Susie and Anne stand beside their Jeep. It's stacked with what will pass for forty crates of gold coins, ten thousand total, $30 million US. The lids are off all the crates. Five million of it's real. The shine is what you'd expect, golden.

Anne and Susie both have pistols in their right hands. Anne braces her hip against the Jeep's door but seems to wobble anyway. Susie has her suicide-vest trigger switch in her left hand, her thumb on the button.

She and Anne glare at an armored UN Humvee.

Behind it are three gunmen aiming short-barreled submachine guns.

Behind them is a smallish light-brown man. He wears sunglasses, jeans, and a sport jacket with no shirt.

I can't smell or hear him; no way to tell if he's what was in my monastery cell with me.

Sweat stings my eyes. I try to hear what's being said but can't; the crater's too deep. Didn't think I'd die like this, a multimillionaire with my own hockey team, doing the final scene in *The Good, the Bad and the Ugly*. My knees ache. Both feet want to move. But move means a sniper bullet. Dry swallow. This is it, the bet-it-all moment all horseplayers crave and hate. If I held win tickets they'd be crushed in my hand.

Clear as day I hear Arlington Park's John Dooley say: "They're all in the gate. They're all in line—"

***

SUSIE DEVEREUX

The .45 is cocked in my right hand.

My left hand has the suicide-vest detonator.

I point the detonator at the Gryphon's three gunmen. Anne looks across her duct-taped arm at me. I step three feet closer to the gunmen. "Go ahead, pull the trigger, kill you some white meat for dinner."

Another step closer.

"C'mon, let's all see if that Humvee's armor came from Rumsfeld."

Anne coughs. "Eyes on the prize, dearie."

The "prize" is the monster behind the Humvee. Other than the bone pearls around his narrow lumpy neck, his clothes are unchanged from the last time he had me. I use his real name, shout over his protection: "Feel it, Marcel? Fuck it up here and it's end of the line. You'll be in hell before you know I sent you."

The Gryphon's gunmen bristle. They really, really want to shoot me.

The Gryphon speaks, his tone the emotionless confidence of old-world French aristocracy. "It is you, Susan, who must be sure. For your partners, their families, their friends."

His voice chills my back. My thumb tightens on the detonator. "Don't think so. You won't have the reach after you're dead. And you're gonna die where you're standing unless I find Jesus in the next few minutes."

Anne says, *"Susie."*

His breath is twenty feet away, but I can smell it on my lips, all over my face. He says, "Deliver my gold, and I will allow you to walk away, face your demons on any ground you choose."

"Step out here, eye to eye. Make me a believer."

"Prove the gold you display is real."

I nod Anne away from our open Jeep. "C'mon, then. Take your look." Plan A is *move back* to the edge of the ravine behind us.

Anne whispers, "Sail together; finish together."

One of the Gryphon's three gunmen steps forward, eyes me, then looks over my shoulder to Anne behind me, then continues past me to the Jeep.

He inspects everything that's visible; pops the glove box; pops the hood . . . looking for a cache of explosives large enough to possibly kill his boss, regardless of the Humvee.

Satisfied that the threat isn't there, the gunman inspects the gold, removing random coins from five different boxes. He steps backward several steps until he can pass the coins to the Gryphon at the far end of the Humvee.

Anne wobbles off the Jeep's fender to move back—

The Gryphon dives behind his Humvee's rear wheel. Two of his .50-caliber rifles boom from the west rim.

I spin; don't see Bill standing where he was. Submachine guns roar on Tania's rim. I jump back and hook Anne's neck with my gun hand to keep us where we are. The Gryphon's three gunmen are crouched to light us up—

My heart's pounding. Anne blinks, confused, but doesn't fight. She hip-slides us past the Jeep's door to the front bumper, where we have to be if we intend to kill this monster and survive.

The Gryphon stands but stays behind the Humvee. His voice is still calm, calmer than when he had me naked on his table: "If your intent is to carry on as agreed, step away from the gold."

Anne straightens her neck, stares at the Gryphon, and says, "And who would you be, tellin' Anne Bonny her business? Your gold's here where we said, $30 million in coins; maybe $10 million if Susie's vest makes 'em pieces, assumin' a digger could find 'em all."

The Gryphon doesn't move.

Anne spits blood and saliva at the gunmen. "Not much of a man, your Gryphon. Two women got his tongue *and* his feet." Anne shoulders us off the fender and past the bumper. We both stumble—like we are supposed to. I jerk us backward—

We fall five feet over a narrow ledge into the crevice directly behind us.

Anne lands hard on her back. I land on Anne and punch the button.

The Jeep doesn't explode.

Submachine guns rake Tania's and Bill's rims. I punch the button again. And again. *Goddammit,* my vest detonator was actually rigged to *the Jeep* via a remote sensor, not the vest. The Jeep's oversize tires and seats on the passenger side are packed with four hundred pounds of C-4 that won't fucking explode.

Tania's LAW rocket doesn't fire.

Bill's LAW rocket doesn't fire.

Anne moans. I roll off her chest. She paws for her .45 and rolls to her stomach. I rise in a crouch, then peek between the top of our crevice and the bottom of the Jeep. "Cease fire! Cease fire! We fell, that's all! We're here. Stand down and we'll come out."

Up high on the rim behind the Gryphon, two children crawl over the caldera's edge and slide down the rocks toward the bottom. Then another child, then another.

Anne pants, sucking for air that the fall knocked out of her. Her face is taut, eyes clouded with pain.

I try to figure the detonator. It clicks but won't fire. Must be the goddamn sensor.

At the bottom of the crater, ten children waddle-walk single-file to the Gryphon's Humvee and cluster behind him. He motions the nearest boy to stand in front, places a hand on the boy's shoulder, draws a serrated knife, holds it blade up, the hilt resting on the boy's shoulder.

Anne makes her knees using the .45 to push upright, then stands, crouched below the lip of our crevice. "He's a clever bad one. Give me a moment and I'll see to 'im."

I tell her, "Seen this lineup in the desert. He's gonna put their heads in the sand one at a time."

On the rim behind the Gryphon, the Tontons break into two groups. Eight run to our left, toward the rim with the ramp/road, then disappear.

Eight run to our right, toward the rim where Tania's supposed to be, then disappear.

Anne spits, trying to focus.

More Tontons appear on the rim behind the Gryphon. They aim across the crater, over our heads at where Bill was before the .50s fired at him.

Anne says, "They're gonna engage Tania on our right, block the ramp on our left, circle past it to kill Bill if he's still alive. Then come down for us."

I nod. "Start beheading the kids to draw us out . . . away from the Jeep."

"Can ya fix that detonator?"

"Think it's the sensor. If the detonator's good, I could attach it direct to the vest, spike it with the backup cord. Would work for the tires too—"

"No. Ya'd have to spike the tire, then punch the button. Be shot before ya could make the second move."

Exhale, squint at the rims, the ten kids. "Without the Jeep's C-4, my vest is twenty pounds; won't kill him for sure unless he's out front of the Humvee."

"If I bait him out, can you throw it? My good arm's strugglin' with this pistol."

"Throwing won't work. No way to detonate it other than this button."

We both glance under the Jeep—see ten kids, three gunmen, and the Gryphon.

Anne says, "We gotta make a move."

I nod. "Once they're behind us, it's over." My hands fumble to connect Tania's backup cord to the detonator button. I suck a deep breath—so does Anne. I stab the cord's spike into the vest's C-4.

We don't explode.

I grip Anne's shoulders with both hands. "Vest is live."

She nods to the high rims around us. "Aye. 'Tis a witch's cauldron he's in." Anne grins through the pain. "And we're the Witches."

AKs roar on Tania's side of the crater. A *huge* explosion answers. The AKs cut to just spits. A chunk of Tania's rim is on fire. No voices shout Kreyol.

I check the ramp side opposite Tania. No Tontons are visible yet. But they're there. I yell behind us, "Bill?"

Distant: "Yeah!"

"They'll be coming on your left—"

Distant: "Already here!"

"Forget plan A. Use the rocket to stop 'em."

"Doesn't work! Piece of shit won't fire!"

Anne spits blood, wobbles. "I'll climb out first. If they don't shoot me, I'll position at the back bumper, use the tire for cover. You stand at the front. That'll split two of the gunmen—"

"What good's that do? The only way we're sure he dies is this vest. Stay here. I can bluff him."

"I'll not be stayin' behind—"

I yell over the Jeep, "Start killing kids and we all die—" turn to Anne. "Stay put. Trust me, stay put till I yell for you."

Anne inhales to argue.

I shove her off her feet, then scramble out of the crevice using the Jeep for cover.

From behind it I yell, "Twenty pounds of C-4!" then jam my left arm up above the Jeep's hood where they can see my thumb on the button. Slowly, I stand—don't get shot—loop the Jeep toward the gunmen, stop, and tell the monster behind them:

"Should've shot me coming out of the crevice. At ten, I kill us all. I make it eighty-twenty your Humvee is UN papier-mâché; these kids go to heaven instead of back to the veal crates with you. *Or* you can send them up the ramp, take your gold, and build yourself another red-market paradise. Up to you."

I point at the children, then the ledge ramp.

The children don't move.

"Ten. Nine. Eight—"

The Gryphon speaks in soft Kreyol. Half the children run/waddle weak legs toward the ramp.

I wait for the children to reach the ramp and scramble up to the rim. "Seven. Six. Five. Four. Three." I extend the hand with my thumb on the button. "Two."

The remaining children break for the ramp.

When they are over the rim, I lower my hand.

The Gryphon says, "Perhaps what you truly wish is to come home, assist in the reconstruction of Dimanche? Be America's interrogator again."

My thumb flexes on the button. "Don't think that's where you and I are headed."

"There are worse outcomes."

"Nothing's worse than you being alive tomorrow."

High up behind me on Bill's rim, his rocket tube *booms*; I duck; the far edge of Bill's rim explodes in a fireball; the Gryphon ducks back behind his Humvee's wheel.

Anne scrambles for the Jeep's rear bumper and tire.

The Gryphon's three gunmen crouch, focused on the fireball.

Bill yells from the rim: "Got 'em! Flyers rule!"

Anne rolls out into the open from underneath her end of the Jeep. In her right hand is another detonator button. It's attached by a four-foot cord to a spike detonator she has buried to the hilt in the rear tire. She makes her knees, then wobbles to her feet, collapses to a knee, looks at me, and says, "Always have a backup. I'll drive from here."

I scream: "See that, Marcel? Quarter ton of C-4 in those tires. You bitches ready?"

The Gryphon doesn't move.

Anne says, "Step back, Susie." She coughs blood. "Feels like I'm goin' either way. Would prefer to take this man with me."

I glance up toward Bill, hoping he can see me pull his talisman off my neck, grip it tight in my right hand, then step back next to Anne. "Love you, Annie."

Anne winks, sags against my shoulder.

I turn to the red-market monster trapped behind his Humvee, show him my forearms, stare into his pig eyes until I'm absolutely certain this thirty-year horror show knows it was Anne Bonny and Susie Devereaux who killed him.

The Gryphon stands, confident that his next move will save him and kill us.

I wrap one arm around Anne. "They say hell hath no fury . . . Believe it's time we carved that in stone."

The Gryphon answers: "Sadly, Susan, you've always lacked the courage—"

Anne and I count, "Three, two, one," and punch the buttons.

***

BILL OWENS

Susie and Anne both click their detonators. The caldera erupts. I duck. Jeep and Humvee fragment into razor shrapnel. The heat blast hits my rim, blows high over my head, and sucks all the air out of the sky.

***

Bloody blond hair. "Up. Up."

"Huh?" I push away, scramble, rub volcano out of my eyes. "What the fuck—"

Tania Hahn says, "We gotta go. Your LAW clocked the Tontons on the south rim. Susie and Anne did the rest. C'mon."

I roll to my stomach, make my knees, cough smoke, and she helps me to stand. Lotta smoke; smells like a forest fire in a salvage yard. "Where's Susie"—wobble, cough—"and Anne?"

Tania jerks my arm. "Make your feet run or you're gonna die right here."

I wave smoke out of my face, look left and right. "Where are they?"

"At the plane; come on. We gotta go."

Chapter 37

BILL OWENS

Tania skid-stops her Jeep under the Lear's wing, helps me out, then up the plane's stairs. Susie and Anne aren't there. They're not inside when Shelia Lopez buckles me into a seat. Tania bangs the door shut and shouts *"Vamanos!"* to her pilots. The Lear's engines roar and the torque blasts me into my seat.

"Wait, where are they? We can't—"

The Lear screams down the airstrip, lifts off, and banks hard north, the wings almost perpendicular like we're gonna roll. We snap level out of the bank and climb into the sun. Every part of me hurts.

Lopez throws Tania a towel. "Okay?"

Tania nods, wipes grit from her face and neck, looks at the towel for blood, exhales deep, and tells Lopez, "We need new rockets. No more French shit unless it's got a Michelin star."

Lopez looks me over like a battlefield medic might, then pushes a warm, unopened Presidente beer at me. "Drink one. You're alive; trust me, I can tell."

"Susie and Anne?"

Tania leans in close and checks my eyes for focus.

I think she says, "We're running the DR west, then the north coast of Haiti—stay this course until someone starts shooting at us—then veer north, fly the Old Bahama Channel between the Bahamas and Cuba, put down in New Orleans if I can wire it from the air. If not, there's a strip on Eleuthera at Governor's Harbour we can use; figure New Orleans while we refuel." She opens her brown bottle. "To the Witches of Eastwick. I take back what I said; some serious badass girls in that crew."

Reality hits me; what I saw; what I know. The exhale empties me top to bottom. My eyes close. I rerun the 8 mm movie behind my eyes. "You're sure? Maybe . . ."

"Gone, Bill. Went out big."

I want to stay in the dark, but don't.

Tania nods at me slow and small, then accepts another beer from Lopez, toasts again, and chugs half.

I twist off the beer cap but can't. Lopez does it for me, then clinks her bottle to mine. Tania does the same. We drink to . . . being alive, to all the shit that should've been, that won't be.

My beer has no taste. "He died with them? The Gryphon?"

"Vaporized. The Witches should get a monument. That was one straight-up evil motherfucker who needed to go."

The plane bucks hard. Tania checks the window, then points. "Hurricane and the Rebelyon have half of Haiti on fire."

I look down at what might be Haiti's north coast, then farther west at what has to be Cap-Haïtien. The last thirty-six hours have not been kind to Haiti. If this plane had a bomb rack, I'd use it. I look back from the window. "The kids he had with him? They're dead?"

"Probably not. Not from the blast; no telling what the surviving Tontons intend other than hunting gold fragments till the Dominicans we tip off get there." Tania looks at Lopez, who's already on a sat phone doing that, then back to me. "That kind of country, Bill. Add natural disaster and revolution; gonna be all nine circles for a while."

I show her my palm. "I know what kind of country it is."

CHICAGO

Chapter 38

BILL OWENS

Loef Brummel and I stand on the backside of the Jardine Water Purification Plant at the Ohio Street seawall rocks. Lake Michigan's September breeze is cool on my swollen face. It's not doing much for Loef's. Our end of the plant's parking lot is under construction and empty, other than the two bodyguards at my back and Lieutenant Denny Banahan's Crown Vic idling at the Ohio Street curb.

Loef's scarred fingers count his money—currency, not gold coins. He closes the Flyers gym bag, then says, "What else?"

"Have a nice day?"

Loef sniffs his bent nose, then spits. "Not happy, Bill."

"Maybe see a therapist?" My smile is genuine, probably the Myers's Rum and hydrocodone tablets.

He looks at the gym bag's logo. "I lost people. They got families, some of 'em."

"I lost people too. Two women in particular. Could've married either one. Would've died young but happy."

Loef inhales to threaten me.

I wave it off. "Save it, okay? In an hour I'll be in the hospital. Five minutes after the docs are done and while I'm still IV'd to the bed, my lawyer and I get to do an assistant state's attorney showdown for my exit last week—the police seem to think I'm involved in Dave and Barlow's bloodbath up here. Assuming I survive the hospital and the ASA, then I have a hockey team to save." My smile flattens. "And some shit I need to forget. How about we leave it at that?"

"People talking, Bill. Saying you found a lot of money."

"Could be I found enough to pay you what I didn't owe. That what you mean? Kinda hoped you'd be happy. But should you decide not to be—say you decide to put the arm on me, or one of your Belfast assholes threatens the Flyers again." I crank my thumb over my shoulder at Lieutenant Banahan's Crown Vic. "I'll drop a house on you—every word I can write down, every phone tape, everything a US attorney might want to tee up a RICO run for the roses. And if that doesn't get you the death penalty, I'll tell your childhood neighbor in the Crown Vic that I saw you shoot his partner at Nick & Nora's."

Loef's lips peel. "Talk like that could put a guy in a Canaryville basement."

"Yeah, it could. And so you know, that's the kinda place I went to get you your fucking money; saw stuff that'd turn *your* head sideways. The Bill Owens who made it back is not the guy who left here last week. Don't fuck with me, Loef, and I won't fuck with you."

***

One week later

Track announcer John Dooley PAs the paddock apron: "THEY'RE IN THE GATE FOR THE SIXTH RACE AT ARLINGTON."

Standing with me in the paddock, Jonathan Eig stirs coffee from a paper cup he hasn't sipped. There's no sugar or milk in the coffee, so stirring it seems stupid. Jon Eig isn't stupid. He lowers his cobalt-blue Maui Jim sunglasses and says, "Rough trip, huh?"

"Every bit of that."

Eig glances at the two formidable fellows who came with me, now thirty feet away. "Hear it was Haiti."

"Might've been."

Eig chins at someone in the crowd. Not a look-alike, but similar. The new guy walks over.

Eig introduces us. "Bill Owens; Jonathan Eig."

"Jonathan Eig" no. 2 extends his hand. I cut back to the original. "Who are you?"

Original Eig says, "Barlow died before he could pay those bills I mentioned." He backs into the crowd. "You and I never met."

Jonathan Eig no. 2 sips a beer. "So, the deal you're offering is . . ."

The crowd swallows my ghost. I tell Eig no. 2: "Gimme your wallet."

He does.

It's filled with "Jonathan Eig" cards, including two photo IDs. I call the number on one. A phone rings in his pocket. I hand him his wallet. "Who's my ghost?"

"Don't think you want to know."

"You'd be wrong."

Eig stares, relents. "My guess? Ex-spook. Blood on his hands. Looking for absolution or revenge, or both."

I know the concept; sift the crowd again, as do my bodyguards.

"So, Bill, your deal, as I understand it, is you'll tell me the whole story. I write the book and keep whatever it pays. In return, your hockey team and its coach get my personal best at media spin—whatever your lawyers say they require to keep the county off your team's back?"

"Forever."

"What if—"

"No *what if.* Forever."

Eig lowers his beer. "Don't think I can guarantee that. The Hurricane Lana smoke hasn't cleared, and already there's some pretty scary chatter. 'CIA' and 'red market' could be awfully explosive if your story's part of that."

"Possibly *Mary Poppins* suits you better? Always best to write about what you know."

He smiles under a Panama stingy brim that suits him, then winces. "The Barlow shooting. Then his murder in some kind of vodou ritual." Headshake. "Nine dead at Nick & Nora's—some of them foreign pre-op transsexuals *with a brand*?" Bigger wince. "Dave Grossfeld's ritual murder on his boat in Haiti . . ."

"You're right, Jon, better I give the story to someone taller."

Eig doesn't inflate or stop his Jimmy Olsen cub-reporter impression. "In Haiti, the Dominican Republic, and Jamaica, they're reporting—"

"You're gonna believe 'reports' coming out of Haiti?"

"Who's the Gryphon?"

"No idea."

"Cranston Piccard?"

Shrug.

"If they were in your story, would you be talking about them?"

"If they were in it, yeah, I would."

"And Barlow and the CIA would be part of it?"

"If they were."

Eig sips more beer but doesn't avert his eyes. "On a scale of one to ten, how dangerous is your . . . story?"

Shrug. "Don't know, maybe *a hundred*? Hide in a hole the rest of your life and hope the forces of evil are busy elsewhere?"

He contemplates the risks, then allows voracious-journalist/author DNA to overwhelm his education and spousal responsibilities.

"And the gold?"

"Jesus, Jon, did you hear what I just said?"

"I did."

"The *story* isn't scary enough?"

"Haven't heard it yet."

I look up at the paddock odds board. *This* Jon Eig is crazy. The diminutive, intellectual act is thinner than varnish. "You're probably gonna surf the Banzai Pipeline."

"Already have." He touches the scar on his forehead.

Headshake. "Okay. Rumor is, part of Anne and Susie's share went to an orphanage on Rum Cay in the Bahamas, sprucing it up to first world. Plan is to take in one-third Jamaican kids, one-third Haitian, one-third Cuban. Think it's a trade school for boats and sailing, and an adventure school as well; something like that. Like what Oprah's millions did in Africa."

"But you don't know."

"Nope. You could call Kayak Jim Jordan at the Grand Hotel Boblo; think he'll be running the adventure-school part. Some kind of Outward Bound for—"

"Kids with issues, right. Like your Flyers."

I nod. "Maybe I heard something like that."

Jon stares. "And your friends? Susie Devereux and Anne Bonny?"

I think about that before I answer. Anne died in the way she would've wanted to go. Same for Susie. Part of me thinks Susie allowed the Gryphon's people to grab her in Chicago; that at some point she'd decided the money wasn't gonna do it for her. She was willing to buy a ticket to hell just to get close enough to kill him. I think I kinda knew after she finished with the suicide vest before we went to the crater to do the O.K. Corral, when she cut her friends' names into her arms.

Exhale.

I look at my bandaged palm and the carving that isn't there anymore. "Well, Jon, the Witches of Eastwick would *be* the story, wouldn't they?"

Epilogue

BILL OWENS

Summer 2012

Inside Johnny's IceHouse, Coach Kenny Rzepecki stands straighter with his new hip. Outside on West Madison Street is a new yellow Hummer that Kenny can now get in and out of with no trouble. When his ride's not parked here, it's at his new house in Park Ridge. Kenny smiles more, possibly because he and Patty Prom-Night now have a curvy forty-five-year-old assistant who knows fuck-all about hockey but clearly a whole bunch about making Kenny happy. Kenny's odd for a rich middle-aged white guy, working the same hours he worked when he was a poor middle-aged white guy. He's his father's son, a man who a number of us in the city owe a lot.

Kenny's rich because he's my new partner in the hockey team previously known as Grossfeld's Flyers. Our team now has twenty-two players, twelve Americans, ten Haitians, two of them HIV-positive. We have a team doctor and a team psychologist and a pit-bull lawyer on full retainer.

As is happens, Down syndrome kids are good mentors for Haitian kids who've never met civilization. Or hockey. Or cars, sky, endless white people, TV, et cetera. The Flyers are good mentors because they don't freak out as easily as civilians who have Western expectations of the people they deal with. The ethereal combination of ice, safety, and Flyers is a work in progress for the Haitians. The Flyers, on the other hand, are living like rock stars compared to our pre–Witches of Eastwick adventure, and they know it. Our goalie, Lisa "The Wall" Saunders, high-fives all twenty-two Flyers before and after each practice, grinning and overpronouncing our team motto from kissing distance into every face:

"We sail together; we finish together."

Grossfeld's Flyers have been renamed the Valkyrie Flyers. They have their own clubhouse adjacent to the grounds at Hawthorne Race Course, which is next door to the ghost of Sportsman's and six miles from Johnny's IceHouse. On the walls we have a life-size photo of the Witches of Eastwick—the rugby shot of Susie, Siri, and Anne. We also have the Mary Read–Anne Bonny painting from the Sazerac Bar in Port Royal. We have our own team bus and a pontoon-deck boat that we dock a block away on the Sanitary and Ship Canal, known to some as the Chicago River. Every Saturday after practice we sail the river with Anne Bonny's flag from the Sazerac Bar flying from the masthead. Patty Prom-Night will soon have her captain's license. She says we aspire to a bigger boat.

The Flyers have a skybox for the Blackhawks home games and once a year, a full-uniform, pre-game parade. In the spring, we have a lifetime reservation at the Grand Hotel Boblo in Rum Cay, beachfront bungalows for Bobby Little and Kayak Jim's Burning Man festival held there every May. The Flyers wear their road jerseys. On the wall above the hotel bar is the last photo ever taken of Susie Devereux and Anne Bonny, taken at Lake Arenal in Costa Rica on September 9, 2009. The photo isn't signed.

***

Me, I've been writing poems and songs, publishing them on the internet. Odd, huh? Given that I have no more talent for either form than

Eddie O'Hare did. Most afternoons I come to a Chicago cemetery and write for an hour or two, my back leaned against the four-person mausoleum I built next to my brother Mike's grave.

Carved above the mausoleum's door is: "PENDELANE." Inside, visible through the gated door and above the grave vaults, is a map of the Corazón Santo and "HELL HATH NO FURY." Under that are the names "Susie Devereux, Anne Cormac Bonny, Florent Dusson-Siri, and Tafat Pendelane."

Their mausoleum's nice—my construction company still does good work even with Lisa Reins running it—but this mausoleum's not a necropolis monument. After a lot of thought about Tania Hahn's "monument" comment, no structure I could conjure felt like it would be sufficiently Mount Rushmore. Then, listening to Kenny Herbert do songs off the Beatles' *Abbey Road* album while I did my rehab, it came to me—Anne's whole "Paul is dead; let's quit school to figure it out," epic-Beatles cryptogram from 1969:

Susie and Anne's Mount Rushmore should be a treasure hunt.

Their mausoleum is a clue.

It fits somewhere in an intricate series of clues to an already hidden cache of gold bullion; bought with coins the four women and their friends died finding.

Eight years from today, on September 20, 2020, a blind trust based in Queen's Ferry, Scotland, will announce to the treasure world that the Capone gold was found on September 9, 2009, on a small uninhabited atoll in the Corazón Santo. The announcement will say that the opening clue to the gold's current location is in a Kenny Herbert song about the "Bargain" and its "pirates."

However long the treasure hunt lasts, and whatever publicity it gets, the hunt will shine a light on the "Rotten Bargain"—the endless government/crime/business partnerships that govern our planet—and that all four of the girls were born to and died living.

But more important—to me at least—the hunt and its eventual treasure, and the legends that will surround both forever, will be a lasting monument to four women who took turns rescuing me, who walked it like they talked it; who, when the final bell tolled, probably were the Valkyries of Norse legend, the angels of the battlefield who appear out of the smoke and fire to pick who lives and who dies.

In many ways the Valkyries were, and are, the balance, the karma police when the pendulum has swung too far. And given mankind's endless tryst with the Bargain, it's even money that in one form or another, all four women are together somewhere in the ether, preparing to come back.

Privateer: "A commission granted by a government to make reprisals; to gain reparations for specific offenses in time of peace, or to prey upon the enemy in time of war."

The Barbancourt Clues

Tick tock, tick tock.
 Rue the day
When the ship will stop.
 —EJO

Cacos, bracero, and Charlemagne, too
Sixty-Five cannout match
 Mon Major who

left the ship with skeleton crew.
 —EJO

Only the Rhum beards know
 The long and the latte
His partner names
 Just bits of the trap.
 —EJO

The pieces float; the pieces drift
    Turn back
If I did not send you
No false heart survives my gift.

Forever bound by Code Noir
Maroons, multâre, and mara-bou
Births the crocodile as sailor's star
           — EJ̶o.

A star to fear And to find
    the one true race.
    who grows the vine.

Go over the mountains of the Moon
Down the Valley of the Shadow,
Ride, boldly ride,
The shade replied —
"If you seek for El Dorado."
— EJŌ

But in the wind eat the herb.
Only they avoid the slaughter
Beyond the cape, Fish the shallows
For they swim in freedoms tomorrows.
— EJŌ

Drink your fill The pirate's will
Trust only the vintner
And his hare contraire
Never the shade
Nor his fille fille de joie."

"The treasure travels from bank to bank,
Where the frigates sail and sink,
Her Majesty is the season; La Vilora the reason,
The shade is there, me thinks."
— EJC

"Soldiers, slaves and sailors, all have drowned
under the weight, the end is the end, circles
the friend, and like all thieves, death
is your fate."

Illustrations: Robert Bucciarelli, RobertBDesign

Acknowledgments

THE BOOK

Bill Owens.
    My partner in BAM (Back Alley Maulers), our first street gang. Candy cigarettes rolled into our shirtsleeves, "LOVE" and "HATE" in washable ballpoint on our knuckles, corrective shoes our mothers made us wear, and one block on Central Street we decided was ours.

Billy Thompson.
    If you're gonna race thoroughbreds or borrow money from loan sharks, might as well make it fun.

Kayak Jim Jordan.
    Sky pilot every way you can mean that.

Miami Jon Eig.
    Love child of Mike Royko, Studs Terkel, and Margo Godfrey-Oberg.

Deena "The Beast" Telley.
    She says Susie Devereux knows why, but that I couldn't say.

THE LIFE

Brian Rodgers.
    First in; never out.

Murad Siam.
  Zen Prince of the Pirate Cove and Cosmic River.

Bob Bucciarelli.
  Co-conspirator. A boy, a guitar, and a paintbrush.

Sharon Bennett.
  Editor in Chief.

Douglas J. Bennett.
  MacGyver's Lost Boy.

Eric Meyer.
  Anne Cormack Bonny's Charleston scion.

Simon Lipskar.
  The Southern Cross of this voyage, and the others. Believer, confidant, life preserver in the endless twenty-footers.

Easy Ed Stackler.
  Best red pen in the business.

Meghan Sailor Harvey.
  When the first publisher enters the America's Cup, she'll be their captain.

And
My pal, James B. Loef.
  Jimmy lived it fearless and fast, and when I was with him, when we were kids and pals and he looked after me, he was as tough and as good a kid as I ever knew.

About the Author

Charlie Newton is a Chicago native, a writer known for a global life on the road and extended MIA absences. When he does publish, Newton's heart-pounding, gritty, and witty realism has been a starred-review favorite of the critics and a finalist for the Edgar, the Ian Fleming Steel Dagger, the Macavity, and the International Thriller Writers awards. Newton is the author of *Calumet City* (Simon & Schuster, 2008), *Start Shooting* (Doubleday, 2012), and *Traitor's Gate* (Thomas & Mercer, 2015).

Help new readers discover *Privateers* by sharing this book. Please take a moment to post your review on Amazon, Goodreads, or your social channel of choice. #privateersthriller

We hope you enjoyed this book, as well as the knowledge that you supported an indie author by purchasing it.

www.girlfridayproductions.com

CPSIA information can be obtained
at www.ICGtesting.com
Printed in the USA
LVHW052109040720
659750LV00002B/332